CROWN
OF
STARS

Also by Sophie Jaff

Love Is Red, Book I of the Night Song Trilogy

Praise for *Love Is Red*,
Book I of the Night Song Trilogy

"The kick of this ridiculously entertaining book is the haze of delirium it creates in the reader's brain, which is buffeted throughout by wild plot twists, abrupt shifts of mood and verbal style, sudden narrative somersaults, all flashing by at vertigo-inducing speed. . . . Jaff's woozy supernatural saga is effectively scary and great fun to read." —*New York Times Book Review*

"Intelligent, poetic, captivating, and chilling, this is a book that begs to be read aloud; the mystery at the core of *Love Is Red* is so gripping you will find yourself carrying the book around with you until you're done. Savor it, devour it, recommend it, but don't lend it to your friends, because you will want to reread it as soon as you're finished."
—Elizabeth Haynes, *New York Times* bestselling author of *Into the Darkest Corner* and *Under a Silent Moon*

"*Love Is Red* is a tornado of a novel. Jaff twists through so many suspenseful places that the book threatens to blow out of the reader's hands. I couldn't turn the pages fast enough, but I wanted to linger too. This is seriously scary stuff, offered up in high style and with wild narrative invention."
—Laura Kasischke, national bestselling author of *Mind of Winter* and *The Raising*

"I read it in one sitting. I cannot remember the last time I was so completely enthralled with a book. . . . It's good. Real good."
—Smart Bitches, Trashy Books

"One of the most unique and amazing books I have ever had the pleasure of reading. . . . Simultaneously beautiful and terrifying."
—Fresh Fiction

CROWN OF STARS

OF

STARS

BOOK II OF THE NIGHT SONG TRILOGY

SOPHIE JAFF

HARPER

NEW YORK · LONDON · TORONTO · SYDNEY

HarperCollins books may be purchased for educational, business, or sales promotional use. For information, please e-mail the Special Markets Department at SPsales@harpercollins.com.

FIRST EDITION

Library of Congress Cataloging-in-Publication Data
Names: Jaff, Sophie, author.
Title: Crown of stars / Sophie Jaff.
Description: First Harper Paperbacks edition. | New York, NY : Harper Paperbacks, [2017] | Series: The night song trilogy ; book 2
Identifiers: LCCN 2016044094 (print) | LCCN 2016055149 (ebook) | ISBN 9780062346285 (softcover : acid-free paper) | ISBN 9780062346308
Subjects: LCSH: Women--Crimes against--Fiction. | Paranormal fiction. | GSAFD: Occult fiction. | Horror fiction.
Classification: LCC PS3610.A358 C76 2017 (print) | LCC PS3610.A358 (ebook) | DDC 813/.6--dc23
LC record available at https://lccn.loc.gov/2016044094

ISBN 978-0-06-234628-5 (pbk.)

17 18 19 20 21   LSC   10 9 8 7 6 5 4 3 2 1

For my mother, an ocean away,
and yet always there when I need her.

For some learned men propound this reason; that there are three things in nature, the Tongue, an Ecclesiastic, and a Woman, which know no moderation . . .and when they exceed the bounds of their condition they reach the greatest heights and the lowest depths of goodness and vice. When they are governed by a good spirit, they are most excellent in virtue; but when they are governed by an evil spirit, they indulge the worst possible vices.

—Heinrich Kramer, *Malleus Maleficarum*
(Hammer of Witches), 1486

Margaret

I wake in darkness. I smile. The time has come at last.

I press my palms against the heavy weight of stone above me. I push upward with all my strength and the lid moves slowly until there's a slim lip of gray light. I work one hand out, and then the other. My fingers grip the sides of the coffin as I slowly sit up. Here, in the crypt, torches flicker with blue flames, though they cast no heat or real light. Stone angels stare with sightless eyes. The air is tepid, with a faint tang of dust.

This is a place that even the dead have forgotten.

I emerge. Vertebrae stacking one upon the other, muscles, tendons, fibers, blood, bone, and flesh. I stand. Then, slowly, one foot in front of the other, I begin to walk. One foot in front of the other, one step leading to another. Each more sure than the one before. Faster. Faster now. I run. Up the stone stairs and through the passageway past the Great Hall, my palms sweeping along the rough-hewn walls, my footfalls echoing dully in the silence.

I remember tiptoeing down to the crypt that night, careful to blend with the shadows, careful not to be seen, but now I look neither left nor right as I fly past the black maws of the cavernous hallways. There is nothing to see. There is no one here to see me. No lords nor ladies in their finery. No servants scurrying on errands, knights in the courtyard nor horses snorting in the stables. No fires smoking in the hearths. No tapestries stirring against the walls or rushes whispering upon the floor. This is only the shell of a memory.

I run from the castle to the world beyond. With a single step I cross valleys and fields, mountains and oceans. I run from the Old World to the New World. The world of here. The world of now. And I am within it again.

The breeze is soft upon my bare flesh. I thrill to it. I run on. He is close.

There, on the shore of the lake, a small boat waits for me. It waits to take me to him, on the other side of the water. I row and row. I relish the strength in my arms each time I plunge the oar through water. Each stroke pulls me closer. I could be blind yet I would still find him.

I reach the far bank, the sliver of beach, and run into the small wood beyond. The earth is damp beneath my feet. It teems with life. I trail my fingertips against the trees. I hear the faint rustle of the leaves, and the hum of insects.

The wood dissolves to a path of small stones, pale in the moonlight. Up ahead is a dwelling from which bright light shines out, eclipsing the moon.

He is there. God alone knows how long I have waited for this. God alone knows what I have sacrificed.

I do not stop to marvel at the two monstrous hunks of steel, the size of oxcarts, looming just off the path. I have waited too long. Instead, I slip through the open door and up gleaming wooden steps, which lead to an outside balcony.

Through the dimness I can just make out a figure lying motionless upon a pillowed bench. Another one of his victims? But no, as my eyes adjust I can make out the broad shoulders and tapering torso of a sleeping man.

Something catches the corner of my eye. My quarry's victories must have made him careless. Why else would he have left it gleaming upon a table?

I slowly, reverently, pick it up, savoring its heft within my grasp. I press my thumb lightly against the blade and delight in the bead of blood.

There is a muffled thud beneath my feet, and a creak followed by another. He is coming.

I slink back into the darkness. A slight tremor shakes the balcony, and there he is, the one who I have waited for.

He approaches the man who lies upon the bed. He is so intent that he does not notice the absence of the knife. He does not sense me at all. He clutches an ordinary carving knife, and I suddenly understand. He would not use his sacred blade upon the body of a man.

He raises the knife above him.

I step out of the shadows.

He turns. His eyes widen in surprise, and could it be fear? I grin.

"Katherine?" His voice holds a question, holds doubt. "Katherine, my heart?"

A growl wells and swells deep within my chest. My lips draw back; I bare my teeth. I will rip his eyes from his face. I will tear his skin from his bones.

I lunge.

He is caught by surprise, but he struggles. I claw at his face, his throat. He is fighting hard, holding me back. Again he calls me by a name that is not mine.

"Katherine!" he cries.

I spit and hiss. I am a silver serpent. I am burning coil and poisoned fang. I will crush him in my folds, I will crack his bones, I will strike his neck, I will suck him of life.

Then his face softens. He stops struggling, turns limp. The Thing that defends itself drains away, and he opens his arms up to me as my own lover once did, a lifetime ago.

"Please," he begs.

I do not stop to question why he would surrender, for now it is my time. For the spilled blood and the wasted centuries, the slaughtered children and innocence defiled, for the warped and twisted lives left moldering on the scrap heap, for the agony and injustice suffered by all he butchered, and for my own life too, I scream. I scream out all my rage and pain as I drive his knife in up to its hilt, splintering bone and severing sinew, twisting the curved blade deep into his heart. It is vengeance. It is ecstasy. It is mine.

His eyes roll back, and I cry out with joy. A million voices join my song in triumph.

Now someone else is screaming. The man on the bed has woken and he screams and screams. But he is of no importance to me.

I have kept my vow. And again, for a while, I can sleep.

First Trimester

1

Katherine

"Tell me a story," the little boy says.

"What story would you like?" she asks.

"You know the one," he says.

She does. It's a story about Princess Katherine and Prince Lucas and their quest to find a magical treasure that grants health and happiness to those who discover it. The treasure is hidden in the dark, cold castle of King Spear, guarded by a Griffin and a Sorceress and a Giant Toad. The little boy's favorite part of the story is when the Giant Toad falls in love with Princess Katherine and tries to give her great big, slimy toady kisses. He giggles and squirms as she imitates the Toad's blubbering croak and gives him a raspberry on his neck. Then the story is over. The Princess and Prince escape, thanks to their courage and bravery, to search for the treasure another day. Meanwhile, it's bedtime.

The woman tucks the little boy up under the covers. She tells him she loves him. She gives him a good-night kiss on the forehead; then she gets up and turns out the light. She is careful not to close the door all the way as she leaves, careful not to leave him in full darkness. She's promised him a night-light when they finally find their own apartment. Until then she leaves the door open a crack. That will have to do.

Once outside, she takes a moment, stands on the opposite side of the door. It seems as if she is listening for something, but for what, she cannot say. At any rate, there is nothing to hear. She gathers herself together and walks into the next room slowly, almost wading through the air, and now that she is alone and does not have to tell stories, we can see how tired she is. She falls, arms outstretched, face forward, onto the bed. She wonders where she will find the strength to undress, to brush her teeth.

"How am I doing, Andrea?" she asks the silent room.

There is no answer. Why would there be?

Andrea, the mother of four-year-old Lucas, who now sleeps in the other room, is dead. She's dead, and these days the dead stay quiet.

There was a time, not so long ago, when this was not the case. But Andrea Bowers, the eleventh victim of David Balan, a serial killer known as the Sickle Man, is dead, and Katherine Anne Emerson, his only survivor, is tired. She's bone-tired after working all day as a temp at Sterling and Spear Investment Fund Management. She knows nothing about investments or funding, only knows that she has none and needs some.

Katherine's life is ruled by ifs. *If* she does a good enough job in her temporary position, maybe Sterling and Spear will make it a permanent one. *If* she becomes permanent she can get health insurance, and if she gets health insurance she can afford to go to the doctor. She doesn't want to go to the doctor, but she needs to go to the doctor. The small plastic stick with the two pink lines tells her she must.

And she'll have to tell him. Him, the man she loves, Sael de Villias. Possibly the most pretentious name ever.

"It's pronounced 'Sah-*el*,'" he had told her, staring at her with his merciless, pale eyes, when she had mistakenly first called him Saul.

Sael, who proposed; Sael, the man she thought she would marry; Sael of forever and ever. Sael, who now hates her.

She can't remember much of that night. "Post-traumatic stress disorder," the shrinks say, all of them, and there have been many . . .

She was running, naked and terrified, through the woods, and then came those strange images, nightmares that made no sense. A figure in a boat. A castle. A coffin. The woman in the green dress.

She doesn't remember how she got back to the cabin, though apparently she used an abandoned rowboat, nor how or where she found the strange, curved knife.

She doesn't remember plunging it into David's chest.

But after that, she remembers more than she wants to. She remembers Sael screaming. She remembers David falling backward over the balcony. The crunching sound of the wooden rail breaking, the soft thud of his body hitting the earth below. She remembers the way Sael looked at her as he cradled his friend in his arms.

You killed him, you killed him, you killed him!

In the world's eyes, Katherine is a heroine. In Sael's eyes, she's a murderer.

David was his best friend. David had also been her friend, and also more than a friend. The truth is, it doesn't matter that she acted in self-defense, or what horrific acts David had committed. The moment she killed David, she severed the bond between herself and Sael. He couldn't get past it, couldn't look at her in the same way again.

Katherine will survive. She's a survivor, only she knows that surviving isn't the same thing as living. There have been days, many of them, when she didn't think she could make it out of bed. Had it not been for Lucas, she would have stayed there, maybe taken too many of the tranquilizers she'd been prescribed. But there is Lucas, and now there's a little plastic stick that confirms what she's known for a while.

She'll have to tell Sael. Soon.

2

Margaret

It is said to be spring, but Old Mother Winter will not be so easily banished. She rattles at the doors and shrieks down the chimneys and scrapes her bony knuckles against the shutters. Luckily, in the King's Head, the doors have been fastened and barred against her. For tonight there is a celebration, the wedding of the most popular man for miles around and his young, beautiful bride. The whole village is here, at least those who endured the bitter cold, the illnesses, and the meager portions.

They are here because everyone knows that when the tavern owner is wed, the drink is sure to flow, and they are not disappointed. John Belwood is generous to a fault, and his ale is famed throughout five counties.

If it were not for me, my father would have been wed an age ago.

The women wear their finest dresses, the men their best tunics, bright reds and blues and greens and yellows. They have even washed for the occasion, hauled bucket after bucket from the well, stoked the fires, heated jugs, scoured themselves with tallow and wood ash. After the long, harsh winter, everyone has a pale, plucked look to them, scrawny fowl scarcely fit for the pot. Still, tonight they're happy. There's a pipe and tabor, a fiddle and dancing. There is drink and food for all. The evening is filled with laughter and songs and toast upon toast to the bride and groom, but especially to the bride. Toasts to her pink cheeks, and toasts to her blue eyes, and above all to her golden hair, which is almost as famous as the Belwood ale.

My father grins as he sits at one large table, already in his cups, accepting those slaps on the back along with the good-natured ribbing that must come when a much older man marries a young and beautiful girl.

And where is Cecily, the bride? Why, she's there, surrounded by her friends, a gaggle of girls who giggle and coo. The older women watch indulgently. They are ready to give advice, to reminisce about their own wedding days, to whisper of the failures that took place in the marriage bed. Occasionally they will glance over toward their husbands to make sure that they have not been overheard. But there's little chance of that, what with the clamor of lumbering young men attempting to dance with their squealing partners and the roar of laughter at stale jokes freshened, for a time at least, by ale. Meanwhile, Cecily remains extraordinarily self-possessed for one so young. She sits calmly enough through the gale of teasing and advice and compliments. She lowers her eyes fetchingly, letting her lashes graze against her soft cheeks. She knows that she is the most beautiful, most desirable girl in the county. She knows she has made a good match. And she knows she can afford to sit and smile and simply let the praise rain down upon her.

I wonder, not for the first time, what my mother would think if she could see her.

Pretty, she might have said. *Pretty as a bird, and as cunning as a serpent.*

I bite my lip. Surely my mother would have wanted my father to be happy. It is only I who stand and watch with such bitterness in my heart.

But no, I look over and see another who sits by herself. She is young, but her pinched expression makes her seem older than her years. Her hair is yellow, but not the gold of Cecily's. More the color of soiled straw. Her watery, pink-rimmed eyes remind me of a mouse's. I silently name her Mouse Wife, although I know who she is, as everyone in the village must. Her true name is Bertha, and she is the collier's new wife, after his first died in childbirth along with the baby. It is unspoken, but generally agreed, that this was a lucky escape for her and her child. Upon their deaths, the collier left town and a few days later returned with this thin, sad thing. I feel sorry for her, married to the collier. I think of his thick, grimy fingers reluctantly working the coins from his purse, how his small, rheumy eyes crawl over my breasts and hips. He is known to be rough when drunk. As if on cue, he roars at a jest and the Mouse Wife flinches. I wonder what would happen if I went and sat next to Bertha, offered her a cup of ale. Perhaps she would look at me and smile. After all, Bertha has not yet been poisoned by the others. For a moment, I let myself imagine what it would be like to have her as a friend. I picture walking with her to the marketplace, exchanging gossip and stories as we go the way the other women do. I would make a poultice for her bruises, be there when she needed to cry. Bertha in turn would defend me when the women talk.

Pay them no mind, she might say, *for what do they know?* She could help me keep my temper.

The dream is a heady one. But why not? On the day of my father's wedding, perhaps I too could have some luck. I swallow and rise to fill a cup to the brim; then I take a step toward her. The Mouse

Wife looks up and, miraculously, she meets my gaze. She sees my outstretched hand holding the cup and a little grin flickers at the corners of her mouth. Really, she is not so mousy after all when she smiles. She rises, opening her hand to receive the cup, but before she can do so Mistress Faye swoops down like a great black crow and sweeps her up and away to the older women's table.

Her rescue is executed with astonishing speed. I am left standing, cup in hand. I watch as Bertha the Mouse Wife is ushered into the group, watch how they move over to make room for her. I know that, if it weren't for me, Mistress Faye and her lot would have taken their time, been slower to welcome Bertha to their circle. After all, she is still a stranger. But even a stranger must be protected. Even a stranger must be warned.

The women gather in. Any moment now they'll tell Bertha why they rescued her. Why she must never speak with me. It will be Mistress Faye, or Mistress Bigge, or the old crone Webb who will tell her all about the night I was born. How the heavens flashed with light and rolled with thunder, how the wind wailed and the sleet sliced like daggers. How the pigs screamed and the horses bucked and the dogs howled in despair. How grown men shook in their boots as women shrieked and tore their hair out by the roots, convinced that the Day of Judgment was upon them. How the midwife who had delivered me was found dead the next day, her black hair turned white as snow, her face frozen with horror.

Then they will tell of my mother, Isobel, whom they had all adored. And of her fate.

Even when I was a little girl, she would take me foraging in the wood south of the village for wild mushrooms. On the day that began no different from all the others, she and I had set out for wood ears and slippery jacks and scarlet hoods. Nightfall came, but brought neither of us home with it. My father led a search party of village men, and it was he who first discovered my mother's body, near dawn, at the far edge of the wood. She was naked and ravaged. Her throat had been sliced from ear to ear. Most fearsome of all, intricate symbols had been engraved deep into her flesh. They could find no sign of me. They said that my father's face was an open grave of sorrow. His neighbors could barely look at him, so terrible was his anguish.

Three days later, I returned, crusted with dirt, loam and leaves in my hair, but nary a scratch upon my body. My father wept; then he pleaded with me for my story. Who had attacked us and killed my mother and why had I escaped? They say that I would not speak, but in truth I *could* not speak, for I remembered nothing.

I still do not remember.

After that, the other children in the village would not play with me. Instead, they ran and hid, the older ones behind the hedges, the younger back to their mothers' skirts. Their parents shuddered when they saw me. Even my father was too sore of heart to look upon me. I was a reminder of the evil done unto my mother. I had come back, and my mother had not. To the people who had buried and mourned her, I was a reminder that the world was not safe. I was a lonely, pitiful little thing, reviled and neglected, my father still too steeped in grief to care for me.

It was Father Aiden who found me in the long grass outside his cottage, eavesdropping on the lessons he gave to the sons of wealthier merchants. He must have thought my passion to learn curious, although it was the attention he lavished upon the students that I craved. He decided to teach me the rudiments of reading and writing, I am sure for his own amusement rather than a true desire to help. After all, he soon began to teach me other lessons too, his gnarled fingers inching closer and closer. I would bite my lip and stare at the thin, swooping lines on the faded vellum, trying to withstand the indignities, but this betrayal grew too much to bear. I became a mongrel cur snapping and snarling at whomever came near. When my father sent me away to a nunnery, I am sure the villagers young and old sighed with relief. Now they could go on with their lives and forget.

How sorry they were when I returned.

I know the villagers can only speculate. How bad must I be for even the nuns to cast me out? What terrible evil could they sense? My father and Widow Clancy were to be wed, but after I returned she refused. It is no secret that I frightened her. I frighten them all.

At this point in the story, the Mouse Wife appears to ask a question. I cannot hear her, but I wager it concerns the fate of my father's new bride. The older women glance as one toward the table of girls where Cecily no longer sits. She excused herself with a blush and smile only moments ago. After all, she is not used to drinking so much ale.

The women cluck and ruffle, a fierce brood of mother hens, protective of their charge. But even *I* would know better than to ply my wiles upon such a sweet and innocent girl. The village would not stand for it.

Surely the Mouse Wife will want to know of my dark deeds. The women will hesitate; real proof is hard to come by. Still, there are rumors; soured milk and sickened children when I crossed their path, odd and awful dreams when I looked in their direction. There are those who claim to have been stung by wasps, or wrenched an ankle, after somehow displeasing me. And so these women will talk on and on, their eyes growing bright with malice and drink. On and on and on.

I imagine what would happen if I walked up to them, jug in

hand, to offer more ale. They would scarcely dare to blink, let alone shake their heads. For a moment I am tempted, just to see, but then I turn away. What is the use? Bertha is lost to me now. Instead, I head down to the cellar.

It is cool down here in the dark. I close my eyes and lean my head against the damp wood of a cask. Above me I can hear muffled shouts of laughter, the pounding feet of the graceless dancers. I wait for my flushed cheeks to cool, for the sour taste at the back of my throat to subside. I still see their spiteful faces shining in the firelight, hear their endlessly wagging tongues.

"Mother," I whisper. "Mother."

It would be a relief to cry, but I hardly ever do, and have not since I was a little girl. Not since that night. What is the use in crying? Still, if tears do come, no one will hear me. I am safe in the cellar.

There's a noise. Not the scrabble of rats, but a strange ruffling, panting sound. I peer forward into the darkness, and can just make out the shape of a woman and a man in a passionate coupling. They writhe against the wall. With a small gasp I draw back behind the barrels again, but they must have heard me, or else sensed my presence, for they both fall silent. I hold my breath, willing even my heart to still.

After an eternity, I hear sharp, furtive whispers. The fun, for now, is over. One of them begins to ascend, and the light falls on the broad back of a young man as he turns his head and stalks up the steps like a tomcat. The girl holds back, taking a little more time to set her dress straight, to run a hand over her hair and wipe her face. She climbs quickly and nimbly, and then at the last moment she peers back into the cellar. I only take in a glimpse of her, but it is enough. Her narrowed eyes are hard as she searches for the intruder. It is she who should be fearful, abashed, and yet somehow

I am the one crouching in the dark. Finally she turns again, and heads back into the light and laughter.

I stand, but do not move to leave yet. Instead I wait for a long while thinking of her cold eyes, the grim set of her rosebud mouth, her beautiful golden hair. And I know.

I have been seen.

3

Katherine

At four, Katherine is sitting and waiting in a diner.

The diner is nothing special, just one of those diners you can find anywhere in midtown Manhattan—lime-green booths, cracks in the faux-leather, dull Formica counters, a massive laminated menu, Greek salad, eggs any way you want 'em, a meatloaf special. So far, all Katherine has ordered is a cup of coffee, milk on the side. She really just wants water, which comes in one of those tall, clouded plastic glasses so specific to diners, but she has to buy something in exchange for her seat. Her eyes are fixed on the door. She got here early, 3:45. Told the office she had a doctor's appointment, but nobody cared anyway. She's only a temp.

At 4:04, the door opens and she sees him standing there. Dark, angular, somehow pulling all the energy in the diner toward him. He looks around. She half lifts her hand in an "over here" gesture, a little ridiculous with the place so empty, then puts it down again, unsure of what to do with her limbs.

He sees her and comes over, but hesitates a moment, as if he needs her permission.

"Sit," she says.

He slides in opposite her. He's wearing jeans, a dark sweater, a light peacoat. She sees he has new lines; he looks tired, drawn, too thin. He bends his head down to study the menu.

I'm over him, she thinks in triumph.

A waiter approaches. He looks up.

"Coffee," Sael says. "Black."

The waiter lopes away. He's seen this kind of setup before; he can bet no one's going to be eating.

They stare at each other.

"Katherine."

He makes her name a sentence in its own right. He smiles, and she knows that all is lost.

"Sael."

"How have you been?" He asks as if he really wants to know.

She thinks about the nights she lies awake, the weight of worry squeezing the breath from her chest, her heart pounding in her mouth. The days of staring at computer screens but not seeing anything. Praying to a god she doesn't believe in. Wondering how they'll survive.

"Hanging in there." Only by the tips of her bleeding fingers.

"Good, that's good."

"And you?"

"I've been okay." He's grave. "Some days are better than others."

After these lifeless platitudes offered like limp bouquets, they sit in silence.

It's clear he's gathering his strength, gathering his thoughts.

"I wrote to you because I wanted to see you, I wanted to talk."

She says nothing, only looks at him.

"I wanted to apologize for the things I said that night, for cutting you out of my life. I blamed you. I guess you can understand that. But some of the things I said . . . I was wrong, completely wrong. And when you reached out, when you wanted to talk, I shut you down. I wouldn't, I couldn't at the time, but I know that wasn't right. I just didn't know how to handle it. I'm sorry."

She's been waiting to hear this for so long. She's not sure what to say.

"Can you forgive me?"

She thinks about a time they made pancakes. She'd burned two, but he ate them anyway, insisting they were good. The small kitchen was flooded with sunlight. He had pulled her down onto his lap, his kisses tasting of pancake batter.

Now he sits opposite her in the diner, a stranger apologizing.

"Yes," she says. "I forgive you."

The relief on his face is painful to see.

"I can't tell you what that means to me."

"It's okay. I really do forgive you," she says again. She wonders if she'll ever be able to say anything else.

"It's important for me that I told you how I felt because . . . You see, the thing is, I'm moving to England."

Katherine just looks at him.

"I've been offered a position in London, and I've decided to take it. It might be time for a fresh start, maybe leave New York for a while."

She nods, but he's stopped talking, so she'll have to say something.

"How long will you be gone?" Her mouth is bone-dry. She tries to take a sip of her water, but her glass is empty. There's never a waiter when you need one.

"Depends." He shrugs. "It's all up in the air at the moment, for six months to a year at least. Then we'll see how the project is going, how I'm feeling."

Katherine has never really understood what Sael does, something highly technical to do with coding and computer systems. Something, apparently, that has him in great demand, and that pays extremely well.

You can't do this, she thinks. "That's great," she says.

"I'm glad you think so." He is earnest now, more earnest than she has ever known him to be. "I really wanted to talk with you."

The thing is, he does look glad.

"It's good to clear the air," he continues.

Katherine smiles and murmurs something. She excuses herself and heads to the bathroom, passing a booth where an old man sits, engrossed in the newspaper.

He glances up at her approach. "Best keep it to one cup."

"What?" she says.

"You shouldn't drink more than one cup of coffee, it's not good for the baby." He seems lost for a moment in a memory, then comes back to the present. "Now usually you could probably drink two cups in a day and that would be fine, but I've been coming here for fourteen years and I know this coffee, this coffee is strong."

"Excuse me, sir." Katherine's voice is icy. Her spine almost crackles it's so stiff.

The old man is unperturbed. He smiles gently at her. "Also, it's best not to get upset. It raises your blood pressure, that's no good. It will be okay."

He goes back to his paper as if nothing had passed between them.

In the bathroom she examines her face in the mirror, looking for any telltale signs, although what they would be, she has no idea. A maternal glow? A flush? The old man's crazy. He *must* be crazy. But how did he know?

She braces herself for a further encounter on her return, but he's once again absorbed in his paper.

Sael looks concerned. "Everything okay?"

"Yeah." She tries to manage something related to a smile.

"You were talking to that man . . . You seemed sort of upset?"

"It was nothing, he's a little eccentric."

"Oh. So how's everything going with you?"

Now that Sael has unburdened himself, now that she has given him her blessing, he's eager to talk and share. Now he wants to know.

"Pretty good." What's one more lie now she has begun? "But it's a real change taking care of Lucas." She takes a certain, hard pleasure in mentioning Lucas.

His whole face changes. "I wasn't thinking of that. Wow. I imagine it is. To suddenly be taking care of a little kid. I mean, I know you love him, but it must be overwhelming at times."

Sael's sudden, genuine sympathy makes her want to howl. Serves her right for using Lucas as a weapon. "It's hard sometimes, but I do love him, and speaking of that, I need to get back to him pretty soon."

"Where is he now?"

"With a friend in our building, but—"

"Oh shit, I should have come to your place, I didn't think."

"It's okay." She doesn't want Sael around Lucas, not after what happened.

He leans forward. "You know, I wanted to see you. It's not just my shrink persuading me."

"That's nice to hear." Her face feels stiff, unnatural.

"The thing is, is that—"

You still love me and you want us to be together.

"It was important for me to know that you were okay, that you were doing all right."

"So far, so good." She wants to get out of there.

"So you're okay, though? You're handling everything?"

She hears the hum of the air conditioner, faint laughter from back in the kitchen. Someone, somewhere, is able to tell a joke, make someone laugh. It seems incredible. She looks over and sees that the man with the newspaper is gone.

She hasn't touched her refill. The old man was right. This coffee is strong.

She looks again at Sael, the love of her life, the unaware father of her child. He is trying to move on. He is doing the best he can.

"Everything's fine," Katherine says.

And that seems to be the end of it. He has already deftly paid for the coffee. They're standing up, slipping into their jackets. It's not cold yet, but it's getting there. There's a slight nip in the air. The promise of winter soon.

"You're looking well," he says, finally.

"Thank you." She remembers when he knelt in the moonlight. When he offered her now and forever.

They walk together to the subway. It dawns on her that this may be the very last time they will meet. She sees by the expression on his face that he realizes it too.

"So you're really okay?" he asks.

"Yes." What else can she say now? "Really. I promise."

"Well." He bites his lip. "It was good to see you."

"It was good to see you too."

Unexpectedly, he hugs her. His smell, his Sael smell of clean skin, and the very Sael-ness comes back to her, and she is tempted to scream. *No, I'm not fine. I'm pregnant, and I lie awake thinking about Lucas, and how we're going to find another place, and I don't know if I'm going to get health insurance, I'm lonely, I'm all alone and I'm frightened and I can't do this, help me, hold me, be with me, take me back, love me again please, please, or just take me back, make it okay please.*

Then he lets go.

"Well, take care of yourself, Katherine."

"You too, Sael," she says, and plunges down into the subway.

She doesn't look back.

The subway is crowded. It's rush hour, 5:20 p.m. Everyone hates everyone, and everyone just wants to go home, home, home. People's faces are carved in stone with that "don't fuck with me" look. The stout accountant and the hip young thing, the rumple-suited businessman and the wilted-skirt saleslady, the pretty jean-jacketed girl, everyone is pacing and tensing and waiting to spring at the doors, and the trains are packed, packed, packed. The whole of midtown is thinking of what to make or order or warm up for dinner, of how they'll turn the TV on in the background and get sucked in by its siren song.

As the train she needs draws up to the platform, Katherine sees a car that doesn't seem too crowded. She tries not to get her hopes up. If it seems too good to be true, it is. The door opens and she takes a small, tentative sniff, but smells nothing too offensive and so steps on. She needs to get home to Lucas. It's not full, but there aren't any free seats. She'll have to stand.

After the third stop she begins to feel faint. She holds on tightly to the pole, but there are floaters in front of her eyes and the humming in her ears grows louder.

"Hey, do you need to sit down?" A nice-looking guy, dark hair, dark-framed glasses, green sneakers, a backpack, looks up from his iPad.

Katherine is too grateful to protest, though surely she doesn't *look* pregnant yet? She sits, mouths, *Thank you.*

He shrugs it off and gestures to her still-flat belly. "Of course, in your condition . . ." He smiles and looks away.

Katherine feels cold. *It's like that old man. How do they know?*

A high, harsh monotone jars her out of this unpleasant thought.

"God, our Most Holy Father, is angry with the wicked every day. I am living testimony of the truth of the wicked sinner, because I came to the foot of Christ, and Christ burned me pure with His holy flame. God will judge you according to His perfect, absolute laws. If we want to be saved, we must be born again, we must be born again!"

Oh no, she thinks. *One of those Bible-thumpers.* Or, worse, the Heaven's True fanatics. Rising to prominence after the Sickle Man's summer of slaughter, spreading their terrifying gospel, convinced the End of Days are near. They are everywhere now, putting up posters, handing out pamphlets, and the worst part is that they seem normal. Until they begin to talk to you.

She closes her eyes.

"It's the Truth and the Word is the Truth and God said you will burn! God is love, but God is also a jealous God, and He sees you all worshipping your false idols and He will smite you down in the fire pits of Hell! He sees you sinning and will smite you down! This is the Word and the Truth, the End Times are here, my friends, and you will all burn."

The Bible-thumper is getting closer. Katherine can see him now. He wears a thin white shirt, untucked, and a gray jacket and tan pants. His skin is the color of faded leather, pulled tight across his bones. He is gaunt to the point of starvation. The whites of his eyes are wet and shiny, like fried egg whites. Sweat gleams upon his forehead. His nostrils flare and his tongue darts out, lizard-like, to wet his lips as he preaches. There is a fire within him. One skeletal hands waves and jerks as a conductor's might, and the other grasps a well-thumbed Bible.

"Turn back to Jesus, turn back to Jesus, you filthy sinners! You will burn in Hell! Mock not the Lord and the Word of the Lord, you sodomites!"

"C'mon," sighs the immense man sitting on Katherine's right. His shirt strains against his bulk. All around her the stone faces of the passengers are beginning to crack.

"You sinners, you slaves of the devil all around us, the sins of the sodomites! Homosexuality and drinking and drugs . . ."

He's getting louder, as is the *ca-shunk ca-shunk ca-shunk*, and the rattling roar of the train as it picks up speed, shooting through the blackness. It's going express, and there's no way out of this car other than pushing through the packed riders to the door at the end of it.

We're trapped like rats. She thinks.

The thumper's voice rises in pitch, in volume, until it's almost a shout, grating against her ears. There is no blocking it, no tuning it out. The only thing she can do is wait until she can get off at the next stop.

And then he is there. The footsteps stop, but the harsh voice carries on. *What makes a person do this?* Katherine just wants to go home and nurse her wounds. Maybe she'll even have half a glass of wine. She deserves it.

"Sinners! All of you! And you will burn—"

He breaks off abruptly. She glances upward. He's standing directly in front of her.

"Oh God! Oh Great and Glorious God in Heaven! I see, I see you have blessed us! You are come, She is here! Holy, holy, holy. Oh blessed day! Oh God, you have not forsaken us! You have blessed us and blessed us with the Light and the Truth!"

The Bible-thumper sinks down upon his bony knees in front of her amid the passengers, his arms stretched up, palms splayed, the Bible aloft. His head thrown back in rapture.

"Hail, thou that art highly favoured, the Lord is *with* thee!"

Katherine tries not to panic. *Don't let him touch me. I'll die if he touches me.*

"Back off!" Her massive neighbor, his bald head gleaming, veins popping in his arms, rises up, looking angry. "Back the fuck off from her, man."

A rumble of assent echoes through the car, but the man now kneeling in front of Katherine pays no attention. He is crying, tears coursing in wet streaks down his face.

"Oh God, You are coming to us through this Most Holy Vessel—"

"That's enough." A woman seated just opposite Katherine dressed in black yoga pants and an off-the-shoulder pink-and-blue-tie-dyed shirt, a cross between a gypsy and a middle-aged hippie, reaches out to her. The woman's already tired face is further worn with concern. She has the largest hoop earrings Katherine has ever seen. "Come over here, honey."

Katherine would like to get to her, but she doesn't think she can stand without touching the weeping man, who is now prostrating himself at her feet.

"Blessed art thou among women!"

"I mean it, man. Back off!"

The large guy is furious. He's lost his chance to be the modern day superhero. His authority unheeded, he is now reduced to red-faced impotence.

"That's it! I'm calling the cops."

Another man, possibly a construction worker in his paint-splashed pants and massive tan boots, takes action. He rises and gently takes hold of the Bible-thumper's shoulders. "Come on, buddy, get back, stop this."

The murmurs of agreement are growing louder now, banding together.

"Don't you see? Can't you see her light? How beautiful it is? Oh God, You have not deserted me, You have not deserted us. Oh Christ, you are returning!" His high voice rises higher, his words speed up, become incomprehensible.

Oh fuck! He's speaking in tongues!

And finally, finally the train slows.

Stops.

Almost everyone, including Katherine, gets off.

"You okay?" A thin woman wants to know. Her hair is unnaturally black and her breasts seem insanely large and high, but the concern in her eyes is the real thing. "You okay, sweetie? Jeez, that guy was freaky. You wanna sit down?" She gestures to a bench on the platform.

"I'm okay, just a little shaken." Katherine is more than shaken, she is faint with nausea, but she needs to keep moving.

"Nuts," offers a sharply suited guy as he passes. "They're all nuts these days."

"An 'only in New York' moment, am I right? You sure you're okay, honey?"

"I'm okay," Katherine repeats.

The black-haired woman purses her pink lips. She doesn't want to let go of the drama.

Katherine needs to move, fast. "Thank you so much! Sorry, I have to pick my kid up." She merges with the crowd surging up the stairs.

Then she's outside and it's good to be outside in the fresh, sharp, almost-evening air. It shakes off the craziness. Out here, she's just another person hurrying to pick up her kid, hurrying home. She passes a woman sitting on the corner. Her head is down, matted gray hair covers her face. One thin, mottled hand clutches at the multitude of filthy shawls and blankets forming a cocoon around her. A dirty, dog-eared cardboard sign with the words ANYTHING HELPS is propped up against the curb next to a plastic cup, which at a glance holds two limp dollar bills and some meager change. *There's a person who's had a worse day than I've had*, Katherine thinks. She takes out her wallet, hesitates over the one, then gets out a five. On the off chance that someone is up there watching, maybe they'll put in a good word for her.

"Here." She bends down to place the bill in the woman's cup.

The old woman does not raise her head. "Thank you, Katherine."

Katherine stops, wheels back around. "*What* did you say?"

There is no response. The old woman's head is still down. She slumps, a heap of old age huddled in old shawls, a posture of total defeat. The world has beaten her. Or maybe she's just drunk.

"Miss? Hello? Sorry, did you say something? A name?" Katherine leans in a little closer, bracing herself for the smell of old age and drink and dirt. Surprisingly, there's only a faint tang of lemons, and no answer. "Miss?"

Still nothing.

Katherine sighs and turns to go.

A skinny, wrinkled hand, shoots out from within the layers of stained fabric and grabs Katherine's wrist. The old woman raises her head. Her hair is wild and her forehead is seamed with lines, but her eyes—Katherine cannot look away from her shining, silver eyes.

Her voice is low, rasping, but her words are clear. "Do not fear the Annunciation."

Katherine jerks back with a cry. The old woman releases her grasp and her head sinks down once again. Her mottled hand returns to the folds of what is now not a collection of shawls but a velvet starry cloak.

Katherine turns violently away, her heart in her throat. She walks quickly, almost running. *Keep going. Just keep going. I'm not going to think about it*, she promises herself. *The whole of today is best buried and forgotten.*

But that night as she lies in bed, the treacherous little voice begins to whisper: *Silver. The old woman's eyes were silver. No human being has silver eyes.*

"Shut up," Katherine tells the little voice out loud. "I imagined it. It was a rough day. Go to sleep."

And, after a surprisingly short while, she does.

4

Margaret

I am outside feeding the pigs when my father finds me. He comes to me there so I cannot protest. Nothing must upset his new bride, his new love. Over the sows' grunts and squeals, he orders me to teach Cecily how to brew. She must come with me to the market to learn what spices to purchase. His mouth is turned down in a scowl and his eyes are hard. He is readying himself for a fight, but I give him none, for I see that he means it. Still he pauses, as if he wishes to say something more. He stands there, silent, as the chaff from my bucket floats in the sunlight and the pigs root happily in their muck. Then he turns away. I am glad to see his back, for the relief in his eyes is wounding.

Even my own father is afraid of me.

Before setting out I was unsure what would we talk about, but the answer became clear. She does not talk and so neither do I, though I glance over at her pretty sullen face. Her blue eyes gaze at some point in the distance, her cheeks are flushed and her mouth pursed tight. I wonder what she is thinking. There is no way of telling, but it is of little matter as we can hear and smell the market even before it comes into view.

Cecily's step quickens, as does mine. The squawks and clucks, bleats and brays of the livestock swell in chorus with the trader's shouts and cries and whistles. I catch the reek of the tannery, the dark tang of leather, then the sharp, thin smell of cheese and a lovely earthen scent of fresh bread. Underneath all of it is the slightly sour odor of sweaty wool. The market is unusually busy. Pilgrims of high and low birth, distinguishable by their clothes and their retinues, or lack thereof, and servants of all ranks rub shoulders with wealthy town merchants and their wives. There are many who have come to buy and sell, but still more who are only here to stretch their legs, to feel the weak sun upon their faces and to be in the company of others. Cecily's face blossoms into a smile. She's spotted two of her friends and she runs toward them as if released from a prison. There is no question of whether I would like to join her. I would not, nor would she have me.

Cecily says something to the girls and gestures in my direction. The three of them begin to laugh. I turn away; I have spices to buy. If she was by my side she could see how I recognize each spice by its color and smell. How I am able to measure quality from the snap of cinnamon sticks, to the nutmeg's heady pull. Nor is she there to learn how to barter with the spice merchant, who does not like me. Perhaps something about my face troubles her, or maybe she has heard the rumors and stories that linger behind me like a shadow. I do good business with her and always try to pay a fair price, and still she fears me. I can only take small comfort knowing she will not try to hold her thumb on the scale.

Spices bought, I wander through the main market street, past the fishmongers and the furriers, the butchers and the bakers, the cheesemongers and the cloth merchants. It is packed with a rough, rowdy, merry throng. Stray dogs and small children have grown bold and weave among the legs of their elders. Men of wealth keep their fat, sweaty hands upon their purses, as pickpockets abound. I see a cluster of women surrounding a colorful green stall, cooing and exclaiming. A new merchant must have arrived in town. I can understand their excitement as I draw closer. The cloth on display is wonderful. Not just the usual fare of scratchy, discolored wools, but fine fabrics. A few bolts look to be silks, even satins, though no one dares to finger them. Women have been flogged for wearing that which is only to be worn by nobility.

The stall is watched over by an old crone with a face like a withered apple. She sits sourly as we marvel over cloth most of us will never be able to afford. I do not want to give her the satisfaction of showing any interest, but even I am tempted by a ream of rich red fabric that sings out to me. Almost against my will, my fingers reach out to caress it. They have barely alighted upon a fold when I hear a shout and my hand jerks back as if from a hot coal. After a moment I hear another shout and another, then a yell and laughter. I turn to see what the commotion is about.

People have formed into a makeshift ring blocking the main street of the market. I join other townsfolk in the ever-widening circle, curious to watch. I cannot see much, but I manage to squeeze my way to the front.

There, in the center, an old drunk beats a large man with a stick. I recognize the drunk as Old Warren; a fixture of the King's Head for many years, he was finally banned over a fortnight ago, more for his filthy temper than his inability to settle his debts. My father cannot stand the sight of him. Old Warren must have found something strong elsewhere, as now he's thoroughly soused, red-faced and frothing. Drink only serves to increase the vigor of his blows, which rain down as he curses the other man. He shows no signs of tiring.

Old Warren's victim is twice his size. He has a sloping brow and the bewildered eyes of a child. It is clear the man is a fool, and help-less. Now he cowers down, whimpering, his huge hands trying to ward off Old Warren's fists. The crowd is delighted. They hoot and cheer. Some encourage Old Warren to hit him harder, while others urge the fool to strike back. It is fine entertainment, better even than a dancing bear. I look at the spectators and my eyes fall upon Cecily, standing among her friends. Her cheeks are flushed with excitement, she's breathing heavily, and her eyes are shining. She laughs and laughs. A bitter taste fills my mouth.

As I turn to go, there is a commotion across the ring, a shifting and parting, and a small boy, his ugly freckled skin drawn tight against his bones, pushes his way through. He must be fearless or mad or both, because he charges head down toward Old Warren. The old man stumbles, but manages to give the boy a mighty crack with his stick and he flies backward to land almost at my feet.

The boy lies there, motionless. I wonder if he will rise again, but then incredibly he sits up slowly, dazed and blinking. The spec-tators clap their hands, their bloodlust red and roaring. The boy looks directly at me, his eyes, bright with unshed tears, begging for help. I see now how young he is. His cheeks are filthy. I can make no move to aid him. What good could I possibly do?

As he stares at me, Old Warren stands and lurches toward him, stick upraised. Before I can cry out, he brings it crashing down upon the boy's head. The stick only slams the packed earth. The boy is no longer there. Something in my face must have warned him, and he's rolled away to scramble back on his feet. Old War-ren swings again and again, while the boy ducks and weaves, both locked in a brutal dance. Finally Old Warren, lunges wildly and the boy twists sideways and leaps onto the mad drunkard's back. The crowd hollers its approval. It seems they have a soft spot for the underdog, after all.

Old Warren flails, but now that his air supply is being cut off, he's turning purple. He teeters and totters, bellowing like a wounded bull. The boy hangs on grimly. Finally, the old man drops to his knees and then sprawls facedown in the dirt. The onlookers go wild. The boy is the victor, but he takes no joy in his triumph. His first action is to comfort, to console. He scrambles over to the feeble giant, who sits, enormous shoulders shaking with sobs. A rumble now from the back of the crowd; the sheriff's men are here, and they will spoil everyone's fun. There are halfhearted protests and grumbles from the spectators, but eventually they begin to dissipate. It's been enjoyable, but enough of the day has been squandered. There are still goods to be sold and bought, and deals to be done.

I look back at the boy and the giant, already forgotten. The boy speaks quietly to the fool, who gazes at him with worshipful wet eyes. I can see that boy means everything to this man, that he loves the boy and the boy loves him too. They are each other's world. My heart aches. I wonder what this boy and his fool would do if they knew that someone envied them.

I glance at Cecily, who is avidly talking with her two companions. As I walk toward her, one of them glances up and extends her index and little finger and curls the rest, a gesture to ward off evil. The other girl looks down at her feet, ashamed and fearful. When I greet them, they barely acknowledge me and soon move away. Cecily sighs, resigned to her fate, and we walk back to the stalls to finish our purchases. On our way, she manages to buy not one but *two* meat pies with the coins my father has given her. She makes no offer to share as she eats them in quick greedy bites, sucking the pastry crumbs off her fingers. It is not a fetching sight, but she does not care how she appears now. After all, I do not count as company.

Down in the cellar of the King's Head, Cecily seems a trifle green. Keeping my promise to my father, I begin explaining how to make the ale. How the grains must be mashed, how much yeast to add. Cecily is nodding, but all the while her cheeks gleam, white and dripping as candles. When I prepare the mixture she begins to gag. She tries to get ahold of herself, tries to cover her mouth, but it is no use.

"The smell," she begins to tell me, "the smell—" then with a gasp of pain, clutching her stomach, she leans over and vomits; pastry crust and meat pool in wet stinking chunks on the dirt floor.

She turns with a cry and runs, clambering up the stairs, leaving me alone in the darkness.

I stare at the slimy mess. She may say what she will about the smell of the grain, or perhaps she will blame it on the pie maker, but it is clear now what her true condition is. Whether she learns to make ale or not makes no difference, because she holds all the power she'll ever need within her womb.

My days in my father's house are numbered.

5

Katherine

It's 5:30 a.m. and Katherine is sneaking around the sublet, trying not to wake up the five-year-old sleeping in the next room. It's funny, it's Lucas's birthday, and yet she's the one who's overexcited. Terrified, more like it. *What the hell am I doing?* she wonders, but there's a satisfaction in it—the phrase "go big or go home" comes to mind as she gets ready in her jeans and shirt, clothing cherished because it isn't office attire. She pushes back his door and begins to sing:

> *Happy birthday to you!*
> *Happy birthday to you!*
> *Happy birthday, dear Lucas,*
> *Happy birthday to you!*

He's up, eyes bright and alert. Katherine wonders how much sleep he got.

"Hey, kid!"

"Hey, Kat!"

For a moment, she stands in the doorway, unsure of what to do next. On his last birthday, there were piles of presents. On his last birthday, his mom was alive. On his last birthday, Katherine was happy to give him a hug and a kiss, happy to watch from the sidelines. Now she's in center field and all the stadium lights shine on her.

"Well," she says.

He looks nervous, as if she is going to change her mind, sit on his bed and say, *Now Lucas, I need to talk to you.*

Instead, she smiles. "Let's have breakfast and be on our way."

Breakfast is not a success. Lucas watches his cereal grow soggy, while Katherine picks at her toast. Both of them are too keyed up to eat.

Finally, they decide to pack two apples, some small cheese sticks, and granola bars for the journey. It's one of those magnanimous bright blue days that September likes to give out as summer's parting gift. Lucas is fizzing with excitement. It's hard for him to keep still; he shifts from foot to foot. To the tune of "The Wheels on the Bus," he sings: "We're going to get a dog today, dog today, dog today. We're going to get a dog today, a doggie doggie dog!"

Katherine hasn't seen him so happy since before Andrea died. Despite her anxiety over how they'll actually take home a dog, his joy makes it all worth it. She smiles at him, and then resumes thinking about her plan. She's thinking a small dog. Not an aggressive little pillow dog, but it's going to have to be small or else how are they going to manage? Lucas understands that he'll have to take care of it himself, feed it, and so on. But she also understands that while he may have the best intentions in the world, he's still only five. He's starting to comprehend responsibility, but she'll need to be there if (when) the going gets tough.

They can't afford professional dog-walking services. In this neighborhood, children are taken care of by immigrants who get paid minimum wage, but dogs are walked by people with master's degrees from Columbia. However, she has her eye on a teenage neighbor whom she thinks will do nicely. Actually, it doesn't seem like such a bad career, dog-walking. The sun, the dogs, staying in shape, getting to know the city, notes about infamous clients stored later for some wildly successful novel. Do dog-walkers have health insurance?

"Kat?" Lucas looks up at her, perhaps sensing her drifting.

"Oh, sorry, honey, I was daydreaming."

It isn't convenient. It isn't going to be easy. But he's in a new school and a new neighborhood. His mom is dead. A dog seems like a small concession.

They get the subway uptown. Lucas grips her hand tight. Katherine is happy for him, but now she begins to worry. How will any dog be able to meet these expectations? This little boy's happiness seems as fragile as an eggshell, or a taut, bright balloon ready to burst.

It's an uneventful train ride. That is to say, there are no religious freaks kissing her feet or speaking in tongues. No silver-eyed women. The train is full, crowded for the weekend. Sure enough, there's an announcement about construction; the last leg of the journey is all local stops, anticipation building with each one. Lucas squirms in his seat and tries to get up at every stop, hope leaping in his eyes.

"Not yet," she says. "Almost there."

She tries to remember when she was this excited about anything. *Meeting Sael. You were excited about that*, she reminds herself. It's no fun being an adult.

Eventually, it's their stop. Katherine and Lucas walk out of the subway into the sunny, chilly morning. Finally, they are at their destination, a white building with murals across its walls. Inside, the odor of disinfectant covers any real animal smell, but the cacophony of barking, whining, and yapping is nearly deafening.

They stop by the front desk, where a plump girl with a ponytail sits. Her name tag reads KENDRA.

"We're getting a dog!" Lucas informs her.

Kendra smiles at him. His enthusiasm is contagious.

"That's great," she says. "Is it going to be your first dog?"

He nods violently. "Yes, and it's my birthday!"

"That's wonderful." She turns to Katherine. "Got all your paperwork?"

Katherine hands over her ID, proof of residence. She's already filled in her preferences on the form: not a puppy but an older dog, one that needs a good home. She can totally relate. *We also need a good home, me and Lucas. We're housebroken and we don't shed, so please, oh please, take us in.*

This is a good thing, she repeats in her head as she watches Kendra go over the paperwork. *I'm doing a good thing. I'm getting an orphaned boy a dog. I'm saving a dog. Anything to make Lucas smile, to make him laugh like he used to. These are good things. Well done, me.*

So why is her skin creeping with this sense of dread?

With the paperwork in order, the door opens and they follow Kendra down a long corridor. *To death row,* Katherine can't help imagining, and then reprimands herself. Then through a series of passageways until they reach the sign that says VISITORS. She sees another couple looking for a dog, pausing by each one of the cages. A couple choosing their first dog together, no rings yet but surely not long now.

Katherine feels a pang. *That could have been Sael and me*—the thought is unavoidable. *Sael, who's moving; Sael, who needed closure. Maybe I can train this dog to sniff out anyone who has the potential to break my heart. I can sic him on to mankind; he'll give a piercing bark to warn me of romantic danger.*

It's only then that she registers the total silence. No barks, no whines, no whimpers.

Lucas realizes it too. He looks up at Kendra. "Why aren't they barking?"

Kendra licks her lips. "I, uh, I don't know."

Their footfalls are amplified as they walk along the row of cages. Pit bulls; Labrador-like dogs, mostly short-haired; a small grimy Maltese. The other couple has disappeared. No one says anything. Dogs that only a minute ago were pacing, leaping up against their cages, are now sitting, then lying down as they pass. Heads between front paws, perfectly still, perfectly quiet.

"Um . . ." Kendra clears her throat. She seems torn between acknowledging what is happening and denying it. She decides to push forward with the latter, her voice growing louder and falsely bright, almost maniacal, as she talks faster and faster. Like a real estate agent trying to sell a haunted house. *Heck no, what poltergeist?*

"So we're going to check out Lucy. Lucy is a sweet white pit bull. Now I know pit bulls get a bad rap, but the good ones, well, Lucy is the best, aren't you, sweetheart? We've only known her to be gentle with other dogs, and she loves people."

Please bark, Katherine prays as they approach the cage. *Please just bark like a normal dog.* But Lucy doesn't make a sound. As they approach, she scrabbles back into the corner of her cage. Her head wags from side to side, then goes down between her paws. She cowers, desperate.

"Lucy," Kendra calls, her voice echoing in the terrible silence. "Lucy, come on, girl." Then she's in the cage, trying to pull Lucy out. "Lucy, come on, girl. Lucy, what's going on?"

"What's the matter with her?" It's the guy from the couple. They have stopped looking at dogs to stare at Lucy as she scrabbles away from Kendra and Katherine and Lucas.

Kendra doesn't answer him, only keeps on at Lucy, trying to get her to come out. It's no use. Lucy whimpers and crouches. Finally, Kendra wipes her face with the back of her arm.

"I guess Lucy is having a bad day," she says, her voice flat. Then she straightens up and tries to smile. "Well, there are other candidates for you."

She and Lucas back up, and it seems to Katherine that Lucy relaxes a little. The farther away they get, the happier Lucy will be. Meanwhile, every sound is magnified. The guy breathing through his nose, his girlfriend chewing her gum. It makes Katherine want to slap them both.

Lucas tugs at her arm. "Kat, why aren't they barking?"

Now the girlfriend is whispering something to her boyfriend, who's unabashedly staring at Katherine and Lucas.

"I don't know, honey. Maybe they just feel like being quiet?"

Kendra turns to Katherine. "I've never seen this before. Are you wearing something? Some pheromone perfume or whatever?" She sounds angry.

Not angry, Katherine suddenly realizes, *she's frightened*. "No, apart from my normal deodorant, nothing."

The walk is endless, but they finally arrive at the last cage to the right. The nameplate on the front says BORIS.

Kendra clears her throat. "This is Boris. Boris is a three-year-old, a Catahoula leopard dog mix," she recites.

The three of them look down into the cage, down into Boris's fuzzy, brown face. *Please don't open the door, please just let him be.* But Kendra is already bending down. Katherine hears the seams of Kendra's jeans creak as she kneels, the harsh jangle of her key chain, her heavy breathing.

A film of sweat forms on Kendra's upper lip. "Come on, Boris," she breathes. "Come on, boy."

Boris retreats to the back of his cage, trembling.

"Come on, Boris, be a good boy."

"Holy shit," someone says behind them, "that dog is fucking terrified."

Katherine turns around. It's the guy from the couple, both of whom are riveted. Her stomach sinks further.

Kendra is dragging Boris out by the collar. He is curled into a small, miserable ball of rigid muscle. She seems baffled.

"I don't understand it. I've never seen him behave like this."

"I gotta record this! This shit is unbelievable." The girlfriend is holding up her phone.

Please, Katherine tries to say, but her tongue flaps like a piece of rope.

"Hey!" Kendra looks up. "You're not allowed to record anything here."

The woman takes no notice.

Lucas bends down and tentatively puts out one hand. "Boris?"

"Excuse me, miss!" Kendra is trying to get authority back, and is building up steam. "You're going to need to put that away."

The woman swings her phone around to focus on Lucas, crouching by Boris's side.

"Miss!" Kendra's tone is sharper. "I'm only going to tell you one more time to stop that. Recording is strictly prohibited on the premises."

"This is fucking crazy shit," her boyfriend mutters, transfixed. "Like *exorcist* shit."

Lucas's head is close to Boris's, he's speaking quietly.

"Hey, Boris." His voice is soft and sweet. "What's wrong, boy? Tell me." He cocks his ear to Boris's muzzle, as if he is waiting for the dog to answer.

"That's it!" Kendra explodes, "I'm getting my supervisor. Hold on for a moment," she says to Katherine and Lucas before turning and almost running back up the corridor.

Katherine looks again at the couple, the woman still engrossed in filming Lucas. There's a harsh drone of wasps in her ears. Rage fills her like black smoke, and her voice erupts from somewhere deep within her.

"Leave him alone!"

Suddenly the girl squints at her phone, pressing a button.

"Shit," she hisses to her boyfriend. "My phone just died! Try yours."

The guy pulls his phone from his back pocket, then frowns. "Mine's dead too. I just charged it this morning!"

They gape at their lifeless devices, at each other.

Katherine turns her attention back to Lucas, who is still whispering to Boris. Then he looks up, a strange detached, expression upon his face. Icicles slide down her spine. She tries to swallow but her throat is filled with glass and stones.

"Lucas? Honey?"

His gaze, so alien a moment before, now clears. He becomes himself again.

Thank God for that at least, she thinks.

"We have to go," he mutters, and slowly he gets to his feet.

She wonders if they can just leave Boris there, coiled up and quivering, but she doesn't think they'll be able to move him without distressing him further. She senses that, as with Lucy, the farther away they get from the dogs, the happier they'll be.

"We have to go!" Lucas is more urgent now.

Her stomach roils and heaves. She wipes her forehead with the back of her hand. *Forget about the dogs—the sooner we leave, the happier I'll be.*

"Okay." She holds out her hand. "Let's go."

Lucas stands. His expression is both sorrowful and resigned. He is far too young to wear it. He takes her hand and turns to the small unhappy animal.

"Bye, Boris," he says.

They retreat up the row, pushing past the couple, who are now bickering, their frustration with their phones turned on each other. Katherine tries not to look at them. Then she sees Kendra and a thin, frowning woman with short spiky hair coming toward them.

"What's going on here?" The spiky-haired woman, presumably Kendra's supervisor, is pissed and ready to unleash hell on anyone.

"It's not them." Kendra says. "It's those other two, through there."

The shock of relief is so strong, that Katherine's knees almost give way. Kendra isn't going to mention the strange behavior of the dogs.

The woman nods and moves on toward the couple.

Katherine lays her hand on Kendra's arm.

Kendra flinches.

Katherine swallows. "I think it's best that we try this at another time."

"Yeah." Kendra is blanched. "Perhaps that's for the best."

"We can always come back." Katherine knows that they will never come back.

"Maybe that's better. I'm sorry, I don't understand it."

Katherine attempts a smile. "I'll remember to use a different perfume."

"I'm sorry," Kendra says to Lucas. Her regret appears genuine.

Tears prick at Katherine's eyes. "Me too," she whispers.

"Take care," Kendra tells them, but this isn't just an automatic dismissal.

It feels like a warning.

Katherine hears it as they exit, an exuberant howling. Then they're outside in the cold sunshine of a September day, where the rest of the world is carrying on around them as if nothing has happened.

"Honey?"

Lucas rears away.

"Lucas?"

He still won't look at her.

"Lucas, talk to me. We promised each other we would use our words."

He mutters something inaudible.

Katherine crouches down. "What was that?"

"He was scared." Lucas's tone is reluctant. He still won't look at her.

"Who was scared? You were scared?"

"Boris. Boris was scared."

"He did seem scared," Katherine admits, though she's aware that's an understatement. *He seemed terrified.* "Do you know what he was scared of?"

"He told me."

"He told you? What was he scared of?"

Lucas shakes his head.

She's on the edge of something crucial. She presses him. "Lucas, you can tell me. What was he scared of?"

He mumbles something, but she's unsure whether she's heard him correctly. "Me?"

A nod.

The dogs were scared of her. The horror of it knocks her back, winds her, leaves her breathless. *How can it be? It can't be, can it?* "Oh, sweetheart." A wave of helplessness washes over her. It's impossible, it's unfair, but Lucas believes it. Maybe it's better that he does. *At least he can blame me, blame someone. At least there's some control in this scenario.*

"I'm so sorry, Lucas." And Katherine is sorry. She's sorry Andrea is dead, and she's sorry that those other women are dead too. She's sorry that Sael doesn't love her anymore. She is sorry, sorry, sorry.

He scuffs his shoe furiously in the dirt.

"Come on," she says, and gathers him into her arms. "Come on, it's okay." Even though it's not okay, and it never will be okay.

Eventually, the tears come. Katherine hasn't seen Lucas cry like this before. It's something she's spoken about with the child psychologist. *Is he holding all his emotions back? Will it turn into anger? Is this normal?*

But how could anyone handle this kind of grief? He's only five today. He weeps and weeps. She cries too. The city streams around them, the sun is still shining, but they are under their own cloud of sadness and there is nothing to do but cry until—

"Katherine?"

Sael is standing in front of her. How did he get here? Is this even his neighborhood? She isn't sure if he moved or not. He's in track-suit pants, a sweatshirt. He must have come from a fitness class. Katherine remembers that he used to like something to do with riding stationary bikes in a darkened room to hard-core music, but she can't think of the name. There must be a studio around here.

"Hi," she croaks, still holding Lucas, shielding him from the world as best she can.

"What's wrong? What happened?" Sael's face screws up with concern.

"Oh, nothing, we're okay." Katherine wipes her eyes with the backs of her hands, and digs in her pockets for tissues, or paper napkins, or *something* with which to blow her nose, blow Lucas's nose. "We just had a rough morning."

"Wow. It must have been." Sael crouches down, and very gently he addresses Lucas's small, woeful figure. "Hi, Lucas."

Lucas sniffs. Turns away.

"Lucas?"

Lucas stares at his sneakers.

Sael stands up, wiping his hands on his legs. "Well, I'll tell you what I do on rough mornings. I turn to hot chocolate. Sound good?"

Katherine is about to decline when Lucas tugs at her hand. She looks down.

"Want to go and eat something?"

"Yeah." He sounds so small and lost that she almost starts weeping all over again.

"Well, I know of just the place. This cool little café. And you know what? I think they even have a cat there!" Sael sounds genuinely excited.

I forgot how kind he can be, she thinks.

"Really?" The idea of a café with a cat has momentarily distracted Lucas.

"Yeah. Wanna see?"

"Okay." Lucas takes Sael's hand, his little paw swallowed up by Sael's larger one.

Sael straightens, and then with his other hand he helps Katherine up. "You can tell me about it there."

The sun warms their faces as they walk to a small coffee shop. Katherine and Sael order croissants and coffee, and Lucas gets a hot chocolate and a donut.

Katherine mentions in passing that it's Lucas's birthday, but downplays it. *Please*—she wants to beam her thoughts, laser-like into Sael's brain—*please don't make a big deal about it*. Sael, to his credit, doesn't. He has, after all, just seen them sobbing on the street.

They talk instead of comfortable meaningless subjects, the weather, the cat that is currently sleeping on the bench outside the coffee shop, until Sael asks, "Now, what happened?"

Lucas shifts and shakes his head. He sits, mute and miserable.

Katherine can't bear it. "Want me to start?" She looks at him.
He nods.

"Well, we were planning on adopting a dog today, because of . . .
Well, you know. But unfortunately, we didn't find one. The dogs
were sort of acting . . . *strangely*."

"They were scared!" Lucas is direct.

Sael turns to him. "Scared? What were they scared of?"

Lucas looks at Katherine. She's too exhausted to keep making up
stories, building walls against the growing darkness.

"Lucas thinks they were scared of me," she says. Voicing Lucas's
accusation is an unexpected relief. He hates her. She has let him
down. She's the worst excuse for a mother ever. Let the world know.
She has nothing more to give, come what may. She leans back, emp-
tied out.

Sael has opened his mouth and he's about to say something, but
it's Lucas who speaks.

"No."

"No?" Katherine sits back up and stares down at him.

Lucas is shaking his head, as though he's a little surprised,
maybe even annoyed, that Katherine got it so wrong. "They weren't
scared of *you*. They were scared of the baby."

Sael wields around to Katherine. "The baby?"

She opens her mouth, but only a dusty squeak comes out.

He turns to Lucas. "What baby, Lucas?" His voice is cool.

Lucas is matter-of-fact. "The baby that's growing in Kat." But as
soon as he speaks, he turns to Katherine, his eyes round, his hand
clapped over his mouth, appalled. "Oh! I forgot! It's a secret!"

"That's okay, love." Katherine's voice is weak. It would be comical if it weren't so catastrophic. "I'm not mad at you." *Oh. Fuck.*

"Katherine? What baby?" Sael asks calmly, rationally. Somehow,
this makes it worse.

She turns to him. Panic makes the blood in her ears sing and her skin cold, as though she has been thrown into a swimming pool. "The baby that I'm having."

"My baby?" His eyes are wide, astonished. He asks not cruelly, but in disbelief.

And then he sees the answer in her eyes.

There is pressure on Katherine's arm.

"Kat?" Lucas's worried face peers up at her.

Some birthday, she thinks. "It's fine, honey. It's okay. We're just talking."

It's impossible to read Sael's expression.

Eventually, he says, "Okay. Katherine, we'll talk later. I need to process this."

"Okay." Her tone is as dry and practical as his.

He gets up. "Happy birthday," he says to Lucas, and then he's gone.

"Kat?" Lucas says again into the vacuum left by Sael's abrupt departure. "I'm sorry."

"Lamb, don't worry about it. It doesn't matter. It really doesn't matter."

Katherine is reeling after this apocalypse. She takes a deep breath, then another. She can't show Lucas how she feels. She has to keep it together.

"But why do you think the dogs were scared of the baby?"

She wonders if, maybe, Lucas is scared of the baby. Jealous? Unhappy? They haven't talked about it since he mentioned it to her when they were sitting in the park, just over a month ago. She has no idea how he knew she was pregnant when she herself had only a glimmer. She hasn't questioned him, though.

After he'd begun drawing the murdered women, and demonstrating a preternatural ability to pick up on her thoughts, her energy, she just accepted it—whatever *it* was. She'd hoped that this frightening ability would recede like the tide when the terrible summer ended, that he would go back to being an "ordinary" little kid, preoccupied with superheroes or trucks or animals or the latest thing kids liked these days.

Now, deeply troubled, she stares at him and waits for him to answer.

"Boris told me."

"Boris? You mean the dog? He spoke to you?" How much more can she take today? Is this yet another form of regression? But knowing Lucas's history, his *ability*, she can't discount it.

This actually, amazingly, brings forth a watery smile from Lucas. "No. Dogs can't talk, silly."

"Oh, that's right." She tries to smile to show how foolish she was. *Silly me.*

"No, no, he showed me."

She wonders if she should ask, how far she should take this. There will be no going back. "How, Lucas?" A pulse pounds in her temples.

"When I put my face close to his, he showed me." Lucas is becoming frustrated as he tries to describe it to her. "With pictures."

"Pictures?" "Like the ones you drew for me?" Katherine battles to understand. Her mind darts briefly to the drawings of "the ladies," with their huge howling mouths and squiggled red lines but again Lucas shakes his head no.

"Like on television or the movies."

"What did the pictures show you?" She can't believe she sounds so calm. A spring of hysteria bubbles up in her chest. She fights to keep down the screaming spray of laughter.

"They were . . . They were kind of fuzzy. There was light." Lucas has forgotten his sadness for now. He is determined to explain this to her.

"Light?"

"Very light and it hurt my eyes and the ground shook and the sky . . ."

"The sky?"

He seems unwilling to go on. Finally, he mutters, "It was the wrong color."

Katherine swallows. She cannot show him how his words terrify her. She wrestles to get her voice back under control. "Well, I can understand why the dogs would have been scared."

He nods. "The dogs knew and they didn't want to go with us."

"I'm sorry to hear that." *It's true. I am more sorry than he could possibly know.*

He just looks at her, his eyes warm with an awful understanding. It seems to Katherine that she is now the small, disappointed child and he the adult who must comfort her.

"Maybe we can try again later, at another place."

Lucas is shaking his head. "No, they won't ever do that. They'll always be scared."

Katherine remembers the shivering dogs, the thick reek of fear, their total, paralyzing surrender. The howling as they left. She would like nothing better than to crawl into bed and pull the covers up over her head, but it is Lucas's birthday after all. She must do what she can.

"I know it's been kind of a horrible day so far. What can we do to make it better?"

Hours later, Lucas is almost asleep, lulled by the new book they bought and read twice through. They also saw a movie, an animated classic, and she hopes it was a balm, however temporary. Katherine begins to rise from the bed when he seems to jolt awake.

"Kat? Is it true?"

"Is what true?"

"What Boris showed me? The storm and the sky?"

"Honey, I don't know. But we'll keep an eye out, okay?" How can she answer questions she cannot begin to understand? *Please*, she prays, *please let him forget about that. Please let us leave this day behind.*

"Yes, but—"

"But what?"

"I dunno." He sighs. "I feel sad."

"I feel sad too." *What can I give you?* Katherine wonders. *What else can I give? A goldfish seems like a poor substitute.*

But then he's asleep, and it's just her waiting for her phone to ring. She sits and waits.

Her phone rings.

Still, she pauses. Ironic, isn't it, that only yesterday she would have given anything for this call.

She picks up.

"We need to talk," Sael says.

6

Margaret

I never meant to come back to these woods, but there is nowhere else to go.

I knew that they would come for me. I knew it as soon as I heard that the boy had died. They would come for me at night, out of respect for my father. They would come at night, and they would come quietly, but they would come. There is nothing else for it. I take what little I have and flee.

I think about how it will unfold. They will knock, and my father will come to the door. He will tell them that he has not seen me since the morning, and it will be the truth. His manner will be grave, his mind puzzled. But underneath it all, I think he will be relieved. He has never known what to do with me. I have been a burden to him for so many years now. He will be a little sad, though, I think. At times I still remind him of my mother.

Cecily will also appear saddened. Her eyes will be downcast and her mouth solemn. She will turn away, but inside I know she will be dancing with glee. It is Cecily who drives me out. She's done it cleverly; I'll give her that. She's whispering tales to her mother,

her friends, the women at the market, my father's customers. She expels lies as easily as breath of how I stare at her and mutter incantations, how I draw strange symbols in the dust and how she fears for her child growing inside her. Her bastard child.

Her lies are so wonderful that even I am tempted to believe her, to believe in my own power, that I would be capable of such acts. Her audience is a willing one, for they have never liked me and Cecily's lies are vinegar, curdling their fear into hatred. No one will meet my gaze or even do business with me. Only their love for my father has held them back, but now Cecily has spun her web of deceit, and the boy is dead.

I do not think they will search too hard for me here. They fear the woods. Sunlight must battle to pierce through the gnarled branches. Bandits are known to hide within these thickets, bandits and wolves.

My mother loved these woods, and she would always bring me here.

My mother, with her dark hair and shining eyes, her bright way of cocking her head to one side, like a robin. She laughed often, and my father said that when my mother sang, even the songbirds would fall silent with envy.

The villagers loved my mother, although she was a Traveler and they usually hated the gypsies who came to the town to sell their colored beads and bangles, herbs and philters, to tell fortunes and trade horses. But she met my father and they fell in love and she stayed.

She possessed knowledge, handed down through generations, of which plants could heal and which could harm, depending how they were used. The villagers would come to her with all kinds of troubles: their toothaches and heartaches, their backaches and sleepless nights. Sometimes she made up tonics and powders but most often my mother would listen and give counsel, how to flatter and bargain, what to say to sweeten a sullen spouse, how to catch the eye of an intended.

She began to teach me the ways of her people early on. "Like most folk," she'd warn, "flowers can do good or evil."

We would walk through the fields and woods and she showed me where to pick rose hip and hawthorn, how bitter rowan berries could be turned to sweet wine, and how to avoid the blood-red charms of the butcher's broom and spindle.

"Make the wood your friend, my Maggie," she would say. "She is alive. Be good to her and she will be good to you. You must listen to her."

"Can she talk?" I would ask.

"Yes," she always responded, "but not with words of men. She will speak to you through the breeze in her trees, and the water over the stones in her brook. If you listen and love her, she will tell you her secrets and share her gifts with you."

More than once, we would see movement through the trees, a glimpse of fur, and while I always startled, my mother would just smile.

Do not take fright, for they know we wish them no harm.

With my hand in hers, I was never afraid. I loved and trusted my mother, and so I loved and trusted the woods too.

Until the night she was murdered in the very place she had promised was safe.

After that, I never went into the woods again.

Now, I have no choice. The wood is a hungry mouth, and it will swallow me up. I am cold and frightened. I trip over craggy roots and twisted branches catch at me.

"The trees will protect you," my mother always said. *"Let the trees stand guard."*

But the trees did not protect her that night. Why would they protect me now?

I run until I can run no more, and then I fall forward, curling up and covering my face with my hands.

When I wake, the breeze is soft against my skin. A canopy of leaves glows green above me. A bird sings. Another answers. I am hungry and thirsty, but I am alive.

I listen to the rush of water over stones. It grows louder and louder as I pick my way to a brook. The water is clear, icy, and sweet. I drink my fill. My thirst now slaked, I search for food. I stoop and find some berries, glossy and black. As I reach for them I hear my mother's voice

Belladonna. Deadly nightshade. My hand drops to my side.

I remember the warm firm grip of her fingers curled over mine as we made our way through the woods. I remember the sound of her singing, the melody true and winding, clearing a path beneath our feet and how the trees bent their branches aside to make way for us.

I know what I need to do.

It is so long since I sang and it's hard to begin. I cough and falter at first, but then a kernel within the seed sown deep down within me soaks and swells, grasps and curls, unfurls, sprouts pale shoots pushing through a deepening rosy pink, flood with color lengthens and reaches, buds burst up and out, and out rushes a song of green and growing. My gift to the woods. My song. I sing as I walk along the damp, leaf-strewn ground, and soon my foot kicks at something. A nest, two eggs remaining in it, and by their smell I know they are not rotten but abandoned. I can eat them. A brilliant cluster of rowan berries winks orange-red through dark green leaves. Pale mushroom caps peep up beneath my toes. They smell rich and of the earth.

And so it begins.

I remember a little more each day. Where the streams meander through, the trees that protect me from the wind, under the leaves, that give me shade. I offer up my song and am rewarded with mushrooms, berries, wild garlic, burdock, nettles, and dandelion. At night I sleep with moss and leaves under my head, the heavens spread out above me. I stare up and I can hear my mother as clear as a church bell, telling me about the night I was born, how, after the storm, the sky was aflame with stars.

"My people once told me . . ." her voice had trailed off.

"Told you what?" I had asked.

"Never you mind," she had said. "Only know that you are special, for upon your birth the heavens sang and rang with stars in an ancient and glorious song, a night song. You were surely meant for great things when the night sings and your destiny is writ golden in the skies."

My mother. The locked chest of my heart is slowly creaking open.

And so it goes for eight nights; then I have the dream.

He crouches over my mother's body, holding his curved knife. Intent on working its blade, his face is creased in concentration, but still wears a little smile. I try to hold my breath, but a whimper escapes and he looks up. He has black holes instead of eyes. He lets her arm drop into a pool of blood on the ground. Dark and thick, it has left a smeary stain on his sleeve.

"That boy was but nine years old," he says. "His wounds festered and his tongue turned black. His mother is sick with weeping."

The man's voice is light and tender and full of laughter as if imparting pleasant news.

I wake up, my heart hammering.

I remember the boy.

I was returning to our village from the market when they began following me, a gaggle of urchins as small as sparrows, dirty and neglected. They kept a safe distance, whistling and giggling and calling out foul names, daring one another to go closer. It was maddening. I was hot and tired, and each time I swung around they would stop in their tracks, staring at me with insolent eyes. As soon as I turned away, they would begin again. The worst part was knowing that if I couldn't stop them, no one else would. After all, it was their parents who had taught them to hate me.

A sharp stone hit me on the back of the neck. With a cry I stumbled forward to the ground, scraping my palms and knees. I scrabbled up and around to see the boy, his hand still raised, unsure of what to do now that he finally had my full attention. I touched the place where the stone had struck me. My fingers came away, red with blood. The boy could see that I was wounded and perhaps not knowing what else to do, he grinned.

His short life had thus far most likely been a hard and hungry one. It must have been intoxicating for him to feel so powerful, even if only for a moment.

It was the last straw.

My shell cracked, and the words swarmed out. Ancient and twisted, beetle-black, and gleaming green with pincers and stingers and poisonous pointed barbs. They came from a pit of rage festering inside me, ever since my mother's death. They were meant for the villagers who shunned and scorned and hurt me, they were meant for Cecily, but in that moment only this boy was there before me, and I cursed him. I had not known I was capable of such an act. My mother's spirit turned away from me in shame.

"Travelers must use their words with the greatest care," she had warned me more than once. "The fires they ignite are not easily banked." The children scattered every which way, shrieking in terror. The boy froze; then he too turned and ran. I had been goaded beyond endurance, but I would have done anything to take my words back.

I watched the small figure stumbling away and prayed that nothing untoward would happen.

He died on the sixth day.

It is hard to sleep. I lie in the darkness for a long time. I try not to think of the man from my dream.

In the morning, though, all feels well again. The birds are chirping; the wind murmurs through the trees. There are no hateful looks or spiteful comments in these woods, only the brook, low and laughing, to keep me company.

I wake in the night, and do not know why. I stare into the blackness, and then I see them. Yellow eyes watching mine. I take in his huge shape, his fur the color of smoke. I slowly push myself up.

We look at each other for a long time until he pads away, melting into the darkness.

The wolf comes again and again. Each time he gains a little ground and stays a little longer. Tonight he has brought his mate and their three cubs. The cubs roll and, with small squeaks, bat softly at their mother's muzzle. I sit quietly upon the ground, hugging my knees to my chest and beaming. To know that there are living beings in the world that trust me, even take pleasure in my company, that is something worth living for. I have not felt such peace since my mother died.

The next day, I see men in the wood. I count twelve rough, cruel faces in total, wearing clothes that are dirty and patched, the fabric dark to blend in with the undergrowth. They are not from the village. I have heard tell of men like these. They hide deep in the woods at night and by day they prey upon those who travel on the main road.

I follow them, watch as they make camp. It is good to know where they are. The leader does not work, only stands and growls orders. His face is the vilest I have ever seen. He must have come too close to a fire, for his skin is blistered and burned, his cheeks and chin crawling with livid pink and purple scars. What teeth he has jut out jagged brown points. I must be careful now; death would be far sweeter than being at the mercy of him or his men.

I wake to a strange glow. Fire. I sit up.

The firelight is coming from the men's camp. Something is amiss; the men would not usually stoke such a strong blaze for fear of detection. I push my way through the ferns, avoiding the tree roots, my feet soft upon the leaves. As soon as I am close enough to hear the flames crackle, and the raised voices, I drop down behind a fallen tree and peer over it,.

I need not have taken such precautions, for they are too intent on their meal. I squint and see a large carcass spiked on a spit across the fire, next to three smaller ones. I must stuff my fists into my mouth to keep from screaming.

The men are laughing and jesting as they grasp handfuls of cooked meat. Fat smears their lips and oozes between their fingers; bits of gristle lie tangled in their beards. What mother would leave her cubs? I imagine how many of them it took to corner her. Fights must already be brewing over the pelts.

I watch for a long time. I realize that I am crying.

There is a low, deep growling. The wolf is here beside me. His hackles are raised, and thunder rumbles in his throat. He readies to spring. Without thinking I place my palm on his massive side. He turns and I stare into his yellow eyes.

Cows and horses convey little; contentment, weariness, and a dull, grinding hunger. Birds are flighty and fevered and leave my head ringing. I have never tried to go further with any other creature. Now I take a deep breath and let myself fall.

His wild eyes are a living gold, a glinting stream of grain. I am diving deeper. Faint memories: a deer leaping out, the flash of hide through the undergrowth, his mate running low and close; his mate lying on her side suckling their cubs, gray balls of squeaking fur. She licks one with a lazy tongue.

Then his vision bursts through. He is launching forward, tearing open the scarred throat of the leader, his snout dripping with hot, red spray.

Reaching to the depths of myself, I bring forth my own pictures. Sharp sticks with wicked points, men's faces contorted with hate, his body sprawled in the dirt, fur matted with blood.

Wait like a pool of water, still and quiet. Wait, or they will kill you too. Wait. I promise you that you shall have your revenge. Wait.

He blinks, half shakes his heavy head, then gazes again at the men, the spits, the fire. What reason does he have to trust me after what they have done?

Abruptly he turns and disappears into the darkness.

I sit there a long time, listening to the shouts and drunken laughter. Then I too slink away, defeated.

I am weary unto the bone.

My eyes are gritty and swollen. Three low gray days have passed since they killed her. My heart is heavy. The woods no longer seem friendly. For the first time in a long while, I wish for human company. But I am alone, helpless.

There is shouting, a sudden commotion. Men are running, calling to one another as their leader barks out orders, harsh and furious. Something has happened. What has stirred up the hornets' nest? I duck down into the undergrowth, my toes digging into the wet loam, the bristling stems scratch at my face, their thorns poking into my skin. I shut my eyes and try to become invisible. I pray they will not see me.

I am parched and starving, but I stay hidden. There are too many men loose in the woods. There is nothing for me to do but sleep.

My arm is roughly shaken. Someone is here. The men have found me. I am done for.

I open my eyes and come to my senses. It is not a bandit but a terrified little boy whose filthy face stares into mine.

"Please," he gasps, "please help me. They've taken Rudd."

7

Katherine

Michelle is taking Katherine out to dinner at the Orpheus. "It's been too long," Michelle said, and Katherine agrees. Michelle is one of the friends who hung on after all the bad stuff happened, after all the shit went down.

It's been hard for Katherine to maintain her friendships—ever since she found out she'd dated a serial killer; ever since she found out he brutally murdered her roommate, her friend. These events have tipped the balance of her relationships. Grief is boring; it drains all the color from the world, the oxygen from the room. How do you get back to an everyday life? How can you relate?

And she's a mother now, of a five-year-old. Motherhood was thrust upon her. How does she feel about that? Who really wants to know? Her friends love her, but they have their own lives. Her friends are moving to Chicago, they're buying apartments, they're changing jobs, they're getting promoted, they're earning their PhDs, they're getting married, they're having children, they're having their second child and their third child. They're living their lives. Katherine is a reminder that things can go wrong, horribly wrong. She is a reminder that there is madness out there, that the people around us cannot always be trusted, that the world doesn't make sense.

Michelle, however, hangs in.

"We're having dinner. I'll book."

Katherine is excited about the prospect of a grown-up dinner. She has arranged for Lucas to have dinner with Anthony, a gorgeous little boy who lives in their building. Anthony is the poster child for his chic parents, Greg and Melissa. Greg has a luxuriant beard and Melissa is stunning. Anthony is angelic. He wears a shell necklace, and apparently one of his first words was "olive oil." Katherine would normally hate them but luckily Greg and Melissa adore Lucas.

Katherine loves the Orpheus. It's old-school enough to have kept things right for its regular patrons, but it still appeals to couples who come on first dates at the bar. They have great steak frites, and even greater martinis. It's a pity she won't be having either, but she can still soak up the vibe.

She is the first one to arrive, but is not alone for long. Michelle swoops in, dressed in her lawyer gear, which, Katherine notes, is like administrative assistant gear but better quality, with superior tailoring. She sits down, and their waitress approaches, blond hair pulled back in a ponytail from her pleasant, weary face.

"Can I bring you ladies something to drink?"

"A martini, neat," Michelle says, and turns to Katherine. "And for you?"

Katherine holds up her seltzer water complete with lime. She got it from the barman and hopes that it looks enough like a vodka tonic to defer questions for a while. She wants to get past the first trimester before she shares the news.

"Excellent," says the waitress, and, "Can I bring water? Still, sparkling, or tap?"

"Two glasses of New York's finest." Michelle doesn't even bother to look up.

"Sure thing."

The waitress shoots Katherine a look she can't quite put her finger on. Is it irritation or amusement? Michelle doesn't notice because her attention is fixed on Katherine.

"Okay." She leans forward when the waitress departs. "Now tell me everything!"

Katherine had mentioned to Michelle on the phone that she and Sael ran into each other a while ago. She did not mention how he stumbled upon her and Lucas sobbing in each other's arms outside the shelter. Now, she tells Michelle about Sael asking her and Lucas to come to England with him.

"That's awesome!" Michelle is elated. "Clearly he still loves you."

Katherine smiles wanly. Nothing could be further from the truth. She thinks of the incessant phone calls, the tense meetings and emails. Sael was livid about her not telling him she was pregnant, but he's been controlling himself. Really, he's just being practical. He won't be able to concentrate on his new position if he has to worry about her.

"So, you're going, right?"

"I'm not sure yet. I have to think about it."

"Really? What in hell is there to think about? Apart from missing me?" She sees Katherine's expression. "Okay, okay. I guess it is a big change, and I know there's Lucas to consider, but if I were you I would jump at the chance. I'm sick of this shithole town."

Katherine has to laugh. Michelle is a die-hard New Yorker. Not even the apocalypse could drag her away.

The waitress is back with their drinks and more water. "And are you ladies ready to order?"

This time she sees Katherine looking at her, and bares her teeth in a forced smile.

Michelle looks up from the menu. "I'll have the steak frites."

The waitress, now amiable and neutral, turns back to Katherine.

"I'll have the hamburger."

"Oh, shut up." Michelle is imperious. "Order the steak frites, you know you want it."

"But—it's so expensive!"

"She'll have the steak frites." Michelle is firm.

"How do you like it?" asks the waitress, clearly bowing to the alpha female.

"Medium well." Katherine says. Sometimes she hates the kind of person she's becoming.

"Medium well?" Michelle looks horrified. "Who are you? What have you done with my friend?"

"Don't judge. Or I'll be forced to stab you with a knife."

"All right, but I've got my eye on you."

The waitress seems bemused by their little exchange, but she's shifting uneasily. It's as if she's trying to act normally, to hide something behind her smile. It's unnerving.

Michelle has her head down, and doesn't see.

"Two steak frites, one medium rare, one medium well, got it!" She takes their menus and leaves.

"Did you notice anything strange about our waitress?" Katherine asks.

"Our waitress? No, why?" Michelle looks at her, surprised.

"She just seems . . . off."

"Probably wants to murder everyone here. It's how I feel most of the time."

Actually, Katherine thinks, *that's exactly how she looked.* She tries to laugh, but doesn't quite manage it.

"You okay?" Now Michelle is scrutinizing her across the table. "You seem kind of on edge."

"Just a bit stressed out."

"I'm not surprised. Moving is insane, and you've had a lot else going on."

"Tell me about it." She changes the subject. "And you? How's work going?"

"Jesus, what a nightmare. Remind me again how much I want health insurance."

"Trust me, you want it." *Unless you like staring up at the ceiling at 4:00 a.m. wondering which kidney to donate to pay for a doctor's appointment.*

"I'll take your word on that."

"How's the poker going?"

Michelle brightens. "Not bad actually. I played a game last weekend where I didn't do badly, not badly at all."

Katherine grins. Michelle is a semiprofessional poker player. Her specialty is flirting to butter up her male opponents and then taking their asses to the cleaners.

The waitress is back. "Here you are, ladies!"

Her delivery is matter-of-fact, but yes, on closer inspection, Katherine can see a layer of perspiration on her forehead.

"The medium rare for you, and the medium well for you." On the word "you," she carefully, almost tenderly, places Katherine's plate down in front of her. Then she stands there staring at Katherine, the corner of her mouth twitching. "Enjoy!"

"Thank you," Michelle says pointedly.

The waitress doesn't move.

"I think we're good," Michelle tries again in a "Can you please fuck off?" tone.

The waitress gives a little jump. "Oh yes. Let me know if you need anything else."

"We're fine for now." Michelle catches Katherine's eye.

The waitress finally turns away and walks jerkily back toward the kitchen.

"What the fuck was that?" Michelle is incredulous.

"I told you she was off."

"Well, you were right." Michelle doesn't sound particularly thrown by the exchange.

"I thought she was going to watch us eat." Katherine tries to make this observation more neutral than paranoid.

"Yeah, maybe." Michelle shrugs, and picks up her knife and fork.

"She might still be watching us." Katherine peers toward where the waitress stands.

"Really?" Michelle cranes her head. Lowers her cutlery. Interest revived.

From somewhere in the back, Katherine hears raised voices growing louder. There's a definite commotion. Diners are craning their heads. Loud Spanish coming from the kitchens.

"Is someone having a *fight*?" Michelle can't really see from where she's sitting.

Katherine looks towards the kitchen doors in time to catch sight of a short dark guy in kitchen whites gesticulating wildly at their table. A lean, elegant man, clad in a tailored suit with an air of authority, glances at them, nods curtly, and then, sure enough, he's bearing down on them. Fast.

"What do you think is going on?" Michelle asks. She has resumed slicing her steak.

"I wouldn't eat that," Katherine says, a cold current icing her veins.

Michelle halts, startled, her fork in midair.

"Ladies!" The elegant man is now upon them. He's smiling, but it's strained. "There's seems to have been a misunderstanding." Without hesitation he picks up both of their plates.

"Hey!" Michelle is indignant.

"The kitchen," he says shaking his head in paternal exasperation.

"Excuse me." Michelle's pitch has risen several notches. More diners turn around. "That doesn't tell us anything! What's going on here? What *is* this?"

"All apologies, but you were given the wrong order. This was supposed to go to table twelve."

"But this is what we ordered!"

The manager has removed a meal from a hungry corporate lawyer, and Michelle is gearing up for a serious scene. But he is practiced at dealing with clientele like this. He doesn't hesitate.

"Dinner is on us," he says. "Would you like the same order? Can I bring the menus for anything else? We'll bring you a new round of drinks."

"You can tell us what happened." Michelle's tone has taken on a steely quality.

"There was a mix-up. Entirely our fault. Kenny!" He beckons to a young guy with a simpering, ratlike face. "The wine list, please."

"But they were correct!"

Katherine looks at Michelle with admiration. It's impressive to see her friend in action; she's like a terrier, her jaws firmly clamped on a rat.

"We're so sorry."

Sorry, but not sorry. Katherine has to hand it to the guy. He would make an amazing politician. And his apology gives Michelle time to draw breath. Finally, the reality sinks in.

"Wait, so it's on you?"

"Yes, whatever you desire, and again, please accept our apologies. Kenny!"

Kenny appears at the table and presents a huge wine list. He gets right to business as the manager leaves, even nailing his employer's soothing, flattering tone.

"May I recommend the Cabernet? It pairs excellently with the steak."

Katherine doesn't care about the Cabernet. The waitress's manic grin is still seared in her mind. Her stomach is balled into a fist and her temples throb. "What happened to our waitress?"

Kenny also doesn't hesitate. The master has taught him well and his reply is prompt. "Unfortunately, Candice had to go home."

"Is that it?" Michelle pounces. "Is she sick or something, touching our food?"

"No, no!" He sounds shocked, appalled that they could even think such a thing. "It was a personal matter. She received a phone call, bad news."

"Oh." There's not much Michelle can say against bad news and free food. Whatever happened has happened, and an expensive wine has been suggested. "Well, I hope this doesn't run late." She nods at Katherine. "It's a school night for some of us. Along with my steak frites, I'd also like a green salad and a French onion soup." She turns to Katherine. "You?"

Katherine's about to say no, how could she think about eating, when she realizes what she could bring home. "I guess the soup as well, and along with the steak frites I'd also like the BLT sandwich to go."

To Kenny's credit, he doesn't flinch. "Of course."

Michelle is all business now. "You'll have to give me a minute with the wine. How long will this take?"

"It will be out quickly, I promise."

And it is, with the help of a solicitous Kenny presiding. There's even dessert. Michelle has the lemon tart, and Katherine has the chocolate brownie. She has a thing for chocolate these days. *I need chocolate the way a crackhead needs a fix. One bite*, she promises herself, *and I'm taking the rest for Lucas. We'll eat like kings for days.*

Finally, they're heading home. Michelle is getting up to go to the bathroom. Not surprising—she had four full glasses of wine.

"Here's our stub." She hands it over to Katherine, who hands it over to a tired hostess, who goes off to get the coats.

Katherine waits. It seems to take a long time. The other hostess smiles at her. She's in her early twenties and impossibly thin. Her smile gives Katherine confidence. "Do you know what happened with the waitress tonight? Candice?"

The hostess plays dumb. Or maybe she is dumb. She shakes her exquisite head. "Sorry, I wouldn't know."

Right.

Michelle reappears, swaying a little.

"Are you okay?"

"I'm good," she says. "I'm just peachy keen. Peachy keen! Although we shouldn't have had the bottle—I can't believe you made me drink all of that!"

"I'm on antibiotics."

"Nothing like a beautiful glass of red to help you over whatever ails."

"Right," Katherine agrees as they head outside into the bite of an early October evening.

"All right, honey. It was so great to see you and hear all your news. Also nice work on getting the meal for free." Michelle's cheeks are flushed—she's not quite sloppy, but she's close.

"They don't call me a cheap date for nothing."

"Damn straight."

"Well . . ."

"Don't be a stranger. Let's talk this weekend." She suddenly hugs Katherine fiercely. "It will be okay."

Her reassurance brings tears to Katherine's eyes. For all her tough-girl bluster, Michelle is amazingly kind.

"Love ya."

"Love ya too."

Michelle hails a cab and Katherine heads off to the subway. Cabs are a luxury she really can't afford these days.

The wind picks up, she jams her hands into her pockets, and encounters a small crunch of paper. She removes the scrap. Her heart sinks. She strains to read the spidery writing, but it's too dark outside.

In the fluorescent light of the subway car, she tries again.

Le puso vidrio en la comida. Que Dios la acompañe.

Katherine translates it in Google when she gets home.

She put glass in the food. May God go with you.

She doesn't let herself think about it until she's finally lying in her bed. Then there's nothing for it. What happened tonight will have to be faced.

Katherine remembers the waitress's jerky, puppet-like movements, her flat voice, her unnerving rictus grin. *Her eyes*, she realizes. *They were like the construction worker's eyes.*

She has tried her best not to think about what happened with the construction worker either, but now in the dark it floods back.

She had been walking past a group of construction workers, on her way home from work, dreading their catcalls—or, worse, *no* catcalls. She was almost at the end of the block when she heard one of the men cry.

"Miss!"

Great, she'd groaned, but deep down there was a tiny surge of relief. *I still have something.* But she kept walking.

"Miss! Miss!"

The shout was louder, more urgent. Whoever was calling out to her was directly behind her now. He must have run to catch up.

"Excuse me, miss?"

Katherine swung around to confront him as he stood before her in worn jeans and boots. Not her type, but his face was definitely appealing: surprisingly pale skin; short, close-cropped dark hair; and the kind of inadvertent designer stubble many metrosexuals would pay serious money for. But there was something about his eyes, a fixed, robotic look and it made the hair on the back of her neck stand up. He had taken off his hard hat, and was gripping it in his hands.

"Miss?"

"What do you want?" She kept her voice cold. *It's broad daylight*, she'd reminded herself. *People will help me.*

"I'm sorry, miss, I'm sorry, but . . ."

"Yes? What?"

With great effort he manages "It's my sister."

"Your sister?"

"Please, she's got cancer. It's bad."

He bit his lip, and Katherine, glancing down, could see that his nails were white from the pressure of his grip on his hard hat. She looked back up to his face to see that his eyes with their fixed blankness were swimmy with tears. "My mom, she just called to tell me. Holy Christ. It came back. She can't do chemo again, and she's got a little boy, Donny, he's only seven, God help him. Her husband's in the military, and he doesn't get leave for two months at least. Please."

"What?"

Lying in her bed, Katherine remembers the feeling of a weight upon her chest, pressing her flat.

The sky was unquestionably blue, and the cheerful sunlight beat down on the crown of her head. Her feet were pressed firmly on the pavement. A taxi hooted, then another. She tried to clear the rubble lodged in her throat, tried to breath, tried to shade her eyes with her hand, although her limbs were filled with concrete.

"I don't understand. Why are you telling me this? What do you want me to do?"

Her question seemed to throw him. He shook his head, like a dog trying to shake off water.

"I dunno, I just . . . I just needed you to know."

Katherine swallowed.

The man's face slackened as he stared at her still-flat stomach. "I just thought maybe . . ."

His outstretched hand inched toward her.

She couldn't move.

It was like a nightmare. One where someone is chasing you but you can't run.

And then another man had come up to them, calling, "Mickey, Mickey, what the hell you doing?"

He is bald, a year or two older than Mickey, not fat but huge, with a friendly bulldog's face. A guy who would be the life and soul of the bar. He caught hold of his friend, seeming more mystified than annoyed.

"What's wrong with you, man?"

Mickey was shaking his head again, his hand frozen midair.

The second guy turned to her.

"Ma'am, I'm sorry. I don't know what's going on with him." He was holding Mickey firmly, but not angrily, by the arm. "Come on, Mickey, stop bothering the lady, c'mon."

Mickey stood transfixed still staring at Katherine's stomach.

"Jesus Christ, what's going on, Mickey?" He tried to steer his friend away, but Mickey wouldn't move.

"Please help her," Mickey said to Katherine, his voice suddenly clear and strong. "I know you can. Please."

"Seriously, dude. Come on! What are you, drunk? Are you high? What the fuck, man?"

"I'm sorry." Pity for Mickey, for his sick sister, had welled up inside Katherine. He must have been desperate to approach her. "I don't know how to help you."

Mickey just stared at her.

Then, the words had come. She had never uttered them before, but she knew they were the right ones. "I'll pray for her," Katherine promised. "And for her son, and for you."

"You will?"

"Yes."

Now she remembers him folding her hand in his large, damp one. *He was so young, so young. Younger than Lucas is, in a way. Like a child.*

"God bless you."

"God bless you too." She no longer felt afraid.

Mickey wiped his eyes with the back of one hand, smearing sweat and dust across his cheek. His other hand still held the hard hat. "Thank you. His voice was husky with gratitude. Thank you, from the bottom of my heart."

"Jesus," said his friend. "Jesus." He turned to Katherine. "I don't know, his sister, he found out some bad news . . ."

"I heard," she murmured. "You better help him."

"Yes, come on, man, let's go."

The guy looked far more shaken than Mickey. Mickey who had offered no resistance when his friend had put one huge arm around his shoulders to lead him away.

Katherine pictures the other construction workers. How they had stared at her as if Mickey's breakdown were her fault. It must have been the trick of the sun but she could have sworn one worker's eyes flashed silver. She turned away abruptly, wanting to get as far from them as possible. Almost running.

Dear God, she wonders, *what is going on?*

8

Margaret

I stare into the boy's swollen eyes. He is covered with bruises and cuts so that it hurts to look at him. He seems familiar, but I cannot place him.

"Rudd?" I stammer. "Who is Rudd? Who has him?"

"It's all my fault. I left him there!" With this confession, the boy folds over in a fit of grief, his thin frame wracked with sobs. He is not capable of telling me anything yet.

"Come," I say. I try to take his arm but, still howling, he pulls away. I murmur over and over, hushed and soft, as I would to any frightened animal. "Come. Come with me."

Eventually it works, I am able to lead him through the green tangle of ferns and bushes to the brook.

"Drink slowly," I warn as he frantically scoops up handfuls of water, but I doubt he can hear me.

At last he begins to slow down, his thirst quenched. He makes as if to rise.

"Sit," I tell him, grasping his upper arm and wincing at how thin it is. I point to the wounds upon his face. "Let me tend to these at least."

He sinks down again to the damp edge of the brook, but twists under my grip.

"Be still." I am stern. "Do you want these to fester? You must be brave!"

This seems to do the trick. He flinches a little but does not turn away as I rinse his cuts and scratches with the clear, cool water. Luckily they all seem shallow enough. Soon I have washed away enough grime to tell from where I know him. He was the boy in the marketplace who fought Old Warren.

Sharp red marks wrap around his wrists.

He notices me looking at them and lowers his eyes.

"From the rope," he mutters.

I nod as if I understand.

When I have tended all his wounds as best as I can and pressed dock leaves upon his nettle stings, I guide him back to my tree. There, I offer him mushrooms and some leaves of wild sage. With a little moan of hunger, he falls upon them.

"You must go slowly," I remind him again, "lest you sick it all back up and waste this good food."

He tries, but it is clear that he is starving. While he eats, I set about gathering comfrey leaves to make a poultice. I tear some strips of cloth from the hem of my skirt, then crumble the leaves into fine pieces. I trickle a little of my stored brook water upon the pieces and mash them into a paste. It would be easier if the water were warm, but I dare not light a fire. The smoke could draw the bandits' attention.

By the time I am done he has eaten his fill, and some color has blossomed in his cheeks.

"Here." I show him one of the poultices.

He looks doubtful, wrinkles his nose.

"It will help," I assure him, and his eyes widen with relief when I apply them to his arms and legs. "Now, let me hear your story. From the beginning."

And at last he tells me

His name is Thomas. His father died of fever, and his mother, a widow with a small holding, married Old Warren three years ago. She did not live long at the hands of her new husband, who drank and beat and starved her. Remembering how the old bastard acted when in his cups, I'm not surprised. Rudd was not Old Warren's son. Thomas thinks he bought him from a couple who had too many mouths to feed with the intention of setting him to work on the small holding. The two grew close, despite Rudd's lack of wits and the years between them. In Rudd, Thomas found the only other person in the world who would be kind to him and they became like brothers. After his mother's death, he took care of Rudd as best he could.

When Old Warren finally finished drinking away what little money they had, Thomas was forced to steal. Theft turned out to be his dubious talent and thanks to him, they were all able to survive the bitter winter. Of course, all the boy stole flowed right into Old Warren's tankard, and when he could not lay hold of Thomas, who was becoming as slippery as a fish, he would beat Rudd all the harder.

Thomas began to plan their escape, managing to hide a pocketed coin or two in a secret crack in the cottage's wall. Then my father banned Old Warren from our tavern, and the old man grew more violent. The scene I witnessed at the market was a near-everyday occurrence.

One night soon after that public fight, Old Warren discovered Thomas's hoard. He had taken Thomas by surprise, his huge hands nearly choking the life out of the boy, until Rudd pried him off and pushed him away. Old Warren's head hit the stone wall of their cottage with a sickening crunch, and he had crumpled lifeless to the ground.

There had been nothing for it but to seize the stolen coins and flee. As hated as Old Warren had been in the village, he would still be missed, and the sheriff was sure to try and bring his killers to justice. Thomas told me how he and Rudd had run into the woods and right into the hands of the bandits. The men stripped them of all they owned but their nightmare had only begun.

After realizing that Rudd was a fool, they had roped and staked him to the ground like a dog, marveling at his size. There was much argument as to what was to be done with him until their leader decreed that he would train Rudd to fight, pitting him against dogs or other men for money. He would do it by force if needed, with pokers and sticks, feeding him only raw meat and scraps until he begged. They had little use for Thomas. Some wanted to slit his throat, but then one shouted that it had been too long since they had had a woman, and what else was the lad good for?

Thomas's voice sinks lower, and he begins to tremble. I do not want him to dwell on this memory. There is a danger he will not be able to continue if he does.

"Go on," I encourage him as kindly as I can manage. "How did you escape?"

Thomas describes how he worked the ropes that bound him, twisting and turning at them, trying not to scream. Finally he managed to slip one bleeding, chafed wrist free. And then, at last, the other. He ran and ran blindly through the woods, nearing exhaustion, until he almost fell upon a sleeping figure.

"And I woke you," he says.

Now he is desperate to rescue Rudd, poor Rudd, who sits weeping in pain, bewildered and helpless.

It has taken Thomas much to tell his tale, and now he gnaws at his thumb, thinking of Rudd. "We will go tonight?"

"No," I say. "We would be caught." I catch at the whisper of an idea, faint as the hum of a bee.

He leaps up. "I cannot leave him!"

"Sit down." My mind is stirring furiously. "We will not abandon him, but we must use our wits. What good will we be to Rudd if we are caught too?"

He slowly sags, the fight draining out of him, his face crumples.

"Thomas, look at me."

He drags his eyes reluctantly to meet mine.

"I give you my word, we will save him."

Still, he cannot believe me.

"Why would you help us? What could you gain from it?"

It is an honest question. I will only be putting myself in more danger by helping two strangers, and yet . . .

I remember a small girl lost in the woods, the only person who loved her brutally ripped away. "I was once in need of help. I was once like you."

Something in my face must have convinced him.

"It is a debt we can never repay" he says. We will owe you our lives." He swallows. "What should we do?"

"For the present there is nothing more we can do."

In truth there is already a plan brewing, a dangerous plan, but I can think of no other way. I will let it ferment overnight, and visit it anew in the morning.

"All you can do is sleep."

Even as he protests, his head is falling, his eyes drooping, and soon he has surrendered.

I lie awake, looking out into the darkness.

By morning, my scheme has taken shape. We go to the brook again, and I show him what flowers to pick.

"See the small white blossoms blooming in clusters?"

He nods.

"We need their roots, the ones streaked with purple."

"They are pretty," he offers.

"Yes," I agree. "Only do not touch your mouth or eyes as you dig them out. Keep rinsing your hands in the brook or it shall go ill with you."

While we gather the plants I sense him looking at me.

"What is it?"

"It is nothing," he stammers, then turns away. "Only, I think I know you. You are John Belwood's daughter."

There is nothing for it except to tell him the truth. "Yes, I am she."

He still stares. "Only . . ."

"Only what?" I ask him.

"You are not a bit like what they say."

"And what do they say?" I can only imagine what monstrous tales he must have heard.

He glances away. "They say you are a witch, that you have dealings with the devil," he mutters.

"And what do you think?"

"It is no matter to me who you deal with. I would still rather be with you than Old Warren!"

He is earnest, and I smile. High praise indeed. As we pick blossoms together, my heart lightens.

I show him how to lay out the roots so they dry under the sun. Then we return to my makeshift camp to wait.

Thomas is running just a little ahead of me when he stops, midstride.

"What is it?"

"Look." He points to a dead rabbit, which lies neatly upon a log. "Who did this?" He spins around, peering high and low, scouring the trees. "Who else is here?"

"There is no one but us in this part of the woods." I speak easily and my tone is placid enough for I know who left me this gift.

"It's a trap! The men! They followed me and they know we're here!" His voice rises in agitation.

"Think!" I am scornful. "Why would they bother to lay a trap for us when they could have lain in wait? What purpose would it serve? Besides—" I pick up the rabbit's limp body and show him the fatal wounds on both its neck and side. "No man killed this creature."

"Then how did it die?"

I hesitate wondering how much he is capable of understanding. "Perhaps you will see, in time. Meanwhile, we will eat well tonight."

Thomas draws breath as if to speak, and then pauses, exhales.

At any rate, he now has rabbit to look forward to.

It is late at night when the growling wakes me from my sleep. Thomas half-crouches, rigid, his fingers gripping a large stone. He is mesmerized by the shape outlined against the moon.

"Thomas." I force myself to remain calm. "Thomas, drop the stone."

He does not move.

I do not know if my words can penetrate the dense wall of his terror. "Thomas, listen to me. Our lives depend on it."

Thomas does not look at me. "He will tear our throats out."

"He is not our enemy, Thomas," I whisper. "You must trust me."

The growling continues. Thomas is white. He takes a deep breath. Then, very slowly, he lowers his arm and lets the stone tumble from his fingertips.

The woods hold their breath.

After a long while, there is only the rustle of an animal slipping away into the undergrowth.

"Is he the one who brought the rabbit?" He is hushed, awed.

I nod. In the moonlight, I can see him gaping. "Why do you look at me like that?" I ask.

"I have never known a wolf to act like a dog." Thomas's eyes are very round. He has not yet stirred from his spot.

"He is not tamed as a dog would be. He comes and goes as he pleases."

"But why . . ." He wants me to explain but doesn't dare outright ask.

I say nothing. There is nothing to say.

The rest of our night is a quiet one.

9

Katherine

As they stand pressed up between the fairy princesses and the killer clowns, Katherine questions if this was a good idea. *It's difficult with a five-year-old at the best of times, but how,* she wonders, *do you explain all the ghosts and zombies to someone who has actually seen the dead? Who has spoken with them?* She looks down at Lucas, who stands by her knee. She holds his hand. She wonders what he is thinking.

She believes she's come to terms with Lucas's "abilities," his gifts. God knows she loves him and she knows that he would never hurt her. She thinks that he is like a conduit, or even a barometer, able to communicate and forecast the unearthly conditions surrounding them. There are still moments, though, when he turns his dark and luminous eyes toward her that her breath still catches in her throat.

Women who died at the hands of the Sickle Man gave him messages, left him pennies, told him secrets. He drew pictures of these visitors, naked women with rusted, crusted lines dug deep through their flesh. "The ladies," he called them, "the ladies" who were "hurted."

Can he tell the difference between fake blood and real blood? What if he asks why a person would pretend to be bleeding or pretend to be killing? she worries. *How do you explain it?*

But then again, how can they hide from Halloween? Especially in a city like New York? How can they ignore the giant pandas, Dorothys, and witches who ride the subway? How can they pretend not to see the pumpkins and the skeletons and fake spiderwebs in every store window?

You don't, Katherine decides. All his classmates are trick-or-treating, dressing up, and surely the kid is entitled to a little ordinary magic. Real magic, she isn't so sure about, but candy, yes, he is definitely entitled to eat too much candy. It is his God-given right as an American. Still, she's a little nervous as they stand on the sidelines of the jostling crowd, waiting for the parade to begin. She knows all too well the fierce Bacchanalian bent of the city on Halloween. It's an "anything goes" and "everyone does" kind of night, hormones and beer and breasts and paint and feathers and rubber faces and fake blood. Which is great when you're out for a crazy night, but not when you're shepherding a five-year-old around. She checks her watch. It's already 7:10. Luckily, the army of spectators in wild and wonderful costumes is a good-humored one. They laugh, and call to one another; they text, take and pose for photos.

There is also a vigil for the Sickle Man's victims tonight. They could have gone, but Katherine decided not to. Lucas seems to be doing well. These gatherings tend to get taken over by protesters wanting to make statements about the oppression of women, or by angry family members who will never have closure. Lucas and Katherine would be the reluctant center of attention. So she opts for the parade instead. *And yet,* she notices, *the ripples are still spreading.* She thinks she sees fewer people covered in blood this year. Twelve women viciously sliced open tends to take the fun out of the whole gore-covered-costume thing. There are plenty of other costumes to make up for it: Ghostbusters, nurses, guys in military gear, and homemade costumes involving clever puns; A man in a blood-sprayed apron and grimy chef's hat wears a sign: VEGETARIAN CHEF while the words on his apron read: I ONLY EAT PEOPLE. Someone else, through the clever use of cardboard, has turned herself into a walking online profile.

There are harlequin clowns, and ninjas, and obviously an inordinate number of sexy cats and bats, and of course the couples. A mouse and some cheese, a King and Queen of Hearts, and Frankenstein with his bride all jamming in close, and closer. Katherine is relieved to see that there are plenty of little kids here too, enough little kids that the crowd is somewhat monitoring itself. It's almost 7:30 now, and a murmur is rising. The parents want their princesses and superheroes and little monsters home and in bed at a decent-ish hour.

Then, with a roll and a flourish, the zombie drummers strike up their drums: *BOOM, BOOM, BOOM.* The drums light up purple and green and red when struck, and the excited crowd roars with joy as the parade officially begins to march.

"Can you see okay?" Katherine asks Lucas.

It's an unnecessary question as they've made it to the front, so really it's her way of checking in. She doesn't need to worry. Lucas can barely keep still. She thinks the kindergarten tried to monitor his sugar intake, but he's still one candy-stuffed little Dalmatian.

"Why a Dalmatian?" she had asked.

"Because it's the fireman's dog," Lucas had told her solemnly.

"Why firemen?"

"Because firemen save people."

"And you want to save people?"

"Yes," he said.

It's an answer that would have made his mother proud.

As for herself, she's used a black eyeliner pencil to draw a nose and whiskers across her face, jammed some pointy cat ears on her head, and called it a day. It's lame, but it will have to do. They stand, a firehouse Dalmatian and a grown-up cat holding hands, while the massive skeleton puppets and their amazing puppeteers rattle over.

"I'm so cooooold," moans one.

"My poooor booones," cries another.

The little kids shriek in glee, safe in the company of their parents.

Katherine looks down at Lucas, who is laughing with delight. They watch as silly monsters and pumpkin-heads and men on stilts, and marching bands and gyrating bunnies and killer clowns and unicorns, pass by. The parade is a success, and her shoulders descend with relief. She finally made the right call.

She is still smiling when there's a tap on her shoulder. Snow White—the Disney version of Snow White, with black hair and a yellow skirt and a red ribbon—stands behind her. Her costume is eerily perfect.

Snow White beams at Katherine and whispers something. The music is deafening; the marchers are breaking out into a flash mob dance, carefully choreographed to Michael Jackson's "Thriller."

"Sorry, what?"

Snow White leans in, and so does Katherine. The girl smells nice, like expensive perfume. Her breath is cool with peppermint chewing gum. Her eyes are warm and friendly.

"You need to die," Snow White says, and dimples.

"*What?*"

The world around Katherine turns sticky and slows, stops. She can't have heard right.

"You really need to die, as soon as possible. You should kill yourself." Snow White's tone is mild, almost tender.

"What?"

The girl is sweetly patient. "Maybe an overdose. It doesn't have to be painful."

Katherine feels as if she has just been struck. Her ears buzz, and her lips feel numb.

"What's wrong with you? What the hell is wrong with you? Why are you saying this?"

A momentary flicker of confusion crosses Snow White's face. *Oh God*, Katherine realizes, *she doesn't know why she's saying this.*

Then Snow White shakes her head, the way a horse would shake away a fly. "I just know you should." She presses her hand to her heart. "In here."

Each detail of Snow White's face crystalizes against the now-dimmed backdrop of the parade. Katherine can make out the thick mascara clinging to her eyelashes, the pores on her nose, the smudge of lipstick on her lower lip. And her eyes, her vacuous, varnished eyes.

Like all the others. Katherine's stomach clenches, her gorge rises. She begins to shiver, can't stop.

"Fuck off!" she hisses. She shouldn't be swearing in front of Lucas, but she needs to make this woman shut up, to get away.

"I'm just saying what all of us are thinking." Snow White shrugs apologetically. She glances down at Lucas. "You should probably take him with you when you do it."

No one threatens Lucas. This is cold water. This is electricity. This is the metallic click of the barrel of the gun. "Back. Off."

Katherine's voice isn't loud, but Snow White's eyes widen. She grimaces as though, for a second, her real self is breaking through. And then her expression glazes over and she is swallowed up again by whatever it is that wears her like a skin. "Okay. I just felt you should know. The longer you wait, the worse it's going to get."

A harassed Cinderella elbows up to Snow White. "Stace, we have to go."

"Okay," Snow White agrees. "I'm coming."

She turns back to Katherine, almost regretful. "Look, sooner or later one of us will kill you. Even if we have to die to do it."

"Get the fuck away from us." Katherine's voice is hoarse and shaky. She wonders how she's still breathing, still upright.

Snow White, Stace, appears puzzled, even a little hurt. "Have a good night."

She moves away, and a cheerful-looking clown rapidly fills the space.

"Kat." There's a tug on her hand.

"Yes, honey? What's wrong?"

Lucas shakes his head.

"Want to get out of here?"

He nods.

They begin the slow, torturous fight out of the crowd. All the fun of the parade has darkened. Everyone is endlessly coming and going and pushing, yet somehow they manage to squeeze through.

His pressure on her hand tightens.

"Kat? I has to go to the bathroom."

Great, she thinks. *Like any of the bathrooms will be available for a five-year-old kid tonight.* "Oh, honey. Okay."

She tries to work out where they could go. The bars are bursting at the seams with costumed drunks, axe-wielding murderers, mad scientists, and fiendish ghosts. She and Lucas are heading toward a slightly less hectic side street, and maybe there's a diner around somewhere that's not so packed.

She spots one and they walk in. Immediately, she sees the sign: BATHROOM ONLY FOR PAYING CUSTOMERS. Shit. There's no open table they can sit at, of course.

She takes a deep breath, and walks up to the register with Lucas.

"Please, he's only a little boy, he'll pee himself, I'm *begging* you. I'll buy something to go."

The old guy with the hooded eyes at the register begins to shake his head; then he sees Lucas and stops. Sighs. Gestures to the back.

"Thank you, thank you."

But he doesn't turn around again.

They walk to the back.

"Okay, honey? I'll be right outside the door."

While she waits, she tries to calm down, but can't stop replaying what just happened in her head.

I'm just saying what all of us are thinking.

Jesus, what was that? Who was that freakish girl? What did she mean by "all of us"? Katherine glances toward the entrance of the diner; then she returns her focus to the bathroom door. Her forehead is clammy, and she has to clench her jaw to keep her teeth from chattering like one of those stupid gimmicky toys. A scattering of brilliant dots swims before her eyes, the first sign of a whopper migraine descending.

Sooner or later one of us will kill you. Even if we have to die to do it.

The toilet flushes and Lucas emerges.

"All good?"

"Yes. But . . ."

"But what?"

"I'm hungry."

Katherine is about to tell him they'll get something at home when her stomach growls, and she realizes that she's starving. Suddenly she's craving matzo ball soup. Or chicken noodle soup. Something soup. Warm and comforting and practical. Nurturing food. Pregnancy strikes again.

She glances around the busy diner. *Fat chance of finding a table here.* They'll have to go somewhere else. As they make their way back to the front, a massive man seated with a female companion reaches out with one great arm and bars their way. Katherine steels herself. *What other presents does the night have in store?*

The man, who must weigh a good 250 pounds, is dressed as a Viking, complete with a huge beard and braids. His face is one of a battered warrior, with eyes that are a startling pale blue. Nordic eyes, winter-day eyes. The woman is on the wrong side of fifty. She has a wonderfully hooked parrot nose, which dominates her face underneath long blond hair and militant bangs. Her sleeveless leather vest reveals equally leathery skin. Katherine has no idea if she's in costume or not. They both wear a certain dream-like expression that she has come to know and dread.

"Miss, miss! Take our table," the Viking offers.

"We're finished here anyway," says his friend.

Katherine looks at their half-eaten burgers, the almost untouched sides of fries. No one leaves that many fries.

"Oh no, we couldn't." She means it. She glances down at Lucas, who is staring at the giant—but not, Katherine senses, in fear. *Well, at least that's something.* Of course she shouldn't be using Lucas like a canary in a coal mine.

"Please," urges the Viking. "You should be sitting, in your condition."

"It would be our honor," the woman adds.

It's a bizarre thing to say but Katherine doesn't crack a smile. Their unexpected, old-fashioned chivalry should make her feel better after the encounter with Snow White, but somehow it makes her feel worse. Some want to protect her, others kill her. It's all wrong. Short of running out of the diner, though, there's nothing to be done.

"Thank you," she says weakly.

The man, all six feet five inches of him, rises and tries to bow; the woman follows him, strangely bobbing in a sort of curtsy. They smile, widely, vacantly and then turn to go and pay the man up front.

She nods at Lucas and they slide into the turquoise booth. Almost everyone here is in costume. A busboy comes by, but his eyes, Katherine is thankful to see, hold no strange gleam. He clears away the couple's abandoned food. Katherine nearly asks him to leave the fries, but she holds herself back.

Lucas orders the mac and cheese, and Katherine has chicken soup and fries. She's tempted to order some wings. And maybe chicken tenders too. *Definitely a pregnant thing*, she sighs, and then her attention is drawn to one of the main booths, where a group is laughing, being loud. They're hot hipster types, these guys, good-looking, seemingly educated. They all wear various robes, and most have beards. They look familiar, but she can't figure it out. Many photos are being taken. Sometimes they pose for them, and in between shots they eat.

"She couldn't help it," Lucas says, bringing her back to their table of two. "Saying those scary things. None of them can help it."

"Who couldn't help it?" Katherine asks, dread surging in the depths of her stomach.

"That lady who looked like Snow White." Lucas pauses, eats a fry and then adds, "And the people here too, the giant."

The hair on Katherine's arms prickles. She tries to release the breath that has caught in her chest. "How do you know?"

But now a guy sitting in the loud booth, who wears a red robe with a blue shawl over it, rises. His hair is long, and his chin is cradled by a partial beard. Katherine finally works it out. He's Jesus, and the others in the booth are his dining companions at the Last Supper.

"As the Lord and Savior, I would personally like to bless this establishment," Jesus says.

Katherine has to grin. It's pretty cool. She remembers studying da Vinci's *The Last Supper* for art history class. There was a whole lecture dedicated to it, where they learned how both Christ's and Judas's hands are reaching for the same bowl, how one of Jesus's hands is turned up and one down. How Judas's neck is turned away, because he is the traitor. The guys have put some effort into their costumes, even sitting to match the positions of the Disciples in the painting. *Lucky the booths are big.* She smiles to herself.

"Sit down, Josh, and shut up," another guy at the table says.

Katherine thinks it's Judas, but she can't be sure amid all the laughter, which is drunk but not malicious.

Josh-slash-Jesus has no intention of sitting down. "My children. You are all my children."

"Shhh! C'mon! Sit down, asshole."

"You are my children, yet you would dare to call your Lord and Savior an asshole. Tsk, tsk. I proclaim thee not cool. And I proclaim this table next to me very cool. And I proclaim that table with two sexy zombie nurses most good, most good indeed. And the two hard-core dudes chatting up those girls, they cause no offense to my eyes."

He is loud and he is intoxicated, but he's not an asshole. Katherine guesses being God could understandably go to one's head. The girls giggle, and the tough-looking guys shoot him side-eye. The majority of diners in the diner do what most New Yorkers do, which is to pretend to ignore the scene while watching it. It's free entertainment.

"What's he doing?" Lucas is curious.

Andrea and Katherine never really discussed religion. Lucas, men, what they were having for dinner, TV they liked, books they loved, exhaustion, hilarious things they saw on the street, yes, even celebrity scandals, but somehow God didn't make it. All Katherine knows is that Andrea came from a hard-core Baptist family. One that didn't approve of a single mother and rejected her son. So she's unsure if Andrea would have wanted Lucas to find the Lord; she thinks Andrea was more concerned about him eating his vegetables and having a good day in preschool.

"He's dressed up and he's fooling around. Kind of showing off. He'll probably stop just now."

Or get thrown out, she thinks. *He's bound to offend someone sooner or later.* But then again, this is New York, and it is Halloween, and he's not being rude. Just a little stupid and drunk, mostly high on the thrill of wearing a cool costume and all the potential the night holds.

Katherine takes another spoonful of the soup that's just arrived, and looks up to see that Jesus has wandered over to their booth.

He beams at her and winks at Lucas. "And I pronounce you . . ."

Then he twitches.

He stands, swaying slightly, and when he speaks again his tone is grave, and he speaks as if he is reciting a passage of text by rote.

"And there appeared a great wonder in heaven, a woman clothed by the sun, with the moon laid under her feet and a crown of twelve stars upon her head. Her time was near, and she cried and pained to be delivered of a Child, who was to rule over all nations, and was to be caught up unto God, and to His throne."

His voice swells.

"Then she beheld a great red dragon having seven heads and ten horns, and seven diadems upon his heads. And with the dragon came war. Michael and his angels fought against the dragon; the dragon and the dark angels who served him fought back. The woman fled into the wilderness, where she had a place prepared for her by God Himself."

The diners are not happy now.

"See to yo' boy," one of the tough guys snarls at Judas. "Get yo' *friend* under control."

But the diners at the Last Supper are frozen, like the Disciples in the painting.

"Josh?" one of them asks, but Josh-slash-Jesus is now convulsing.

"Oh Jesus, oh Jesus, oh Jesus . . ." one of the zombie nurses moans.

The fluorescent lights of the diner flicker, darken.

"She carries the Lamb, and the Prophet shall be their guide! The Lamb and the Prophet shall lead us in war against the Beast! The time of reckoning has come!"

Katherine feels Lucas's small hand takes her own, and it shakes her awake from this terrible dream. Except it's not a dream.

She rises to her feet. She won't have him scaring Lucas. He will not scare Lucas.

She is calm now, filled with a quiet certitude. He will not scare Lucas. She is flooded with strength. All her focus, all her will, is fixed upon the shuddering figure in front of her.

"Stop," she says.

But Josh rants on. "The dragon is the Serpent, the dragon is the Devil, the dragon is Satan, and the Child is—"

"*BE STILL.*"

Josh's hands scrabble at his neck, his eyes jerk backward in his head, and he crumples to the floor. There is a pop as the light bulb explodes above him in a shower of glass.

He writhes on the ground.

"Help him!"

"Help him!"

And they rush forward, all of them, just young guys in robes made out of bedsheets who are terrified for their friend.

"Oh my God!"

"Josh! Is he having a seizure?"

"Fuck, man, call an ambulance."

Katherine frantically flings some money down next to their barely touched plates, and swings Lucas up in her arms.

"Wait," someone tells them, but they don't, and they are gone out the door into the dark, hectic Halloween streets. Katherine keeps hold of Lucas and walks as fast as she can.

She does not slacken her pace until they are safe at home.

It's two hours later, two hours too late, but Lucas is in bed. As she tucks him under the covers, she steels herself for his questions.

"What was the matter with him?"

"I don't know, honey. He was drunk, I guess, and sometimes drunk people do silly things."

"It's the baby, isn't it?"

"What do you mean?" Her voice is sharp. *Calm down*, she reminds herself. *You want him to be able to trust you, so just calm down. You can handle this.* "What do you mean, Lucas?" she asks again, this time willing herself to speak softly. Her heart aches for this little boy who will always see what others cannot see, who will always know too much.

He gazes at her, patient in the face of her blindness. "He was talking about the baby, the one growing inside of you."

Katherine must say something, but he'll know if she's lying and she can't lose his trust. "Lucas, here's the truth. I don't know what's going on. I only know one thing. I will never let anyone hurt you. That's the promise I give to you."

"You promise?" The words very faint in the darkness.

"I promise. Okay?"

"Okay."

"Think you can sleep now?"

"Yes. Will you leave the door open a little?"

"Of course I will."

"Night, Lucas."

"Night, Kat."

"I love you."

"I love you too."

She gets up very quietly and walks out.

She walks to her room and sits down on the bed.

The baby, Lucas says, they're acting that way because of the baby.

She closes her eyes, trying to gain strength for what she is about to do. She has made him a promise. She needs to keep it.

Right now it's there, growing inside her, a collection of cells and fibers swelling and forming, multiplying and dividing.

She picks up her phone and presses a button, dials.

There have been so many reasons for not wanting to go. Tonight they have all been wiped away.

It's hiding there. A chrysalis held fast in the deep, wet, darkness of her womb.

He picks up after the second ring, as if he has been waiting for her call.

"We'll come," she says.

10

Margaret

By the following morning, the roots are dried and ready for further preparation. I leave Thomas sleeping to collect them. The sun shines just as brightly as it did the day before, the brook still chuckles to itself, but my heart is heavy as I work. I hear my mother's warning.

We must do good. Most people cannot do what we do. They do not have our gifts. They cannot help themselves.

She had taught me which plants were poisonous so that I should be safe, not so that I should do harm. But what choice do I have?

I return to Thomas, who is just waking. I greet him, and we eat our breakfast of berries.

"Thomas," I ask, choosing my words with care, "how far would you go to save Rudd? Could you kill a man?"

Thomas stops, thinks about the question.

"Yes," he says at last. "If that is the only way."

I nod and, after a deep breath, tell him of my plan. He is frightened, but he does not question it.

*   *   *

That night I am again shaken awake. I open my eyes, and Thomas's face peers down into my own.

"You were crying out in your sleep."

I feel my forehead. Drenched. My heart knocks against my breast.

"Did you dream?" He is wide-eyed.

For a moment I think of saying nothing, but to finally have remembered! I must tell someone.

Still, at first, I struggle to find the words.

"This is not the first time I have hidden in these woods," I begin. "Years ago, when I was a little girl, I would come here with my mother.

"We would pick mushrooms, blushers, and Queen Boletes, and princes. She always encouraged me to try and find the horn of plenty. They are the hardest to spot, since they grow best under fallen leaves."

I smile at the memory.

"Back then, I was not frightened to venture too far, and on that day I wandered deeper and deeper into the woods until I spotted a cluster of them." I cannot help the note of pride that creeps in. "After I crammed my basket close to bursting. I grew tired. I planned only to rest my eyes for a moment or two . . .

"When I awoke, it was cold and the sky was dark. I had been gone too long, and Mother would be worried, so I hurried back the way that I had come, but the woods did not seem so friendly now. It was the quiet. No birds sang, and even the wind held its breath.

"I was almost at the clearing when I saw him. A man crouched over something. Not something, but someone. My mother. She lay like a snapped branch. He had a knife. He was holding her arm, intent on guiding the curved blade into her flesh as a carver etches a wooden staff. The blade was red. Blood pooled underneath her, staining his sleeve. I opened my mouth to scream, but nothing came out, no sound at all.

"He sensed me there anyway, watching him, and looked up, grinning. He released my mother's arm, and it fell, limp. Dead. My mother was dead. He had killed her. This man, a stranger with a sickle knife, which the village men use to reap their wheat, had killed my mother.

"I turned and scrambled back through the trees. 'Margaret,' he called to me. His voice was light and sweet. He knew my name. 'Margaret, there's no need to run.' But I did, madly I stumbled, rose, and kept going. Each beat of my heart crying, 'Mother! Mother! Mother!'

"I could hear his voice echoing through the woods. 'Margaret? Margaret? Come back!' Down into the deepest part of the copse I ran, down where no one could find me, until I slipped and tumbled down a slope into a thicket. I crawled inside an old hollow tree trunk, and I waited. Rocking back and forth in that damp trunk, I waited. His voice was gentle. 'Margaret, you do not need to fear me.' I heard the smile curling his words. 'It is not your time. Not yet.'"

Thomas is silent, staring. "How did he know your name?"

I shake my head, for I myself do not know.

"I am sorry," he says at last.

His sympathy causes my throat to ache, my eyes to burn. I have never told this story to a living soul before tonight.

It is the first time I have remembered.

Now there seems nothing else to say.

"We should try to rest. Tomorrow will be a long day."

He seems uncertain, as if he wants to ask me more questions, but I close my eyes and feign sleep. After a long while, I hear him settle back down.

As great a relief as it was to tell him, I did not dare share the whole of it.

I stayed in that hollow trunk till a thin, restless sleep overtook me. I woke, terrified, cramped, and cold. I saw through the rotten gaps in the trunk that the moon had risen. Shaking off the beetles and spiders, I pushed my way free, only to see him standing in the moonlight.

"I have found you, little rabbit," he said.

I willed my feet to move, but they would not, could not.

His face glowed kind and serene. "You had no need to run." He sounded wistful. "I only wished to see you for it will be a while before we meet again."

"My mother . . . ?" My voice fainter than a mouse's squeak.

"Your mother is dead. When I found her, she was searching for you. Did you know that? You were a wicked girl to wander so far away.

His manner changed from chiding to reminiscent.

"Her colors were glorious. Her anguish was the rusty orange of an unclean blade. It cut like the wail of a starving infant, it stung like the salted sweat left on the hangman's noose. I could taste her lineage in her veins, that old knowledge rich as velvet wine.

"Still . . ." He grew grave, as one about to impart a confidence. "She was nothing compared to you. What you will become. But you must grow and you must bloom before I find you again. When you turn red, I will come for you. Now," he said with faint regret, "you may run."

I did not wait, but turned and fled far, far, far away into the woods. I did not know how much time had passed, and with each step I left what I saw and what I heard farther and farther behind me until it disappeared into blackness. I knew only that I must get home. I must get home.

And I did, leaving the chaos and the horror of that night buried deep in this place.

The day dawns cool and blue. A day for action.

Thomas and I say very little as we make our way to their camp, both of us steeling ourselves for what lies ahead. Thomas holds the leather pouch tightly. I clasp a wineskin, thankful that I had brought it and thought to save the contents to trade. Above our heads the sun shines; the birds carol as if all is well. When we come to the fallen trunk, we crouch down. We wait.

The men are chatting, laughing, shouting at one another. We can hear them making ready to depart for the main road. A few will remain on lookout, but in truth they will sleep in the sun's warmth.

If I lean out from behind the log, I can see a large man staked to a post. Two men pass by, and he squints up through reddened eyes. One gives him a vicious kick, and Rudd cries out weakly. They laugh.

"Down, dog!" the other says.

Thomas leaps up, fury contorting his features, and I must drag him down again. "Not yet," I hiss through my teeth, "or else you mean to kill us all."

"Those bastards!" He trembles. "Those filthy bastards."

"Quiet." I shake him a little. "You'll do Rudd no good if they hear us." Then I look at him. "Now, remember. You must—"

"I must empty all the contents of the pouch into the pot," he says, "as you have told me a hundred times." He is as jumpy as a flea.

"Keep a cool head." Though I feel as fluttery and panicked as a bird in a cage. "Think of Rudd. I wish you luck."

"What's to stop the cook from catching me?"

"He'll be otherwise engaged," I promise grimly, and hope that it will be so.

When I am sure the main group has left, I move silently to the fringe of the clearing where the men have made their camp. The cook, sweaty and straining, stirs a great cast-iron pot on the fire. Standing in his line of sight, I take a breath and bring my foot down hard snapping some small branches to gain his attention.

He stops stirring and stares at me, mouth agape. It would be comical if I were not so fearful.

Pressing my finger to my lips, I beckon him with my free hand. He waddles over, breathing heavily, his eyes never leaving my face. I wince inwardly at the noise he makes, hoping he will not draw undue attention. I try my best to smile and pray that he will not wish to share me with his fellows until his own needs are satisfied. And here he is, panting before me with the sweaty, bristly complexion of a pig. His grin reveals stumps of gray, broken teeth and I can smell his fetid breath.

I trail my fingers lightly down my neck, across the tops of my breasts. His chest heaves with excitement. I hold out my wineskin, put it to my lips, and pretend to drink while being careful not to swallow. I raise it in a toast, then pass it to him. He clutches it willingly. For a wonder he does not question the fortune of finding a willing maiden who would bring her own drink—another piece of luck for him on this bright morning. He takes a cautionary sniff of its contents, sweet and heady, like dandelion wine, and then tosses them back. I watch his thick throat working as he swallows.

When he has gulped his fill, he wipes his mouth on his yellowed smock sleeve and lurches forward. I step back playfully, tossing my hair over my shoulder, and so we continue until we are well into the trees. After a few steps he stops and stands still. His face is suddenly frantic as his hands tear at his throat; then his eyes glaze over and a dull green foam oozes from his mouth. He topples.

My heart pounds loud and fast in my ears. I stare at his lifeless body. I have done this. *I have done this.* Somewhere close, a bird warbles.

Perhaps he has a wife and children somewhere. Perhaps he was not such a bad man, only trying to survive.

But I will never know now. There is no going back.

I am the first to reach the trunk. I sit in its shade, trying to still my thoughts. Waiting has never been so hard. It seems like an eternity, but then Thomas is here, ducking down next to me, breathing heavily.

I know something is amiss the moment I see his whey complexion. "What is it?"

He only shakes his head, unable to gain the breath to tell me.

I have to clasp my hands together in order not to wring the answers from him. "Thomas, what is wrong?"

Eventually, he answers. "Not all went into the pot," he mumbles.

"What?!"

Now it is his turn to silence me.

"My hands trembled so, and the wind took it."

"How much?"

He does not answer.

"*How much*, Thomas?" Only the knowledge of the camp nearby prevents me from shouting.

"Half," he finally mutters.

Oh God, I think, *we are in trouble.* What shall we do? There's nothing we can do except sit and wait. So we sit and wait. We wait while the men return to their camp, while the light fades from the sky and the darkness closes in. The cook is, of course, nowhere to be found. The men grumble, but do not seem unduly worried. He's probably sleeping somewhere and, after all, the stew is here and still warm. They help themselves, and sit around eating and drinking.

"What if they give Rudd the stew?" Thomas whispers suddenly.

I shake my head decisively, though this is a new and terrible thought. "They will not want to waste food on him. Did not you tell me that they will starve him to make him fight?"

Thomas nods, but his eyes are fearful. I am fearful myself. Nothing is certain.

As the night draws in, the fire spits and sputters and we continue our vigil. No one falls facedown as the cook did, but I hear groaning, and whenever I feel bold enough to peer over the trunk I see men slumped on the ground. Finally, there is quiet enough for me to shake Thomas awake.

"We only have a very little time," I murmur. "Go now."

Thomas nods, pale but determined, and then rises to make his way to the silent camp. Soon he is nothing but a shadow fading into the others. I wait and wait some more, my ears aching for the slightest noise. But there is only stillness.

He's taking too long. They should be back by now. Images float before my eyes: Thomas lying in a pool of blood; Rudd, a huddled mass of broken bones; the bandits, now alerted, creeping toward me and ready with daggers.

I hear it then, a faint cry. I cease to think and run past the sprawled bodies. There is no other sound. This must be as a battlefield looks.

Then I see Thomas, but my relief does not last long. He is bent over, shaking the motionless bulk of Rudd.

"I cannot wake him," he hisses.

My heart sinks. If these were better men than I had thought and they fed Rudd, I have doomed him. I bend over Rudd, and as I do so strong hands circle my waist from behind.

"Got you," a man spits into my ear on a gust of vile breath.

I try to twist around, but I already know that voice. He is the leader, the one who barks out commands.

Thomas steps toward me, his features grim with determination, but there is a sharp, painful pressure across my throat.

"Get back." The leader's voice slurs a little. "Or I'll gut her like a fish."

I can see him now out of the corners of my eyes, his burned and blistered face drained of its redness. Vomit cakes his chin and covers his chest, yet he is standing firm enough, and judging by his grip around me, he is still hellishly strong.

"I tasted the stew and I knew something was amiss. All around me my men are falling, but I—" He leers. "I made myself expel it. You rotten whore, I'll make you wish your mother had never suffered your father's weight."

And then we hear it. A rumbling so deep that our bodies tremble with it. Leaves shiver on their branches, and clumps of dirt roll beneath our feet. The leader's hand shakes a little, but his grasp does not falter.

The thunder reverberates and swells as a giant wolf, ten hands at least, thick with muscle and as broad as an ox, pads through the trees toward us. His ashen coat gleams in the moonlight, and his eyes are two glowing embers that fix upon the leader. My heart halts. I gaze in awe.

I feel the leader catch his breath.

"No," he exhales. "What devilry is this, you witch?" He stumbles backward, raising his free hand either to finish me or to defend himself.

With a roar the wolf lunges forward and up at the leader, knocking him back onto the earth. Slick wet fur sweeps against my cheek, and a hot, rank animal cloud envelops me before I too am flung forward, shaken but unharmed. Now the wolf is upon him, but not attacking, not yet. Pinning the man down with his front legs, the wolf merely mouths at his throat, almost delicately, as a mother cat would her kitten.

"No devilry." I swallow and find the words. "But revenge."

As if in agreement, the wolf flings back his great head and howls. Every hair on my body stiffens. He howls and howls again, and I wonder that the sound does not pierce the moon to bleed into the night, that the trees do not shed their leaves, and the brook's waters freeze in their courses. Then the wolf returns his attention to the man on the ground.

Silent as ghosts, the other wolves emerge from the woods. They slip across the camp, great warriors, the sheen of their fur mottled in shadow, their eyes barely banked fires. Each one sits by the side of a fallen man, an executioner waiting patiently to carry out the final sentence.

Tears slide down the leader's cheeks. "Please," he croaks. "Please, call them off. I will give you all we have. *Please.*"

"I have no power over them," I say, for it is the truth. "They are not mine to command."

Rising, I move over to Rudd. I bend forward and slap his face. He stirs, grunts.

"Thomas, help me!"

My voice breaks through to Thomas, who has been cowering down behind his brother's bulk, stupefied with fear. He crouches over Rudd and slaps his other cheek. Rudd grunts again. He has been given some of the food, but this is a good sign. His immense size must have saved him. Together, tugging and pulling, we help him to stand. He sways, about to topple over, and it takes all our combined strength to hold him upright between us.

"For the love of God," moans the leader, still on the ground, "have mercy. Do not leave me here to be torn to bloody bits. I beg of you, have pity and call them off."

I look inward to see if I can find pity, and can find none. "I told you before, there is nothing I can do," I repeat.

Propping up Rudd between us, we turn to leave.

"Then may my bitterest curse be upon you, you bitch!" His choked cry echoes through the silent camp.

When I stop in my tracks, Thomas must stop with me or let his brother fall. I turn to look at him, truly look at him. I look down at the doomed man, past his furious face and shivering limbs, beyond the meat and bone of him to the center within.

The memory of a bloody carcass roasting upon a spit floats before me. Rudd tied to a stake, cringing as he is kicked. A body so badly beaten that it no longer resembles a man; a kneeling woman, her hand outstretched. A young girl, scarcely twelve, shrieking. Pieces of an infant's blanket, stained red, scattered upon the path.

And now he dares to lay his curse on me.

A gully whirls within me yawning wider and wider, pulling me into a blizzard of ash and snow consuming everything in its path. I am a wailing tunnel of black wind, my clawed currents sweeping him up and skinning him alive unraveling him like a woolen skein till only his bones are left, bare.

"You!" I intone. My arm rises, my hand extends, my fingers tingle and glow.

His face curdles in terror. His mouth opens and shuts, as a dying fish.

"Margaret," Thomas says, sounding very small.

Abruptly, I am brought to my senses and the darkness recedes like a dying storm. Thomas looks at me with fear.

"Come, we must leave this place. The wolves wait for us, but they will not wait much longer."

Thomas nods, desperate to be gone. We turn slowly, Rudd between us, and begin our walk back into the trees and the safety of our camp. It will be a difficult journey, and there is a long night ahead.

THE MAN IN THE WOODS

You stand and watch the three figures, a huge man propped up between a woman and a child, clumsily, awkwardly move toward the woods. They do not turn around. They do not want to see the wolves take their meal.

Perhaps this is just as well, for it means they do not see you as you lean against a tree. You would be hard to spot anyway, deep in the shadows, cloaked in dark wool.

You prefer watching to being watched.

They do not see the way your fingers lightly caress the curved blade of your knife. Nor do they see the slow and winsome smile that plays upon your lips.

It is hard going, but they keep at it, and you wish you could applaud their efforts. But perhaps it is better not to distract them.

The first anguished shrieks drift up from the camp. You sigh with pleasure. The wolves have begun to feast.

Then you gaze back again, and sure enough the three figures quicken their pace, stumbling as fast as they dare. Desperate not to hear their suffering.

Unlike you. You envy the wolves.

Ah, well. Soon enough you'll be able to kill again.

You were called forth from the darkness for just such a purpose. You've missed it so, the sting of the salt and the tang of blood and the soft surrender of flesh under your blade.

Give praise, give thanks for the Glorious, Glorious Hunt!

She'll be ready, soon enough.

11

Margaret

The tavern's name, the Black Ewe, is painted on the wooden sign underneath a picture of a stout black sheep. The sign swings violently in the wind. The storm has reached its peak.

The heavy front door bangs loudly behind us. We stand, drenched and shivering, on the threshold. A silence drifts down upon the room like a cloak as the rain puddles on the floor. I can only imagine how we must appear to those who now sit and stare.

A short, fat woman with a massive bosom and a terrible scowl bustles our way. She has the bossy air of the innkeeper's wife. With one glance of her piggy eyes she takes our measure from dripping head to dripping toe, and announces, "We're full up, no room here."

I have opened my mouth to argue, to plead, to *beg*, when Thomas speaks.

"Forgive our rough appearance, ma'am, but we were set upon by bandits in the woods."

"Bandits?" a small, rheumy-eyed man asks.

"Aye, they ambushed us along the main road, made off with our horses and our belongings."

The woman scoffs. "The only bandits hereabouts are Blacwin's gang, and they are at least twenty men strong."

"Twelve at most. Or were," I add as an afterthought.

The woman's scowl deepens and she turns back to Thomas. "You lie. Those bastards leave no one alive."

"How fortunate we were able to persuade them otherwise." Thomas's voice is solemn but I can see the impish gleam in his eye.

This rally brings forth an uneasy laugh as everyone takes stock of Rudd's size.

"Their leader," another man, sitting on a bench calls out. "What did he look like?"

The innkeeper's wife rounds on him. "I will hear no more of this!"

But I can answer the question, as I will remember that face all the rest of my days. "He had burned and blistered skin with scars coursing from cheek to chin."

"That do sound like Blacwin," the man concedes cautiously.

His neighbor, squat and bearded, wrinkles his heavy forehead with the effort of understanding. "Are you telling us that your trio alone has felled the most murderous fiends the county has ever known?"

Thomas nods. "Aye. Their bodies can be found in the woods." He pauses. "That is, those not already eaten by the wolves."

A large, stooped man lumbers to his feet. He has kind, almost sad eyes set in a cavernous face. "I will know more!" he declares.

"Surely you cannot believe this madness!" The woman is full of scorn.

"Be quiet, Dryllis." He does not speak loudly, but he is firm.

Her little eyes waver, and she closes her mouth with a snap.

The man looks directly at us. "Those whoresons killed my brother, his wife, and their two young children on that road. Slit their throats and left them to die like vermin. If what you say is true, I'll gladly pay for your drink and board."

Dryllis glowers, but she can scarce refuse now. "By all means, then," she snipes. "But it will be upon your head, Master Alun, if we are all murdered and robbed in the night."

It seems a dreadful thing to say to him given what we have just heard of his history, but another drinker, small and merry with plump, flushed cheeks, pipes up.

"Yes, and if they survive your cooking that will be miracle enough."

There is much laughter at this and the room seems to ease and settle.

Dryllis shoots the jester a venomous look. "You are welcome to drink elsewhere." She heaves around abruptly and goes back to the kitchen.

"Come," Alun beckons us.

We make our way to his bench, where there is a great shuffling to make room for us. It is no small feat given Rudd's size, but finally we are all squeezed in. I am seated between Rudd and the little, jolly-faced man who teased Dryllis about her cooking.

He introduces himself as Cefwin the Baker. "Though truly I should have been a potter—if only I did not love my own wares so much." He twinkles at me, and I smile back, my heart warming. It is good to be the heroine and not the witch for once.

"Now, boy, from the beginning," orders Alun. His manner is amiable enough, but his gaze never leaves Thomas's face. He is hungry for details.

And so Thomas begins. His silver tongue amazes me. Listening to it, I am half inclined to believe him myself. In the tale he spins, Rudd is the hero while Thomas and I play more minor roles diverting the bandits and setting various traps for them. Not for the first time tonight, I marvel at his wit, for it's a clever move to make Rudd seem so capable of defense. Men who may wish to take advantage of us will think twice in the face of such bravery. He does not mention poison, for which I am glad.

During the course of Thomas's story, a sallow, sour-looking girl of about my age brings us mugs of ale and bowls of pottage and thick crusted bread.

"Her name is Ayleth," Cefwin informs me. He drops his voice slightly. "She has the visage of her father and the temperament of her mother, the lucky wench with the ability to turn milk to cheese with a single look." Then he laughs uproariously.

No matter what has been said of the food, we eat well and drink better. Although I was so hungry for anything from an oven I would have wolfed down thin gruel and hard rye, this pottage is rich with meat and the bread is made with finer flour than I would have given Dryllis credit for. Again and again our bowls are filled and we sop up the gravy with our crusts. For the first time in a long while, the three of us have full bellies and dry feet. Rudd yawns.

"The weight of our journey bears down upon us," Thomas apologizes, and yawns himself. "I think we must all go to bed."

As the two make their way up the rickety staircase, I pause to thank Alun again for paying for our bed and board, but he brushes my gratitude aside.

"It is I who owe you a debt," he whispers in my ear. "Judging by Dryllis's looks, you've made an enemy tonight. If I were you, I would leave at first light." He sighs ruefully. "My wife and I would gladly have you, but our small home is bursting at the seams as it is."

At the door of our room, I am halted by the innkeeper. As Cefwin said, he and his daughter share the same complexion. He has pale staring eyes, thick wet lips, and a weak chin.

"Do you have everything you need?" he asks.

"Yes, and I thank you." I try to open the door, but he stands in front of it, blocking my way.

"If you should want for anything, anything at all," he simpers, revealing a small stub of gray tongue, "you need only fetch me. My wife is a sound sleeper, but I wake easily."

His meaning is all too clear.

"Thank you, but this is more than sufficient."

He smiles again. "It is no trouble, I will be awake for some time still." He pauses. "It is lucky that you were not defiled, a girl as lovely as you."

"There was my brother to thank, sir." I try to remain cool, though my flesh is crawling under his gaze. "He was easily able to defend my honor."

He laughs unpleasantly. "I'm glad there was any to defend. Your brother, big lad, silent, isn't he?"

"He does not speak unless he has something to say."

"I do not think that would be often."

"Good night," I say firmly, and this time I am successful in forcing my way by him and into the room, and pivoting so that I straight-away shut the door. There is no bar against it, though, nor chair or chest to brace it. Rudd is already snoring and Thomas is dead to the world as I lie upon my scratchy pallet and wait for the fleas. I think of Dryllis's anger and of her husband's leering smile. I think of Alun's warning. Tomorrow, I vow, we will depart first thing.

But when the morning dawns, it's raining too hard for us to travel anywhere. We cannot go back into the woods. There is noth-ing to do but wait it out.

I try to talk to Ayleth, the whey-faced daughter, but I make little progress. She is just as Cefwin described her, in turn both sullen and vicious. I keep to our room as much as I can, but when I de-scend to the tavern I feel the innkeeper's eyes constantly upon me. I retreat to a bench in the loneliest corner and watch customers come in from, and go out into, the deluge.

Word has spread of our encounter with Blacwin's gang, and

despite the weather a steady stream of souls is eager to see the ones who defeated the bandits. Dryllis can hardly complain of the customers, but for all that she still hates us. Ayleth is just as bad, with her undercurrent of sighs and complaints. Rudd does what chores he can, lifting barrels and moving sacks, and Thomas is content to weave his fabulous story to new audiences, but I am not used to sitting by idly. My hands itch to brew or to serve or do *something* of use. The walls seem to close in around me.

In the late afternoon, the innkeeper corners me once more.

"Have you given thought to means of payment for this second night?" He makes so bold as to reach his hand out, caressing my waist, wandering up to pinch my breast.

I slap it away. "Do not lay hands upon me again or—"

"Or you'll set your brother on me?" He smirks. "I think not. In daylight it is clear to me that the boy is missing his wits." He reaches for me again.

This time I strike his face, but he is quick to grab my wrist.

"The she-cat has her claws out," he croons; then his face hardens as he pulls me in closer to bite at my neck and fill my ear with his slimy tongue, the reek of foul meat on his breath. "Listen to me, you little slut—"

"Garreth!" Somewhere, Dryllis is screeching. "Garreth, come and help me!"

Garreth releases me, but not without giving my breast a vicious pinch.

"Later you shall give me what you owe, or else I will fetch the sheriff and have you all thrown in the gaol. You know what they do to women in there."

There is no escape but the room. I crawl upon my pallet and shut my eyes tight. I listen to endless rain and pray for it to end. Tonight we will have to make our escape, rain or no.

It seems but a moment until I am being shaken awake. It is much darker now, and from below there are echoes of loud laughter and talk. Thomas is staring at me impatiently.

"Margaret, you must make haste and come down!"

"Why?" I close my eyes and turn over. The last thing I wish to do is spend more time in the company of Garreth and his family, but Thomas will not let me be.

"There are men here, the steward and his men." He dances from foot to foot, his words tumbling over one another.

"And what is that to us?" I keep my eyes closed, hoping that Thomas will take my hint.

"It might be everything, according to Ayleth."

Faint curiosity stirs within me. "What do you mean?"

"She did not want to tell me at first, oh, she was happy to lord it over me, but I teased and goaded her until she did!" He sounds amused.

"Tell you what?" I am exasperated now. "Thomas, speak plain!"

"Why, only that the lord is soon to return to his castle and they are in search of an alewife! They are calling in at all the taverns in the county."

"Oh?" I roll back, open my eyes, and see him grin.

"Dryllis has put her daughter forward, but there might still be a chance for you."

"Oh!" I sit up.

Thomas laughs and thumps the pallet. "In truth, you are slow! I have sung your praises while Dryllis prepares their meal, but now you must come down and present yourself."

There is no time to linger, so I smooth down my hair and make sure no soot stains my cheek while Thomas watches with a critical eye.

"I suppose that will do." He sighs.

I have to smile, he is so different now from the terrified beaten waif I first encountered in the woods.

"Come, come!" He grows impatient.

As I climb down the steps I can hear the steward's men before I even see them. They are merry, full of ale and Dryllis's best meat. These men seem larger than the villagers, they do not look like they have ever known hunger or want. They wear tabards, fine woolen hose, and tunics of good cloth. They speak with loud, commanding voices, and laugh louder.

Painfully aware of my unkempt appearance, my rough stained dress and my worn and muddy shoes, I advance timidly with Thomas by my side.

"And so this is your sister you speak of?"

It is easy to pick out the steward, for he is the hawk-like man with a curved beak of a nose and sharp, appraising eyes.

"Yes, sir." Thomas is meek, no sauce to him now.

"Come closer." It is a command. "Your brother has been speaking well of you. Of course, that is to be expected, but he claims you brew the best ale in five counties, and that you brewed for your father's inn."

"That is true, sir." I raise my eyes to look him full in the face. "I am confident that you would not find my efforts wanting."

"I'm sure he would not!" Leers a large, ruddy man in the steward's party. "I myself would be keen to taste *your* ale!"

There is much laughter.

"Be quiet," the steward snaps, and the men, chastened, do.

I flush and lower my eyes. I long to shrink back into the shadows, away from the hungry gaze of these men. Then I plan to murder Thomas.

The unnatural silence alerts Dryllis that something is amiss, and she rushes in.

"And what is this?" she cries in dismay upon seeing me at the steward's table.

"Another candidate for the position, mistress," the steward responds dryly.

"But I have already told you, sir, that Ayleth is perfect for the post!"

"Let's hope her brews are sweeter than her countenance," mutters the florid-faced man.

Agitated, Dryllis turns to the steward. "It has all been arranged," she insists.

Her tone seems to irk him. "Nothing is binding yet," he retorts.

"Sir, I beseech you, do not believe a word they say!" Dryllis is desperate now, her thick fingers clutching at her apron. "They are full of trickery and falsehood without a coin to their name, and she"—here she points—"she is nothing but a hedge-born slattern!"

"What about a competition?" The suggestion is proffered by a thin man, also in the party. He looks leaner, more thoughtful, than his companions.

The steward seems inclined to hear him out. "A competition?" he asks.

"Yes, for I'm sure there are others in the county who would like to try their hand at this work. You can assume the main role of taster, sir, and judge for yourself." He smiles. "In this way Lord de Villias will be certain of receiving the finest ale the county has to offer. After all, knights must joust to earn favor in court, so why should these women not have the chance to prove the same?"

Dryllis's scowl is mutinous. "That is not what we had agreed upon," she protests, turning again to the steward, but it is in vain.

"Nothing has yet been agreed by myself or by his lordship. Unless you do not think your daughter's ale can be measured against others?"

She takes a breath to protest but, seeing how the land lies, knows she has no choice but to accept the challenge on Ayleth's behalf.

"And you?" The steward turns to me.

"I accept," I say.

"A joust, a joust, a joust of the alewives!" one man bellows, and several take up the cry.

"It is decided. We will taste the ale in three days. We can leave it no longer, for we must be about his lordship's business."

Three days? I quail, wondering what can be brewed in only three days. Dryllis is clearly fuming, but there is nothing either of us can do. The date has been set. She glares at me with pure loathing and waddles back to the kitchen. Thomas begins to count under his breath, and when in a moment I hear a loud slap and then a wail, I understand why. Of course Dryllis would vent her displeasure upon the hapless Ayleth.

I thank the steward and pull Thomas with me into a far corner of the room, away from their table.

"Ow!" Thomas winces and looks at me reproachfully. "I thought you meant to squeeze my hand off its joint."

"I still might, for I have nothing to brew in and no oats nor barley, nor money to buy them, and I am certain Dryllis is not likely to lend me much!"

"And how can you doubt our Dryllis's warm and generous nature?"

I spin around. Cefwin the Baker grins, for he and Alun have joined our little circle too.

Alun also smiles. "I think we might be able to help you, at least in part. I can loan you a kettle big enough to brew in, and Cefwin can spare you the grains. Only it must be done in secret, for if Dryllis got word that we had helped you . . ." A comic look of horror comes over his face.

"You see, this is the only tavern for miles," Cefwin informs me solemnly, but his round face cannot suppress his natural mirth.

"And yet it is such fine sport to vex Dryllis, I swear it is good for the blood."

"It will have to be done well away from the village, out by the wood. Will that suit?" Alun's expression is hopeful, anxious.

Their sudden kindnesses, Thomas's belief in me, make me catch my breath. The task seems impossible, but for once there are those who are on my side. I am unable to speak. I nod and try to smile, for I do not wish to dismay them by crying.

For the next three days, I toil in a secluded thicket out on the edge of the wood. Alun brings his kettle, and Cefwin brings me what he can. At the King's Head I could purchase what I wanted at the town market, and inspect the goods firsthand, but now I am reliant on others. A handful of oats here and there some malted barley. I search for wild pepper and blue ginger and sage. I must try and work out what proportions to use, how to build strength and draw out flavor. I mash and stir and strain as Thomas and Rudd fetch pails of brook water and stoke the fire under the kettle.

I do not return to the Black Ewe. There is no rest or safety to be had for me there, nor could I pay. I am only grateful the rain has stopped, as I will be a little cold, but not wet through. Alun gives me a blanket and Cefwin gives me bread. It will not be for much longer, one way or another. A neighbor of Alun and Cefwin, Abel the Miller, has entered into the spirit of the joust and has offered to house Thomas and Rudd in his barn for the remaining days. Thomas assures me they are quite comfortable and have all they need. He flits back and forth to bring me news.

"Dryllis is in a foul mood, and woe betide anyone who gets in her way. She has done little else than stir and shout orders. Ayleth makes for a sad ghost, alternating weeping and sighing, and pretending that her mother is only aiding her."

Late in the evening of the third day, Thomas comes for the final time. Word of the contest has spread through the county, and many will be coming on the morrow to taste and judge for themselves.

"How does it go?" he asks hopefully.

I shake my head. I do not want to dash his hopes, but I fear the worst. After he has gone, I taste my ale again. It's no good, weak and sour.

If it falls short, and it will, our one means of escape, of survival, will be gone.

As despair overwhelms me, I sit on a stump beside the kettle and think about my mother, who brewed the ale that first made the King's Head famous. I close my eyes and try to conjure up what memories I have. She knew the art of brewing, but I was still so young when she died. There was so much more I could have learned from her.

"Mother," I implore. "Mother, what would *you* do?"

Her answer comes in the sigh of the wind whispering through the branches of the thicket.

Sing. I would sing, my Margaret.

"But what must I sing?" My chest is tight with the ache for her.

Let the song come to you.

My tune weaves and dips, trembling at first before finding itself and then gaining strength. I sing of the flowering summer, the smell of the earth under the warm sun, and then the ripening of autumn, when the green turns into golden grain. I sing of malt and the pale oats. I sing of sweet honey, humming bees, and the churning brook. I sing of growth and fermenting and of full cups brimming with plenty.

Then a great weariness overtakes me. I curl up next to the kettle. I have done my best, and cannot do more.

I sleep.

The sun has not yet reached its peak when I see Thomas and Rudd cresting the hill, cups in hand. Thomas is almost skipping. I wish I shared his confidence.

They are closely followed by Alun and Cefwin and then most of the locals from the Black Ewe, but there are soon many faces that I do not recognize, a seemingly endless parade of villagers from around the county toting their cups and bowls and tankards. There is an air of a festival, even among the men rolling the barrels. They groan, complaining about the weight, but all seem to be in good humor. I spy Dryllis walking next to the men who roll her oaken barrel. She barks instructions at the men who lug it here for her, while Garreth and Ayleth look on sourly, sulking. Finally the steward's party arrive, full of vigor and bearing cups too. It is fine for them, I think with sudden anger, for they have nothing to lose and everything to drink. They play with our lives as if this were a game of fivestones.

I watch as the growing procession makes its way over to us. I can only wonder what I must look like, emerging from the woods as a wild creature in my one worn green dress that will never be clean again, its ripped hem now stained with dew my hair long and tangled. I have done the best that I can, but I know I fall woefully short. We stand in line, waiting to serve. The crowd cheers and then falls silent as the steward announces he wishes to begin.

He first tastes the ale offered by an old woman who calls herself Mistress Edda. She is bent with whiskers upon her chin. The steward dips his cup, sips. Then he purses his lips, spits, and wipes his mouth with the back of his hand in disgust.

"It has not yet had its full growth," whines Mistress Edda as his reaction unfolds.

"That may be, but it should be put to death before it grows legs and slays us all."

There is much laughter at this, and the audience readies itself for his next tasting. I begin to sweat under the unrelenting sun. The next two barrels are none too bad, and from the corner of my eye I can see Ayleth fidgeting, sighing heavily. Dryliss does not seem worried, only bored.

The fourth cask is pronounced intolerable and the fifth, passable. I try to keep my hands busy stirring my kettle so they will not wring each other for the terror of it. I croon softly to myself, snippets of my song from the evening before.

> Grown from the earth,
> Golden in worth,
> Barley and wheat,
> Belly full sweet.

Thomas looks up at me, curious.

"A snatch of verse my mother once sang," I confide, for I cannot tell him the whole story.

Thomas nods. "Perhaps it will bring us luck," he says.

"Perhaps," I answer, but we can no longer meet each other's eyes.

It is now Ayleth's turn to be judged, and a hush falls over the expectant crowd. Dryllis stands at attention, her ample breasts and stomach jut forth, her simpering face red and round. Ayleth's complexion is that of moldy cheese, but she stands rigid like her mother, only the pinch of her nostrils shows that she breathes.

The steward dips his cup and drinks. He drinks again and

smiles, and in a loud voice he proclaims, "The best by far! The most fit for my lordship's table."

Ayleth crows with glee, and Dryllis's vastness visibly swells.

"Thank you, sir," she twitters. "You do the house of the Black Ewe great credit."

The villagers, including Alun and Cefwin, cheer, for however much they may dislike Ayleth, it is a source of pride that the Black Ewe's ale has been marked with distinction. They will be able to boast that one of their own will brew for Lord de Villias himself, that they will drink the same ale as his lordship.

My heart sinks as the steward turns away. Thomas bites his lip. How can we hope to match this praise? Will the steward even bother to keep tasting?

"Wait!" It is the lean, clever man who first suggested the competition. "Sir, with greatest respect, I trust you will not proclaim a victor before tasting all the brews?"

Dryllis opens her mouth. "*Surely* there is no competition here. Master Steward knows what he wants and likes!"

The villagers already lined up, cup in hand, to drink the winning brew nod vigorously, but the steward is shaking his head.

"You are right, Landon, and you speak the truth. It would not be fair, although I cannot conceive of any ale that could match that which I have just tasted."

Dryllis's stare is one of pure, hateful triumph. Ayleth smirks.

I swallow, for there is nothing I can do now but pray.

He walks slowly to where I stand by the kettle. "Well, mistress, do you still offer me a drink?" he asks. "Or do you forfeit?"

In answer I take his cup, dip it into the kettle, and hold it out to him. He takes it and sips. A strange expression passes over his face.

"My God." He sips again. He clears his throat, and when he speaks his voice is husky, almost a whisper. "One summer morning, when I was a boy, I ran away from my duties and spent the whole day fishing. I caught a huge trout, and though I was beaten for my willfulness, that night we ate well."

He laughs, and indeed for a moment his face is the face of a boy again, glowing with mischief and gleeful pride. His musing is quiet enough, but each word carries to the now-silent crowd. "It is as if I can hear the sound of the river, see the sunlight upon the water, feel the weight of the fish in my arms as I carried it home."

With these words he drains his cup to the last drop, then holds it out to me. "Again," he orders. "And fill it to the brim."

THE MAN IN THE WOODS

You watch as she stumbles into the clearing before bursting into an angry torrent of tears. Her one chance is gone, stolen away by a stranger. Now it will be that slattern who brews his lordship's ale. No matter that Ayleth cannot herself brew; she and her mother would have settled it somehow. The fact is that she must stay here in the village, a slave to her mother and a burden to her father. Unwanted, unwelcome, and unloved.

Self-pity is the color of curdled milk. It roars like other people's laughter, tastes like the ends of wet hair sucked, and the bland chew of fingernails. It mewls like a newborn kitten, it burns like bile at the back of the throat.

It takes a while before she realizes that you are leaning against a tree, watching her. She recognizes you, and is embarrassed that someone so high should witness her thus.

"Stop gawping and leave me be!" she snaps.

You do neither, only ask, "Why are you crying, fair maid?"

No one has ever given her a compliment. She squints at you through her swollen red eyes to see if you mock her, but no, your expression is grave, concerned.

"Surely you must know?"

You shake your head. "Tell me," you say and offer your hand to help her up.

She hesitates for a moment. You are, after all, a stranger. What would her mother say?

But then a gust of rebellion sweeps her up. *And what of it?* she thinks, gnawing her lip. *I am a grown woman and know my own mind.*

Rebellion is the sky's final hue of purple flame before the day runs out.

She takes your outstretched hand, allows your warm, firm fingers to close over her own. You smile at her then, and she sees that you are handsome. Here is a handsome man of good position taking an interest in her. Perhaps she has not lost her chance after all. Perhaps her salvation will come another way.

Hope smells of fresh mint, and tickles of murmured promises. Hope is a cool green swallow.

She begins to tell you of her woes. You are a good listener, understanding, sympathetic. You are, in fact, so attentive that she no longer pays attention to where you

are going. She does not question the wisdom of walking deeper into the wood with you as the sun begins its
descent. She is only happy to be in your presence, only
happy that someone is paying attention to her.

Insecurity is lavender. It pipes merrily at weddings
that will never be yours. It scoffs and pulls your ear down
with firm, unforgiving fingers.

And so you wander farther and farther away from
where the villagers drink and dance and make merry,
where they will do so until dawn.

It will be more than a fortnight before they find her
desecrated body, strange and savage symbols carved
upon it.

Her throat slit, her skin a tapestry of red.

12

Katherine

As they roar down the runway and climb upward, Katherine's most pressing thought is not about the magnitude of leaving (escaping) New York, nor about the life she's abandoning. It's not even, much to her shame, about how this move will affect Lucas. It is about whether or not they'll be offered a turkey dinner tonight. And if so, will it be edible? She thinks both are strong possibilities. It is, after all, Thanksgiving. And they're flying first class. First class. The most she ever strove for was business. Not that she's ever flown business either. She can count on one hand the number of times she has flown overseas. She always thinks that first class seems a crazy waste of money. Everyone is on the same plane after all, so if you're going down, you're going down together. Now, sitting in her spacious pod, being offered champagne and orange juice, she may reconsider.

She glances over at Sael. The seats are so huge and distant, she actually has to turn and look. He's got his laptop out and he seems engrossed. Lucas sits next to her, plugged in and content, watching some animated movie. It's his first flight and his first, possibly last, time in first class. She's not sure he appreciates any of it. She wants him to appreciate it and love it, but she also doesn't want him to freak out or get sad. He can't understand the implications of this flight. How can he, when she doesn't truly understand the implications of all this either?

"England, huh?" everyone says. "That's great!"

"At least they'll speak English," her friend Liz had teased her. "And I hear that's very similar to American."

Lucas seems to be happy about the journey, but not wildly excited. That's probably a good thing. He's taking it all in his stride, like he did when she told him about the move. After fielding a bunch of questions, she thought the best option was to let him watch something. She thought *she* might enjoy watching the endless lines of passengers grimly make their way to the back of the plane, but now that they're floating in their seats she doesn't feel the gleeful smugness she was counting on, but instead an anxious sympathy. *I totally understand where you're coming from*, she wants to say. *We shouldn't be here either.* And that's the truth, because why would they be going to England if it weren't for Sael? They wouldn't be going anywhere. They would still be trapped in a cold and hostile city with eight million residents. Without thinking about it, Katherine places her hand protectively over her belly.

"Good evening!"

Katherine starts, looks up. An elegantly coifed flight attendant is there. Perfectly made-up and smiling, she reminds Katherine of someone.

"Sorry to startle you, but I wanted to share our dinner choices with you tonight." She hands Katherine a cream-colored menu.

A menu! On a plane! Katherine wants to share the ridiculous amazingness of this with someone, but Lucas is not going to appreciate it, and sharing it with Sael wouldn't be much fun either. She will have to gloat alone. She checks out the options. A full

Thanksgiving turkey dinner (she knew it!) or salmon. She shyly makes eye contact with the flight attendant, unsure of how to proceed. Should she ask her what she, the stewardess, prefers as if she were a maître d'?

Before she can say anything, the flight attendant adds brightly, "Our salmon is very nice, but obviously, in your condition, turkey might be preferable."

Katherine wonders if Sael has heard, but he's still staring down at his laptop screen.

"Thank you." Her mouth is dry. She gestures to Lucas, who is laughing at the antics of a small blue dog with large floating eyebrows. "He'll have the turkey dinner too."

The stewardess nods affably enough. "And to drink? Obviously, you won't be having wine."

It's her eyes, Katherine realizes, *those glassy, marble eyes.*

"A ginger ale." She keeps her tone level, pleasant. "Please. And he'll have some milk."

The stewardess nods, and then moves over toward Sael.

Katherine rubs the bridge of her nose, trying not to cry. *It's not stopping.* She has to admit it. *It's not stopping. Here we are on the plane and the stewardess is going to bring us our turkey dinners and we're trapped and it's not stopping.* Because she had thought it would stop once they left New York. She had secretly hoped that somehow the sterile environment of the plane would kill it off, a quarantine.

She's gotten all too good at recognizing that slack look, that vacuous gaze. There are those who would revere; Mickey with his outstretched hand *I just wanted you to know,* the Bible thumper prostrate *Holy, Holy, Holy.* There are those who want her dead, Candice sprinkling glass on her food, Snow White regretful but matter-of-fact *Sooner or later one of us will kill you.* The worshippers may seem harmless but in truth they are almost as frightening.

She has triggered something within them but it's not *her* that's the trigger is it? *None of them can help it* Lucas told her.

It's the baby.

And as the baby grows, will their murderous urges and devotions grow stronger? Deep down she thinks knows the answer. She has never been so afraid.

Will it be like this England? She can't breathe; she needs a moment. She grabs her purse and heads to the bathroom.

Katherine tries for the door, but it's too late. The stewardess is suddenly beside her, her eyes now clouding over. She's smiling, but tears are coming as the words tumble out.

"You're so lucky to be pregnant. I've frozen all my eggs, the ones they could get to. Eggs on ice. My potential babies in some deep freeze, and there's only a minimal chance of it working. You do it to yourself. The injections are huge. You pump yourself full of hormones. Like a turkey. Like a Thanksgiving turkey on steroids." She laughs a little, but it sounds more like a sob.

Katherine reaches for the door again. The handle seems to be jammed.

"He's never going to leave his wife," the stewardess continues. "I'm getting too old for him anyway. It suited him at first, my schedule, the long distances, the endless flying. God. I just want to stop flying." She reaches out and touches Katherine's hand.

Of course, Katherine observes in the midst of her panic, *it's the perfect hand for a stewardess.* It's soft but not too soft, warm and professionally smooth.

"Could you help me?" the stewardess beseeches her. "Please help me?"

"I-I-I have to use the bathroom, I'm sorry," Katherine stammers, and miraculously the handle clicks and she opens the door, gets inside, and locks it. She stares at herself in the tiny mirror.

"Now what?" she asks aloud.

She had thought it would end. That was the main reason for saying yes, for leaving. She had thought it would stop. It hasn't, and it's getting worse.

Katherine rummages around in her purse for her eye drops, for some lipstick. She'll straighten herself out and then she'll go back. She'll have to go back. The bathroom is tiny. First class or no first class.

Something pricks her thumb and she draws back. *Shit! What was that?* She reaches into her purse again, cautiously, and her fingers close around a metal brooch. The ring brooch that Sael had given her when he knelt in the moonlight those endless months ago.

Katherine, will you wear this, now and forever?

She had said yes.

And now she stands in a tiny bathroom stall, thousands of feet above the ground, staring at the ring brooch in her palm, at the delicately coiled silver snake, its mouth forever fastened on the tip of its own tail.

She had said yes to Sael and she had worn it. But she had taken it off after what happened. The memories were too sad. The weight of it dragged her down. She wonders how it got here, loose in her purse. She had agonized over whether to return it, had lost count of the times she had opened her rosewood box where it lay gleaming, and steeled herself to do so. But then there had been no need.

Still, she could have sworn she had zipped it up safely in her jewelry traveling case when she was packing, but here it is, round and solid within her hand.

Will you wear this, now and forever?

Perhaps it could serve as a reminder of how once he loved her and wanted to spend his life with her. *Or perhaps this is a sign, a sign that we're meant to be together and that all is not lost.* She is almost dismayed by the way her heart lifts at this sudden thought. He won't see it if she wears it underneath her shirt. No one will.

It's the most beautiful, most precious piece of jewelry she owns, and yet she pauses for a moment longer. Then she lifts its chain and hangs it around her neck.

The ring brooch gleams. It is light, but she's aware of its presence on the slinky, silky chain, its cool weight between her breasts. It feels like she found something precious she didn't know she'd lost. It feels right.

Katherine finds herself staring at her own reflection. She laughs, shakes her head. She must have zoned out there for a moment. As she opens the door, she braces herself for the stewardess, sure that she'll be standing there still. *I can't do this*, she thinks, but then the infinitesimal pressure of the ring brooch upon her skin somehow gives her comfort. A miniscule anchor holding her steady, or a compass guiding her true. *I won't listen to anything that comes out of her mouth*, she decides. *I'll say, "Excuse me, I don't want to hear this."*

Except the flight attendant isn't there.

Relieved but puzzled, Katherine makes her way back to her seat. Sael looks up as she returns.

"Hey." He's put away the laptop and is going through some papers. "Everything okay?"

She nods. "It's fine."

"Good." He returns to his papers.

Lucas is engrossed in his movie. Katherine turns one page of her trashy novel, and then another. All is well.

"Excuse me?"

It's the flight attendant again. *Here we go.* Katherine shudders and resigns herself to whatever may follow: more confidences, more pleadings, more tears. But although only moments ago, cornered in the bathroom, she had felt terrified, after discovering the ring brooch she knows she can handle it. Somehow she feels stronger, more sure of herself.

"I know that you asked for a ginger ale, but are you sure I can't offer you another complimentary beverage?" the flight attendant asks. "We have wine, red and white, or a cocktail, a glass of Prosecco?"

"But . . . but . . . you said . . ." Katherine is totally thrown. The woman who was just warning her about the dangers of eating salmon while pregnant, who just told her she couldn't have wine, is now back to offer her a choice of alcohol. Katherine scans the flight attendant's face, her professional "I'm doing my job, and you're taking far too long to answer the question, but I'll stand here smiling until you do" demeanor.

"Is it possible to have a Bloody Mary?" she asks at last.

The flight attendant doesn't blink. "Absolutely."

"Actually—" Katherine smiles. "Sorry, I'll make that a Virgin Mary. Drinking can be dehydrating on a flight."

"Of course," the flight attendant replies, pleasant and detached as if she has no memory of what happened. "I'll be right back."

"Are you sure you're feeling okay?"

Sael is staring at her. He's not as absorbed in his work as she'd thought.

"Yeah. You?"

"I'm all right."

"Big changes."

"You could say that."

She wonders what it's like to be in his shoes. Two months ago, he was off to England for a fresh start. Now he has a pregnant woman—a woman he wanted to leave behind—and her five-year-old adopted child in tow. Katherine knows he's not sure how he feels about any of it. She wants to say something comforting. She wants to say, *It's cool. We'll be okay.* She wants to say, *Thank you.* But she can't seem to say any of these things.

Instead, she reaches out and touches his hand. He looks up.

Looks at her. Really *at* her, as if suddenly seeing her, Katherine, not as a woman he wants to forget, but as a woman he wants to remember.

Please, she prays, *please. You once reached out to me and I reached back. I need you.*

He gazes at her for a long while; then he takes her hand in his own warm dry one. Then looks down again at his papers but his face has relaxed a little, almost into a smile. After a long moment he releases her hand, but the small smile remains.

"Happy Thanksgiving, Katherine."

"Happy Thanksgiving, Sael."

It is enough. They don't say anything more for now.

She stares out at the gathering darkness. They are now well above the clouds. Good-bye, New York. Good-bye to the streets and the traffic, the buses and the subways, the endless mass of people walking, talking, laughing, shouting, shoving past. Pushing strollers and begging on corners and chatting on cell phones, walking their dogs and walking other people's dogs and lining up for brunch, waiting in pharmacies and delis and coffee shops and bars, at restaurants or at the Met or at concerts. Running along the river, in Central Park. Good-bye, good-bye, good-bye. *I loved you.* She thinks. *My heart is breaking, yet I am thankful.*

She *is* thankful and she also gives thanks that with every moment they are flying farther and farther away.

Thousands of feet below, other people are traveling, are arriving home on trains and buses and planes, winding, steering, flying to boyfriends or girlfriends or in-laws or friends. They will be greeted with hugs, with recriminations, the scent of turkey, and that warm, welcoming smell of mashed potato. Dogs, small and big, barking, leaping up. All these things are happening, but they seem to Katherine not just far away, but also in the past, as if distance equales time. They cannot hurt her now.

Second Trimester

13

Margaret

I wake before the dawn. It is dark, still, and I lie for a moment staring up at the underside of the thatch. He will be here by tonight, and the ale, the ale is not yet ready.

Thomas is usually the first to wake, but today it is I, for I have things to do. I rise, as quietly as I am able. I glance around, shivering, for the mornings are still a little cool. Our cottage is simple enough, with no more than two rooms, but it is ours. No Cecily watching and waiting, her small blue eyes scheming with new lies; no Old Warren stumbling through the door, his fists ready to swing. Here, at least, we are safe. I pull on my new dark brown woolen dress. Soon I shall have enough to buy material for another new one, if the lord is pleased with my ale.

I close the front door behind me, and walk to the smaller stone arch by the main castle gate. The armored guards know the sight of me by now and merely nod sleepily. It is early still and they are waiting to be relieved of their night duty. I cross the cobbles of the inner courtyard. It is strange to think that we only arrived here two weeks ago. I remember staring at the rough stone walls climbing up to the heavens. Now, if I lean back far enough, I can just make out the parapets where the archers and long bowmen stand guarding us.

I do not know if I will ever become accustomed to the size of this place: the dim, cool, never-ending corridors that lead into dim, cool solars; the staircases that wind, up to the lord's private chambers. When we first arrived the steward hurried me past the Great Hall. I would have little business there, keeping mostly to the kitchens and the buttery, but I caught a glimpse of the bright silk standards fluttering in the rafters, of the vivid wool tapestries lining its walls.

I find the staircase I seek, and descend into the belly of the castle. As early as it is, the kitchen is already teeming with life. Tonight, Lord de Villias returns, and there is a banquet. Many hands are already at work around the endless stretch of tables, which bear the weight of piled iron pots and skillets and instruments, most of torturous design: knives for skinning and peeling and scraping, mallets for mashing and pestles for grinding, sieves for straining and tied twigs for whisking. In baskets below are heaps of onions and apples and turnips. It is hot down here, and just as in hell the devil himself presides; the head cook roars like an ogre, torturing the legions of scullions who live to serve him, right down to the poor little spit boys who, because of the fire's flaming heat, often wear nothing at all.

I am careful to avoid the cook, who has but two humors: foul and fouler. He is huge and bald, though black bristles sprout upon his chest and back, and his clothes are stiff with stains and smears of grease. When I first laid eyes upon him I was frightened enough, but I have since learned that he has more of an eye for a pretty spit boy than he does for a woman, and as long as I keep out of his way I am in no danger of his attentions.

I slip into the bakehouse, which is next to the brewery. Here is yet more heat, and the warm animal smell of yeast rising. Faces are flushed, and I look for Warin, who has quickly become a favorite of Thomas and myself.

"You're up early today." Warin raises an eyebrow. "Your brother has yet to come in to claim his portion."

I feel a pang of guilt. "You will save a good piece, won't you?"

"He'll take what I give him," Warin says gruffly, but his voice holds a smile. Everyone likes Thomas. Within days of our arrival he had befriended the butler, the brewers, the guards, and all of the scullions with a nimble wit, fast tongue and a sympathetic way of drawing out others' troubles. He's learned the woes of Folant the Cobbler, what ails Dyl the Blacksmith, who is fighting with whom, the nature of each and every man serving the lord and how best to please him. It is thanks to Thomas that Rudd has had such easy passage. At first sight, many had been alarmed by his size.

"He'll eat at least two men's portions," grumbled one of the guards.

"Yes," Thomas had shot back. "He'll eat for two, but he'll work for five, so you'll have three men's work out of him. You couldn't make a better bargain!"

Even the guard had laughed at this. Since then, Rudd has been treated well. Each day he reports to the castellan, who puts him to work unloading carts and lifting sacks of grain and moving stones when ramparts need repair. No one can be offended by Rudd's cheerful smile and simple silence. As Thomas puts it, Rudd is the best listener by far.

I often wonder how Thomas has smoothed my path. No doubt he has had to field some questions, even defend me, but perhaps it is better not to know.

I thank Warin and, clutching my small loaf new from the oven, I move over to my vats. For two weeks I have been sifting and straining, trying with all different grains and spices to make an ale worthy of Lord de Villias himself. I taste it now. It is good, no one could say otherwise, and yet, and yet . . . I stir and sweat through the better part of the day, and then Thomas clatters into the brewery.

"Margaret!" he cries.

"What is wrong?" I wince at the thought of trouble.

"Come, come quick, he is here!" He grabs my hand and pulls me, running, up and into the main castle courtyard.

There is much commotion, horses snorting and pawing in the late light and knights and messengers and pages calling good-natured greetings.

"But where is the lord?" I ask. "I cannot see him in this madness."

Thomas points. High on a great white horse he sits, haloed by the last of the sun, and he is golden, golden, golden. His fair skin glows, and his tawny curls glint in the waning light. His eyes are radiant. His features are firm, proud. Lord August de Villias, August by name and august by nature. He throws back his handsome head at a jest from one of his men, and his laughter is full and innocent as a boy's.

Instantly, I know.

If he would but smile at me just once, I would happily walk into fire for him. There are flashes before my eyes, as if I have been staring unguardedly into the blazing summer sun.

"Oh, Margaret." Thomas is awed. "Is he not splendid? What would you not give to serve him?"

I nod and swallow. For once, I have no words. It is all too much. I turn abruptly, for it hurts my heart to look upon him.

"I will see you later," I tell Thomas.

I must go to the garden. I understand now what the ale needs.

There, I breathe in the scent of sage and parsley and try to keep a cool head. I must let my heart guide me. I snap stems of rosemary and lavender, and clutch them tightly to my chest.

The castle has caught my fever. Servants scurry here and there under a volley of shouted orders in preparation for the night's banquet, which is almost upon us. The kitchens are bedlam, though the smells are heavenly. The spit boys turn huge joints of lamb and swine, pots are bubbling, and the stone ovens are crammed to bursting. I make my way to the brewery, where my casks are ready to be filled to their brims. I drop the lavender and rosemary into the cauldron and stir as the song flows from me:

> *Heart to heart,*
> *Bone to bone,*
> *Each cup-filled cup*
> *Make thee my own.*

I am tired but there is no time to rest, for I know now that the ale is ready and it must go out to all the men.

I wipe the sweat from my forehead and begin to fill the casks, which servants grunt and strain to lift.

As the last of the sun fades from the sky, the banquet begins. There is roasted fowl and spitted lamb, stewed beef and braised hare, turbot and baked herrings, bone and marrow pies, brawn in mustard and meat fritters made with the finest entrails. A suckling pig and a baked capon in pastry are served, alongside boiled venison in almond milk and Lord de Villias's favorite dish, roast curlew and martinets, which is followed by pyramids of honeyed fruits and bowls of stewed damsons, pears poached in wine. Wafers and shelled nuts are presented on dishes of silver and shining pewter.

Watching the parade of delicacies travel up to the Great Hall, I sit in a corner of the kitchen to eat my own meal, having scavenged a discarded wing of fowl and some fatty end bits from the joint. I am drowsy from my work and the warmth of the ovens, and doze . . . until I am woken by a page dressed in good cloth.

"The new alewife is summoned to the Great Hall!" he calls out.

My heart is in my mouth.

"What could he want with me?" I ask, but I am told only that I must appear before the lord and his men.

I am dirty and sweaty from my labors, but there is nothing for it. With my palms, I wipe the smuts from my face as best I can and let my hair down around my shoulders.

When I finally enter the Great Hall, I am speechless. Fires illuminate the rich colors of the heavy tapestries, the long tables draped with linens embroidered in silver and gold thread and an endless array of dishes. More candles than I have ever seen flicker and smoke amid the platters. The Hall is filled with sound, minstrels accompanied by lute and pipes and fiddles, and the laughter and talk of the knights and nobles, punctuated by shouts to servants to bring more dishes, to refill their cups.

I make my way through this joyous din, carefully stepping over the carpet of rushes strewn about the floor, which still smells sweet and fresh even though now it is blanketed in bones and bits of gristle that even the dogs would not have. Slowly, I approach the main table. Clad in green and silver, he sits, leaning back a little, among those who love him best. His steward stands to his right. Lord de Villias gestures and the steward bends down and whispers into his ear. The lord nods and smiles. The music ceases, the talk dies, and the silence that follows is immense.

"What is your name?"

His voice, though not loud, carries clear and confident across the Great Hall.

It feels as if the whole world is waiting to hear my answer.

"Margaret Belwood, my lord." I pray my voice will not betray my trembling limbs, my hammering heart.

"Well, Mistress Belwood."

My name from his lips is exquisite like cold, sweet well water. He lets his eyes move slowly up and down my form before fixing his gaze upon my own.

"I have summoned you to commend you on your most excellent ale. I swear I have never tasted its like before."

With my eyes lowered, I curtsy as best I can.

"Thank you, my lord," I murmur.

The flames of the fire and the candles bathe him in gold. He smiles, and warmth rises within me. Would that I could die now, when I am so happy.

"What reward, what payment, might I give you to show you my pleasure?"

I do not need to think of what to say because the words are already there. "My lord, your satisfaction is reward enough for me."

I dare to lift my gaze to his. I see surprise, surprise and genuine gratification. I believe he did not expect this answer. His mouth curves into a smile.

"Well then, Margaret Belwood," he says softly, "I thank you." His eyes shine more brightly than the silver upon the table.

I curtsy again, then take my leave. A strange silence drags behind me as I exit. I am a few steps into the passage when the musicians and minstrels strike up their tunes. The voices grow louder—one splits into shards of laughter—and I am once more alone.

I head for the cottage, not walking but floating. I am just past the main gate when I float into a wall, only it is not a wall but the solid bulk of a man's back. It's a guard, drawing from a wineskin.

He turns with an oath, and then he sees me. His face breaks into a pitted leer.

"Well, what have we here?"

When we came to the castle, the steward warned me of the dangers.

"It has been a long winter," he had said. "The men have grown restless. I have told those who work in the household that you are under my protection, but I cannot account for every man here. You would do well to keep to your quarters when you are not at work."

The guard reaches out with thick fingers, pulling me close. He is well into his cups by the reek of him.

"Let me go!" I wriggle, a hooked fish.

"Not without a kiss," he smirks. "My lips are parched for love. It is too long since I've lain with a whore and you'll do nicely."

"Let me go!" I cry again, but he only laughs, pulling me off into the darkness.

"Unhand her!" It is the lean, long steward's man, with a voice of iron.

The guard looks up with a grunt, he stumbles forward, still clutching me, ready to fight. "And what is it to you?"

"I am Landon, the steward's man, and I make my report to him."

He had been affable when I saw him last, but now he stands cold and straight, authority itself. There is something in his manner that I would not wish to cross.

"But why should you care for a whore?" The drunken guard appears bewildered at Landon's vehemence.

"She is no whore! She is the new alewife, chosen by the steward and owed all due protection. Why, his lordship himself summoned her tonight to praise her work. I doubt he would be pleased to hear of the woman he personally showed favor toward being handled so rough by one of his own men."

The guard takes a step back.

"Forgive me, sir, I did not know," he mutters, chastened.

"It is not for me, but for her to grant you forgiveness," Landon declares.

The guard mumbles something, churlish.

"I could not hear, speak up."

I want to protest, for Landon has made a bad situation worse, but I dare not.

At last the guard speaks to the ground. "I beg your forgiveness. I did not know."

I nod.

"Now, be gone from my sight!"

Like a dog with its tail between its legs, the guard shuffles away, turning back but once to shoot me a venomous look before skulking into the night.

Landon smiles tightly, steps toward me. "Any true harm done?"

I shake my head. "None. I thank you."

"Must I always be saving you?" He gives me a crooked grin, and I think again of him deftly ensuring that the steward would try my ale even after he seemed to declare Dryllis and her daughter the winners.

"It would seem so," I admit.

"You did very well tonight."

"Again, I thank you."

"What do you think of his lordship?"

"Why, he is like the sun," I blurt out before I can think the better of it.

He nods. "It is true that he is the best of men. But be careful, lest you come too close and burn up. Now, go home quickly. It is not safe out here when the hour is so late."

It is clear that our exchange is over, and I continue into the darkness, still so rattled by my encounter with the guard that I do not think to wonder why Landon was out here at this hour.

Though it is late, Thomas is waiting up for me. Rudd is snoring loudly, but he has a hundred and one questions and makes me tell him exactly what happened, for word has somehow already reached him of my audience with Lord de Villias, and the offer of a reward.

He is by turns pleased and bewildered, even angry.

"But why?" He keeps his voice low for fear of waking Rudd. "Why did you not ask for some small reward? He is certain to have given it to you and now the chance is lost forever!"

How to explain it to him, still a child? If I had taken what was offered, that would have been the end of it.

I lie upon my pallet. I close my eyes, and see him as he smiles at me in the firelight and I know. I know.

This is just the beginning.

14

Katherine

They are exhausted after the flight. It's raining.

"Welcome to England," their driver had said when he met them at Heathrow. Now he pulls up in front of a line of white houses, guarded by black railings, that stand quietly in the rain. Katherine notices a small park, soft and damp and still green even though it's almost December.

They get their bags in, and then, even though they are tired, they explore their new home. The open kitchen has a massive white marble island in the center, which separates it from the dining room. The walls are off-white, and the floors are pale wood. There are cream and pale-gray couches with tan and cream cushions, and large terra-cotta pots holding white orchids. *As if we were drowning in milk*, Katherine thinks. It's one of the most elegant and beautiful spaces she's ever seen.

On the long wooden dining room table is a huge white ceramic bowl of gleaming grapes and peaches and apples. Lucas helps himself to an apple, and Katherine almost screams, *Stop! Don't touch anything!* Then, collecting herself, *I guess he's allowed an apple if he wants one. It's his home, after all.*

Sael opens the shining stainless steel refrigerator. He whistles. Its spotless white interior is stocked with milk, eggs, several different cheeses, vegetables.

They walk from room to room.

Sael seems mildly pleased. "It will do."

Katherine is silent. She has never lived in a place as nice as this. In one of the bedrooms there's a huge bouquet of lilies, white again, and Sael stands by the bed looking not pleased but concerned.

"What's wrong?"

"I think George thought that we'd be staying in a room . . . together." His eyes veer away and he frowns.

"Aren't we staying in a room together? That's what I thought too."

Katherine has the real sensation of the floorboards tilting away under her feet.

"Oh . . . I mean, I just didn't know how you felt."

She wants to say, *Sael, I miss you, I want to be in bed with you*, begins to say this, but just then Lucas comes running through.

"Kat, Kat, come! I think I found my room!"

"You did? That's great!"

"Well, he's coming around later to meet us, so we can talk with him then." Sael doesn't meet her eye. "The company brought him in kind of last minute anyway. We've been emailing on and off, but I guess there's always going to be stuff that doesn't translate."

Lucas grabs her hand and pulls her out of the room before she can ask just what 'stuff' he's talking about, how he'll explain their situation.

She's dragged into Lucas's room, where a very cool-looking model airplane, a Paddington Bear, and several books—one called *The Horrible History of Britain* and two big picture books, one that seems to be about castles—sit on his bed.

George, I don't know how Sael feels about you but I think I'm in love.

"Wow! This is awesome. But you know what?" She collapses on the bed. "I think this is my room."

Lucas smiles shyly. "No, it's not, it's mine."

"Nope, this airplane, this bear"—she hugs the Paddington to her chest—"clearly mine."

"No, it's—"

"Wanna wrestle for it?" She reaches out and pulls him in, hugging and tickling.

Lucas shrieks with laughter. "Stop it! No, it's mine! It's mine!"

Katherine grins into his hair. She's suddenly seized with wild optimism. Maybe this could work, after all.

"Guys?" Sael stands in the doorway. "I'm starving, want to grab lunch?"

As if in reply Katherine's stomach rumbles and she clutches it, grimacing with embarrassment. Lucas giggles.

"I guess that's your answer. Should we make something with what's in the fridge?"

"We could, but I kind of want to stretch my legs." He crouches down to Lucas's height. "What do you say, kid?"

"Okay!" Lucas is still in giggle mode. *He's pretty excited, maybe overexcited,* Katherine worries, and then decides, *but what the hell, it's not every day you immigrate.*

They take a walk, taking two umbrellas that they find neatly stacked by the door. The rain isn't that bad now, more spitting than pouring. There's a whole array of shops and cafés two streets down, and Katherine's heart lifts again. Sael heads toward a trendy restaurant that looks chic yet cozy. The lunch-hour crowd fills it up, but they get a table near the back.

"Well, we're here," he says. "For some reason I sort of feel like breakfast food."

"That's because it's morning in New York," Lucas informs him sagely. He turns to Katherine. "Right, Kat?"

"That's right." She glances at her watch. "It's about six in the morning. Right now I'd be saying grumpy things to the alarm clock and waking you up." She reaches over and rubs his head. "Time to wake up!"

Lucas grins.

Again she allows herself to believe that maybe this will be okay.

She orders an avocado-and-crab sandwich, Sael gets bacon and eggs, and in a bold move Lucas orders fish-and-chips.

"You're the most English of us," Katherine tells him.

When their food comes, the piece of fish seems to be the size of his head. Lucas looks nervously at Katherine.

"Don't worry," she reassures him. "You only need to eat what you want."

"And I thought the portions in America were big!" Sael winks at Lucas. "I'll help you out."

Katherine sits back. She's loving this exchange between them. Mostly they've been communicating by using her as a translator. Sael has been nervous. Little kids are not his normal target audience. Lucas likes Sael, but he's shy.

"So," says Katherine after the initial attack on their food is over. "Who is this mysterious George?"

Sael shrugs. "I'm not sure what his official title is, but he's like an in-house facilitator. When the company hires people from overseas, his job is to make sure they can settle in as quickly and easily as possible. He also facilitates their transition into the company. Shows the new kid around the school, so to speak. A lot of organizations have them these days."

"That's nice." Katherine tries to sound neutral. *Money. If you have enough money you don't have to deal with anything.*

Perhaps Sael hears something in her tone, for he becomes a little defensive.

"Well, it's really to their benefit. They don't want you wasting time with finding a place or dealing with all the admin cra—" He glances at Lucas. "Pain of moving. They're paying you to work for them, so it's in everyone's interest."

Katherine imagines George to be a good-looking but painfully shy man. She sees him dressed in tailored suits, sort of like a modern-day butler. Maybe he's gay, or maybe he develops a passion for her, but is too timid to ever act on it, like a late 1980s or early 1990s comedy. Maybe he's endearingly plump and sort of looks like a rabbit. She looks up to see Sael yawning hugely.

"The jet lag is taking over." He smiles. "This is the most dangerous time. Nice full meal, sleepy weather.

"Jet lag?" Lucas looks up, alarmed.

"It just means when you're flying between countries you might want to sleep in the day, but it's best to sleep at night."

"When else would you sleep?" Lucas is curious.

"Well . . ." Sael struggles. "You might want to take a nap beforehand."

Lucas is scornful. "Naps are for babies."

"I agree, and I feel like a big, big baby right now." He yawns again, and Katherine finds herself yawning too. "Oh no! It's contagious!"

Lucas laughs at both of them.

It was a joke, but now Katherine can't stop yawning. Her eyelids feel like lead. *Maybe I'll just lie down and read for a little while,* she compromises. Once on the bed, she negotiates with herself. *I'll just shut my eyes for a second.* She shuts her eyes. *Maybe Sael will come in. Maybe he'll lie down next to me. Maybe he'll see that I have my eyes closed and maybe he'll very gently lean over and kiss my forehead, so lightly that I don't wake. Maybe a wave of tenderness will wash over him and he'll touch my hair . . .*

Katherine wakes. She lies there staring up at the ceiling with no sense of who, what, where, or how. Knowledge drifts back in little snatches and chunks. England. Traveling. There's still some light—the sky is draining white—but very little of it. She looks at her watch to discover it's already four p.m. She succumbed to jet lag after all.

Rising, she walks to Lucas's room. He might have fallen asleep too. *You shouldn't have slept so long,* she worries, *but maybe after the trip and the meal and the excitement it was all too much. You'll wake him up gently, he's bound to be grumpy.* Katherine feels kind of grumpy herself. Her mouth is dry. She's dying for water.

She opens the door, but Lucas's room is empty. His airplane lies untouched. The bear's eyes gleam blackly back at her. Then she hears voices coming from downstairs. Sael sounds relaxed, happy. Lucas soft and sweet, and there's another voice, a woman's. Their laughter is coming from the kitchen.

Sael is sitting at the dining room table, elbows up, clutching a mug of tea. Lucas is also at the table. He's got his colored pencils out and appears to be making good use of his coloring book. A tall woman stands at the stove, her back to Katherine as she pours boiling water into the kettle. Katherine can see she's slim underneath her snow-white shirt and black leggings. Her auburn hair is knotted in a casual bun, soft strands escaping. She half glances over her shoulder to makes a comment, and they all laugh again, like a family enjoying one another's company at home on a rainy evening.

Katherine has a strange impulse not to be seen. She turns to go back upstairs, but Lucas looks up and Sael follows.

"Katherine!"

There's nothing for it now. She continues down the last few steps, feeling oddly nervous.

"Hey." She tries to sound casual, but instead sounds croaky. Her mouth is insanely dry. She coughs.

The woman turns, and Katherine can see that she's not much more than a girl, still in her early twenties. She comes over, hand outstretched, and Katherine takes in her loveliness: her flawless skin, high cheekbones, shining eyes fringed with dark lashes, and full-lipped laughing mouth.

"Oh my God, I'm so sorry, did we wake you?" She has a beautiful English accent, plummy enough to indicate true class.

Katherine notes the "we" as she shakes her head.

"No. But it doesn't matter. I shouldn't have been sleeping anyway." She turns to Sael and Lucas. "I can't believe you guys let me sleep!"

It's a comment that's supposed to sound lightly jovial, but it comes off as harsh, accusatory. Cranky. Lucas winces and looks down.

Sael clears his throat. "We should have woken you, but you just seemed so tired and I thought in your condition . . ." He trails off. "Sorry," he finishes.

It's not a big deal, she tries to say, but starts coughing.

"Let me get you a glass of water," offers the supermodel.

Katherine wants to tell her that she'll get it herself, but she can't stop coughing. She sits down by Lucas.

"Hey, kid," she croaks in between coughs.

"Hey, Kat." His expression is one of apprehension.

She tries to smile.

The supermodel hands her a glass of water. "I'll make you a cup of tea," she says.

Katherine downs half the contents of the glass. She can breathe again. The first thing to do is reassure Lucas.

"Phew. Better." Then she looks up at the gorgeous woman who happens to be in their kitchen. "I don't think we've met."

"Oh, I'm so stupid!" The woman laughs. "Forgive me, I'm George, or Georgie, whatever you prefer."

"George?"

"Yes, it's a bit of a blow. Christened Georgiana, I'm afraid, but I beg you not to call me that. Reserved only for my parents, or for my teachers, when I was in serious trouble. They would say, 'Georgiana Benniton-Harris, get down off that desk and come here!' It was awful!" She gives Lucas a huge, saucy wink. He laughs.

"Oh." Katherine's imaginary butler stands in the corner, holding his immaculately packed suitcase with one hand and giving her a mock salute with the other, mouthing, *Good luck with this one, my dear.* "It seems we have you to thank for the flowers, and all the amazing presents for Lucas."

"Thank you," Lucas says, serious again.

"Oh." George waves their gratitude away with one slim hand. "It was my pleasure. I always think flowers make a place feel like home. Milk, lemon, sugar?"

Home.

"Milk, thanks."

Sael clears his throat. "Georgiana—"

"Georgie! I beg you."

"Oops, sorry."

Lucas giggles; Sael smiles.

"Anyway, Georgie—"

"Thank you."

"—was just telling us about the house in more detail."

"Well, really you'll meet Mrs. Bailey tomorrow, and you can go through everything with her. She's the housekeeper we hired," she says in an aside to Katherine. "She's fantastic, very organized."

Mrs. Bailey, Katherine repeats to herself, imagining a plump, bustling mother-hen type of woman in a long dress, with an apron and a little cap. *She'll call us her "ducks," and we'll have cozy gossip sessions, and I can lay my head on her soft shoulder and weep.* Then she thinks of her fantasy about George, and wonders how this dream will be destroyed.

"Great."

"I just wanted to come over today and meet you all and work out when would be a good time to go through various options regarding doctors, schools, all that fun stuff, right, Lucas?"

"Yeah," he agrees.

"Lucas, let's not say 'yeah,' let's say 'yes.'" The words come out of Katherine's mouth before she can stop them. She sounds like an uptight bitch.

"Yes." The word sounds small, his eyes are cast down.

There's an embarrassed pause; then Georgie turns to Katherine.

"We were thinking that I could bring Sael to the company offices tomorrow morning and then come back and meet up with you and Lucas both in the early afternoon and take it from there. That way you could take it easy and get your bearings a little. Does that work?

That "we" again.

"Perfectly."

Georgie leaves soon afterward, and in her wake silence and awkwardness descend. The ease and lightheartedness of the day is gone. Sael turns on the television, maybe to bring back some noise into the house. It's time for the BBC News broadcast, and Katherine notices there is less of a theatrical bent to the nightly news unlike the States. And the English accents make everything feel more official, more solid.

She listlessly makes them a salad, an omelet, some toast. The meal has a sad Sunday-night feeling.

"Kat, look." Sael nods toward the couch, where Lucas has fallen asleep.

"Oh man, he must be wiped." Instinctively she bends to pick him up, but Sael stops her.

"Let me carry him."

Katherine watches as he gently lifts Lucas up and against his shoulder. He *is* good with kids when he doesn't worry too much. That's lucky. She feels like crying.

It must be the hormones.

She follows him upstairs and into Lucas's room. Together they take off his sneakers and socks and tug off his jeans. She debates about waking him up to brush his teeth and then dismisses it as madness. He can also have a shower tomorrow morning. He's five years old, after all. It's been a long day.

"Night, Lucas," she whispers. "I love you." She kisses his forehead, hopes in his sleep he'll hear her.

Back downstairs in the kitchen, she starts tidying up the remnants of dinner.

"I can do that," Sael tells her. "No worries." He rinses the dishes and places them into the dishwasher. "Not sure where the soap is. I guess the housekeeper will let us know tomorrow."

"I guess so," she answers.

They stand quietly now they have run out of things to do with their hands.

"Long day."

"Yeah." He turns and gives her a sharp look. "Or should I have said 'yes'?"

She winces. "I just realized how American we sound."

"Well, we are American."

She doesn't want to fight with him, doesn't know how to explain that she felt threatened, how she didn't want them to seem like dumb hicks.

"That's true, we are." Her voice is soft, placatory.

They look at each other, unsure of how to proceed.

"Anyway, she seems nice," Katherine concedes.

"She's insanely organized. It's amazing."

Of course she is. Katherine scowls inwardly, forcing herself to nod. *It's important to keep the peace when you're so tired it's easy to start a fight.* "So, are you coming to bed?" She tries to keep the question light and not loaded.

"I will soon, I still have some paperwork to do."

"You must be exhausted."

"It's not so bad. I prefer to try push through till ten or eleven, if I can."

"Unlike me." She sounds harder than she means to be.

He shrugs. "I'm not pregnant."

This is undeniable. She is pregnant. It's the reason why Lucas and she are there. The fact of it seems to move Sael too.

"How are you feeling?" he asks in a gentler voice.

"I'm okay. A little tired maybe."

"Well, take it easy."

"Yeah, I'll try."

"Yeah?"

"Yeah. Yeah, yeah, yeah!"

He grins and she grins back at him.

Sael, she wants to say, *I miss you, don't do the paperwork, come to bed with me. Let's just hold each other in the dark the way we used to.* Instead, she says, "Well, don't work too hard."

"Okay."

"Night, Sael."

"Night, Katherine."

She stands there for a moment longer. Uncertain. *Now would be the time to go to him,* she thinks. *Put a hand on his cheek. But he's right, it's been a long day.*

She turns and walks up the stairs.

15

Margaret

When I wake, the day tastes different. The breeze is softer, sweeter. The light is brighter. But it is not just the day. As soon as I step within the castle walls, I can feel it.

This cold, crenellated shell has become another world. There are servants everywhere. Running up and down the winding stone spiral stairs and along the passageways, delivering messages and carrying plates of food or baskets of soiled linen for the washerwomen. In the main courtyard, knights banter loudly over the crash and clank of swordplay. Eager squires cheer their masters on, and little pages squeal as they wield their wooden blades. The blacksmith's iron rings out again and again. The stables echo with the snorts and neighs of horses.

In the kitchens there is even more activity, with so many more mouths to feed. The head cook bellows, the spit boys sweat and turn the cranks, the scullions scour pots and platters. There is no time now for them to tease one another or scratch small drawings into the walls. We are all happy to be busy, for with his return Lord de Villias has brought a renewed sense of purpose. He carries within him the fire of regal youth, and it has ignited us all.

I go to my vats and begin my work. As I have done nearly every day since I came to the castle, I stir and strain, call for more water, more malted barley. The tasks are still as backbreaking as they have always been, but today I marvel at how easy it feels and wonder at the change. I still sweat as I pour and stir and stoke the fire with new logs, but I am smiling and singing all the while. I am brimming, as full as an ale cup, with happiness.

When Thomas runs in, he is breathing so hard he can scarce get the words out. "Margaret, come quick!" Before I can ask him he continues.

"The cottage," he gasps. "We are being expelled."

Suddenly, my cup is tipped over, its contents poured out.

Sure enough, a stout, red-faced man stands firmly on the threshold. He only has one thing to say but makes up for it by endless repetition.

"This place is mine."

"How can this be, you fool?" Frustration has driven Thomas's good manners from him. "You can see plain that we live here!"

"It's mine." He remains stubborn. "It were *promised* to me."

"He is right."

Landon appears behind us. I did not hear him approach.

"But how can this be?" I implore him.

"You are to be moved," he says shortly. Thomas opens his mouth ready to protest, but he continues. "My lord heard tell of your adventure last night when you returned home. He deems it dangerous that you should travel so far late at night as your duties so often keep you until after curfew."

Today he is brisk and businesslike.

"He heard tell from you?" I hazard.

Landon allows the ghost of a smile.

"What adventure?" Thomas turns to me.

"All in good time." I brush him aside, for I am more concerned by what is happening now. "So where are we to go?"

"Follow me."

Now that Landon is involved, we go meekly enough, hastily collecting our belongings and leaving our usurper to gloat over his new home. We walk back toward the castle on a smoother path, one that's less isolated, and then Landon stops.

"Here."

My mouth falls open. The cottage is perfect, with solid stone walls and a new, tightly packed thatched roof. He opens the thick oak door, which I notice has a sturdy iron bolt on the inside, into a room filled with light. There is a large cooking hearth, and it is already furnished with a wooden table and two benches, a spruce chest with an ornate iron lock, an ewer and basin, a stack of pewter plates, and pots and spoons and ladles of all different sizes. Thomas and I run about the chambers that open off each side of the hall, one for Rudd and Thomas and one for myself. Painted cloths decorate the walls in bright reds and blues. There are actual wooden bedsteads, and when I touch the coverlets—coverlets!—my fingertips tell me they are linen and not rough hemp. I doubt if Thomas or Rudd have ever slept upon a proper bed before, let alone one with a feathered mattress instead of one stuffed with straw.

I walk through the wooden door in the back wall of the hall, and there, oh marvel of marvels, is a small garden already planted with vegetables. Protected by a fence of wooden boards, it is perfect for growing herbs of my own.

Thomas looks pleased, but he is aware enough of the world to be puzzled by this sudden change of luck. He glances at Landon, but says nothing.

After Landon thinks we have had enough time to admire our new home, he shows us a little path that leads off through a small entrance in the garden fence. "This will lead you to the keep," he says. "Truly, it is only a stone's throw away."

Tonight will be the first in our new home. We sit around the table as a family might. I am still overwhelmed with the luxury of it. There is a small oven next to the hearth so that we may bake our own bread, and with the spices in the almery we can make our own pottage with the onions, leeks, celery, and peas from the garden. Rudd is round-eyed, and even Thomas still sits silent.

Once we have eaten, I bid good night to Thomas, who seems troubled.

"What ails you?"

"Nothing. Only . . ."

"Only?"

"I cannot make sense of it. Why would we be moved to so pleasant a place?"

I look away so that he will not see my flushed cheeks and give no answer.

Over the following days we ease into our good fortune, finding new treasures, saffron among the spices, embroidered cushions, smooth ceramic jugs, even a pair of fine pewter candlesticks upon the mantel. Each day I hug my happiness tightly to myself as I go about my work in the brewery.

Then, one early morning not long after our move, I sense someone's gaze upon me as I stand in line with Thomas at the well. A woman with a pale, trembling mouth and raw red eyes stares at me. Next to her is a man, presumably her husband given the small child teetering about her feet. She may be pretty beneath her distress, but it is impossible to tell.

She is about to start toward to me when her husband grips her arm and mutters something in her ear. Tossing her head, she seems

ready to defy him, but then he speaks again and abruptly her arms
fall limp at her sides. If she could, I'm sure she would spit upon me,
but there is her family and their livelihood to think of. Instead she
shoots one last furious look as her child begins to wail. Gathering
him in her arms, she croons to him, in tears herself. We are tempo-
rarily forgotten.

The scene dumbfounds me. "What is the matter with her?"

Thomas's face is miserable, ashamed. "That is the wife of Guy
the Candlemaker. I hear that it was to them our cottage was first
promised."

I feel sorry for the woman, but I cannot pretend that I would give
back the cottage. Never before have I had a sanctuary where I have
felt such peace and safety. Never before have I been the mistress of
my own home.

The incident is soon driven from my mind. Having worked a full
day in the brewery, I return to the cottage and walk straight into my
chamber. There, lying neatly upon my bed, is a rich rainbow of soft
linen smocks and kirtles. Spruce green and evening blue and, best
of all, a warm and vital red, they glow like jewels. Even the wealthy
merchants' wives whom I have seen wandering through the market
could never afford the garments that are now displayed before me.
I am so stunned I cry out.

Thomas runs into my chamber. "Margaret! What is it?"

When he sees what is on my bed, he too is spellbound. For a moment I am back at the town market on the day I took Cecily, standing at that stall with all its sumptuous bolts of cloth, not daring to
touch the vivid wools and silks while the old woman scowls at me
with sunken, sour eyes.

"Is that *silk*?" Thomas is awestruck. He reaches out one hand,
returning me to the present.

"Stop!" My voice is sharp.

He glances at me, suddenly afraid.

Again I see the old woman's grim face.

"The fabric is so fine," I explain softly. "We would do best to make sure our hands are clean."

Slowly the hurt fades from his face, but he does not return to my chamber again to touch them.

Once the dresses appear, I know it is now only a matter of time. I cycle through the same tasks each day, but inside I am warmed by small flames and spiked with cold shivers. It is like a fever. What will happen next? To wait and wonder is delicious and maddening. When next? When next? When next?

I stir the cauldron, drifting into a dream.

"How do you fare?"

I start, look up. Landon is leaning up against the wall of the brewery, watching me. I do not know how long he has been there. He has a habit of blending in until he wants to be seen.

"Very well, sir."

"The cottage, is it to your taste?"

"It is indeed."

He nods. "You found the gowns in your chamber?"

Now it is my turn to nod.

"His lordship would like to see how his gift becomes you."

"Oh!" I exclaim, then press my lips together.

Landon displays no emotion. "I will come and escort you this evening."

There is some forewarning, at least. I must prepare as best I can.

For the rest of the day I cannot settle my thoughts.

As dusk drifts down I hurry back to the cottage with an extra bucket of water, trying not to slop it out. In my chamber, I take off my russet smock and scrub at my skin with a hemp cloth, trying to rid myself of the patina of sweat, ale suds, and soot. By the end of it I am raw and smarting, but I am clean enough to put on the red dress. I have not tried it on before, for I have been too afraid. The silk is cool and light on my fingers. I comb my hair with my hands, and then I leave my chamber and show myself to Thomas and Rudd. I give a mock curtsy such as I imagine a real lady might. Thomas's mouth and eyes open wide. For once he seems speechless.

"Have you no words?" I jest, though I tremble as I speak.

He shakes his head slowly, gazing at me from head to toe and up again.

"I will take that as a compliment, then."

"You look well," he says, filled with some emotion that I do not understand.

Rudd claps his hands with delight, right as there is a knock upon our door.

"Take care."

Thomas seems unusually solemn, but I do not give it much thought.

Landon has no such reaction, and we walk together toward the keep in cold silence.

Finally, I can bear it no longer.

"It was most clever of his lordship to know what size of dress I would take."

"It was I who told him your size." He delivers this information coldly.

"And how would you know?" His insolent manner stings me.

"I am most clever too." His mouth is taut until he sees my expression and relents a little. "I have a sister about your size. I am glad I am proved right."

Our silence is more companionable after this. As we enter the keep and cross the courtyard into the castle, there are not many around. It is dark, and with no evening festivities planned, most servants have gone home to their cottages, the knights and pages retreated to their chambers. I wonder where Landon is taking me, and then suddenly we stop at the foot of a staircase.

"I will leave you here," he tells me. "It is the first room past the stairs."

Then he turns and disappears back down the passageway through which we came.

And so, alone, I make my way to his lordship's solar.

In the bright light of the fire burning in a carved hearth, I discover a chamber more magnificent than any I have ever seen with golden arras rugs and rich red tapestries. There are damask cushions, embroidered with unicorns and bulls in silver thread, and birch chests bound with iron and carved with intricate leaves and flowers. A red silken-canopied bed, looms in the center of the room, a massive island of dark oak draped with yet more damask cloth. But most magnificent of all is Lord August.

His eyes run over me, he seems almost as surprised as Thomas.

"That will do very well." He takes a step closer. "Is it possible you are one and same maid?"

A great weakness engulfs my limbs. "Aye, my lord." My mouth forms the words, though I can barely summon enough air to carry them.

His smile is slow, but broad. "You seem sure enough though I cannot believe it."

I stay silent. My wits seem to have scattered like a flock of startled sheep and I have lost all ability to speak.

"And how do you like your gowns?"

Speak, you fool, else he will think you do not care for them! My fingers tug at each other with painful urgency. *Speak!*

"My lord, there are not words to express how much I like them."

He regards me critically. "I, for one, believe they have a plain look."

"My lord?"

He comes closer, then closer still, one hand held behind his back. I smell faint musk and sandalwood. He places a palm upon my waist, and I can feel its heat through the folds of silk. To be touched by him is almost more than I can bear.

"This may help," he whispers, the warmth of his words sweet in my ear, as he withdraws his hand to reveal a jeweled belt.

He places it around my waist, and the hammered silver buckle glints in the firelight.

I have never before been given such a gift. To think that I now own something as fine as this. All my words are caught in my throat, like chicks struggling to flee their nests.

He steps back and studies me. "That is *much* better."

"My lord, how could I ever thank you?" Would that I could fashion a crown of moonbeams, or offer a goblet brimming with light. Anything to feel his touch again.

"If I have given you pleasure, that is reward enough for me."

"These are words that were spoken to me not so long ago." Coming forward again, he gently cups my face with his hands. "You look as any lady might, only . . ." He pauses, and then continues, "There is something about your eyes. They are like a wild animal's." He stops, alarmed. "You are trembling!"

I cannot meet his gaze.

"Your shyness suggests you are not used to the attentions of men, which I can scarce believe."

"Never, my lord." He must know that I am still a maiden, that I am pure. For is that not what men desire?

In truth, my virtue is still intact not because I have been modest, but because I have never sought nor craved a man's touch. Until now.

"Never?" He narrows his eyes; then abruptly he turns away and crosses the room to the hearth. "The ale you made for the night I returned. It had a flavor I could not place."

"Lavender, my lord."

"Lavender?" He turns, now facing me. "A strange choice."

"Yes, my lord."

A cloud has covered the sun; the sky has darkened. My soul droops and wilts, a flower deprived of light and warmth.

"What made you choose such a thing?"

I hesitate. "I felt in my heart that it was right."

"You were led by your heart?" His tone is mocking.

"Yes, my lord."

"And are you *often* led by your heart?"

I do not move, for I am unsure whether to nod or shake my head.

"I have heard that is a dangerous guide." He sighs then, and stares down into the flames. "I am glad you are pleased with the gifts. Landon will escort you back."

He does not look at me again.

Clearly, I have done something wrong. "M-m-my lord," I stammer, but when he raises a hand, I fall silent.

His dismissal is obvious enough, and I turn and leave his chamber. Landon is standing outside. I wonder how much he heard of our exchange. All of it, I have no doubt.

Neither of us speaks as he escorts me back to the cottage. When we reach it, I am in a hurry to retreat inside, but Landon takes my hand.

"Margaret."

He has never called me by my name before.

"Do not be sore of heart."

I bow my head, humiliated.

"It will all have a way of coming right."

Then he leaves me at my door.

Thomas waits for me inside.

"Did his lordship admire your dress? What did he say? Will he make you other gifts?"

"He admired my dress." I am curt, but cannot help it. "He was pleased." Then I go to my chamber and with shaking fingers undress. I crawl into bed. I stare dry-eyed into the darkness.

I know what he wanted and I would have gladly given it to him. I feel again the heat of his palm. I would give my all for him.

I do not sleep.

The next week passes in agony. The days are heavy and long. I see his smile before me; his whisper echoes in my ears. Nothing eases the tightness in my chest. My head aches; my heart pains me. I am cross with Thomas and snap at poor Rudd, who stares at me with wounded eyes. I want to stop, but I do not know how.

I am so lost in my sorrow that it takes me a while to see the lovely little page standing in the doorway of the brewery. Spellbound, he gazes around this new terrain, and I wonder how he got past the head cook's grasp.

"Come child." I beckon him forward and he runs to me.

"Please, mistress." His hand trembles as he passes me a folded piece of white linen.

I open it very carefully. A sprig of lavender nestles inside it.

"His lordship gave it me himself!" The page is awestruck, despite his fear. "He said you would understand."

I nod. "Yes. Now, best you make a run for it before you attract Cook's notice."

In a heartbeat, he is gone.

I stand, gazing at the small fragrant strand in my hand.

That night I once again approach the staircase. The sconces are out and I worry how I will be able to climb the steps in the darkness, but then I see the stub of a white candle flickering bravely on the third stair. Up two more stairs and another candle, and then another, tiny sentinels lighting my way to the top. As I climb I do not think of anything at all. My hand pressed against the cold stone, my tread soft upon the steps, one above the other, and then I am there.

The corners of his chamber are in shadow, but its heart is made bright by a multitude of candles. He stands in the center, and when he speaks his voice is full of passion.

"I have tried, I have tried in vain to keep away. To forget you. But it is no use. You are a madness that courses through my veins. You are a fever that will not break. I close my eyes, but you are still before me."

I cannot move. Then all at once he is here, his lips upon my skin; his fingers digging deep in my hair, pulling me down, down, down as he whispers in my ear.

"I will have you."

And for a long time, neither of us has the need to say anything at all.

16

Katherine

It's three days after Christmas. Katherine is in Hatchards bookstore, crying her heart out. She stands facing a bookshelf, trying to be quiet, but her shoulders are heaving.

"It must be a very sad book," a man says. "May I see it?" His manner is light and gentle, detached. Soothing, somehow.

Wordlessly, she hands it to him and he reads the title aloud. "*How to Train Your New Puppy in Just Seven Days*! Dear God!" he cries in mock horror. "No wonder you're weeping, that is tragic. No, no, this is too much to bear!"

Katherine laughs, but it comes out as more of a sob. "I'm sorry." She makes an attempt to wipe her eyes. "I'm so sorry."

"Don't apologize, take this," he says, handing her what feels like a piece of silk. She looks down and sees it's a monogrammed handkerchief. *MV*.

Katherine is horrified, shaken from her misery. "I couldn't! I would totally ruin it!"

"Well, darling, I never use it. The whole point of carrying a handkerchief is to find a damsel in distress so you can look gallant. And

I believe I detect an American accent? If you're a Southern belle, I really will have died and gone to heaven."

"Sorry to disappoint, but I'm from the Midwest. However . . ." Katherine bats her waterlogged eyes. "I have always relied upon the kindness of strangers." She tries again to laugh.

"That's it, Blanche DuBois." His tone is firm. "There is only one solution to this."

About twenty minutes later they're seated at a small, white-clothed table set with light turquoise plates and cups. A man is playing "Smoke Gets in Your Eyes" on the piano, and a stand of sandwiches towers between them.

"Frightfully cheesy, but I adore Fortnum and Mason, and as Wilde once said, 'Give me luxuries and I can dispense with the necessities.'"

Katherine is getting into the spirit of the endeavor. "Or as Aristotle once said, 'Whatever floats your boat.'"

He smiles. "Exactly."

She surreptitiously studies her knight in shining armor. She doesn't know when she last met such a beautiful man. His dark blond hair sweeps impeccably across his forehead above slanting gray eyes and a bone structure that would make anyone weep. His deliberate drawl makes her think of peat-smoked whiskey, as though he is a luxury himself. There *is* something wickedly indulgent about him. His jeans fit him flawlessly; his shirt is a tailor's dream. And he clearly has time to spare.

"I'm Matthew, by the way."

"I'm Katherine."

"So, Katherine, I have to ask why are you weeping over puppy-training manuals—not that I blame you?"

"Oof. It's a long and boring story."

"Nonsense."

"Well, it's probably not that long, just boring."

"Darling, I would never ask if I didn't actually want to know. I'm far too self-absorbed for that."

"Okay, but I'm warning you."

She had wanted Lucas's Christmas to be wonderful. At least she had wanted it not to be terrible. If she was honest with herself, she would admit that she'd gone completely overboard. They'd visited the Winter Wonderland festival at Hyde Park, gone to a Christmas pantomime, checked out the Christmas Grotto at Harrods, and marveled at the Christmas lights on Oxford Street. She'd filled their white-and-cream apartment with drawings and decorations and glitter.

"Maybe you need to dial it down," Sael had remarked one evening when they were in the kitchen putting away the plates. She'd been telling him about all about the reindeer they had seen in the Wonderland festival.

"Huh?"

"It just seems to be a lot. Maybe you're overdoing it."

She glared at him.

"Sorry, I mean you know best, but—"

"But what?"

"The whole thing might be a bit overwhelming, you know? New country, new school, new life . . . It's a lot for anyone to take in, let alone for a five-year-old."

"It's really good to know how you feel." She hated the way she sounded, icy and defensive.

"I'm just saying. I mean, he's your kid, you're in charge, but it's not just about him. I'm thinking of . . ." He trailed off.

"Tell me."

He looked at her, apprehensive. "I mean, you also have to adjust, take it easy."

"I wouldn't say visiting the Christmas Grotto is particularly taxing."

"Well, it all adds up. Then there's Santa's live-in roommate, Santa's villa, his holiday house in Maui."

Katherine smiled despite herself. "Yeah, okay. I just . . ." It's hard for her to find the words.

"What?"

"I guess I just . . ."

She thought of Andrea and Lucas coming in through the front door of their apartment, Lucas exhausted and Andrea tired but satisfied. They had waited in Macy's for four hours to see Santa, just so Lucas could sit upon the famous lap and tell him of his wishes. She remembers going to Rockefeller Center, with Lucas perched atop Andrea's shoulders, and trying to glimpse the star upon the top of the tree. All of them freezing but grinning like maniacs. She recalls Christmas Day itself, Lucas yelling that Santa had come, bouncing up and down, trying to open his presents. She had given him a coloring book and crayons. It had been a big hit. They'd all eaten too much, and when Lucas fell asleep on the couch she and Andrea watched *It's a Wonderful Life* and *Groundhog Day* until they also fell asleep.

But all she said was, "I don't want him to miss Andrea. I don't want him to think about what Christmas means without his mom."

In truth, she didn't want him to wake up with a pounding heart. She didn't want him aching and sad and tearful every time he hears one of those stupid Christmas songs. The way she did.

"I just want him to have a good time," she finished, a little lamely.

"He is, I'm sure of it. I just want you to take care of yourself, okay?"

"Okay." She nodded.

"Okay." He touched her cheek.

He hasn't touched her in so long. Katherine holds her breath. *Please God*, she prayed, *could you just freeze time. Stop everything? Please.* They stared at each other.

"Kat?" Lucas was calling her.

Still they held their gaze.

"Kat? I'm ready!" Lucas's voice drifted from upstairs, announcing he's in bed and waiting for their bedtime ritual.

"Coming, honey!"

The moment, as fragile as a soap bubble, was gone.

After Katherine read him his story and pulled up his covers, she asked him casually, "So, what do you think Santa's going to bring you?"

"Oh, he knows already."

"He does? How? Have you asked?"

"No, but I'm going to write a secret list and put it somewhere that only Santa will find it and that way we'll know he's for real."

"Want to give me the list so I can mail it to him?" She aimed for total nonchalance.

Lucas was scornful. "No, because then I'll have to tell you and only Santa can find it!"

"Oh yeah, right!"

Note to self, she thought, *search Lucas's room and tell Mrs. B to be on the lookout.*

"Kat?"

"Yes, hon?"

"Will you sing me a song?"

"Of course I will." She sang Joni Mitchell's "A Case of You." Then she gave him a kiss on his forehead and headed downstairs, where she found Sael inexplicably drinking a glass of milk.

"Bartender," Katherine drawled, "I'll take one of those, heavy on the ice."

"Sure, lady, sure." He poured her a glass and she downed it. It tasted of childhood. "Hey, lady, easy on those things," he protested in a drawl of his own.

"Fill her up again!" she demanded.

"Sure? This is strong stuff!"

"It's been a tough day, starting from ten minutes ago."

"What's up?" Sael poured her another glass.

Katherine dropped the saloon act. She groaned. "So now he's written a secret list for Santa."

"A list, huh?"

"That he's hidden."

"Well, of course he's hidden it. It's a secret."

"How am I supposed to get him his present?"

"I'm sure anything you get him will be wonderful."

"Yeah, but it's always nice to get what you want, especially when you're a little kid."

"I think it's nice to be surprised by something even better."

"That's a good point, but I really just want his first Christmas here to be special."

"I'm sure it will be." He had a thoughtful expression. After a moment he asked, "And what do you want?"

"Me?"

"Well, I thought about asking the other Katherine, but I guess you'll do."

And what does she answer? *You. I want you. I want to go back to the way things were.* "You don't have to get me a present."

"That's not the answer to my question."

"Then surprise me." She smiled.

He smiled back. "Okay."

Christmas Eve was wonderful. They got a tree and spent a happy afternoon decorating it with the eight million baubles they bought at the Christmas market. Less is not more for once. Katherine managed to drag Sael downstairs, and for about half an hour he was off all his devices as he reached to the very top of the tree to place the angel. He was surprised that the tree could still stand up, he grumbled, but he took great care. Finally, the angel was in place and they turned down the lights so that the tree would twinkle and glow.

Lucas and Katherine both said, "Oooh," and it was wonderful.

They heard carolers and even attended an early church service. They watched *A Christmas Carol* on television. Lucas swore he'd never get to sleep. He was wriggling with excitement.

"When will it be tomorrow?"

"Soon enough," she told him. "Shut your eyes and it will be here before you know it."

"But then I'll be asleep and miss him!"

In the darkened bedroom Katherine rolled her eyes. *Sometimes,* she admitted, *this kid is way too smart for his own good.*

"Well, shut your eyes for the moment, and if you wake up maybe you'll see him. I won't stop you if you want to chat. Fair?"

"I guess so." He sighed.

She laughed. "Okay." She leaned over and kissed him.

"Kat?"

"Yes?"

"I love you."

"I love you too." Her heart will burst out of her chest with love for him. *It is dreadful,* she thought, *how much I love this boy.*

"Kat?"

"Yes?"

"I hope Santa gets you what you want."

"Thanks, honey. I hope Santa gets you want you want!" *Believe me kid, you have no idea how much I hope.*

She gave him another kiss for good measure. His eyes were closing, and then he was finally falling asleep. She rose as silently as she could and headed out of the room.

A figure leaned in the doorway. "Ho, ho, ho," he said softly.

"Hey! You startled me! What's up?"

He just stared at her. They were standing very close now, his eyes looked down into hers. "I wonder what Santa will give you?"

"Maybe Santa will surprise me," she answered, and then they went into the bedroom together.

He swung her up onto the bed with absolutely no effort, pregnant though she was, and she was in his arms. *Oh my love, oh my Sael. How I've missed you.* She has missed him so much. But Sael was uncharacteristically nervous.

"I don't want to hurt the baby."

"You won't," she said.

"Are you sure?"

"Yes."

He looked down at her and his face softened.

"Hey," his voice was rough with emotion. "You're still wearing it?"

For a moment Katherine did not realize what he was referring to, and then her fingers glided over the smooth silver shape of the ring brooch, a constant weight against her skin that almost feels like part of her. The question needed no answer, and Sael bent to kiss her.

It was a gentle coupling, skin on skin, soft and sweet. She was crying with relief because they were back together, beyond the words that have held them apart. They were again themselves in the dark, in each other's arms, and when she slept, it was deeply and without dreams.

Until she was awakened at around six by a joyful shout.

"Kat!"

"Holy shit!" She sat bolt upright, heart pounding. "Lucas?!"

Sael called downstairs. "Everything all right?"

Lucas's voice came floating up. "Come see! Come see what Santa brought!"

She didn't think she had ever heard him sound so excited. He must really love the plastic armor and sword she got him. Then again, what five-year-old didn't like swords? In fact, what man on the planet didn't love a sword? Still, his almost hysterical joy was amazing and perfect to hear.

Sael lay down again with a groan. It was 6:15, but Katherine couldn't stop beaming. *I guess I got it right*, she marveled. She couldn't believe it.

"Kat?!" Lucas called again.

"Coming!"

"Nope!" Sael wrapped his arms around her. "No, you're not. I refuse to let you go in exchange for say three more hours."

She laughed and snuggled down into the best hostage situation ever.

"Kat! Sael!"

She turned to Sael. "I guess you're summoned too."

He sighed, but he wasn't really mad. "Damn, Santa has a lot to answer for. If I find that hairy bastard . . ."

"You weren't nearly a good enough boy," she murmured.

"I wasn't?"

"You were fabulously bad."

"Mmmm." His arms tightened.

"Guys!"

"Okay, okay, we're coming!"

They pulled on pajama bottoms and T-shirts and headed downstairs. Katherine couldn't wait to see Lucas swinging the sword, grinning from ear to ear. He was sitting under the tree next to her unopened present. In fact, all his presents were unopened apart from one crate.

Crate?

Something moved under the tree among the tissue paper, and a small brown-and-white furry face peered out. Lucas cradled the puppy in his arms.

"What's this?" Her legs were shaking. She had to sit down.

"Santa!" cried Lucas. "Santa knew! He knew!"

Sael came into the room and plopped down on the floor.

"Let's see who this is." He picked up a large card that was on the crate and read it aloud. "'Hello! I am an English springer spaniel puppy. Santa brought me all the way from the North Pole. I am yours, please have fun and be good to me. My name is Cordelia. Merry Christmas!'"

The puppy had liver-colored patches over her huge brown eyes.

Lucas buried his face in her soft, squirming body. "He knew! Santa knew!"

Katherine stared at Sael. "I can't believe it. How did Santa know?"

He smiled. "Sometimes Santa just knows these things."

"Look, Kat!"

She instinctively opened her arms and took the puppy without thinking. Immediately she tensed, catapulted back to that day at the pound, but Cordelia did nothing but squirrel her warm, wriggling body against Katherine's.

"She's adorable," Katherine said faintly as she looked again at Sael. Sharp needles sank into her finger. "Ow! I guess she's teething. She's going to be a great guard dog, Lucas." She passed the puppy back to him and saw small red dots well up on her skin. "I think I might need a Band-Aid."

"Want me to get it?" Sael maked as if to get up.

"No, I'm good. You stay there."

She left them sitting with the puppy. *Sael got him a puppy. It's really wonderful,* she told herself. *He really cares about Lucas's happiness. It is an amazing present.*

So why did she feel like crying?

"I can't believe you managed to organize that," she told Sael later.

They were in the kitchen fixing themselves breakfast. Yogurt, fruit. Lucas was still playing with Cordelia.

"You mean Santa," he said.

"Okay. I can't believe Santa managed to organize that."

"Well, Santa admits that Georgie had a big part to play."

"What?"

She stopped slicing the banana and whipped around to face him, but Sael had opened the fridge and was rooting inside it.

"Yeah, once I told her that Lucas wanted a dog, she went and did everything! It was great."

"Oh."

"What?" He closed the door, looked at her.

"I just thought that you had chosen it."

"Well, I wouldn't know the first thing about where to go or how to get a dog here."

"Yeah, yeah. I know."

"Is there something wrong?"

"No, not at all," she lied, remembering how tightly Lucas had been gripping her hand as they walked from the subway toward the pound. "I'm just impressed. She managed to do such a great job."

Lucas had sung all the way there on the train. She had worked so hard to budget, fill out all the forms.

"Really? You say that, but your tone of voice tells me another story . . ."

She shrugged. "I was just thinking about when Lucas and I tried to get a dog in New York."

"Yeah, I remember there was a problem that day with getting one? They were acting up or something? So y'know, that's why I thought of it." He spoke with real pride.

Katherine said, "Awesome," but all she saw was Georgie and Sael plotting on the phone, working out the details, the seamlessness of it.

She glanced over her shoulder at Lucas. He was totally and completely in love. Katherine knew she'd never be able to say anything.

She gazed at her bandaged finger. *Once bitten, twice shy.*

Now, sitting in Fortnum's, she's finally able to confess how she felt to a man she's just met.

"I know it's stupid and petty," she tells him, "but somehow it just sticks in my throat, the thought of them working together on it and—"

"You wanted that to be your thing," he says gently. "I understand."

"You do, don't you? I just, I don't know, it seems so personal. I guess Sael wanted to surprise me too, but I would have liked to be included in the experience."

"It makes sense."

"And somehow, the puppy is a constant reminder of how I wasn't. Anyway, as you see, I'm a horrible person."

"I adore horrible people. I'm one of them." His delivery is so deadpan that Katherine is apt to believe him. Still she protests.

"No, you're not, you're very nice. Very nice and kind to weeping women in the bookstore."

"Honestly, it's never happened before. I must be coming down with something."

"Well, thank you, it meant the world to me."

"You're welcome."

A man comes over, his suit suggesting he's more of a manager than a waiter. "Is everything all right, Mr. de Villias?"

"Everything is wonderful, thank you, Daniel."

She stares at him. For a moment, she's unable to blink, or even exhale.

Matthew sees her reaction and sighs, exaggeratedly. "It's true. I come here too often, clearly."

"No, what did he say your last name was?"

"Oh, my surname? Isn't it wildly pretentious? But there's not much I can do, it's too old to get rid of, so it's just my cross to bear."

"No, no, that's *Sael's* surname. Could you be related?"

"Really?" Matthew frowns.

"Yes, I think he mentioned that he has family from here, a cousin?"

"How fantastic! My long-lost American cousin."

"That's *incredibly* odd."

"It's more than that." He grins at her. "Thank God I'm not feverish after all! I told you I was never normally so nice, but I felt an undeniable pull toward you. Clearly you were destined to be with de Villias men."

Katherine laughs, and finally it's genuine. "Only the most fabulous ones."

"Darling, *all* de Villias men are fabulous, but me in particular. Let's have some more tea and you can tell me all about my cousin and your life. I want to hear *everything*!"

And this is how Katherine meets Matthew de Villias.

THE MAN IN THE WOODS

SHE HAS TAKEN TO WALKING ALONE LATE AT NIGHT. SHE claims it is to draw water from the well when there's no wait, but that's only an excuse. It is madness of course. There's Hervey at home and her husband too. Hervey can be fretful at times, still she can comfort him by putting him to her breast, but Guy will be dead to the world.

He may as well be dead to her too. Any other man would have put his foot down and forbade his wife to journey out after curfew. Guy only sighed, and although he protested that it was too dangerous he did not stop her.

Once she had lain in her lover's arms, their limbs entwined, each kiss a sin, each caress, a secret bliss. Once he had made her promises, and once she had believed him. She believed that a highborn man would keep his word. She had coveted each and every stone, hugging herself over the herb garden delighting in even the thatch. She had spent days and nights envisioning where she would place their belongings, Guy's candlesticks and the one painted cloth her mother had left her.

Soon that cottage would be theirs, be *hers*, and she could arrange things as she liked.

Yearning whispers like fine linen through one's fingers. It grasps like an infant's hand. It sounds like the throaty clucks of the neighbor's fat hen, and tastes like the last sweet sip pooling from the bottom of the wineskin. It is a minstrel's sly croon to those long married, and the jangle of coin in the merchant's purse. It is the deep and rosy pink of a milky nipple, as strong as your father's arm swinging you up, and smells of your lover's hair you once buried your face in.

Overnight, his lordship went back on his word and gave away her home to his new whore. The alewife. She had seen her once as they both waited at the well, pride and insolence itself, and she tried to spit in the slattern's face. Only Guy had pulled her back. He was weak, but not so foolish as for all that. He might have restrained her for the best. Still, she can't bear to think of that bitch inside her house, and so now she walks.

She knows it isn't so safe, but she doesn't brood as much when there's a task to be done. She fills her lungs with the night air, lowers her bucket, and fills it too. Its damp wooden side bumps against her shins as she begins the journey home. Head down, she turns right into you.

The water splashes up and out, dripping down your legs. She laughs. She doesn't mean to, but the surprise on your face was funny. She prays you do not take offense.

You don't. You are courteous to a fault, and insist on

walking her back to the well so she may refill her bucket.
She knows who you are and she is thrilled to her core. It
must be fate.

Scheming is the color of soiled straw, a shadowed
face beneath a cowl. It hisses like a dying fire, it whispers
like the sword drawn from its sheath, it crinkles as a piece
of parchment rolled up tight.

She thinks that if you like what you see, you'll
put in a word for her, perhaps to the lord himself. He'll
be reminded of the nights they spent together. He'll be
ashamed at his lapse of reason. The whore and her son
(for she is sure he is her son) and their fool will be thrown
out, and she and her family, can move in. After all, she
was promised.

You do like what you see. But it is not in your interest to aid her. Instead you say that you'll escort her back.
She is disappointed but hopeful. She thinks there's still
time to persuade you.

There isn't.

You are solicitous. You smile and nod, and she is so
engaged, so wrapped up in indignation, which is the color
of thin gruel, that she doesn't realize you have steered her
off the path and into the hills, out of sight and out of hearing from the castle and its surrounding cottages.

Guy was right. It really is too dangerous for a woman to walk alone at this hour of the night.

17

Margaret

Today we ride. Lord August has given me my own mare, a chestnut whose large dark eyes are set in a delicate head. The stable master was ordered to give me lessons, and at first, he was scornful. Why waste time on a woman when there was real work to be done? He stood there, arms folded, contempt in his eyes. But I earned his grudging admiration. He could not believe that I had never ridden before, and more than once he proclaimed that riding must be in my blood. I did not tell him about my people. I did not tell him how I can see the world through my mare's eyes, how I can feel where she wants to go. It is good to ride.

When I ride I do not think of anything but the rhythm of her hooves on the land stretching under and before me. I do not think about the scowls, the black looks, or what Thomas has told me. I have not spoken with him properly of late. Many of these nights I am not home, and when I return to the cottage he is gone. Bread is brought to us now, bread and rabbit and venison. Still, Thomas chooses to go Warin for his portion, more for friendship than for bread. When he is not with Warin, I suspect he is keeping company with Father Martin, the priest here. I do not understand why he has taken up with an aged priest when he could have the company of pages or squires or apprentices or any of the dozen other boys who always seem to be running around. I do not trust priests or nuns. No one of the cloth.

"Why?" Thomas had asked me when I first challenged him about Father Martin. "How can you judge when you do not know them?"

I have my reasons. I *do* know them. I have eaten at their table and worked beside them and prayed with them on bended knees, and I know what they are capable of. I cannot stop Thomas from speaking with him, though. I can only warn him that many are not what they seem.

He was defiant. "Father Martin says I have a fine mind."

"I have told you that myself. You do not need a priest to tell you so!"

"He says that I might make a fine novice, one who could be taught to read and write."

"Yes, but at what price? Must you give up life and love?"

"Father Martin says . . ." he began, and stopped.

"Father Martin says what?"

"That love should only be between a man and wife. Only in marriage should there be that bond. Otherwise it is a terrible sin."

"And what would Father Martin know of such love? What do any of them know? They pervert what is natural and beautiful. They are warped and twisted through lack of love."

I see again the young girl who thought she was safe with the village priest until she was pulled into his bony lap, his rough robe scratching against her. Then the same girl, only a few years older, kneeling with bowed head before the Sister, her white-knuckles gripping the back of the pew. That girl will never forget the burning pain of the rod, the welts rising, her terror and humiliation.

I blinked back to the present, saw Thomas's uneasy face and lowered my voice. "But perhaps it is not only what the priest says that troubles you."

He would not meet my eye. "There has been talk," he muttered.

"What kind of talk?"

He would not answer.

"You need not be scared to tell me. I know his counselors do not like me, nor many of his knights." I had felt their cold eyes upon me often enough. After all, I had no dowry, nor land nor means to make an alliance between warring factions.

"It is more than that," he had said then.

"More?" A fist squeezed my heart.

"There is talk of something darker." Thomas squirmed, his gaze still fixed upon the table.

"Thomas, tell me what you know." My pride and defiance were swept away by a wave of fear.

"They say that you have bewitched him. Why else would he show you such generosity, such favor, when he hardly knows you? You are but a servant."

I thought about my mare and my dresses of silk and satin, the gold and silver buckles, the pearl strands for my ears and neck, and my sparrow hawk. "Could it not be because he loves me and wishes to make me happy?"

He shrugged. "They say you bewitched the steward and all the steward's men, that you tricked them into bringing you here. They fear you have great power over his lordship, that you have enchanted the cup from which he drinks so he will listen to you above all others."

"But Thomas, this is nonsense! You know that this is nonsense."

"I know." He nodded. "But it is not I who needs convincing. There are knights who do not wish to drink the ale you brew and serve."

I had already gotten wind of this. Lord August had greeted me one night not long before with a face white with fury. His touch bordered on violent, but I accepted it, wishing only to soothe him and he finally told me the story. A knight had refused a cup of my ale, and the insult of it burned a hole between them. In the end, talk of a duel came to nothing, but the knight no longer sat at his lordship's table. Perhaps he was sent away, or perhaps he had fled.

A small, very small, part of me wondered what Cecily would have said if she had learned that Lord de Villias was fighting over my honor. I had felt a flush of triumph, but after Thomas's warning I saw how this became yet another stone in the wall they were building against me.

"And it's not just that. They say you have cursed the castle."

"What do you mean?"

He reluctantly met my eyes. "The dead girls."

"Dead girls?" I was utterly bewildered.

"Found in the fields and in the forest." Thomas peered sideways at me, amazed at my ignorance.

I had been so caught up in my own happiness that I failed to catch the undercurrents. Now I risked drowning. "And what do these girls have to do with me?"

"They say the murders only began after we arrived. They say it is the work of the devil."

"How so?"

Thomas lowered his voice. "They say unholy symbols are carved deep into their flesh with a blade. They say it is the devil's art, that his canvas is skin and that his ink is blood."

I saw my mother returning to me through my dreams in the woods. Her body drained of life. The man working with his knife.

I sank down upon a chair. "When was the first one found?"

"Less than a fortnight after we came."

That night, I could not sleep. I lay awake a long while, hearing his voice over and over again.

When the time is right, I'll come for you.

I knew then in my heart that I should go. Thomas and Rudd would be fine, better than fine, if I left now. With Rudd's brute strength and gentle nature, and Thomas's wits, they would fare well. No one would hold my sins against them. No one would blame them.

But how could I leave? I thought of the sweetness, the joy I had discovered. We hungered for each other. And yet.

How long could I stay before Thomas and Rudd would also bear my burden?

Tomorrow all may end, but today we are hawking. To ride with the wind against my skin, blowing back my hair, to be at one with my mare up and over and down again. We stop at the top of the Downs to view the green and rolling land laid out before us. He who is by my side owns all we survey.

The falconer, whose cruel hooded eyes and beaked nose resembles a falcon himself, places my magnificent sparrow hawk, upon my arm. I admire her sheen of smoky plumage and fierce golden eyes. He guides me as, with a great ruffle and flap, I let her soar into the wind to search for prey. She circles and I stare up at her. She thinks of nothing but the flight and the kill. I wish I were her.

I look over and see Lord August staring at the bird with much the same longing. Perhaps he shares my wish. I think of the councils he must sit through with every petty squabble of fief and serf and landowner and the constant intrigue among his advisers and knights. What would he give to be free himself? Our eyes meet, and an understanding passes between us, a heat rising.

My sparrow hawk returns at last, a limp vole clutched in her talons. She is much petted and praised. Then Lord August sends the attendants and the falconer back, ordering them to take my horse. He helps me up so I can ride behind him, and we canter away. I press my cheek against his broad cloaked back, close my eyes, inhale his smell.

How can I give him up when I belong to him, and him to me?

You cannot, you cannot, you cannot, you cannot, the hoofbeats tell me.

We do not ride far, cannot ride far, only to where the hills shield us. Then he dismounts, looping the reins over a nearby bough. He flings down his cloak and lays me on it, the wool against my back and under it the grass, the earth. He is on top of me a moment later, and soon I am driven to cry out again and again.

"My lord! My lord!"

Another cry, another voice. We lie still as stone.

Sure enough, the shouts come again. "My lord! My lord!"

With an oath he wrenches himself from my arms. The rider is almost upon us.

Lord August is furious, but upon seeing the rider's livery, he calls out, "What is it?"

"Oh my lord I have been sent to you." The messenger is breathless. His face is ashen, and there is foam upon his horse's flanks. "Come quickly."

"What is wrong?"

The messenger only shakes his head. "You must see for yourself, my lord."

Lord August turns to me, meaning to carry me up and back onto his horse. Propriety is forgotten amid urgency, and it is the only way I can return now that my own mare is gone.

"My lord, it would be better for the lady if she did not witness this. It is no sight for a maid's eyes."

"You must stay here and I will send for you soon," he declares before I can protest and swings himself into the saddle. "Lead the way," he orders.

His eyes are hard, his mouth set, but I know that, like me, he is afraid.

I wait. The breeze that once seemed soft now carries a sharper chill; the grass hisses; somewhere a bird cries mournfully. I wait and wait. He does not return. My mind is filled with terrible thoughts and visions. Perhaps the messenger was sent to lead him into a trap, and my beloved, riding in such a state, was ambushed unawares. They will come for me next, I know it.

Eventually I hear the thud of hooves and see a rider cresting the hillock. It is Landon. Of all those to come and fetch me, I would least have it be him. Ever since he escorted me to Lord August's chamber that first night, his manner toward me has changed. He will no longer speak to me and yet his eyes follow me wherever I go. It infuriates me. I wish to slap the mocking smile from his lips.

He has no such look now.

"Come," he tells me. "There is little time to lose." His face is grim.

"What is happening?"

He makes no answer.

I press again. "Landon?"

"They have found a girl. Close to the castle."

There is a buzzing in my ears as the world turns misty and begins to swim before me.

"Drink!"

Landon's voice is faint, and a wineskin is pressed to my mouth. I drink. It is not my ale, nor even wine, but some far stronger stuff that burns as it travels down my throat. I blink and the mist thins a little.

"How do you feel now?"

Landon's face is sharp. My vision has returned. "Better."

"Are your wits about you once more?"

"They are."

"Good," he says. "Then we must ride."

We talk no more on the journey.

It is night when we arrive. I hurry to the cottage and gather word from Thomas, who is bursting with the news. She has been placed in the de Villias chapel, where all will pay their respects. Nuns from the nearby priory will hold a prayer vigil until dawn. We wait for Lord August to speak. Rumors spark flames. *It is a declaration of war. It is the work of bandits. It is a jealous husband's rage.*

I stand with Thomas in the dark. We have left Rudd safe in the cottage, away from this nightmare. The line shuffles forward, step by step. The chapel is cold inside and smells stale, as if dusty prayers have collected in the shadows. Thomas has told me of his love for its murals. No painting, no matter how miraculous, could tempt me back to a life within the church.

As I walk up to the altar where they have laid her out, I try to slow my breath, calm my heart. I command my feet to move one in front of the other. It is not my mother. It is not my mother lying there, but the fear, the fear presses down upon me as a great stone might.

The nuns have prepared her body, closed her eyes. She lies in a shroud of white linen. She seems at peace.

"She was naked when they found her," Thomas had said. "Her throat slit, like the other girls."

When I first saw her, she was glaring at me. *She will have no use for the cottage now,* I think and I am drenched by a wave of shame. I stare at her face. If I stare long enough, perhaps she will open her eyes and name her killer but her life is gone.

No sooner have I melted back into the crowd than a murmuring and shuffling begins as Lord August makes his way to the altar. With great care, he slowly places a single white rose upon her breast. He turns to address us. He speaks softly, but his voice carries. He tells us that this latest unspeakable act will not go unavenged. The sheriff and his men will not rest until the culprit has been found and swiftly brought to justice, no matter the cost.

He beseeches us to pray for her family now that God has called her to His side. At his prompt, all around me kneel down and close their eyes in prayer. I kneel but my eyes stay open. I gaze at his lowered head as he prays with all the others, and then I see one man whose head remains raised, whose eyes are also open. Landon stares back at me with no expression at all.

I shut my eyes in a hurry, and the moment is over.

Lord August rises. He is sure that God will protect us from this demon who now torments us, but no woman is to travel unaccompanied, night or day, until he is caught. Then he turns to Father Martin, bowing his golden head while the priest's voice rises and falls.

I know he cannot look at me, that it would be most wrong, especially here, especially now, and yet I need him to. *Look at me*, I plead with him silently. *Only look at me, make some sign that you know I am here. Only a few hours ago we lay together in the grass, in each other's arms.* But when Father Martin's liturgy ends, he leaves without a glance.

Thomas and I return to the cottage. Neither of us feels like talking. Rudd is already asleep. I lie upon my bed. It has been so long since I spent a night alone.

I close my eyes.

I am at the edge of the woods. It is night. Snow lies on the ground. Stars glitter in the icy sky. A woman stands a little way among the trees. She beckons for me to join her. She is smiling.

I inch closer and realize she wears a shroud. It is Ida, the Candlemaker's wife. She raises her arm to reveal deep cuts dark red and crusting.

"Come, Margaret," she calls out softly. "We are waiting for you."

The trees are becoming women. Their branches stretch into mottled limbs, thin twigs claw to fingertips. Bark peels back as strips of skin, revealing bloodied flesh. Wet white eyes peer out from sunken knots. Jagged tree hollows are gaping mouths stretched in endless, soundless screams. A forest of murdered women, their tears brown, dead leaves, pattering and scattering in the wind.

The man leans casually against one such imploring figure, her arms twisting out, her mouth a dark gash of terror. He cocks his head to one side and whistles a lazy melody. He pares his fingernails with the curved blade of a sickle knife.

"Not long now, pretty maid," he croons. "You know why."

My eyes open. My heart pounds. He is coming.

THE MAN IN THE WOODS

IT'S TIME.

She's red, full-blown, the seed has burrowed deep and taken root, the bud begins to bloom into a rose of flame. You have waited, contenting yourself with lesser kills, lesser colors, lesser hues of self-pity and scheming and hope and yearning, and these have kept you at bay.

But now her redness calls to you, sings to you its siren song, the ocean spray, damp loam digging between your toes, the salt of, and the sweet of, and the bite of and the scent, the holy human scent of redness

As pleasure filled and maddening as a drop of sweat trickling its endless secret way between your lover's upturned breasts, the silken pull of sheets, the glossy flank of a roan, the bite of bone against your teeth, the suck of red rich marrow, the sweet sad thin stringed song on echoing stone, her redness calling you, calling you, calling you home.

You can hardly wait to taste it.

18

Katherine

Katherine sits on a lavender mat in a purple room, although there are several large purple-pink rubber bouncing balls in case the floor proves too hard. At least two of the other women in the room with her are wearing tight V-neck shirts and tanks in various shades of purple, designed to show off their bumps. Clearly purple is the "in" color of pregnancy. Even the antenatal instructor's hair is purple.

Her name is Kate, and she's telling Katherine, along with at least twelve other women, what this course of BellyWise Yoga and Birthing Meditation has to offer. Her eager, acne-pocked face reminds Katherine of an enthusiastic pit bull, and her decidedly violet hair shines every time she turns, expressively and meaningfully, toward each one of them.

Kate has already instructed them to place one hand upon their chests and the other upon their babies.

"Start sending a loving message to your child!"

She informs them that they shouldn't just think of this as a prenatal yoga class. "Consider this another tool to helping you on your personal journey to embrace motherhood and your ties to all women, femininity, and the female earth."

Katherine looks around, hoping that someone else will look as horrified as she feels, but everyone seems to be nodding, deeply and deadly earnest. There's not even one disgusted eye roll. *Oh my God*, she realizes, *I'm in a cult*. It was Georgie who recommended this. *That bitch. If I ever get out, I'll kill her.* The thought of it makes her smile, and Kate sees this and nods her approval, no doubt of Katherine's warmth and general love.

Now that their messages of positivity and joyous visualizations have been sent to their unborn children, Kate announces that the class will go around the room and introduce themselves: "Say how many weeks you are, mention a few of the symptoms you might be challenged with, and share your wishes or desires for your birth experience."

The first woman up is Sonia, who is twenty-four weeks and experiencing back pain and acid reflux.

"Totally normal for the second and third trimesters," reassures Kate. "When we do the open-heart chakras, we'll make sure to keep your head raised and really concentrate on lifting and opening you up."

Sonia smiles gratefully. "That would be wonderful, and I'm having a home birth, so I look forward to a calm and comfortable delivery."

"Excellent." Kate nods voraciously.

Sonia has clearly passed with flying colors. *Not that I should view this as a competition*, Katherine thinks, *but if I can't win, I don't want to come last.*

There's another American here, Naomi, whom Katherine dubs "No-Nonsense Naomi." She's twenty-eight weeks and looking forward to really getting in touch with her primal animal roots by ingesting her placenta.

Katherine blinks, sure she's misheard, but Kate looks deeply impressed. "In what form?" she asks. "Pill or . . ."

"Cooked," says Naomi.

Kate nods voraciously again, her highest hopes confirmed.

However, the next woman somewhat lets the side down. She's a classic English beauty called Fiona and thirty-two weeks along. "But I'll have to do a C-section." She drops her eyes.

"But not by your own choice, surely?"

"A breech position." Her shame is overwhelming.

"Ah, well, perhaps you can still have an intervention massage? Let's talk after class."

Fiona seems almost in tears. Katherine feels for her.

As the introductions continue, Katherine realizes that, along with not knowing about purple, she also never got the memo about black yoga pants and bright, clingy tanks or tees to highlight the belly. Without exception, all the women with long hair sport a single high sleek ponytail, and the women with short hair pin theirs back with adorable primary-colored clips. Katherine's hand wanders up to the back of her head. The only hair elastic she could find broke earlier in the morning, so in desperation she twisted it into a bun and stuck a pencil into it. She also took the website's advice and is wearing comfortable clothing, which means the most unattractive gray, saggy, pajama-type elephant pants and an old, stained Bart Simpson T-shirt. She resolves to burn them both the moment she gets home.

There is a long silence that seems to grow longer. Everyone is looking at her. Kate nods encouragingly, and Katherine realizes it's her turn.

"Oh, hi, um, my name is Katherine and . . ." She's blanked on how many weeks she is. She should have been figuring that out while the others were introducing themselves. *Oh crap.* "I'm, I'm in my second trimester, so I must be . . ." Second trimester means she's over twelve weeks, so maybe it's fourteen weeks, or is it thirteen, or "I think, I think I'm fourteen weeks, or no, uh, maybe fifteen?" The silence stretches out. "Sorry, I've never been good with math," she offers by way of apology.

At this point the silence is so great the chirp of crickets would be welcome. Katherine has no one but herself to blame. She should have expected that when one woman announced she was eighteen weeks, four days, and six hours. Katherine doesn't think she was joking.

"Your symptoms?" Kate prompts.

"Oh, I don't really have any symptoms."

"No symptoms, no symptoms at all? No back pain or heartburn or nausea or headaches or dizziness or dry mouth or acid reflux or frequent urination?" She reels off these complaints with dazzling speed.

Katherine tries to smile. She's pretty sure she can't tell them about those strange encounters she had back in New York and on the plane. They've only been in London a few weeks, but thank God they seem to have stopped, at least for now. The thing is, she hasn't had a single symptom. Secretly, she's even wanted one or two. *Perhaps*, she wonders, *it would make me feel more connected with my body, with the person growing inside of me.* She read that morning sickness was a good sign, but there's been nothing. Something tells her it will not sit well in this group. At the last moment she rallies. "I have had some really weird dreams, though." She knows it's a poor offering, but it's something. Kate's face momentarily softens; the other women nod.

"And your wish for birth?"

"As little pain as possible." It's out of her mouth before she can stop it. Good-bye, all chances at friendship and success in this class.

"Well." Kate is polite but firm. "Here in the *UK*, we try to let birth take its natural course, to limit the number of interventions.

We consider a certain amount of pain to be natural and meaningful in the process." Murmurs of agreement run around the circle. Many of the women look pityingly at her. "I mean, you don't want to be numb to the experience, do you?"

"Yes, but—" Katherine is trying not to get angry. *But we live in the twenty-first century*, is what she wants to say. *Why do we need to suffer unnecessarily?*

"After all," Kate continues, "womankind has been giving birth for thousands upon thousands of years."

"The only problem is that many of them died horribly in childbirth," an unfamiliar voice says.

The observation comes from a small woman sitting in the corner. Katherine guesses she came late to the class. She's got wild curly brown hair, green eyes, a freckled face, and a generous mouth. She looks like a woman who was probably insanely popular in high school, who would always sit at the back of the class and barely study and still manage to get As and nobody would resent her for it. She doesn't drop her eyes from Kate's annoyed ones. In fact, she seems eager for a confrontation.

"Go on." Her look says. *"I dare you."*

Katherine is in love.

Kate narrows her eyes even more. "Well," she says tightly. "We're not here to judge." And having off-loaded that most monstrous of lies, she moves on to the woman sitting next to Katherine, who is clearly far more deserving of her warmth and attention.

Katherine is eager for details of her defender as they continue going around the circle. Her name is spelled "Niamh" but pronounced "Neeve." "Irish names like to do that." The information is delivered in a strong Irish brogue. She's fourteen weeks.

"I'd like to use the loo less than twenty times a day, and my birth plan is to give birth," she concludes brightly.

Katherine has to bite down hard on her lip to keeping from

laughing. She manages it, but it's close. Kate has to gather herself together and rise above this so she doesn't turn human and say something truly nasty.

After class, Katherine puts all her paraphernalia away and then looks around. Niamh is gone. *Shit*, she frets. *You missed your chance. What if she never comes back to this class? Why would she?* She really wanted to talk with her, at least to say "thank you." The other women are in clumps now, phones are out, numbers are being exchanged. They're networking, bonding, the very thing Katherine came here for, but everyone is avoiding her. *Pregnant bitches.* She hates them. She walks up the stairs slowly and into the lobby where someone rises from a bench.

"Hey," Niamh says.

"Hey," Katherine says. She feels like she may cry with relief.

They walk outside together.

"You know what I could use?" Niamh is solemn, earnest.

"What?"

"A drink, possibly a fag."

"Or maybe a big fat joint?"

"Oh no!" Niamh looks shocked.

Katherine kicks herself. *You crossed the line.*

Then Niamh grins, and it's marvelous. "That's nowhere near strong enough. So seriously, fancy a pint?"

"Can we?" Katherine decides to confess. "I never used to enjoy beer, but recently I've started to dream about it." She wasn't going to mention this specific dream in class.

"Of course! We can drink anything!" Niamh pauses. "Well, probably not, but I like going into pubs just to see everyone's expressions."

Katherine doesn't hesitate. Mrs. Bailey—"Call me Mrs. B"— bless her efficient heart, will give Lucas dinner. Mrs. B, turned out not to be the plump, rosy-cheeked Victorian cook of Katherine's imagination, but rather a thin, dour woman on the other side of fifty. However, she is as capable and domestically brilliant as Katherine had hoped for. Then Lucas will play with Cordelia, and Sael will work, and she really has no desire to go home at all. Not that it's home anyway. "A drink, or a pretend drink, sounds heavenly."

They stride into the first pub they find. Katherine is still discovering the warm intimacy of a traditional pub's low ceilings, the worn but still plush patterned carpet, its clusters of old wooden chairs and tables, the lush low jangling of a lone "fruit machine." They end up getting cokes, find a corner table and sit. No one gives them a second look.

"So, class went well," Niamh begins.

"Didn't it?"

Then their faces break and they almost kill themselves laughing.

"Tough crowd. That instructor . . ."

"What an eejit!"

Katherine is delighted with the word. "She *is* an eejit."

"I can't stand it when they start that natural giving-birth-in-the woods shite," Niamh continues.

"Shite" and "eejit." Better and better. Like most Americans, Katherine's a sucker for other accents. "I didn't dare say the word 'epidural.'"

"They're not that keen on them here."

"Really?"

"Yup, but you do get given gas."

"Oh my God, they gas us?"

Niamh grins. "They'll probably make an exception for you. Don't want to be sued by a Yank."

"Well, that's something."

They talk and laugh. *I haven't done this in a long time*, she realizes. It feels good to laugh. Katherine thinks of her friends in New

York. They still "check in," but it's taken on a tinge of guilt and duty. There's the time difference, and they all have their own lives. The things she had in common with them are now more and more in the past. She's in the "here and now," which at the moment is in a cozy pub, where a song is playing, something about our house being a very, very, very fine house. She's sharing a pint and laughing with a new friend, while outside rain has started to flick and spit against the windows, where it gathers into sullen drops. There's a drifting quality, as if they're in space and gravity has no hold. Katherine feels an almost irresistible pull to let go and let all her worries fall away.

"And you really have no symptoms at all?"

"Not really, apart from the dreams."

"I have to say that I envy you." Niamh is rueful. "I didn't even talk about all of mine."

"Well, it's actually not always great."

Katherine wonders how to put it. How to express her ambivalence, the blackness that sometimes comes over her. The strange surrealism of it all. There's a pervading dissociation, as if what's happening in her body is separate from herself. She can't imagine what it will be like to be a mother. She's scared that she'll have the type of relationship with her own child that she has with her mother, cold and distant. Now she struggles to put it all into words.

"It's a little disorienting, you know? It's probably good to get a signal or two from your body. I mean, apparently morning sickness is supposed to be a sign that the baby is healthy."

"In that case I must have the healthiest baby on the planet." Niamh rolls her eyes, then smiles and knocks her fist on the wooden table. "You know what else I hate?"

"What?"

"How the moment other women see you're pregnant, all these horror stories start to come out of their mouths."

"I know! It's like you say, 'I'm going to the dentist,' and they're like, 'Let me tell you about this horrific root canal I had that lasted for thirty-six hours.'"

"No, listen, the other day on the bus I sat down next to this woman who told me how her greatest moment in life was reaching between her legs to feel her son's head crowning through!"

"Get out!"

"Yes, it's true!"

"What did you say?"

"I said, 'I'm not pregnant, I'm just fat.'"

"Oh my God, what did she do?"

"She got off at the next stop! Silly bitch."

Amazing! Katherine loves this girl. For a moment, she toys with the idea of telling her about everything that happened in New York, but decides against it. She'll save those sunny stories for another day, or maybe never. She's so happy to feel normal for once, as far removed from the madness and terror of New York as she can possibly be.

Then Niamh glances at her phone. "Oh shite, is that the time? Cath will be doing his nut!" She answers Katherine's unspoken question. "Cathal, my husband, poor man. He's called several times." She dials. "Cath? Yes? Sorry, love. Yes. No. Just with a friend."

A friend. Katherine thrills at the word. The stars will shine a little brighter tonight.

"Yes, from class, which was dire. Anyway, her name is Katherine, you'll have to meet her." She rolls her eyes again. "Yes, love, I'm coming. Yes, I know it's raining. I'll try not to melt. Jesus!"

Niamh ends the call and looks up apologetically at Katherine. "The joys of being the trophy."

"What?" Katherine is startled.

"I'm the trophy wife." Niamh slyly dimples. "Or, as his first wife says, 'the jumped-up little tart from the council estate.'"

Katherine almost sprays her beer everywhere. "His wife said that?" she chokes out.

"Not to my face. But I have it on good account from his daughter."

Niamh laughs at Katherine's expression and gives a mock shudder.

"Yes, I have a stepdaughter—very Wicked Queen of me, isn't it?"

"That's terrible!"

"I know, my husband and his ex-wife having sex, it hardly bears thinking about."

"No, I meant—"

"I know what you meant"—Niamh shrugs—"but she's fifteen. I was a right little madam at that age."

Katherine has to agree. "Yeah, fifteen was rough."

"She'll probably come right given a year or so and hate her mam. Then I can be the nice one who understands her and buys her cool clothes." She grins. Katherine grins in return but has an unexpected flash of pity for the teenager. Niamh is so pretty, so vivacious. It must be hard to be filled with pimples and rage and have to contend for a besotted father's affection for someone like that.

"It's to my advantage anyway," Niamh continues. "He concentrated so hard on his work the first time round, he's determined to do things right the second time around. Of course"—her voice warms with real affection—"I'm mad about the daft old bugger even though he treats me like spun glass."

Katherine smiles back, but her heart hurts a little. It must be nice to have a husband, a partner so concerned about you. Chances are that if Sael even asks her how class went, he'll be staring at his screen the entire time she responds and then will say something like *Sounds great* without ever lifting his eyes.

Oh well. "I guess we should call it a night?" She hazards trying not to sound too disappointed.

"Let me make sure I have your number." Niamh starts digging through her bag, presumably for her phone, and misses the huge relieved grin Katherine can't quite hold back.

"Let's," Katherine agrees casually and begins digging out her own.

Outside, it's still raining. "Which way are you headed?" Niamh asks. "Shall we spring for a taxi? My call."

"Really?" Katherine tries to avoid taking the taxis here—the very shape of them seems inefficient. Sael has been extraordinarily generous with her allowance, but she can't help but dread the expense. She supposes it's a reflex for all the penny-pinching years in New York.

"C'mon!" Niamh says.

They find a black cab and scramble in. The driver looks at them expectantly.

"Where are you headed?" Niamh prompts again.

Katherine tells her the address of her new home.

"But you can't be!"

Katherine looks at her. "I can't?"

"That's just around the corner from me!"

"You're kidding!"

"I'm not!"

The driver coughs. "Ladies?"

"I'm just around the block," Niamh tells him.

"I love that we're neighbors."

"A nightmare, though, really, because you'll be endlessly borrowing cups of sugar."

"How did you know?"

The rainy night is no longer forlorn. It may be cold and dark outside, but Katherine is not outside. She's inside the taxi with a new friend. She's happy.

The ride is all too quick, and they arrive at Katherine's front door in what seems to be minutes.

Niamh whistles. "Very posh!"

"Oh, shut up, you can't talk! You live in the same neighborhood. Besides, Sael's work found this for us."

She grins. "True enough, I'm very posh too. How did two *hoors* like ourselves wind up in such fancy places?"

"God knows. Anyway, I'll see you soon?" Katherine feels like she's known her forever.

"Of course!"

"Bye!"

"Bye!"

Katherine gets out of the taxi and stands on her new front doorstep. Niamh, still in the backseat, waves at her, and then the taxi speeds off into the wet night.

She remains on the step for a moment. In a moment, she'll go inside. In a moment, she'll go inside and breathe in the perfume of the fresh flowers that Mrs. B will have procured and arranged in a vase on the dining room table. In a moment, she'll go and check in on Lucas, make sure he's asleep and all is well with Cordelia, who will be lying under his bed. She'll pass by the room that's become Sael's unofficial office. The door, of course, will be closed. Then she'll go downstairs and open the fridge to see what Mrs. B has left her to warm up. She'll collapse with her heated-up leftovers in front of the TV and watch a quiz show. The Brits love their quiz shows. But right now she'll allow herself just a moment to stand on the damp steps looking out into the darkness, thanking God, or someone or something, for the simple yet unfathomable miracle of making a new friend.

Then she walks inside and closes the door behind her.

19

Margaret

He did not send for me after her body was found. I understood. He needed to be a leader for his people, to comport himself with dignity. But at night, I ached for him. So I drew on what my mother had taught me, and as I brewed my ale I added anise, for desire, and cinnamon, for happiness. I sang a song of kisses sweet and soft nights, and by the by he sent for me again.

He had summoned me and yet seemed troubled when I arrived at his solar, as if he did not know why I was there.

"I cannot shake you." He would not look at me. "I am drawn to you beyond my own will, as a moth flutters blindly to a flame even though that flame will burn it up."

"Then fly," I told him, "and we will burn together."

And I held open my arms.

He fell into them and then we fell together. I tasted the salt on his skin, felt him upon me and in me. It was all I would ask for.

After a long while, both of us sated, we lay together. My eyes wandered, and in the light of the waning fire I caught the gleam of an ornament that lay upon a wooden chest near the bed. "That's a pretty thing," I remarked.

"It has been in the de Villias family for generations." He seemed proud of it.

I reached out and fingered the brooch, cast silver in the shape of a snake with a gleaming red eye, curving round to swallow its own tail, which glistened with six tiny jewels: blue, green, rose, piercing white, deep purple, and honey. "Sapphire, emerald, topaz, diamond, amethyst, and citrine," he murmured against my neck.

"And the eye?" It was hard to tear my own away from the winking drop of blood.

"A ruby." His arms enfolded me and pulled me down to him again, the brooch still in my hand, and at last I was sure that any frost forming between us had melted away.

Soon after that night, a page comes to the cottage with an invitation; a banquet, which is to be held in five days. Try as I may, I can find no other reason for this invitation other than to make public his affection for me. To dine with him openly and sit by his side as his wife would is an honor I crave above all. I can think of nothing else.

The day of the banquet, I am sent an amber-colored cotehardie, sewn with silver thread and silver-threaded buttons. In the evening, a woman arrives to help dress me. She is the well-born wife of one of his most favored knights. She clearly thinks she is beneath such work, but her husband's fealty is at stake. She sighs heavily as she weaves ribbons until they gleam through my hair.

"That will do," she sniffs grudgingly once her work is done.

I shine tonight. I glow, not just outwardly but inwardly too. Tonight, I shall tell him my secret.

I have never been to a banquet, although by now I have brewed for many. I enter the Great Hall and swallow. I force myself to walk slowly across the newly laid rushes toward the high table so that I may savor the grandeur. Tonight the room is filled with men of high rank. They sit at long tables that are covered with soft linen cloth, and heavy under their burden of silver plates and silver salt cellars, silver knives and spoons and goblets. There are officials and advisers, the sheriff and the steward, Father Martin and his knights attended by their squires.

A heavy hush descends as I approach Lord August's table. My limbs have turned to stone, but he half rises and smiles at me, which is all the assurance I need. Father Martin says grace, and once he has finished, a steady stream of servants make their way toward the high table. There are platters of roasted capons and peacock, stewed venison and honeyed meats, sweet fried fritters of swan, spiced pies with thick flaking crusts, jellies colored yellow with saffron and red with sandalwood, and frumenty. I would love to eat well but I am too nervous to take more than a few bites. I must watch my manners, must remember which hand to use when eating and when I must wait to be served.

The oppressive feeling in the air thickens. Conversation is stilted. I try my best to enjoy the feast before me, but there is a tightness in my throat and chest that makes it impossible to swallow. Lord August laughs, hard and defiant. I wince at how forced it sounds. Our companions at the high table return weak chuckles and jests that fall flat as soon as they are uttered. They are uneasy and unhappy.

Excited as I was, now I can hardly wait for the banquet to be over. As the empty platters are removed, leaving only the dishes of fruits and nuts before us I pray that this evening will come to an end. I curse them all. They may have wealth and titles, but their hearts are no different from the villagers'; they are still the same hateful folk. Soon enough, I hope, he and I will be alone so I may tell him my news.

"And what of entertainment?" Lord August bellows. In the expectant silence that follows, something white kisses my cheek. I start and look up. Soft petals drift down from above, from the ceiling or from the heavens?

"What trick is this?" he demands. The guests exclaim, amazed.

"May I offer my services, my lord?"

Before us stands a stranger. His hair is snowy, shining white, but his age is impossible to guess. In one instant he appears ancient, and the next almost boyish, depending on the shadows. His bulbous nose overhangs a mouth as thin as a piece of string. He wears not red or yellow, as I have seen many of the entertainers do, but a cloak of deepest black, speckled with shining points of silver thread, as if he has cut down a piece of the night sky and swathed himself in a mantle of stars. He leans upon a wooden staff, which is intricately carved with a snake coiling up its length, much like my lord's brooch. A large, glossy raven perches upon his shoulder, cocking its black and gleaming head this way and that. The man turns to me, and I see his eyes are silver.

Lord August is laughing now, truly laughing for the first time this evening. "Caradoc!" he cries in delight.

"My lord." Caradoc bows and then says, "For you, my lady," as he pulls a branch of white blossoms from thin air and holds them out for me. I accept it and nod, doing my best to appear gracious, but I do not smell the flowers or touch their petals. I am terrified of this man, who stares at me with silver eyes. I look again at Lord August, but he seems not to notice anything amiss.

"When did I last see you, you old rogue?"

"Ah, when you were scarcely taller than my knee, a warrior even then and sorely trying the patience of your father!" Caradoc's deep voice resonates in the Great Hall.

"Has it been that long? And yet you are just the same. I still remember the last story you told us. We dined on it for years."

"His lordship speaks with such honeyed words, he does not need my humble skills!"

"Come, you old flatterer, tell us a tale, for I have a hunger to hear one of your stories."

"As you wish, my lord." Caradoc half turns so that he faces all the high tables of the Great Hall. No one need strain to hear him. "Long ago in ages past, there lived two beautiful maidens. One was a daughter of the Sun. Her hair shone as golden gossamer, her eyes were blue as the summer sky and her very touch made the flowers bloom. The other was a daughter of the Moon, whose voice was a mournful wind, her dark locks fell like night upon her brow, and her large eyes were filled with woe . . ."

The story is wonderful, but there is something wrong. And then it comes to me. It is the same as when I sing, the strength lies not within his words but in the enchantment behind them. And he is far more powerful than I. His tongue spins a spider's web, its shining strands drifting down to ensnare us all. It takes everything I have to shut out his voice. I do not know what his intention is in holding his audience so spellbound, but I will not be another helpless fly caught and vulnerable. I glance at Lord August, whose eyes are glazed with wonder, his mouth agape. I look around the Great Hall and see a similar expression on each and every face. Except one.

Landon's eyes are narrowed; his lips are contorted into a snarl. It is a look so full of loathing that I flinch. At that moment, he seems even more alien than the storyteller.

Finally, Caradoc's tale is at an end. He bows, and there is a tumultuous roar of applause and stamping of feet as the Great Hall, in its entirety, cheers.

Lord August wipes his eyes with the back of his hand. "In truth, I have never heard such a tale before. I swear your words will remain in my heart until the end of my days."

Caradoc bows again and smiles. "I am pleased, my lord. And now I must be on my way. But before I go, I wish to tell you your fortune." He steps closer to the table. "Give me your left hand."

The Great Hall settles into stillness again as all crane to hear what lies in store for their lordship. Caradoc seems untroubled by their scrutiny, and he continues to study Lord August's palm.

Then he looks up. "This has been a trying time for you, my lord. Your heart and head are pulled in different directions. And there is an evil presence around you too. One that obscures its true self."

Utter silence. I am crushed by the weight of a hundred eyes upon me.

"But still, be of good cheer, my lord, for soon the slaughter of the innocent will end. The devil among you will flee."

"Thank God," Lord August breathes.

"Yes, thanks be to God"—Caradoc's silver eyes crease up at the corners—"for I see a marriage." The Hall stirs, rapt. "Even as I speak, a messenger is riding to you with glad tidings. A golden bride will soon stand by your side. Like the daughter of the Sun, her eyes are the color of a summer sky, her mouth is a rose in bloom."

Everyone's attention flicks back to me with my dark locks and my dark eyes. As if they needed more proof that I am an imposter whose run of good fortune is about to end.

"Generys," Lord August murmurs. "Her father must have agreed." It is as if I do not exist. Then he remembers his present company, for he composes himself again. "I thank you, Caradoc. Your prophecy is a gift."

Caradoc dips his head. "I am glad my knowledge gives you happiness, my lord, but I have no control nor power over what I see. I am simply passing along a message."

"Still, you have lightened the weight of my troubles and"—he gestures toward the other guests—"lightened all our hearts!"

"Then on that note, I bid you farewell." Caradoc gathers the folds of his cloak around him with one hand as he grips his strange staff with the other. I stare at his bent back as he slowly makes his way toward the end of the Great Hall.

The minstrels strike up their instruments and chatter resumes, although now the guests speak more easily and with true levity. I lean over and whisper to Lord August that I am tired and will retire. He does not even look at me, only nods, not breaking his conversation with his neighbor.

I slip away from the table, descend from the dais, and follow the shadowed back wall of the Great Hall until I reach the kitchen passage. But the old man has not paused for supper to which he is surely entitled. So I hurry on into the garden. And there he stands, his twisted back to me, staring up at the evening sky as if gazing at a map.

"Yes?" he asks, his eyes still turned to the heavens.

I have made no noise, and yet he knows I am here. My confusion and fear and disappointment over the evening whirls up and out into a furious shout.

"Who *are* you?"

He does not answer.

"Who are you?" I cry again, close to losing control, but I have had my fill of icy snubs and haughty silences.

"I am Caradoc, a teller of tales."

I snort and wave his words away. I am not a child to be toyed with.

"Who are you *truly*?"

"You ask questions easily enough. Would you really have the answers?"

"I would." My mouth is dry as a husk and my chest is tight, but whatever the cost, I must know.

"Very well." He pivots, using his staff, until we are facing each other. His silver eyes shine in the moonlight, but I am too incensed to be frightened. "I am an Other."

"And what is that?" I hiss, though I half fear I am demanding sense from a madman.

"I am other than Man, other than an angel, other than a demon. I and my kind are here as witnesses to the words and deeds of mankind. We have been here since the Beginning and we shall be here until the End."

My senses reel, but I cling to my anger—it is the only weapon I can wield. "You accused me of being the devil among them."

He shakes his head. "I would never accuse you of such a thing. There is true evil here, a devil among men. Deep in the marrow of your bones, you know it too, for you came upon him when you were but a child."

Moths of red and black swarm before my vision. "The man who stalks me is here?"

His unwavering stare is all the answer I need.

"But how can this be? Is he also an Other?"

"He is not an Other. He is no mortal assassin, but an Entity disguised as one of you to complete his mission here on earth. A mission that began with the birth of Jesus of Nazareth."

He studies my uncomprehending face. "For what other man could defy the laws of the universe as he did? Jesus, who healed the sick and walked upon the water and rose from the dead, changed the course of this world forever." Caradoc sighs, and age seems to settle upon him like dust. It seems he will not speak again, so long does he pause, but at length he continues.

"But his mother, Mary, was a mortal. It was she, the Virgin, who became the first Vessel. She gave birth to Jesus, and when she did the balance was forever shifted, the harmony of the spheres forever altered.

At the very moment Christ was born, the Entity rose up with

blade in hand. He travels through the ages to ensure no other mortal woman could succeed as a Vessel, no other mortal woman able to bear children who would again test the foundations of the universe. The Entity hunts you because you are a Vessel. You were chosen as the stars aligned at the moment of your birth."

As he speaks I remember my mother's words: *Your destiny is writ golden upon the skies, in the night's song.*

A faint strain of melody and a bark of laughter drift out from the Great Hall. The wandering breeze lifts strands of hair from my forehead. A wave of darkness rises up and threatens to engulf me. I bite down hard upon my lip, and the taste of blood brings me back to the present. I open my mouth and force myself to speak. I will have my answer.

"And this . . . this Entity that you speak of, he is the one who killed my mother?" *Her arm fell back. Dead. She was dead and he was carving her skin.*

"Yes." Caradoc's silver eyes do not look away.

"Was she a Vessel?"

He slowly shakes his head. "She was an Anchor."

"An Anchor?"

"That is true, what would you know of Anchors?" He smiles kindly. "Well then, you have heard tell of ships that sail upon the seas?"

I manage a nod. Amid the insanity, this is something I can grasp. Ships upon the seas, yes, I have heard of them.

"Anchors are great weights that hold ships fast to bottom of the sea so that they do not drift away." He continues to watch me, as if to make sure I am following.

"I do not understand you." I do not understand any of this. In a flash of rage I wish him dead. I wish myself dead or deaf to his voice. My wishes come to nothing. Still I live and still I listen.

"He is not of your world, and so he needed your mother, and countless others, to hold him fast upon the earth until he can complete his task." It is the first time I think I hear a strain of distaste in his words.

"But must he kill them even though they are not Vessels?"

"They too are vessels of a kind. He needs what lives within them."

"Their blood?"

"Their souls. A mortal is made not only of flesh and blood; a mortal possesses a soul. The capacity to feel. The Entity needs a soul. And so he must take it from others. Women. He takes their emotions. Jealousy, passion, tenderness, fear, suspicion, loyalty—all of a woman's experience, her spirit, adds to his weight upon this earth, anchors him in the flesh he possesses."

"How does he know which ones to take?"

My mother.

"Feelings are colors to him. The ancient signs and symbols he carves into their skin release these colors, which he then consumes. Your mother," Caradoc adds, "held both the color of tranquility, the cool hue of deepening twilight, and then also the color of anguish when she thought of you."

"And my color?" My words are hard, my voice cold. Inside I quake and tremble. An immortal killer, an inhuman thing scenting the air to snuff me out. At least I will know what hue has left me naked and defenseless.

"You are red."

Red. The fabric that called to me that day at the market. Berries in the woods, beautiful but often poisonous. The silk dress, the color of fire but cool as water against my skin.

Caradoc stares at me quizzically. "Do you not remember? He told you when you were but a child."

Did Caradoc or his kind stand idly by while my mother was murdered? Did they overhear the killer taunting me in the woods? I cannot bear to think of it.

"Why does he come now?" I ask.

All around me the night is still. Not an insect hums, nor a bird calls. Even the wind has died. Pools of moonlight spill over the potted basil and rosemary; patches of shadow checker the raised beds of sorrel and fenugreek.

Caradoc's raven shifts its weight and again twists its head on one side, the gleam of its inky eyes taking in my measure.

"You know the answer."

Instinctively my hands shield my womb. The secret I was to tell Lord August tonight.

Then a thought occurs and I shake my head with dogged certainty. Here at least is some proof that Caradoc lies.

"I will always remember the face of my mother's killer, no matter how many years have passed, and I have not seen him here."

"Ten or ten hundred of your years is nothing to him. It is a blink of an eye. Time has little relevance. He travels."

"He travels?"

"You saw only the body he possessed. This is how he can endure through the ages, how he can reappear on earth as flesh and blood. He possesses a man's body, lives within that body, but only until he has fulfilled his mission. Then he discards it as easily as you would the skin of a fruit. Often the men he chooses are good, are innocent. Who, through no fault of their own, are forced to commit the vilest acts. He drags them through a living hell and then abandons them to live with the pain and misery and guilt of what they have done, to face the consequences of actions they had no choice but to perform."

"So the man who murdered my mother had no choice?"

Do not run little rabbit.

"None at all." Caradoc speaks with quiet certitude.

"But why?" The words are ripped from me in a wail.

"The Entity delights in chaos, pain amuses him. Remember that he is not of this world. He *has* no soul."

"And you?" I spit out. "And what of your kind?"

"We too must dwell within a human if we are to exist on earth, but we do not act against that person's will. We reside for a spell, but we do not alter that person's destiny in any way. It is not our place to change what is to come."

"Why do you tell me this?"

"Because you asked me and I would tell you the truth. He will come for you, no matter what knowledge you are armed with. And although no Vessel has ever survived him since Mary Magdalene, no one's fate is certain."

He pauses, and his gaze again shifts from me to the sky. His words are almost dreamy.

"If you or your child *did live*, what extraordinary power you could wield, not just over this world but over all worlds." Then his bearing straightens, and he stares at me once more. "You had a right to know." He thumps the end of his staff in the soft earth with defiance.

"I will run."

"He will find you." There is the faintest hint of reprimand now, as if I were a selfish, willful child. "And he will keep killing until he finds you."

"I will find a way." A ray of hope dawns "I will make use of the gifts my mother gave me."

"Yes." Caradoc nods thoughtfully. "You have some power, passed down through your mother, but the power of her people is tied to the things of the earth. His is not of this earth. His power is beyond it, tied to the vastness of everything." His reasoning maddens me as a sting of an insect must madden a blundering ox.

"I will escape! I will travel through the ages, as he does, as you do."

Caradoc may scoff at my spells and songs, but I am fierce and quick-witted and I can learn.

"There is no body that can hold the soul of a Vessel. Only another Vessel could house you, and there is only one Vessel alive in any age." He speaks quietly now.

"So what would you advise me?"

"I do not advise. I merely tell you the truth. I am telling you your fortune."

"But you will not guide me in any way?" I try one last time to appeal to this creature. It is amazing to me that he would offer no aid or advice at all.

He shakes his head. "I am not able to help you. We do not judge. We neither help nor hinder."

"That is of no use to me! He killed my mother and now he means to kill me and my unborn child." I stab a finger at his chest. "You say that there is little chance I will survive, that I will be slaughtered as a lamb." I take a breath and fight to gain control. "But I tell you now, I will not quit this world so easily. I will destroy him, even if it takes me a *thousand* years, no matter the cost!"

Caradoc studies me with a new intensity.

"You would turn away from the light, to the darkness? If a sapling is lashed down, it grows stunted and warped. Would you destroy him if you knew that doing so would destroy what good you hold in yourself? Would you still be willing if it cost you your soul?" His voice holds no judgment or recrimination. It is only gently curious. "Would you?"

My laughter is scornful. "I will do whatever it takes. I have been hunted for one reason or another my whole life, ever since my mother was taken from me. He shall not win this time. He will not have me. He will not have my child. When he least expects it, I shall strike, I shall bring him down, I shall end him." Each word falls from my lips, a bruising stone, a bloody pledge.

"Take care, Margaret. There will always be a sacrifice." It is calmly stated, not as a warning but as a promise.

"Go, storyteller!" I hiss at him. "Weave your fictions and fortunes somewhere else. Leave me. I have no need of you."

Caradoc remains a moment longer. "I am sorry. Would that you lived in a different age, were born under different stars. But we cannot change what is."

He limps down the path between the herb beds and passes under the arch in the garden wall. Soon, the night swallows him whole.

I stand for a long while in the garden, alone. Breathing in the scent of the good and growing things all around me.

"We'll see," I say aloud to the stars.

20

Katherine

The countryside spills out along either side of them, green and lush despite the winter. *If this were New York*, Katherine thinks, *everything would be buried under ten feet of snow*. It's only a forty-five-minute ride by train from London, but it feels like a different world.

She gazes out at the fields and hills and the houses slipping past her for a while; then she looks at Lucas's small curly head as he sits and stares out of the window. He's doing well, excelling at school and making a multitude of friends. He has Cordelia, and Mrs. B seems to have taken a real shine to him, which, no matter her grim demeanor, clearly means she's a person of remarkable intelligence and taste as far as Katherine is concerned.

Sael, she is given to understand, is also performing well at work. It seems to present a near-impossible series of tasks, which suits him. After all, what else does he have to occupy him? All his domestic arrangements are taken care of, and his every other need is attended to by beautiful, competent young Georgie.

And Katherine? Why, she's also doing well. For a start, she

has friends now. She and Niamh text constantly and speak almost daily. They exchange horror stories about the belly touchers, the oversharers of complicated birthing stories, the judgers. And there's Matthew, whom she often meets for lunch. They talk about books and movies, and he recommends places she should visit. She's never had a friend as glamorous or as sophisticated as Matthew. It's like the most popular girl in school has picked Katherine to sit beside her on the bus, or invited her to a sleepover. She wonders what she's done to deserve the attention. She doesn't question it too much, though. She just enjoys his friendship. He's especially riveted by her stories of Sael.

"I must meet the divine-sounding Sael, and you must meet John," he had said one lunchtime not long ago.

"Really?" She knew what an honor this would be. Matthew commutes to the city to see friends and make purchases—nothing, of course, as common as working—but John tends to stay in the country.

"Of course, we would have had you over before, but John's been getting over this filthy flu and I wouldn't want to inflict that upon anyone."

"I would love to," Katherine had replied, already realizing the obstacles. "But Sael will probably need to work, so it would likely just be me. And I'll need to make a plan for Lucas if it's on a weekend."

"Bring him!"

"Are you sure?" Matthew doesn't seem like the most child-friendly type.

"Of course! We'd love to meet him. It would cheer John up. Getting the flu somewhat depressed him.

But when she isn't with her friends, what does Katherine do? She visits castles, manor houses, other historic buildings or sites of interest. It's easy with Lucas at school all week, and it's not as if she can work in England anyway. She's calling these trips "research," but research for what she cannot answer. She only knows she loves the smell of old places, reading the descriptions of how the Romans or the Normans or the Tudors lived, walking where they walked and talked and loved and died. It feels grounding. In the beginning, she was reluctant to travel by herself, but now she finds satisfaction in visiting these places alone. Learning how to negotiate the trains, the buses, reading the maps. Being independent.

It's a good life, much better than she hoped for, and yet. And yet. Lonely. Once the thrill of independence wears off, she is left with the terrible, terrible loneliness. Katherine is uprooted, and she does not belong here. Sael does not want her. He is either at the office, working, or at home, working. He's taken over the spare room, and even sleeps there now. He says he doesn't want to wake her when he goes to bed so late, but Katherine feels his real reason is abundantly clear. He never touches her, not even to pat her shoulder or tousle her hair. Not since their one perfect Christmas Eve.

He does not want you, she reflects, *but he needs to know that you are safe, that you are fed.* She is carrying his child, after all. She's like a prize mare, or maybe a heifer. He is unfailingly polite and attentive. "Do you have everything you need?" he asks, over and over again. "Yes, thank you," she replies, even though inside she's telling him she does not.

You do not have everything you need, Katherine admits, *because you need to be touched. You need to be touched, embraced, and pinned down. You need to burrow your nose against his head and breathe in the scent of his hair. You need his hands on your thighs, your breasts. You need his tongue on your lips, your cunt, and then you need to be kissed and you need to be held.*

You need him to tell you that everything is going to be okay, even if it isn't okay. You need him to love you. You know he lost so much, but you lost so much too. You lost one of your best friends, and you lost your trust

*in other people, and you lost your life back home, and you lost him. You
lost and you are lost, and you need him to find you and bring you home.*

The conductor announces the upcoming station, which is
Matthew's. Katherine sits up. She was drifting to sleep. She grabs
Lucas's hand, and they step off quickly before the train can carry
them away.

Matthew lounges outside the ticket counter, looking long-legged
and impeccable in dark jeans and a cashmere sweater. "Hello! How
was the ride? Did you suffer? Are you exhausted?"

"It was long and hard, but somehow we made it."

"Thrilling, but come, let's away. Bella's waiting."

"Bella?" Katherine tries not to feel a small surge of jealousy that
he's brought another friend. Lucas squeezes her hand. It's creepy
the way he can read her so well.

Outside in the parking lot, inside Matthew's car, is an old black
Labrador with a wistful, sweet expression that transforms into a
grin of delight as they approach.

"I'm afraid it will smell a bit doggy, but then again this is the dog
car," Matthew says as he unlocks the door.

"A dog car?" Lucas shoots Katherine a reproachful look.

"Oof. Sorry, honey." She turns to Matthew. "Lucas wanted to
bring Cordy, but we weren't sure how to navigate the trains with a
puppy, or if you were up for us bringing a semi-house-trained dog
into your home."

"Darling, I'm English. We live only to serve our dogs." He turns
to Lucas. "You'll just have to come back again soon, with Cordy."

"It's nice to have a car just for dogs." Lucas is impressed.

"Imperative," Matthew says with a straight face.

Katherine is not sure if he's joking.

He takes them for a ride through the main street of the village,
which looks exactly like a picture book. White houses with dark

timber beams and small but elegant cottages line the narrow cobbled streets. As they drive, Matthew delivers a running commentary on both the buildings and their inhabitants. They pass a pub with a little green sign swaying back and forth in the breeze.

"That's the pub, and our local landlord is Oliver, who has a notoriously roving eye," he says, but Katherine only catches the word "Fox" before the sign swings back again and they pass it.

There are several cyclists, one of them a little girl who seems only a few years older than Lucas, an old-fashioned butcher's, a tearoom, a bookshop, and old people taking in the weak sunshine.

Matthew laughs at her rapt expression. "I knew you'd love it," he says. Then he waves to a cheerful-looking plump woman with dark hair who's speaking earnestly to a mother pushing a stroller. "And that's Brenda, who is a nightmare gossip."

"Unlike some." Katherine bats her eyelashes at him.

"Oh please, I can only imagine what they say about dear little *me*."

They have soon passed through the village and are now driving on what seem like exceptionally narrow roads with high hedgerows blocking all the turns. Katherine winces a few times, wondering how any car could pass them, but they encounter no one and Matthew seems to know what he's doing.

"I hope you're hungry," he says as he navigates through the hedgerows. "The fabulous, but terrifying, Mrs. Langley has made the most amazing cake, among other various other delicacies, and I will be livid if I end up eating the whole thing at three in the morning."

"Could you eat a whole cake?" Lucas clearly has doubts, but his natural good manners prevent him from saying more.

"Ah, yes, I cannot resist its siren call. It will just croon to me, '*Mattheeeeew, Mattheeew*,' and I'll sleepwalk downstairs and wake up to find myself covered in crumbs and holding an empty plate, and John will be deeply annoyed."

"I think we might be able to help you out. Lucas and I are known to be champion cake eaters."

Lucas nods seriously. Matthew has turned left and slowed onto a long smooth gravel driveway, which seems to carry on for several miles before opening out onto an endless expanse of manicured green lawn and meticulously trimmed hedges. The manor house towers three stories high. Sheets of ivy drape the bottom half of the faded red brick.

"Whoa," Lucas mumbles. His eyes are huge.

"Oh my God." The words are out before Katherine can stop them.

"Home, sweet home," Matthew says. He's careful to avoid yet another dog in the driveway, a fat and complacent yellow Lab, and then steps over a small dusty-looking terrier sitting by one of the massive white urns that flank the equally massive white door. "Now do you believe me? We are overrun with hounds!"

The entrance hall has deep maroon walls contrasting with white paneling. Two portraits flank the outer hallway. The one on the left holds a fat bearded aristocrat got up in gilt-trimmed cobalt blue velvet; the other depicts an equally fat smug pug wearing a jewel-encrusted collar. Underneath the paintings are two curving china vases baring all the telltale Ming patterns of blue dragons and flowers. The floorboards gleam burnished oak and are draped with thin Persian rugs.

"Oh my God," she murmurs again.

Matthew beckons to the terrier, who clicks past them. "Come on, Tilly, let's go and find John."

As they walk past the sprawling, comfortable rooms, Katherine catches tantalizing glimpses of their sunlight interiors. It's a lovely, well-worn old house that wears its centuries on its sleeve, though Matthew's quirky taste and style is clearly visible throughout; velvet couches of olive green and peacock blue, vintage mirrors and rough-hewn coffee tables live seamlessly together. In the corner of a drawing room a series of carved chests are stacked up on top of one another, reminding Katherine of unpacked Russian dolls. In another corner a stately Roman bust resides on a gleaming grand piano, still dignified under the brim of a natty bowler. Scenic watercolors and modernist depictions of squares hang side by side with the Virgin and Child done in oils. Towers of books are stacked next to marble fireplaces, and the whole house has the delicious smell of burned firewood.

"Your home is nice," Lucas announces, delivering the understatement of the year.

"Why, thank you, you'll get the proper tour in due course."

"It's really big, though."

"That too," Matthew agrees. "It's excellent for playing hide-and-seek."

"It is truly beautiful." Katherine's words are ironed flat with envy. This is the kind of chic and witty shabbiness that takes generations of breeding and knowledge to perfect.

"John would be happier dwelling in some monastic cell, preferably from the fourteenth century, but I must admit I do love creature comforts. You know, running water, central plumbing, glass in the windows. So we settled for Georgian."

"Georgie?" Lucas asks, confused.

"Georgian because it was built in about 1773, when George III was king."

"Wow, that's old."

"We've done *some* renovations since." In the back entrance hall he calls up a dogleg staircase. "John, darling? John?"

There is no reply, but Katherine hears a faint strain of classical music.

"John?"

Matthew goes up the staircase, beckoning Katherine and Lucas to follow him. It creaks and cracks somewhat alarmingly, but also somewhat satisfyingly. Then he leads them along a landing and down a hallway to a door, which Matthew knocks upon and then opens.

Floor-to-ceiling bookshelves, all stuffed, line the room. A shaft of light shines in through the windows on an old oak desk, where Katherine can just make out a man almost completely obscured behind piles and piles of papers and more books, these ones larger leather-bound volumes.

"John?"

The man looks up, startled; then his face relaxes into a smile. "Oh, hello!" He rises and comes around the desk to greet them. Tall and thin, almost alarmingly so, he wears wire-rimmed glasses that match his silvery hair. He looks tired.

"Darling, didn't you hear me?"

"In another world, I'm afraid."

"Did the builders call?"

John frowns. "Not to my knowledge."

"Oh God, only I had finally spoken to Peter and he told me he would definitely be calling today to discuss the roof."

"I didn't hear the phone ring."

"That doesn't mean anything."

"Matthew, don't fuss." John smiles again, and his face lights up. Katherine can see why Matthew loves him. When he smiles like that, he's insanely attractive. "I'm sure they'll call back. Meanwhile this must be the famous Katherine, so lovely to meet you at last! And who is this?" He kneels down effortlessly.

"I'm Lucas." Usually so shy, he seems at ease here.

"Lucas, it's good to meet you too."

"You have a lot of books."

"You think so?" John looks around, as if surveying the room for the first time. "I could do with some more."

Matthew groans. "Don't get him started on this."

"Well, you can never have enough books. Don't you agree, Lucas? I'm sure Katherine feels the same way."

"I do." She would kill to spend a couple of hours browsing through these books.

John turns to Lucas, "What do you think?"

Lucas frowns. "I don't know. Maybe. I like books too, but you have so many of them."

"You tell him, Lucas," teases Matthew.

"Yes, well, but each book offers something different. Each book is like a map that can lead you to a different place, show you something wonderful. And books are also like friends, friends who tell you stories, and who can cheer you up when you're sad."

Lucas looks at him. "Are you very sad?"

It's an unexpected question, one that only a young child could honestly ask, and John pauses. In that pause, Katherine decides, *Yes, he's very sad.*

But then John laughs. "No, not too often."

Matthew exhales, and Katherine has a feeling he was also listening intently for the answer. "There, now. I told you not get John started on the subject of books! Let's go down and try to find where Mrs. Langley has hidden the cake."

"Why did she hide it?"

"To prevent me from eating the whole thing!" Matthew takes Lucas's hand. "And if Tilly takes a liking to you, she might even be persuaded to do a special trick!"

"What special trick?"

"Come and see!"

They head downstairs, and John and Katherine stand for a moment in silence.

"We shouldn't have disturbed you," she says.

"Not at all, it was time I had a break."

"I love this room."

"Thank you. It *is* dreadfully cluttered, though. Matthew is right. He keeps begging me to put it in order, but I have my own kind of order, and a system in place to manage my papers."

"You put them down on a surface and hope they remain there until you need them?"

"Basically, yes." John removes his glasses, absentmindedly rubs the lenses on his sleeve, and pushes them back up the bridge of his nose. "So, Matthew tells me you're unfortunate enough to be involved with a de Villias?"

She likes the way he puts it, although it's a little too much on the money. "That's right."

"How extraordinary for you and Matthew to meet the way that you did."

"It was really a godsend. I needed a friend, and there he was." *You sound so earnest and American.* She cringes. "How did you and Matthew meet?"

"I was a fellow at Oxford, and he was a student."

"That sounds wicked."

"Actually, I thought he was a total dilettante. He swanned in late the first day and I gave him complete hell."

"And how did he take that?"

"He blinked up at me and said, 'I shall have to watch my p's and q's.'"

Katherine grins. "Sounds about right. And did he?"

"Well, honestly, I didn't think he would stick around, but he did. I doubted whether he was too bright, thought some parent or relative had pulled strings to get him in, but he proceeded to run circles around the rest of group. I told him to stop showing off. At the end of the tutorial, he came up to me and held out his hand and said, 'Truce,' and so I shook it."

"And the rest is history."

"Yes, he stuck around. God bless him, I'll never understand why."

Katherine does, although John is clearly unaware of his considerable appeal.

"And you and your own de Villias?"

Her own. She wishes Sael were her own. "Oh . . . we met at a party."

"That sounds reasonable enough."

She doesn't mention how they didn't tell each other their names, how one of them ended up naked at the end of their first encounter, how she never expected to see him again but ran into him at a bar two weeks later. "It does, doesn't it."

"To be involved with de Villias men. We're brave, did you know that?"

"No, why?"

"The de Villias curse."

"The what?"

John's excitement bubbles up through his natural English reserve.

"The family's very own curse! Matthew managed to acquire some rare texts for me at an auction recently that made mention of it." He grins. It's an unexpectedly sexy grin. "They'll need further study, so I can't tell you too much about it yet, but it's part of the research I'm doing on the de Villias collection."

A bell chimes faintly in Katherine's memory.

"I think I first saw the name de Villias on a label in the Morgan Library in New York. Before I even *met* Sael. It was for a painting, I mean, not a painting, an illustration, an illuminated manuscript. From the de Villias collection." She remembers going to the Morgan on her first date with David and sneaking into a gallery that was closed. She recalls how dim it was, the ghostly empty display cases, the eerie silence, the sense of wrongness. Even now her skin prickles uncomfortably as she recalls it.

"Was the manuscript called *The Maiden of Morwyn Castle*?"

"Yes!" There's a satisfaction in fixing the name, like slapping a mosquito that's been whining in one's ear. She's startled when John laughs, equally delighted.

"*I* was the one who loaned that manuscript to the Morgan!"

"No!" Katherine gapes at him.

"I swear it!" John's pale cheeks are flushed, his eyes gaining animation.

"What a bizarre coincidence! You know," she confides, "I've never forgotten how the woman seemed to be staring straight out of the page at me."

She remembers the manuscript opened on its stand, the page of ornamented text and then the illumination. The woman, with her tiny black eyes shining out as she stood in her deep-green dress holding a dagger in the one hand and an apple in the other.

"It was an extremely unusual technique for the artist to use, to have his subject looking directly toward the viewer. Almost unheard of, in fact. Of course, the text itself is highly unusual too.

"It is? Why?"

John frowns and runs his hand through his hair.

"Well, there were far more secular texts popular in the fourteenth century than people give the medieval readers credit for. Romances, histories, poetry . . . I would say it's how much the story feels like a folktale, or an 'urban legend' of that time. I suppose the closest comparison would be *Sir Gawain and the Green Knight* or Langland's *Piers Plowman*, but whereas Langland wanted to draw our attention to the corruption of the aristocracy and the church, this story . . ." John pauses and gives an elegant shrug. "It has no obvious moral or social lesson that I can make sense of as yet. And of course the artist who illustrated it was very ahead of his time. I've been trying to track his identity down."

"That must be hard."

"Yes, but there are certain clues that make it easier. Of course the illuminators were encouraged to be seamless, so that the work was flowing and belonged to the whole, but still, artists inevitably tend to leave their marks or a tiny pictorial signature like a mouse or a rabbit in the margins. They were very fond of portraying rabbits for some reason." John is now getting into the swing of his subject, becoming more professorial by the moment. "And obviously there is the extraordinary material he produced, not religious but truly secular with a fairy-tale quality.

"One wonders, who would have commissioned such a work? Or did the artist conceive and create it of his own volition? Imagine that, one intrepid illuminator spending precious time and resources to create his own art, not glorying God or satisfying a wealthy patron, but for its own sake!" He realizes that his voice has risen and laughs, embarrassed. "Forgive me. I tend to get completely carried away when talking about it. Matthew says I'm becoming a fanatic, but really, it's just so fascinating!"

"Not at all." Katherine keeps her voice gentle, though there is something frantic about John's enthusiasm. "It sounds exciting."

"You are kind to humor me," he says, but he looks pleased. "Would you—" He hesitates. "Would you like to see an illuminated page that I'm working on?"

"I'd love to." John's talk has whetted her appetite to see something new. Anyway, she'd like to exorcize that particular ghost from her memory.

"Give me just a moment." He moves to another desk, and gently starts moving papers. "Ah, here it is." He reverently places a piece of glass over a page and beckons her closer.

Katherine walks toward the desk, aware that her heart is suddenly pounding. She remembers thinking that the woman in that illumination seemed to be speaking to her.

Make your choice, her jet-black eyes had glimmered. *Make your choice.*

She suppresses a shudder with difficulty and looks down.

Part of a stone wall, tall and smooth and gray, dominates the illumination dwarfing the two figures in the foreground.

"This is a tower wall," John explains. "I believe you can see the top of the tower in the background of the illumination that was chosen for display at the Morgan exhibition."

Though he stands close to her, his voice seems to be growing fainter.

"You can see here that he didn't display the tower in its entirety, he wanted to give a sense and perspective of its size. Incredible, at that time, for him to do that. Most art from the period doesn't use foreshortening. Perspective didn't really emerge until the Renaissance."

Katherine vaguely recalls learning about this in college, but her attention is focused on the two figures in front of the wall, a man and a woman facing each other. The man is enfolded in a long black robe pricked with tiny flecks of silver leaf. His hood obscures most of his face. He clutches a staff, and a large black bird perches upon one of his shoulders. With her chestnut hair and tiny black eyes, the woman is clearly the same woman whom Katherine saw so long ago, though here she wears an amber gown and there are ornaments in her hair. One of her hands is outstretched, though whether in greeting or accusation it is hard to tell.

"Amazing," she breathes, and the word has a little shake to it.

"Look at the detail," John whispers, passing her a magnifying glass.

Now Katherine can see that the rounded curve of the man's staff is actually a carved snake coiling up it.

"And the bird?" She asks something for the sake of asking, for the sake of hearing another person's voice, for normality.

"It's a raven," John says. "I'm sure it's a raven."

The man appears to gesture toward the forest, that dark swirl in the corner.

"It keeps me awake at nights," he admits, "wondering who the man is."

He is the Storyteller.

"What?"

He is the Storyteller, Caradoc.

"Katherine?"

He tells stories. And he tells the truth, which can be more marvelous and more terrible than any story.

"Katherine, what's going on? Katherine, are you all right?"

Deeper and deeper into the picture she falls, closer and closer to the forest, the darkness.

His eyes are silver.

The clothes she wears suddenly bind too tight, and the stone walls are closing in, collapsing into blooming black roses, petal after velvet petal unfurling, shining and soft before her eyes, and she falls.

"Hey, hey! Hold on!" He reaches out, grabbing her arm before they both collapse. Katherine reaches back, clutches his arm, hands and skin, and she sees—

—John standing in a series of white rooms, dressed in a paper gown. The smell of anesthetic, echoing footsteps. Waiting, always waiting, for someone to come and take him through to another room, another machine. He lies straight, his toe madly itching, but he doesn't move during the rhythmic bangs and thumps. Trying to think of Bach, no, the Beatles, a yellow submarine. This feels like a submarine. Or the Cure, but the whaa, whaa whines of the MRI are like that terrible trance music that was so big in the '90s. He tries not to think about his toe, how it itches. It's almost comical, something

to tell Matthew, but he cannot tell Matthew, he can't think about Matthew. He doesn't want Matthew to panic, or is he being selfish? Telling Matthew will make it real.

And then she is John himself, inside John himself—

—deep underneath his skin, the meat and the muscle, the organ that looks like a little fish, and there, there it is, the thing. The stranger, the invader, the destroyer. Expanding outward, cells eating, feeding, killing, eating, and taking over.

If only she could focus in upon it, gather it all in her mind, and then—

—burn it, pulverize it, eradicate, evaporate, decimate, eliminate, so that even the smallest particle is banished from his internal memory. Be gone, be gone.

Somewhere, far away, she hears someone cry, "Oh my God, oh my God—"

Let there be light, let there be light! And there was light, a white light of heat, burning until all that is evil is but dust, and then the dust of dust of dust, pulverized until there is nothingness and it is gone, gone, gone, gone—

"Stop!"

Katherine blinks, opens her eyes. John is braced against the desk. Her hand is pressed flat against his stomach, and her other hand is gripping his wrist. He gasps, and she lets go.

He slumps backward onto the desk. "What the—What just happened?"

Katherine has no words. Her mind is panicked, blank. She tries to move away, but now he is the one who grasps her wrist. He stares at her.

And then, very quietly, his eyes not leaving hers, he asks, "Who are you?"

"What do you mean?"

"What *are* you?"

"I—"

"What did you do to me?"

Her mouth opens as she tries to answer. But she has no answer.

"John, Katherine!" It's Matthew, calling for them. "Teatime!"

The spell is broken. John shakes his head as if to clear it.

"I—" Katherine falters. She slowly straightens. "I'm so sorry. I guess pregnancy leaves me lightheaded sometimes."

Only silence.

"Hello! There's cake down here!" They can hear Matthew coaching Lucas. "Tell them we found the cake, they'll listen to you."

"We found the cake!"

John looks at her a moment longer, then slowly says, "Well, it's a good thing I was there to catch you."

"Yes, it was."

"I think you'll have to be careful."

"I know."

"Shall we go down for tea?" His tone is casual, light.

Relief floods through her. It seems they'll be handling this the English way. "Yes," Katherine says. "Tea would be lovely."

She walks to the door and he follows her. She doesn't look back as he carefully shuts the door behind him.

The rest of the afternoon is delightful and Lucas has a great time, and they promise they'll come again very soon.

21

Margaret

I am among the crowd when she first arrives. No one sees me, for I have gone back to being invisible. I am good at this.

Everyone looks eagerly toward the gates. At last the procession comes into view. She arrives in a great party with many lovely ladies and knights to attend her. They have staged it well, white horses arrayed in blue and gold. It is an impressive spectacle. The cheering grows louder and louder. At last, the castle will have a mistress.

The procession goes on and on with carts and wagons loaded with possessions; oaken carved chests, reams of fine linen and silk and birdcages fluttering with birds. Finally the Lady Generys appears, resplendent in an open litter. Its wooden sides shine with the golden heraldic crest of a prancing stag. She is seated upon white-and-blue damask cushions trimmed with silken fringes so that when she alights she gives the impression of descending from a cloud. A hush creeps over us as we stand in the hot sun, watching her.

Two golden coils of braided hair frame her face and spots of high color bloom upon her cheeks. Her eyes are like bright sapphires that flash upon a noble's fingers. The sleeves of her kirtle are of violet cloth, and her cotehardie is vermilion and embroidered with golden thread. Even her cuffs and the buttons, which stream down her back, are edged in gold.

Lord August comes forward, magnificent in a velvet doublet and silken hose. The crowd resumes its cheering as he bends to kiss her hand. How far removed he is from me now. Like the sun in the sky. What did Landon once warn me? *But be careful, lest you come too close and burn up.* I laughed then. I thought I knew better.

She is Caradoc's daughter of the Sun, warm and radiant, and I am the daughter of the Moon, pale and bitter with envy.

I turn back to the brewery. After all, I only came to catch a glimpse, and there is work to be done.

The days leading up to the wedding are busy ones. Thomas is constantly full of news. At first, I think, he was wary of sharing stories, since he did not wish to wound me, but I encouraged him to tell me everything he can. I know much of her now, that she loves birds above all other things, that she is fond of taking her retinue to picnic in the castle gardens or the woods, that she is partial to apples, that she often sings sweet songs. They say that her touch can cool a fever and her smile is a gift. To have her look upon you with favor will bring blessings upon your family.

I have never hated anyone as much.

I have not been into the woods for an age and it takes some time for us to remember each other. Ever since Caradoc's announcement and Lady Generys's arrival, my heart has been hot and tight, but here among the trees, I can breathe a little easier.

The undergrowth rustles, and I hear the killer's warning.

When you turn red, I will come for you.

But not today.

A snatch of song grows and blossoms within me while I gather what I need.

Each and every pretty bloom
Will be laid upon her tomb.

It is a simple little melody, and I hum it over and over as my fingers crush and tear the fragrant leaves and roots.

Tonight, as I prepare our meal back at the cottage, I draw into myself and my memory. I think of Old Mother Briggs. The people in our village went to her with their troubles after my mother died though I do not believe she could have helped them. She certainly looked the part, bent with a crooked back, wild gray hair and rheumy eyes, the whites curdled yellow. I wonder what it would be like to have aches in my joints whenever the wind blows cold or the seasons change. I hunch over and hobble, crook my hands into claws. I practice voices low and croaking, high and wailing.

With a start, I realize that I am no longer alone. Thomas and Rudd have entered and are staring at me with round eyes and open mouths, dumbstruck. I have a sudden urge to laugh.

"What are you about? Are you unwell?" Thomas demands.

"It is nothing of importance, just a strange fancy I had."

He still looks uncertain.

"Come," I say, "and we shall eat."

We eat together these nights, Thomas and Rudd and I. Game is still brought to our cottage. Perhaps it is a way for Lord August to purchase our silence, but it is more likely someone in the castle has forgotten to give the order to stop. Regardless, we take advantage of it, and enjoy rabbit stew. I look at them as they eat, the small boy and the large man, and feel a rush of affection for both of them. I am sorry for what is to come, but it cannot be helped. Time will not stop for us, at least not in the way we would wish.

Thomas is full of chatter, as usual. It seems the Lady Generys will be taking a large party to picnic near the woods tomorrow.

"They will eat all manner of delicacies, larks' tongues and roast fawn and stewed curlew served with roses and quinces, and they will bring minstrels who will play tunes and tell stories till late in the day. Does that not sound fine?"

"It does." Only the finest for our Lady Generys.

"It is good that you are back." Thomas's glance is bashful. He directs his words to the bowl before him.

I smile and respond with a question: "Do you still see much of Father Martin?"

"Yes." Thomas looks at me sideways. "Fairly often."

"What is it about his friendship you so love? Or is it the way of the cloth that appeals to you?" My tone is light. His eyes dart up to my face, but I keep my expression earnest. I am gaining ground again, and I have no wish to stir this particular hornet's nest.

"No, I would not take the cloth." He shifts uncomfortably, for he knows what I have said before about the church, and continues. "Father Martin is gentle and kind, but I could not do it, no meat most days and all that prayer. I go to the chapel for the murals, for the wonderful colors. If I knew how to make them, I would not wish for anything else." His bearing straightens, and he lifts his head, caught up in the splendor of this vision . . .

I sigh. Still, it is good that the priest has an eye out for him and would be a friend to him. As for Rudd, he is a favorite of the blacksmith, who thinks of him as his own.

After we have finished our stew and Rudd has gone to bed, Thomas and I sit in the growing darkness. Only two low sunken candles splutter and hiss.

He half rises, begins to bid me good night, but I put my hand out and gesture for him to sit once more. It is time.

"Thomas? I need to speak with you."

He looks unhappy and searches my face for answers. Why would I wish to speak with him at so late an hour?

"You once told me that you and Rudd owed me your lives because of that night in the woods."

He nods.

"You told me that it was a debt you could never repay."

He nods again, apprehensive.

"Thomas, there is a way to repay it."

His eyes fill with hope, with fear. "How?" His voice is scarcely more than a whisper.

"There is an object I will need."

"What is it?"

"Lord August's brooch, the ring brooch he sometimes wears upon his cloak. He keeps it in his solar."

Thomas pales. "Why me?"

"Only you, with your cleverness and quick hands, can get it for me. I trust you."

"You mean because I was a thief?"

He flushes and rises to leave, but I have no time for his shame.

"Yes, because you were a thief."

"What if I am caught? The penalty for thievery is death. Especially theft from a lord."

I shake my head. "You will not be caught. You are nimble. Besides, there are such comings and goings before the wedding and so many new faces, you will manage it easily."

"And what must I do once I have taken it?"

I ignore his hard tone. He has accepted his task.

"You must bring me the brooch."

"But it will be missed!"

"No, for I shall return it."

"How?"

"That is my affair. You need only bring it to me."

"*Only*," he spits bitterly. "*Only*, you say. By asking me to do this, you put my life at risk, unless they feel merciful and merely cut off my hand."

"When you have done this, you will have repaid your debt," I remind him.

He shakes his head. "No! I cannot do it!"

"Why not?" *You owe me. You owe me your life and more besides.* He hears the anger behind my question and cringes.

"I know what you are capable of. You mean to kill him." His lip is trembling. Tears begin to flow. He will not look at me.

I laugh. "On the contrary!"

He starts, surprised by my laughter.

"Thomas." I reach over and place my hands upon his shoulders. I give him a small good-natured shake. "I mean to bless it! I give you my word. As long as he wears the brooch, he will be safe from all harm. I do it as a wedding gift."

"But"—he is bewildered—"I do not understand it. Why cannot you come to him yourself?"

Now I need no pretense. "I would, Thomas, but he does not wish to see me."

He shifts uncomfortably. "I had not thought of that."

"It is better for us to do it by stealth. No one need ever know, least of all Lord August."

He stares up at me, searching my features for any sign of deceit or hidden malice. "You swear unto God that this will not harm him?"

I will not swear to God, for God abandoned me long ago, but I do not say this aloud for fear of shocking him. I hesitate, think, and then tell him, "I swear it upon my mother's soul."

The dying candlelight flecks spidery shadows upon the walls. Inside there is no sound but the monotonous rhythm of Rudd's snores. Outside the wind drums its fingers along the thatch, and somewhere a dog barks once, twice.

Thomas nods slowly.

"So you will help?"

"I will help you."

I try to thank him, but he jerks himself out from under my grasp and leaves the room without a backward glance.

It is late the following day when he comes to me, pride and anger upon his face.

I am sitting at our table and hold out my hand eagerly. "Have you got it? Clever Thomas!"

He begins to hand it over, then halts. "What is this?" He stares at my palm, which is mottled from the juice of berries.

"It is nothing. Only stained with berry juice I made for a balm."

He hesitates still.

"Come," I urge him gently.

He places it into my hand.

Coiled and gleaming, it seems to shine even brighter against my darkened skin. A serpent devouring its own tail. I remember lying upon my lord's soft linen, sweat cooling and sated, my bare arm indolently stretching out, brushing its stippled surface with my fingertips.

"Beautiful, is it not?"

"I hate it."

I am jolted back to the here and now surprised at his vehemence. "At least your debt is paid." I soothe.

"I did not act to repay a debt." His response is a growl. His head comes up, his face aflame, his eyes blazing.

"No?"

"No. I did it for a sister."

I am speechless.

His words come in a rush. "I did it because you asked me to. There is no talk of debt with one of your own kin!" He bursts into angry tears.

"Thomas—"

But he turns and runs.

I stare after him but do not try to follow. I have been blinded to his misery by my own. Still, there is much to do before nightfall.

I hear the party before I see them. Their light and girlish talk, their laughter. The laughter of those who do not know heartbreak, who have not felt hunger. They are alone, save for the minstrels who play alongside them and a few lucky guards to have been chosen for so pleasant a task.

The ladies recline upon soft cloths and velvet cushions, nibble at dates and figs and candied fruits. They braid one another's hair with flowers. I stand in the ragged shade of the trees, watching them. I think of my own village and of the women there. I used to wonder what my life would have been like if I had been highborn, and for a brief while I had a glimpse, but there is no use wondering now.

I watch her. She holds herself with none of the superiority her station demands, yet I would know her at once. She has a certain grace that the others lack. A finesse. I have faith that she will always set a good example for her ladies.

I am counting on it.

I hobble out of the shadows. Her ladies shriek and start when they see me, my visage darkened with the berry juice and etched with charcoal lines. I shuffle forward, contorted as though I am bent with age. My hair is a bird's nest of twigs and leaves and whitened with flour. I did a fair swap with Brun the Beggar Wife, who got the much better end of the bargain, for I am now clothed in her foul-smelling, pitiful rags and she has one of my good work dresses.

I pull the spirit of Old Mother Briggs around me like a cloak, her lame gait, her stiff clawed hand. I have practiced her voice, and now mine caws and croaks like an old bird.

"May I see the one among you who is to be married to his lordship? For I have heard many tales of her beauty and honor, and wish to pay my respects."

My disguise works almost too well, and I am fearful they will all flee. The guards stiffen, and one moves forward, angry that the peace of the day has been disturbed. He is proud and tall, and so he should be, for he is captain of the castle guards.

"Be off with you, hag!" he snaps. "She'll not see you!"

But Lady Generys rises, holding out her lily-white hand. She is imperious, annoyed at being told what to do. "I pray you would not speak for me, good sir." Her tone is cool, measured. "Come nearer," she bids me.

I hide a smile. I am sure this is more to goad the captain than because she desires my company. She would have done better to heed him.

"Oh, thank you, my lady. You are as beautiful as you are kind, and as kind as you are beautiful, just as they say."

She nods her thanks and smiles, wishing her courtesy to inspire her ladies, who draw a little closer, although they are still as skittish as mares.

Now is the time for me to act, before the fancy to be bold leaves her. "I wish to speak with you in private, your ladyship, for I would like to give you a blessing for your marriage."

Sure enough, her ladies' voices rise in protest. She hesitates, but again the captain aids my course.

"She will do no such thing!" He has turned puce, so irked is he by my impudence.

Lady Generys tosses her head, and her cheeks flush a little. "Sir, do not send this lady away without my order. Clearly she means me no harm." She gathers her skirts about her. Even this small action is graceful. "Come!"

It is an impetuous decision, one she may regret if I give her any time, but I do not. I shuffle toward her, proclamations of thanks and humility upon my lips.

"My lady, I *must* protest—"

"We will not go far," she tells him, "unless you feel that your men are unable to defend me against the goodwill of an old woman."

She has pricked him to the quick. His ears glow red as a furnace with fury, but he stands down.

We wander a little way into the coolness of the woods. The eyes of the party and the guards burn into my back. I know I do not have much time.

"I thank you, my lady, for your graciousness. For your kindness to an old woman."

She inclines her head, although there is no smile upon her lips now that her audience is gone. In fact, she looks a little fearful.

"I would like to give you a gift for your wedding day, which I hear is close at hand." I draw out a small parcel of grubby cloth.

"You are very kind, but I cannot accept it." She tries not to flinch back, her mouth a moue of disgust.

I step forward, for I dare not let this moment slip away. "The knowing of this has been passed down to me from my mother, and from her mother before her, and back through till there is no re-membrance. She is from a Traveler family, and this is an ancient recipe that her folk have used time and time again. I wish to make a gift of it to you, for it will grant you sons."

"Sons?" Her eyes are bright. I have her attention now.

"Yes, if you will do exactly as I say. When you are quite alone upon your wedding night, but before you have lain together, mix this into a cup of wine or ale and repeat the words that I am about to tell you, and then drink."

"And I shall bear sons?" She has moved closer to me, revulsion forgotten.

"Aye. With this you will bear three sons directly, all comely of face and form and noble of spirit and deed."

"Three!" She is transfixed by her fortune.

"Yes, a trinity. Only you must not share this. Tell no one, for this must be done in secret." I smile with what I hope is sympathy. "Men do not always understand these things, do they? And if your ladies knew, they would all clamor for the herbs, or burn with jealousy!" She inclines her head. I have her in the palm of my hand. For three glorious sons, what would any lady not agree to? Still, I must make absolutely sure that she does not tell Lord August. "And if Lord de Villias should find out, he might claim witchcraft. The church is quick to punish those who use it."

This sobers her a little, and I can see each thought passing across her face.

Witchcraft is a dire accusation. But this is not witchcraft, not really. Only a wedding gift given to her by a sweet-natured old lady, and if it works, it would be incredible good fortune, but even if it does not, surely there's no harm in trying.

I lean forward to whisper in her ear. All around us, the forest seems to hush.

When I draw back, she is staring at me. For a moment I am wary. What if my voice lost some of its age as I whispered? But then I see that her eyes are wide not with fear but with dreams. The triumph of having three sons floods her with pleasure.

She hesitates, then begins, "I thank you for this with all my heart. If you would return to the castle later, I will show my gratitude."

For a moment, my heart softens. She wants to show her gratitude, but will not insult me by offering charity. She is so young, so lovely, so truly gentle. And then I think of him.

I look again at this beautiful girl, who has never known want nor pain nor fear nor suffering of any kind. This girl who would take him as her right without a thought of who may have been discarded to make way for her, who is as pretty and void of thought as the birds she loves so well.

"I will take no payment," I reply in my cracked, brittle voice. "If I have given you pleasure it is reward enough for me."

At this she beams sweetly, and turns back into the sunlight. She floats away to her group, having concealed the package from view within the folds of her dress. I hear her murmuring the words to herself, making sure of them.

> *Song to song,*
> *Skin to skin,*
> *Lip to cup,*
> *Heart to wing.*
> *Bone to bone,*
> *Day to night,*
> *Blood to blood,*
> *Wish take flight.*

I grin in the shadows. She sings like a lark. It will do very well indeed.

22

Katherine

"So, Katherine, how did you meet Matthew?"

That's the English for you, she notes. *They don't ask what you do for a living, or where you live, or what you pay in rent.* On the whole she enjoys this approach. It's more challenging. She likes to make an interesting detective game of it, listening for casual clues in conversation to find out what a person does. How long will she take to work it out? So far she's deduced that Ben is a lawyer and Gunther, an elegant German, is in finance. She still has Jane and William and Anna to go.

These are all the guests at Matthew and John's dinner party. Anna and Ben are a slightly younger couple; Jane and William, older and comfortable in their marriage; and Gunther—

"Zolo." He smiles. "I'm afraid Kenneth haz a cold."

And Katherine and Sael, the Americans.

This is exactly what Katherine wants: to sit at a large mahogany candlelit dinner table, beautifully set with Derby china and white majolica roses in Flemish glass; to sip Cabernet, or water in her case, from crystal glasses; to be one half of an acknowledged relationship, except . . . except she's not, because Sael has excused himself. Sael is on the phone again.

Katherine pushes back her ivory-lacquered dining chair to go into the kitchen, where Matthew reigns supremely. Ostensibly to help out, but really to have a quick gossip.

She finds him standing under a stone arched fireplace that houses a sleek Aga range. He looks up from the dish of zabaglione he's fiddling with. "My God, Katherine, why didn't you mention that you're living with a film star?"

"What?"

"Don't play coy. Sael! My jaw hit the floor. Do you think we could persuade him to change sides?"

"Honey, if you can get him off his phone for two seconds, you can do what you want."

"Hmmm, now that might be a serious challenge. So what do you think of everyone?"

"Honestly?"

"*Obviously.*"

"They're lovely."

"I know, so boring to have such lovely friends. I apologize. Wish you could have met Kenneth, though, he's darling and a little bit of a terror, always gives the evening some spice. Without him Gunther is a little suspect."

Over her zabaglione, Jane turns to Katherine with eager eyes. "So how many months are you?" She's one of those women who like to talk pregnancy.

Katherine doesn't hesitate. "I'm in my second trimester." She's through with counting weeks.

"Oh, that's a good one."

"So I hear."

"How has it been?"

"Not bad."

"With me, I was sick for almost the entire time—that was my first one. My second, I was good after the first trimester. I mean, good minus all the horrible symptoms."

"Yes."

"Still, once you hold them in your arms, you know it was all worth it."

"So they tell me."

Katherine's monosyllabic answers and stiff body language aren't stemming Jane's flow of questions. Time to go on the attack. She takes a deep breath, turns toward her inquisitor, and forces her lips upward into a bright, plastic smile.

"How do you know John and Matthew?"

Jane falters for a moment at the abrupt change of subject, but rallies admirably. "Oh, I'm John's cousin! We practically grew up together."

"How nice!" Katherine's voice grows considerably warmer.

"Yes," Jane says, and seems about to add some remark when Ben's voice rings out, pulling them both into his story whether they want to be pulled or not. Ben is a little pudgy, but charismatic. He's a bit tipsy, and he clearly loves to be in the spotlight.

"The oddest thing happened to me the other day. I was waiting for the Tube when this gorgeous woman starts flirting with me."

"That *is* odd." Matthew winks at Anna.

"I congratulated myself on choosing my pink tie that morning. I'm telling you, babe, you can't go wrong in pink. I'm also totally gobsmacked because she's gorgeous. But let's face it"—he turns to Anna—"how drunk did you have to be to end up with me?"

"Incredibly drunk," Anna deadpans. "My parents still want to know what happened."

"So, I'm wondering what the hell is going on, but it starts off casually. I can't even remember, it graduated into the weather, the agony of Tube delays, the film advertised by the poster across the track."

"My lord!" William interjects. "How long were you waiting for the train?"

Everyone laughs. Sael comes back into the dining room, sits down by Katherine's side.

Ben refuses to be derailed. "Not long, but that's the thing, she was so smooth! And then she suddenly mentions something like, 'As they say in chapter two, verse eight,' and then she blushes and gives me this fabulous little smile, and I say, 'I'm sorry, *what*?' And *then* she says, 'If you ever wanted to come and see what a meeting is like, here's my card,' and she gives it to me and on the front are two letters, *H* and *T*, and on the back it says, 'Heaven's True.' And I realize that she's an *evangelist*. A gorgeous one, but still, I'm being accosted by an evangelist from Heaven's True!"

"Heaven's True?" Gunther gives a low whistle. "Zey're here in the UK? From vhat I've read about zem, zey zeem zo *American*. From the *Zouth*. Born-again Baptist." He turns to Katherine and Sael. "Of course, no offense to our friends here." He smirks in a way that she doesn't like, with practiced creases at the corners of his eyes.

Sael smiles back pleasantly. "No offence taken, Gunther, but you are totally going to hell."

There's a beat before the table realizes that yes, the American is joking, and then they laugh.

It's William who says, "Well, after all, that pilot was Russian, so I guess they've been getting to everyone."

Everyone is silent after that, thinking about the pilot who flew a plane full of passengers into a mountain.

The photographs of his apartment had been chilling. The walls plastered with copies of the Heaven's True manifesto, and the numbers 22:12 painted over and over on this makeshift wallpaper.

It was a verse from the Book of Revelation: "Look, I am coming soon! My reward is with me, and I will give to each person according to what they have done." The Heaven's True movement proclaimed him a hero. The media had gone berserk.

"So, Ben, what happened with the hot evangelist?" Katherine asks, trying to get the conversation back to a safer place.

Matthew looks at her gratefully.

"I said, 'Well, I'll tell my husband about it.'" Ben turns to Anna. "Sorry, my love, but I thought that would give her a jolt at least."

"Vat did she do?" Gunther leans forward.

"She didn't even blink, that was the thing. She just said, 'Yes, you should bring him along.'"

"Ugh, you'd think at least that would deter them." This is from Jane.

"Yes, but these zealots are particularly nasty. Imagine some handsome man flirting with you, trying to get his paws on *your* soul."

"Unlike me, who just wants you for your sexy body," Anna retorts.

Ben's mind, however, is already somewhere else. "When did they start gaining prominence again?"

Sael glances at Katherine. He knows just as well as she does where this is going.

But it's William, who seems to be the elected foot-in-mouth man of the night, who once again answers. "It was during that whole thing in the States with that serial killer, wasn't it—what was his name?" A look of surprise and pain crosses his face. "Ow!"

Katherine has to suppress a laugh. Jane has clearly kicked him on the ankle.

She guesses he didn't recognize her, or maybe he really doesn't remember that she was involved. Which is a gift. It's nice not to be known, or to have people determinedly pretend not to know you.

"It's all right," she says to Jane, then turns to William. "You're right. They started gaining prominence during the summer of the Sickle Man, particularly in Manhattan."

There's another weighted pause now while everyone desperately searches for another topic of conversation. William still looks a little confused. Katherine feels bad for him. She hopes that he'll only learn the full story later, after she and Sael are gone.

John comes to the rescue. "Anna, how's your book coming along? Or is that a truly terrible question to ask?"

"The book isn't and the question is, you bastard."

But Katherine can see she doesn't mind being asked, and the table collectively remembers to breathe. They have been saved.

"Anna is working on her third book," John informs them.

"Wow." Sael is genuinely impressed.

"Don't be fooled, it's hideously academic."

"What's your field?" Katherine is curious.

"Celtic mythology." She says this as easily as someone might say, *I like to bake cookies.*

"Cool!" Katherine says, then blushes as Anna turns to her. "I'm sorry, that sounded lame, but I mean, I really *do* think it's cool."

"Our Katherine is becoming quite the history buff lately!" Matthew adds.

Anna looks gratified. "It is actually cool. I get to write about various gods, but translating Gaulish is a bit of a blow."

"You could almost say it's a bit 'Gauling'! Whaa, whaa, whaa."

They can tell that Ben has made this joke before, and it earns him an eye roll from his wife before she continues.

"Anyway, you have no right to ask me such questions, John, when a little fairy told me that you too have a book in the works."

"Where is that little fairy? I'm going to kill him!"

Matthew sticks his head around the doorway and grins impishly. "He's here, and don't you dare!"

"That's marvelous, John!" Jane is endearingly enthusiastic.

"We'll see, it's early days still."

"I've always loved your translations." Anna seems thrilled.

"Well, you won't believe this one! It's is based on some newly discovered material by a medieval English priest, written in"—John pauses for dramatic effect—"*vernacular* English!"

His effect is not lost on Anna, who gives a little gasp of excitement. Katherine thinks she sees Ben roll his eyes.

"John calls him the dark priest," Matthew announces.

John frowns at him.

"Oh, sorry, darling, was that a secret?"

"The dark priest! Sounds intriguing." William is eager to make amends for his earlier gaffes.

"Really, I only say 'dark' as in unknown, unrevealed."

Williams shakes his head vigorously. "Rubbish! It draws up lovely images of evil and the occult."

John grins. "That too."

"Sellout." Matthew reaches over to touch John's cheek.

Their love is so clear and so strong that it makes Katherine's throat hurt. She glances at Sael, but he's again staring at the screen of his phone.

Matthew turns to her. "But I'm cross with you! Why didn't you bring the delicious Lucas? Most darling little boy."

Anna is stunned "That's an amazing thing for Matthew to say. He hates children."

"I do not! I *adore* little children, and John and I would fill the house with them if only I wasn't allergic to all except Lucas." He realizes what he's just said and turns to Jane. "And obviously, all your brood."

"Of course," she says wryly.

Now it's Sael who saves the conversation. "Katherine was all set to bring him, but our housekeeper said she'd look after him."

"Your housekeeper?" Katherine wonders if there's a hint of judgment in Jane's voice.

"Mrs. B. Very formidable, but with a real soft spot for Lucas."

"And it would have been no fun for him to fall asleep here, and then have to wake up and take a train ride late at night," Katherine adds, but she's thinking about the possessive way Mrs. B looks at him, the almost proprietary way she held his hand as she and Sael had left.

After the zabaglione, they all retire to the drawing room, spreading out on the vintage leather chairs or curling up on the cushy couches with their tasseled pillows.

Katherine sips her coffee and lets her eyes wander around the room, admiring the glossy black piano in one corner and the large six-paneled Chinese coromandel screen of a white cherry tree in full bloom against a golden background. The wallpaper is a textured red, and heavy green silk curtains flank the windows. Within the grandeur of the room Matthew's quirky humor is still apparent.

Katherine grins when she sees a Royal Doulton shepherdess jostling for prominence with a small plastic T-Rex on the mantel above the marble fireplace.

She is content to lounge back, catching drifts of others' conversations.

"It's been ages." Anna leans forward to John.

"Too long," he agrees.

"But you were quite ill. That ongoing flu really walloped you, I hear."

"My flu . . ." John looks thoughtful. "Yes, it did." He grins. "But I'm better now."

"You look better. I have to say, you look far better than I've seen you look for ages." Anna is earnest, only half joking.

He laughs. "Did I look that bad?"

"No, but now you're practically glowing with health!"

Katherine thinks about the day she first saw John, and how thin she'd thought he was. She agrees with Anna. He *does* seem to glow.

"In fact I even mentioned to Matthew the potential of doing some sort of exercise in the morning."

Anna gasps theatrically. "And what did he say?"

"He threatened divorce or murder."

"I can't say I blame him."

"John!" Matthew, who has been talking to Gunther, leans over. "Have you shown Anna what I got you for your birthday?"

"No, I haven't."

"Why not? What's the use of getting you expensive presents if you refuse to show off?"

"I thought it was for my pleasure?"

"Well, obviously not."

John turns to Anna. "Actually he's right. It's just up your street. And Katherine's too. She loves old things."

"Oh no, I don't want to intrude." She would rather stay in this lovely room, propped up by pillows, indulging in eavesdropping.

"Nonsense! I want to hear her American 'ooh' of awe." Matthew is firm.

"Let's all go and see it," Ben suggests restlessly. *Can't be left out for a moment, can you*, Katherine thinks with some irritation.

Together they troop out into the hall and up the staircase to John's study, which is considerably neater tonight. He takes the lead, but stops at one of the desks and indicates they should cluster around a brown leather case.

"Very dramatic."

"Please tell me it's a cursed mummy's paw!" William sounds half hopeful.

"That's *monkey's* paw." Jane sighs.

"A something's paw which glows when treasure is near, or helps you curse your enemies!" William waves his hand at her, dismissing semantics.

"You're all close." John slowly opens the box. His expression is both sardonic and proud.

They peer in at a knife with a reddish patina.

I don't like it, Katherine thinks.

"Oh my God." Anna sighs with longing.

"Iron," John says, as if answering her question before she asked it.

"May I?" Anna is already reaching out.

He nods, and she bends over it in rapture.

"Oooh," she coos, as if it were an exquisite jewel. "Just look at that triskele."

"The what?" Ben eyes his wife with exasperated affection.

"That triple spiral." She indicates the three interwoven circles carved into the iron, spanning the hilt. "Oh, John, it's gorgeous!"

"What does that mean?"

Anna launches into full academic mode. "A triskele is a symbol depicted in many ancient cultures, from coins to Greek warriors' armor, but of course because it was found carved on a passage tomb at Newgrange, most people associate it with the Celts.

"Oh, of *course*."

Anna doesn't seem to hear Ben's sarcasm. She's on a roll.

"It had, or has, massive symbolic ties with the triple goddess.

"The what?" Katherine swallows hard; her throat feels tight.

"The Maiden, Mother, and Crone." Their titles trip off Anna's tongue. She's totally in her element.

"What a way to sum up the female experience!" William tries for a lighter tone, but Jane frowns at him as Anna continues, oblivious.

"And as Christianity consumed the Celtic culture, it began to represent the Holy Trinity, but obviously this knife dates far earlier. I mean it's a pervading ornament in the Book of Kells. *And* then there's the whole theory that it ties in with the nine months of a woman's pregnancy."

"Ah, Katherine! Now you can feel part of ze action," Gunther says.

"I don't understand." A tightening sensation closes around Katherine's throat. Her skin prickles with what feels like tiny ants.

"Well, there's a theory that each spiral represents three months as the sun makes its journey . . ." Anna stops. "It's all a bit complicated." She takes in the silence of the room. "I didn't mean to go on like that! It's stunning. Wherever did you find it, Matthew? It looks like it should be in a museum."

"My dealer, would that he dealt in nice normal things, like drugs."

Suddenly Katherine can't breathe. She's choking. She needs to get out of there, away from the knife, the dirty reddish hue so much like crusted blood. She doesn't understand why they aren't all sick to their stomachs.

Luckily, everyone seems to be admiring it, so she is able to disappear from the room unnoticed. In the corridor, she glances down to the right and heads toward the first door she sees, which opens into a darkened room.

Once her eyes adjust, it turns out to be Matthew and John's bedroom. She heaves herself up onto the edge of their four-poster bed, and reaches under her collar to feel the tiny links of the chain on which the ring brooch is strung. She often forgets she's wearing it, it's always under her shirts or a scarf anyway, but it seems to have become a part of her even to the extent that she keeps it on in the shower sometimes. If anyone found out they'd think she was crazy, wearing such a valuable antique in the shower. Not that she's showering as much these days. Katherine must be becoming

English, such is her love of baths. *Not too hot*, Dr. Edwards told her, so she tries to keep them temperate, but baths feel good. Just soaking, floating, zoning out. She's been putting in lavender, rose water. It smells so beautiful, so strangely familiar.

Now she lets her fingertips ride over the links, and the tightness loosens, the heat lessens.

"Are you all right?" Jane peers in through the dimness.

"Oh yes!" Katherine looks up, feeling guilty. "You gave me a start!

"Tired?"

Not tired, she reflects. *I'm never tired these days.* "Yes, I guess so." The easiest answer.

"I remember that when I was pregnant, in my second trimester I would be full of all this energy, and then I would suddenly feel these crashing waves of exhaustion and have to pass out."

"That's about it." Katherine tries to smile as naturally as possible. *Please go away*, she prays.

"Oh! That's so pretty." Jane is looking at her necklace.

"Thanks." She's let her scarf slip, and the ring brooch is glittering on her chest in the light coming in through the open door. Katherine desperately wants to shove it back under her shirt, but Jane comes toward her.

"I didn't see this before. Is it an antique?"

"Sael got it for me . . . a while ago." *Back off*, she thinks, *back off now, you nosy bitch.*

Jane is very close. She reaches out. "Could I see it?"

She is so near that Katherine can see her eye shadow, a faint bruised mouse color with a tiny sheen of glitter. Her lipstick is a bit smudged at the corners of her mouth, and there's a tiny speck of it on one of her front teeth. Katherine looks at her pores, which gape wide, her left eyebrow with its two stray hairs below the main brow line. She can smell the wine on Jane's breath, and the faint chemicals of her perfume. She closes her eyes . . .

Katherine wakes with a start. *I'm in a car. How did I get in a car?* she wonders. Outside the window, night stretches out black and smooth and endless. In the front seat, the driver's shoulders, square and heavy, are silhouetted in the dashboard's glow.

"Sael?"

He looks up, the light from his phone screen briefly illuminating his face. "Yeah?"

She stares at him, dazed.

"You okay?" he asks.

"Fine. Yes. Sorry." She runs her hand along the leather interior, gazes at Sael's profile, at the darkness speeding by her window. "I guess I fell asleep."

"That's okay, it's late."

"You didn't want to take the train?"

He shoots her a puzzled look. "It just seemed easier than the train. I did ask you, and you seemed fine with it."

"But isn't—" She glances toward the driver and lowers her voice. "Isn't this going to be insanely expensive?"

Sael snorts, amused. "I'll manage, don't worry." He pauses. "Sorry I had to be on my phone so much tonight."

"No worries. Did you have any fun at all?"

"Sure. They're nice guys, good people."

"Yeah, I had a feeling you'd like them." Katherine has to admit to feeling pleased—then again, who wouldn't like Matthew and John?

"Gunther was kind of a dick, a bit Eurotrash."

"Right."

"But they were cool." He goes back to his screen. "Although that woman was kind of weird toward the end."

"Which woman?"

"What's her name again? Jane?"

"Yeah? Why?"

"When we were saying good-bye, she seemed kind of, I don't

know, *freaked out*. Sort of squirrely. She wasn't making eye contact with anyone. Muttering."

"Weird," Katherine agrees, but she says it mechanically. Jane was super annoying, wouldn't take the hint to shut up all evening long.

The car speeds through the darkness. She leans back.

She doesn't remember saying good-bye, or leaving, or *anything* much after they'd all trotted upstairs to check out that rancid dagger. But they're driving home, so it must have happened. All she knows is that she's exhausted.

It will probably come to me tomorrow, she thinks. Then she closes her eyes and is asleep once more.

23

Margaret

I rise before midnight. Thomas and Rudd are asleep, so I must move quietly. It would not do to wake them. I dress and gather up the pouch of herbs I will need. I take the brooch.

The moon is full and red, a blood moon. It will serve my purpose well. I walk silently, but I am alone. No one will disturb me, no one wants to venture out tonight. No one wishes to look upon a blood moon, lest it bring them ill fortune.

I slip along the path past the keep, another shadow in the night. I stay close to the stone walls, and the guards do not see me. Soon I reach the castle garden with its great hazelnut tree. My mother taught me about hazelnut trees, old and powerful, their roots drawing wisdom from the earth. I stand under its low sloping branches and take a moment to say farewell to the one who grows within me.

What could my child have become? My babe, my small one, my sweetling. Never to be rocked and crooned to, cossetted and coddled. This baby will never know what it is to be kissed in plump creases, what it is to grasp a finger with a tiny hand, what it is to suckle, to smile. I will never know what it is to have a person who loves me full in his own right. Who loves me regardless of my rank, or my nature; who loves me because I am his mother. My beautiful child, never to feel the sun upon his face or the wind or the rain, or to talk and laugh and taste and drink, to rise taller than me and care for me when I am old. Never will he know my love, fierce and tender and all-consuming. Never, never, never.

I am rocking the empty cloak back and forth and back and forth.

I, who never weep, am weeping.

With his knife, he comes for us, but he will never have you. Never, never, never.

I concentrate upon the cold curl of the ring brooch in my palm. I must place myself, my soul, within it. Safe there I will abide, though it may be forever. I purse my lips, and as I exhale the serpent's coils unfurl; the head rises; the reptile eyes, tiny jewels, glint at my own. I stab it into the flesh of my thumb. A single drop of blood wells up, slides down its length.

Take me, take the whole of me, into you, into you.
Take me, and take all of me, blood and bone and soul.

The ring brooch pulls, pulses as a heart must do, and something deep inside me lets go. I scream in agony. It glows. It burns and burns like a rod of iron from the fire, and yet I wrap my fingers around it. I do not let go. I sink down upon my knees as something rips away. I feel a trickle of blood between my thighs. Good-bye, my love, good-bye, my own.

Good-bye to me.

What am I?

I am a daughter. I see my mother's laughing face as she whirls me around, her warm hand clasping mine. The pained eyes of my father, his stammering demands.

I am an alewife. The smell of the yeast. The fine golden-brown barley. I ache from stirring, a drop of sweat beading down my forehead and nose. The clank of tankards, the first sip, its mellow tang, the foam.

I am a lover. Close, his lips upon my lips, his hands thrust deep within my hair. "I will have you, I will."

I am a savior. Standing, proud, as the wolves come and take their revenge. Thomas, his tears. "I did it for a sister."

I am an enemy. Of the jeering boy who threw the stone; of the bandit leader with his useless curses; of my rival, though she knows it not. Her guileless blue eyes look into my own.

I am this, I am more, I am less . . .

I am Margaret.

Would you still be willing if it cost you your soul? Would you?

I would.

I grip the brooch tightly, I am hard, I am a diamond, I am silver. I glint bright in the blood moon's light. I will bear this and any pain, for after this night nothing will hurt me again.

Hold me, take me, I come willing and true, take me, and make me unto you.

And then—

—it is done.

I stand.

I am light. I am lighter than air, than a feather, than a hollowed bone. All guilt is gone; gone is my anguish, my doubt, my despair. I could fly. Only my clothes weigh me down. I step out of my dress, which pools around my ankles. Yes, that is better by far.

The night breeze skims my skin. I bathe in the blood moon's light. I begin to sway and then to dance. I am free. I am free.

The captain of the guards struts along the perimeter. So arrogant, so proud of his power. He will serve my purpose well.

Blood to blood,
Vein to vein.
Keep my love
From fire or flame,
Or wind or rain,
Till we are back
As one
Again.

He comes now, the fool. Fearful, but duty-bound. I savor his fear. He is right to be afraid.

I smile and he stops, struck by my naked skin in the moonlight, my dark and curling hair. Look at him, mustering up the courage to ask me my business.

He begins to speak.

"Behold!" I open my palms as the serpent upon the brooch glitters and gleams and writhes.

He stares and stares. His stupid mouth hangs open. I laugh, for it is a great sport to see. I grasp his rough hand and lead him, dazed but willing, underneath the hazelnut tree. I take pleasure in his fumbling, his hot breath upon my neck, his groping, clumsy hands. I straddle him as easily as my pretty roan mare, and when I see the whites of his eyes I know he has never known such bliss.

As for me, it is but a diversion. I ride him hard and fast and take my own satisfaction. I do not care if he is sated. And then I rise from him and command him to stand. He does, naked and lumbering, his sex still twitching in hope. He gazes at me, beseeching.

"Kneel," I say.

Now a captain of the guard kneels naked in the dirt before the castle alewife.

"Kiss my feet," I croon. "Lick them clean."

And he covers my dirty toes with his besotted lips, lapping at each one as if this were a delectable feast. I know full well he would do anything I desire. For a moment I am tempted to tell him to slit his own pathetic throat, but it passes. I need him to deliver my gift.

"Get up," I tell him. I hand him the ring brooch, which is now keeper of my soul, my being. "You will return this to Lord August early on the morrow. Easy enough to do in the ensuing chaos of the wedding-day preparations. If he has not noticed its absence, you will return it to his bedchamber and slip away. If he has, and questions you or your men, then you will tell him you found it in a corner of the Great Hall or invent some other story, any story, only make sure he has it back. If I do not see it shining upon his breast tomorrow, it will go ill for you."

He nods his head, his eyes begging for another caress.

"Now be off, fool. And cover yourself." I am a little regretful to dismiss him thus. It would give me such pleasure to make him further writhe with shame, burn with humiliation, but I need him focused upon his task.

After he is gone, I lift up my face to the moon, stretch out my arms, and sigh. Reluctantly, I begin to dress. I do wish he could have killed himself, but he'll be dead soon enough.

It is almost time.

24

Katherine

They're surrounded by an ocean of small pink dresses when Niamh gets light-headed.

"Honestly, I'm surprised you didn't have a reaction sooner," Katherine says. "Are you all right?"

"I'll be fine in a moment, just have to sit down."

"Come on." Katherine leads Niamh to one of the rocking chairs and pushes her gently into it. "Here. You know, we're lucky we're not in the States at the moment. There would probably be signs up saying, 'Warning! Excessive cuteness may cause adverse reactions.'" She stops talking and looks down at her friend with concern. "Do you need some water?"

"That would be grand."

"I'll find some."

"I have my water bottle with me." Niamh motions to her bag on the floor.

"Okay." Katherine digs around and passes her the bottle. "Drink up."

"Jesus, you're bossy!"

"That's why you like me."

Katherine and Niamh have given themselves a day of maternity shopping. Clothes for them and stuff for the babies to come. So far they have tried on some truly hideous dresses.

"We'll be just in time for summer!" Niamh had said, practically swimming in yards of loose denim.

"Good Lord."

"Not fetching?" She batted her eyes coquettishly at Katherine and struck a pose.

"Only a friend can get you through the horror of maternity jeans, though I have a feeling that these suckers are going to come in useful."

"And I love the no-fly-or-buttons part, easy access." Niamh winked. "For a shag or a piss, whip these off in no time!"

The saleswoman must hate us, Katherine had thought. *We're acting like wise-cracking, loud bitches of the crudest variety. Too bad for her we have money. I used to hate people like us.*

It was her turn in the fitting room. She studied herself in the full-length mirror, an activity she usually avoids these days. Her hair has grown longer. She's heard that this is normal in pregnancy, but *this* much longer and *this* much darker? It doesn't look bad, just . . . different. Unlike her.

Her skin looks great, not a blemish, although it's paler, though that may be because the English sun has yet to make a true appearance. She definitely scores there—even the small mole just above her right collarbone has disappeared. She stared at the spot it used to be. Where did it go? And it's not just the mole. She leaned in closer, searched again for the tiny triangle on the left side of her forehead, from when she got chickenpox as an eight-year-old. Reading a book, rubbing at her spotted face absentmindedly—

there had been a little plop as the scab fell onto the open page. She had grown used to the scar, even secretly liked it. "You know," her dad had told her once, "if you get up to heaven and you don't have enough scars, the angels send you back." But it has definitely vanished. She's heard that pregnant women's skin often glows, helped by the extra blood coursing through their bodies and any amount of amazing hormones, but disappearing moles and *scars*?

She stepped back from the mirror. Her belly is rounded, but she hasn't put on a ton of weight. Her breasts are fuller, and her nipples are a deeper plum color, but that wasn't the issue. *It's my face*, she decided.

But what *is* it about her face that looks so different? It is a little less round, more oval, a narrower chin. How could that be? Her hazel eyes seem browner. *It's the light in here*, she told herself. *They always have the shittiest lighting in fitting rooms.* She pressed her palms against her reflection's palms, cool and smooth. She wondered why she would expect it to feel different. It was a mirror after all. Touching her forehead against the glass, still pushing her palms against it, she imagined the fingers on the other side curling through and taking hold of her own.

"Hello," she whispered.

"Katherine?" Niamh was on the other side of the door. "Katherine, you ready?"

"Five minutes."

Katherine pulled on her jeans and bellyband, her bra and shirt and sweater, and stepped into her boots.

"Good-bye," she murmured, but she left quickly, just in case anyone decided to wish her good-bye back.

Outside Niamh was impatiently rubbing the small of her back.

"Sorry, I guess I was just—"

"Navel gazing?"

"Something like that." She blinked and tried to keep a neutral face as they teetered to the front with armfuls of clothes.

They should have called it a day, but they had to go to Cuddles. The names of all the mother-and-baby stores are a killer. Eggs. Giggles. Booboo.

Cuddles is overwhelming. No wonder Niamh feels light-headed. Five floors, nearly four thousand square feet. Enough giraffes named Sophie to start a menagerie. An entire area dedicated to wipes, aloe versus muslin.

"Our Sleep section is huge. Not that they ever *do* sleep," laughs a saleslady, who must think she's being funny.

Niamh had been fine at first, until she wasn't. "Just light-headed," she tells Katherine, but her face is pale.

Katherine can see beads of sweat on her forehead. "Maybe we should call it a day?"

"Oh." Niamh clutches the drained water bottle, genuinely disappointed. "Without getting anything?"

"Yeah, we'll come back. Cuddles isn't going anywhere. Unfortunately."

Niamh smiles. "Oh, go *on*, yez big softy. Don't pretend you don't love it."

"Okay, I just love Cuddles, I love it so damn much! Now let's go. You okay to walk?"

"I'm fine, honestly."

But Katherine takes it slow, and Niamh is leaning on her more heavily than either of them wants to admit. "Let's drop you at home and put your feet up. Shopping can take a lot out of you, even when you're not pregnant. We'll grab a cab."

"But the day is so nice, I wanted to walk!"

"Just this once, let's be lazy bitches," Katherine jokes. She feels more anxious than she's letting on.

It's not a long ride, and soon they're back in the safe, chic streets of their la-di-da neighborhood, where Katherine still feels like a stranger.

"I'm not an invalid," Niamh grumbles when Katherine offers her an arm going up the steps.

"You're pregnant and therefore a womanly miracle."

Niamh giggles, then admits, "I could do with some tea."

"Sit on the couch, and I'll bring you some water and put the kettle on." Katherine has accepted that this is the English solution to all problems.

"Are you me mam?"

"Yes, I am. This has all been an elaborate plot."

"Speaking of, how's your mam taking it? Is she excited about being a gran?"

"Yes, she's thrilled." But it's a lie. The truth is that Katherine hasn't told her. "Yours?"

"Over the moon, but driving me crazy. She keeps calling and giving advice and asking me how I'm doing every five minutes and boasting to her friends, and telling me what they say and all about their grandchildren. Then again, what's new?"

"I know, right?" She disappears into Niamh's kitchen. The layouts of their houses are similar, but the interiors are nothing alike. She could tell herself that Niamh has just been here longer, but she knows that isn't really the case.

There's a sterility about Sael and Katherine's place, an aggressive cleanliness that even a five-year-old's mess can't dispel. It's ludicrous to think of a baby crawling over the pristine cream couches or mashing banana on the smooth white countertops of the kitchen surfaces.

In Niamh's home there's a thread of warmth and humor echoed in the large framed art deco posters of women holding perfume bottles, or the shocking-pink orchids found on the wooden tables, or the vibrant woolen throws flung over the couches. Even the bright yellow and blue oversized mugs are cheerful and homey.

As Katherine fills a glass from the tap and then brings the kettle over, she thinks about her own mother's gleaming white coldness. Seeking comfort from her would be like having a one-on-one with the automated voice that presents options when you dial a doctor. "You were always your father's girl," her mother would say.

That was true, not that she saw him much after the divorce. Her father had good intentions, but a weakness for drink. A writer who never made it, he had moved to San Francisco to work as a small-time journalist. She would have liked to tell him about the baby, but now she doesn't know where he is.

Katherine remembers what her mother said when she had called to break the news that they were moving to London.

"What will happen to Lucas?"

"What do you mean, 'What will happen to Lucas?' We're taking him with us."

"Oh, I see."

"Mother, I am his legal guardian. For all intents and purposes he is my child."

"Well, Sael is a very understanding man."

"Yes, he understands that legally and morally it would be wrong to abandon my child. Also, the fact is that I *love* Lucas and would never leave him behind. He's already gone through the trauma of losing his mother."

"Yes," her mother had replied. "Of course. You'll do the right thing."

Katherine could almost hear the snap of the switch and the click of the lock as the lights were turned out and the door was shut. Her mother had taken a risk with her first husband, and he had turned out to be a drunken deserter. There would be no more risks.

Katherine and Niamh are sipping tea and eating cookies—or biscuits, as Niamh calls them—when they hear the front door opening.

Niamh sits up and says quickly, "Don't mention what happened in the store, all right?" She's looking at Katherine with a fierce kind of urgency. "I'll explain later, but just don't, okay?"

"Uh, okay, no problem."

"Niamh, are you home?"

"We're in here!"

A large solidly built man is there in two seconds, leaning over her, touching her cheek. He looks to be in his late fifties with thinning silver hair and keen eyes, which stare out from his craggy, attractive face. "How are you feeling? Are you all right?"

"Fine, love, we just decided to come home a bit early." There's an overly bright, brittle quality to Niamh's words.

"I was overwhelmed by the strollers," Katherine volunteers.

He doesn't laugh. Doesn't look away from his wife. "Niamh?"

"Cathal, *relax*. I'm fine."

"Well." His shoulders descend. "Well, that's grand."

She sighs operatically. "Jesus, don't be stupid. Come on, meet Katherine."

He glances up, unbends a little. "Katherine! Nice to meet you. Niamh won't stop talking about you."

"Likewise."

"I doubt it, I'm only her husband." He sits down on the couch with them, now ready to talk. "So, how was the shopping?"

"Well, never let it be said that there aren't enough sleepers in the world! I don't really even know what a sleeper is anyway. *Everything* seems based around them sleeping, and apparently they never do anyway." Katherine is aware that she's rambling. She glances from Niamh to Cathal and back again, feeling like an understudy who's wandered onto the stage halfway through a crucial scene.

He studies them keenly. He reaches out to cup Niamh's small hand in his huge one, and Katherine wonders what his deal is. She feels a little nervous for Niamh. He's so big and she's so tiny.

"We'll have to go back when I'm feeling better," Katherine offers.

"Katherine was just feeling a little tired," Niamh chimes in with a grateful glance at her.

"I see." It's said easily enough, but his eyes remain grave, watchful.

Katherine nods. "Also, I feel that there's a finite number of teething and breastfeeding products I'm allowed to look at on any given day. Or ever again."

Cathal tries to appear stern, but it's clear he's losing the battle. "You girls need to take it easy," he says.

"Pregnancy is not for the fainthearted, that's what they say!" Katherine has just made this up.

Niamh stands. "And now I have to go to the loo, *again*. Cath, can you put the kettle on for another pot so Katherine doesn't have to get up?"

"I will." But he sits a moment longer, watching her as she walks away. He turns to Katherine. "Sorry, Niamh's right, I do get a little tense. It's just that . . . when you've been down this road as many times as we have, well, no doubt she's told you herself."

Katherine nods noncommittally. Niamh hasn't mentioned anything to her about going down roads, hasn't been anything other than warm and funny, but he doesn't seem to be paying attention.

"All these treatments, all those bloody doctors and specialists, all those injections . . . Still, it will be worth it, right?" He's staring out at something she can't see.

"That's what I hear." Katherine hopes her expression and tone are upbeat. Her heart is pounding a little. She never knew it was such a struggle for them, and she doesn't know how to process this.

"Do you have brothers and sisters?" Cathal continues. "You come from a big family?"

"Not really," Katherine says. "Not at all, in fact. I mean, I have a stepbrother and stepsister, but they're much older than I am and we're not really close."

"Ah, well, I have a daughter from my first marriage, and both Niamh and I come from large families." He leers theatrically and raises an eyebrow. "The Catholics like to do a thing properly. There are seven on my side and five on hers."

Katherine whistles.

"Yep, we both wanted a large brood ourselves, but the way things turned out . . ." He shrugs, looks grim for a moment as though he is caught in a bad memory, and then he shakes his head as if to clear it. "Well, we're here now and we'll be happy with one, provided it has all ten fingers and toes. We've certainly had enough practice."

"Totally."

"Oh God, Cath." Niamh has returned. "Are you putting her to sleep?"

"No." Katherine laughs. "But I might actually go to have a nap soon."

"See what you did?"

He smiles up at Niamh, with such a radiant tenderness that Katherine's eyes smart and her heart gives a kind of whack against her chest.

Niamh turns to her. "Have another cup before you go?"

They drink more tea and eat more biscuits. Cathal is relaxed, more expansive. Niamh teases him mercilessly, but he clearly loves it. They'll be good parents. The kind of parents that any kid would be lucky to have. Cathal will be loving but firm, the one who reads all the parenting books, who is anxious enough for both of them. Niamh will be funny, sweet, and she won't sweat the small stuff. The kind of parents that Katherine wishes she'd had.

She wonders what sort of parents she and Sael will be. Apart from the obvious dramatic gesture of *You and Lucas must come live with me in London*, it's hard to know how he feels. He'll check in with her, how she's feeling, any new doctor appointments coming up, that kind of thing, but by and large he's consumed by work. She envies that. She envies him having something that can absorb him so entirely. Maybe that will be motherhood for her. She hopes so.

She keeps thinking about this on her way home. When they first arrived in London, she was just trying to settle in. The overwhelming emotion was relief at having escaped New York. Now when she thinks about the baby, a strange blankness fills her. Not joy, not panic, not even ambivalence. Something larger and inexplicable. As if she simply cannot comprehend what is happening to her. Seeing Niamh and Cathal together is motivating. She wants to talk to Sael, really *talk* with him, like they used to. She wants to ask him how he feels about her, about everything. She opens her front door full of good intentions. She's ready for warmth, for noise, She's ready for conversation—or, if necessary, confrontation. She's ready to "bring it," as they say, whoever "they" are and whatever "it" is.

The house is dark and silent. There is a note on the fridge in Sael's neat slant.

Went out for a walk and hot chocolate. Be back soon!

Great, she thinks. Now that she is finally ready to communicate, he's gone. *Oh well, I'm home now and maybe a nap isn't such a bad idea.*

As she heads upstairs, she sees three of Lucas's action figures frozen on the carpet by the one comfortable squashy living room

chair. He must have forgotten to put them away. With a little difficulty she squats down to pick them up and studies them. One appears to be part fly—at least his eyes are fly's eyes. Or maybe they're
like a World War I aviator's goggles. He has an extra set of arms,
closer to an orangutan's than a spider's, though, and he wears a
chic leather vest and black shorts. She thinks he must be a bad guy,
and she names him Maurice. Maurice's companion is green and
has lucked out with some interesting animal parts. A foxy snout, a
monkey tail, and bat wings, although his face is more human. He's
definitely an Oliver. The third, clearly a Lenny, is bright orange and
has a gorilla-type aspect to him. One hand, or paw, appears to be
an anvil.

"Hey, guys," she says aloud. "Fancy a ride back?" She scoops
them up, along with a puzzle box and a hooded jacket that was
flung over the chair, and continues up the stairs. She sighs, but
feels a little virtuous. Mrs. B keeps the place so clean there's hardly
anything for her to do.

When she gets to Lucas's bedroom, she puts the jacket and the
puzzle box down on his bed and leans across it carefully to place
Maurice and Lenny and Oliver back on their shelf. Then she notices
another figurine, a woman, way back in the recess of the shelf, as if
deliberately hidden.

Katherine reaches for her. She is considerably smaller than the
others, so she'd be easy to miss. And unlike them, she's not made
of plastic, but rather of a kind of ceramic. Her white toga dress
hangs in perfect pleats, cinched with a gold rope belt, all the way
down to her bare feet, which rest on a frozen mass of white clouds
daubed with a few golden stars. Her eyes are downcast, heavy on
the eyeliner and mascara. They sit above a creamy dab of a nose, a
pale rosebud mouth in a deeper shade of pink. She looks pretty but
weary, like a teenage babysitter at the end of a long evening.

Katherine sits down heavily on the bed, wondering why the

Virgin Mary ended up tucked away on the shelf in Lucas's bedroom. The puzzle box slides onto the floor, its lid gaping, and the pieces spill out in a glorious puddle of color.

"Shit!"

She puts the Virgin down on the bed and kneels beside the box to put the pieces back. One or two have slid farther under the bed. It's not as easy as it once was for her to bend, but she manages to fumble around until her hand touches something hard. It feels like a book. With a groan, she pulls it out and sees the dark brown faux-leather cover, stamped with gilt letters: HOLY BIBLE.

There are several places where pages have been marked with little ribbons.

She sits with it on her lap for a long time, nap forgotten. She sits as the room grows dim as her banking fury smolders and smokes, growing first orange, then yellow, then finally white hot with rage.

Sael is curious. "What were the passages she marked?"

It's around ten p.m. Lucas has long since been in bed. Sael and Katherine are sitting at the dining room table, having a discussion. Wordlessly, she hands it over.

"Wow, she's *big* into Psalms. Well, at least they're the poetic bits."

"That's hardly the point."

"I guess not." He sighs. "So, what do you want to do?"

"I want her gone." Katherine has never felt so certain in her life. The very thought of Mrs. B spending another moment in their flat, changing their sheets, wiping down the counters, mashing potatoes for a cottage pie, makes her stomach heave and her toes curl.

"Really?"

"Sael, look at this!" Katherine gestures to what lies out on the table in front of them. Four crucifixes, three rosaries, the Virgin Mary figurine, and five cards with saints on them.

"Yeah, it's not great." He concedes.

"It's the way they were hidden, so *sneaky*. I don't even know if I've found everything yet."

He sighs again. "I get it. It's creepy."

"It's psychotic!"

"I don't know if it's psychotic, but it's certainly not"—he grins—"for want of a better word, kosher."

He's not taking this seriously, but Katherine feels ill. It had been a horrible hour of searching; she had torn his room up in a rage. Each time she found a crucifix under the bed, a card of a saint tucked among his socks, a rosary at the back of his cupboard, she experienced a simultaneous rush of triumph and nausea, like the world's worst treasure hunt ever.

Sael sighs again. "The thing is, Katherine, that apart from this—"

"Apart from this?!"

"Let me just finish—"

"You mean, apart from this bizarre religious mania, the woman's a total find?"

"Let me finish!" The exasperation on his face gets through to her, and she pauses, hands on hips.

"Okay, what?"

"She's an amazing cook. The house is spotless, and now probably sacred. And she loves Lucas. She loves spending time with him, and he loves her."

"That's exactly my point. Who knows what the hell she's been telling him, what kind of stories she's been filling his head with?"

"We'll have to ask him, but he seems to be doing fine, better than fine. Has he ever mentioned anything to you?"

"No, and I think that freaks me out too. What if she is like, 'It's our little secret?' I don't want him keeping secrets from me."

"Look, obviously we need to speak with her. Tell her that while we appreciate her religious beliefs"—Sael ignores Katherine's snort of disgust—"while she is entitled to believe in what she wants, it's inappropriate to bring these objects into our home, and that we also would prefer she not discuss or talk about religion with Lucas at all. If she's amenable to it, I think she deserves one more chance."

"You're exceptionally calm and easy-going about this. I thought you were an atheist?"

"Well, I am, but it's nice to have some insurance, just to have some coverage." She opens her mouth, and he laughs. "Katherine, I'm kidding. Look, to be honest with you, all I know is that at the moment we have someone looking after our home and Lucas who clearly cares about him and would never harm him. It's probably her way of expressing love." He stares at her thoughtfully. "What bugs you so much about it?"

"I hate the way she hid them."

"That isn't great, but maybe she felt like she was going the extra mile. Anyway, I think we talk about it with her and give her one more chance before letting her go."

"Okay. But I also think we should speak with Lucas and find out how this has affected him."

"I agree."

"And if it happens again, or he starts spouting some weird religious nonsense? Or shows the slightest effect of brainwashing?"

"We scream out, 'Hallelujah, praise Jesus!'" He sees her expression. "Okay, okay. She's gone. Deal?"

"Deal. And I think we also look for another babysitter."

"Fine."

"Fine."

But she wonders if it *is* fine.

Earlier in the evening, when she had been putting him to bed, Lucas had sensed that something was wrong.

"Hey, Kat. Are you mad?" He had squeezed her arm, the tone of his voice anxious.

"I'm not mad."

He had looked at her with a little frown of concern that made her heart sink.

"Okay, well, I was a little . . . upset. But not at you." She decided to tell him the truth. "I found . . . some stuff in your room."

"Stuff? What kind of stuff?"

"Just stuff. Grown-up stuff." She had plunged on. "Um, Lucas? Has Mrs. B ever told you anything and said it was a secret?"

"A secret?"

"Yeah. Did she ever tell you anything and say you shouldn't tell me?"

"No."

"Because you know you can tell me anything, right?"

"Right."

But she thought he seemed uncomfortable. "Does Mrs. B ever say anything to you that didn't make sense, that confused you?"

"No."

"Okay, because if she did, that's all right, I'm not mad, I just need to know. Because I don't ever want you to be confused."

"Okay." Now, of course, he was confused.

Before heading downstairs to confront Sael, Katherine had returned for a final check on him. He appeared to be sleeping, but when she turned to leave his room—

"Kat?"

"Oh, Lucas, I thought you were sleeping! Everything okay?"

"I was thinking about it."

"Thinking about it?"

"What you said about Mrs. B."

She came back and sat down on the edge of his bed. "Yes?"

"I did tell her something."

"Yeah?" Katherine nudged him gently.

"There was one time when I was scared."

"What were you scared of, honey?"

He was silent. This is a child who has been visited by the dead. *The ladies.*

"Lucas, can you tell me what scared you?"

He hesitated a moment more. "It was a lady."

"Like the ladies you saw a while ago?" She remembered his drawing. The woman's yellow ponytail, the big black circle of her screaming mouth, the red squiggles of blood, the angle of her broken neck.

"No, this lady is different."

"How is she different?"

"She's . . ." He'd struggled for words. "She's not, she's not like them."

"I don't understand, honey. How is she different?"

"She's older."

"Like an old lady?"

"No, like older than that."

"What scares you about her?"

"She doesn't like me."

"How do you know?"

"The way she looks at me when she thinks I don't see her."

"Oh, honey." Katherine felt terrible that she hasn't been there for him, that it has been Mrs. B comforting him instead. "And what did Mrs. B say?"

"She said she would help protect me."

Shit. Katherine had kicked herself. *Now you can't even be angry at her.* "Did she say what she would do?"

"No, she just said she would take care of it."

"Well, love, I'm glad you told me and I want you to know you can always tell me when something scares you."

He still appeared a little unsure. *It's as if he's holding something back, something important. But how can she dig further without alarming him? Bad enough he's been confiding in someone else. She won't push more tonight.*

"All right, Lucas, you need to go to sleep now, but let me know the next time you see this lady, and I'll deal with her." *I have no idea how I will deal with her,* she admitted to herself, *but the way I feel now, I know even a ghost doesn't stand a chance. A ghost of a chance. Ha, ha.*

"Okay, but Kat?"

"Yes?"

"Don't be angry with Mrs. B."

"Love, I'm not mad at her, I'm mad at myself because I couldn't be there for you."

"She's nice."

"Yeah, I know."

"And she makes chocolate cake."

"That's true, she does make excellent cake." *Maybe I'll get the recipe before I fire her religious ass,* Katherine decided. *So much for turning the other cheek.*

He saw her smiling. "Promise?"

"Promise what?"

"That you won't be mad with her."

"I promise," she had said. "I promise I'll give her a chance, if you will make me a promise in turn?"

"What?"

"You promise me that if Mrs. B ever says anything or does anything that you don't understand, or that makes you feel uncomfortable, you'll let me know?"

"I promise."

"Then I guess we have a deal." She gave him a kiss. "Night, Lucas."

"Night, Kat. I love you."

"I love you too. So, so much."

Cordelia had growled softly at her as she got up, but she ignored her. If the dog made Lucas feel safe, so be it. She didn't shut his door all the way, careful to let a little light into his room.

25

Margaret

Thomas bounds into the brewery, excited. He has caught a golden coin. He is the envy of all the pages and most of the assembled crowd, though several others have also been lucky. "She threw a handful, Margaret. A handful!"

"Tell me all of it," I demand, "from the beginning."

And he does.

He describes how the procession made its way toward the chapel. How minstrels and musicians on lute and pipe and drum, led with sweet solemnity, and then behind them came all the lords and ladies of the neighboring counties in glorious gowns and tunics and doublets and cloaks of reds and blues and yellows and greens, silks and satins and furs. How her kinsmen and his paced in stately solemnity, arm in arm, followed by Lord August's knights and advisers and finally Lord August himself, walking slowly through a crowd of all the castle's servants, villagers and farmer and traders and merchants dressed in their best clothes. When he reached the chapel door, Lord August stood with Father Martin and waited, splendid in a doublet of emerald and bright silken hose.

"And over *that* he wore an ermine-trimmed cloak, and upon the cloak a gleaming brooch which winked bright in the sun—"

"A brooch, did you say? The ring brooch?" This is the detail I have been waiting for.

"Yes!" Thomas is annoyed at the interruption. "The one I risked my life for, the one you intended to bless as your wedding present."

"That is good to hear. Forgive me, please continue."

"Then the bride approached." Thomas sighs. "Margaret, I swear you have never seen such loveliness. Truly, she seemed to be not flesh and blood, but an angel. Her dress was bright and brilliant, blue as the sky to match her eyes, and upon it was a silver mantle set with gleaming pearls. Her hair was loose and long and circled with a crown of tiny white wildflowers. We all knelt as she went passed, as though she were a queen, and Lord August—"

Abruptly, he falls silent. It seems he has finally remembered who is listening to him. His careless words would have stung me once, but now I only smile as Thomas sings Lady Generys's praises. "Yes?"

Thomas looks guilty. "I do not wish to bring you pain, Margaret."

"Not at all," I say, raising one arm to wipe my brow as I bend over the vat. "I am most intrigued."

"Well then, Lord August also fell to his knees and said—" Thomas sinks onto his own knees and proclaims dramatically, "'My lady, you outshine the sun. No damsel in the land can compare with thee.'"

"Very prettily said," I agree.

He stares intently at my face, but my expression remains serene. "You are different today."

I am seemingly engrossed in my stirring, careful that nothing I say or do belies my words. "In what way?"

He shakes his head, confused. "I cannot name it, but I know."

"Well, I have been hard at work. Brewing this amount of ale is no easy task!"

"You have brewed vast quantities before," he points out.

"But not ale fit for a great lord's table upon his wedding day." I look up and smile. "My reputation hangs in the balance!"

Thomas leans in and sniffs. "I'll grant you, it smells good. What's in there?"

"Marjoram and nutmeg, lavender, chamomile, valerian root, among other things. A special blend—"

Before I can stop him, he has grabbed a cup and dipped it into the vat.

"Stop!" I cry as he raises it to his lips.

He freezes, mouth hanging open, the cup in his hand.

"It is not ready yet," I finish lamely.

"Oh." He pours the contents back, then glances from me to the foaming liquid, an unhappy expression forming.

Partly to distract him and partly from curiosity, I ask, "How will you spend your coin?"

My question has the desired effect of bringing him back to his sudden good fortune. "I do not know yet." He hugs himself with joy. "Perhaps buy a great house so that you will no longer have to brew, nor Rudd and I to work, and a fine steed as Lord August has."

"All on one coin?"

He is a crestfallen.

I am touched by his generosity and have no desire to dampen his dreams. "And why not?"

His face lights up again.

"I wish you well of it. Now, if I were you, I would go and continue to celebrate the day."

He glances at me again, puzzled, but really he needs little encouragement. It is hot down here and growing hotter. I can hear the cook already working himself up into a frenzy of screaming, while outside there is a fresh breeze, and in the Great Hall minstrels and music, drink and dancing, feasting and finery.

At the door, he turns back to me. "Save me a wing of the roast capon."

"I'll save you the nose and the tips of the toes."

Our little exchange finished, he beams at me. I know this will be the last time I look upon his face, and so am glad he is smiling. I smile too. Then I return my attention to the contents of my vat, with another kind of smile altogether.

Engrossed, I stir and stir, thinking of brimming cups and of toasts, of drunkenness. A vision of dark green vines entwining all who drink and pulling them down, down, down to drown in vast red flowers full of wine and ale. Down, down, down to the very bottom, hands rising, hair drifting up in coils, weighted with drink, anchors, merely anchors, as Caradoc once said—

I blink, come to my senses. I am still standing in the brewery, but the kitchen next door is now fully come to life as a great beast. There are plenty of hands to help, more than one voice braying orders, even other alewives, although they brew for the servants, for the guards and all the others. Only I am in charge of ale for the wedding party. Scullions are running frantically hither and thither, and the poor little naked spit boys are cranking for their lives. Underlings and kitchen servants grunt and struggle to lift the dishes, which are sent up one by one. Glazed swans with ginger, plums stuffed in their mouths; lampreys baked in vinegar and honey; brawn in mustard; stewed pheasant; fritters of marrow from the finest beef. Stuffed fowls in a rich wine sauce; a whole roe deer bursting with rabbit and herbs and bread crumbs; clutches of eggs spiced liberally with saffron. Massive golden-lidded pies filled with pigeon, the crusts fluted with silver; great loins of veal; herrings coated in soft white sugar, salmon in syrup, bream in aspic; colored jellies for the different crests of the houses. And throughout it all, continual demand for more soft white bread for their soft white hands to sop it all up.

I take off my apron and wipe down my hands along the sides of my dress. I cast one last look around the bustling, frantic underbelly of the castle. I will never see this place again. Then I walk slowly, slowly, for I have all the time in world, up toward the Great Hall.

The banquet I attended seems like an age ago, and it was a small affair compared to this. The tables are covered not with linen tonight, but with the finest silks in the de Villias colors; green, red, and silver. A firmament of candles burns and splutters and flickers in great silver candlesticks, dishes and platters of pewter and of silver sparkling in their flame, some even gleaming gold. Tonight the saltcellars take the form of huge silver stags. Even the ewers, holding rose water in which the guests can rinse their fingers before drying them upon soft linen napkins, are silver.

More minstrels and musicians than I have ever seen before are gathered here, but while their chorus is loud, the laughter and talk and toasts are louder. I am pleased to see the servants rushing to refill the cups and vessels as they are raised over and over and over. Throughout it all are presentations of wedding gifts. Rings, brooches, swords, bolts of cloth, and caskets of wine are placed before the bride and groom. Then I realize I have arrived just in time to see the triumph of the evening, Lord August's gift to his new wife.

The din ceases as guests and servants alike stare in awed silence. Six strong men are needed to lift it, and it stands taller even than Rudd. A golden cage, covered with golden leaves and blooms of amethysts and rubies and pearls sparkling along its bars. Inside are nightingales, fluttering wildly and filling the vast hall with frenzied song. Lord August looks just as magnificent as Thomas had said, though now I note he is a trifle flushed with drink and pleasure.

He turns to Lady Generys. "For my new bride, who brings music to my heart and gives me wings to fly." And he draws her hand up to his lips as she blushes so prettily.

I need not remain here any longer. The roaring cheers of the guests are deafening, and the musicians strike up again in earnest. Soon everyone will be dancing and my ale will not cease to flow till dawn.

I make my way to Lord August's solar, quick and silent. I know the route well by now, which turns to take through the passageways to reach the staircase. I encounter no one. As I suspected, even the guards are having their own celebrations.

The room is half lit. A smoldering fire in the fireplace laces shadows upon the great canopied bed with its damask covers and silken sheets, where Lady Generys, not I, will make her way tonight. There, next to the bed upon an ornately carved chest I spy a gold goblet, inlaid with ruby and pearl. I pick it up and place it upon a small rounded table. I cover the goblet with a silken cloth that I have kept pressed to my breast, tucked up in my dress. It was given to me by Lord August, a lifetime ago. I know Lady Generys will take it as a sign. Then I glance around the chamber one last time, a room of seemingly endless nights that ended all too soon.

I close the door very gently behind me.

Outside, the guards sway back and forth. They are drinking the servants' ale readily, and there is talk that perhaps Lord August may give them a taste of the banquet ale too, though I hope for their sakes he is not so generous tonight.

I stand in a dark corner of the courtyard, and I take out the knife, the one I filched from the kitchen unnoticed amid the madness. It will not have been missed. When I hold it up to the moon, its edge gleams dully. I am not regretful or afraid, only glad.

All that could make me sad or fearful is now locked within the brooch he wears. My once-beloved love. So it is with delight that I slowly run the tip of the blade over my wrists, the sharp pain is sweet to me. As I work the blade back and forth, I sing one last time.

> Sing me a song of the stars and the moon,
> Sing of the one that was taken too soon.
> A smile in the dark,
> A knife gleaming bright,
> Sing me a song of the night.

I am only sorry I will not see the fruits that this night shall bear.

In the Great Hall the banquet is in full flood. I see as I walk past that all are sodden with drink. The silks drenched in spilled mead. Bones scattered on the floor amid the rushes, and the dogs are snarling. The nobility is unraveling. The music is bawdy and the revelers raucous. No one sees me, hooded and silent. They would not see me anyway, for they do not see alewives. They do not see servants, even ones who leave a thin trail of red behind them.

"A toast!" someone slurs. "A toast!"

The ones who still can raise their chalices do so, toasting with *my* ale, and face the bride and groom. Lord August's face is ruddy. His eyes shine. He laughs. He takes his lady's hand and kisses it.

Another great shout. "A toast!"

I walk on. Still, I can hear it.

"May you bear many sons!"

I smile. I walk on.

It is quiet here in the place of the dead. There is no warmth. There is no noise. A few torches flicker high above me in their iron brackets. I walk past the great stone coffins; I walk underneath the angels with their dead stone eyes. I walk toward the thing that waits for me in the farthest corner, my own stone bed. It will serve me well. It houses another, but I know she will not mind. I am only a servant and not a person, after all.

I push against the lid. The grating of stone across stone, giant teeth grinding together. I push until there is just enough room for me to slide in. I shed my garments, but my wrists remain wreathed in red.

From dust have ye come, and to dust ye shall return.

Easing in, limb by limb, first one leg and then the other. Down into the fetid dark.

Lying on my back in my final bed, I use almost all of my remaining strength to pull the lid back across. My will seeps out from my veins. My fingers slip and scrape on the stone, turn bloody; my arms scream in protest. Finally, finally, with a snarl of grit, the lid slowly begins to give and moves until there is but a lip of air. I need little, for my breaths are now few and shallow. The knife did its work well. I did my work well. The ring brooch is back, safe in his chamber, and though I shall soon pass, they will not find me once the fire has started.

Good-bye, world I knew.

If Caradoc is right, surely he who hunts me can hear me now.

You. You who killed my mother know this. I lost my beloved, was forced to kill our baby, and now have nothing left to live for but you. I shall wait for you. I will wait for you through the ages; through fire and flame and ice and stone, I will wait, held safe and still, curled in silver, until the spheres align and the blood awakens. I will wait for the Vessel that can hold me, and then know this, you killer of women, you destroyer of souls, you fiend, I will come for you.

I will return.

26

Katherine

"Katherine? Katherine Emerson?"

A middle-aged woman with a broad pleasant face and short brown hair is holding a clipboard and calling her name. Katherine opens her eyes. "Oh, sorry, I guess I was dozing off."

"You ready?"

"Yup." Katherine eases herself up off the chair and follows the woman with the clipboard through the hospital hallway.

"Just you today?"

"Yes." She feels she owes further explanation. "My partner"— she always chokes a little on the word—"wanted to be here, but he couldn't. He had a meeting."

The woman smiles understandingly. "We'll try to get some lovely pictures for him so he'll be able to access them online."

They step into a small white room. Katherine hoists herself up onto the plastic bed and sits with her legs swinging. She feels like a little kid again.

"So, I'm Edna," the woman introduces herself, "and I'll be assisting you with your ultrasound today." Edna consults the clipboard again, making clicking noises with her tongue. "Second trimester,

I see. How are we feeling? Any symptoms we should know about, apart from the obvious ones?"

Katherine hates it when people use the word "we" when they mean "I" or "you."

"No, *I* feel pretty good."

"That's the second trimester for you! More energy again, less nausea."

"Totally." Katherine neglects to mention that she never felt tired or experienced nausea even once during her first trimester.

"And are you starting to feel those kicks?"

"Not really."

"Hmm." Edna checks her clipboard. "This is your first pregnancy, correct?"

"Yes."

"Well, it's early enough still, and often in our first time around, we only feel the kicks starting nearer to twenty-five weeks, so don't worry."

"Oh, uh, thank you." This time Katherine is grateful for the "we." It feels inclusive rather than patronizing.

"Now." Edna has become all business. "As Dr. Edwards no doubt explained to you, this is what we call an anomaly scan, which is basically to check the physical development of your baby and to make sure there aren't abnormalities."

"Abnormalities," Katherine knows, is a word destined to make a mother's heart grow cold. "Great." She attempts a lopsided smile.

"It tends to be really exciting and so lovely that you'll get to have a peek!"

This is a bad idea.

Katherine almost turns to see who's spoken, for the thought is so loud and clear in her head.

Don't do this.

The words are sharp, somehow not her own.

Edna picks up on her trepidation. "Really," she says, "a lot of new mums are nervous, but it's fine."

Katherine lies back upon the white plastic bed. The thin white paper sheet crinkles under her. She pulls up her sweater and feels a slight chill on skin. Her belly is definitely fuller and rounder, but she's far from enormous.

As Edna dims the lights, sweat prickles at Katherine's temples, under her arms.

Leave.

She wants to listen to the voice, even louder now, wants to leave, but she finds she can't move her legs, her arms.

"Okay, here we go!" Edna gloops some cool gel onto Katherine's belly and picks up a white device, like an old-fashioned computer mouse. "Now we'll see." She glances toward the monitor.

Don't
do
this.

But Katherine's tongue has withered to an old piece of leather.

Edna circles the wand around back and forth as she studies the screen, which is just out of Katherine's range of vision. "Wait." The wand stops. She peers closer.

Look away.
Tell her to look away.

Katherine blinks. Wets her lips, tries to speak.

"Hold on. That can't be right. Wait just a moment." Edna peers even closer at the monitor. She is staring and staring and staring and—

Stop her.

The paralysis shatters. Katherine pushes herself up and grabs Edna's unresisting arm.

"Don't look! Look away! Look away!" Her voice cracks as if she's only learning to talk again after a long silence.

Edna's nose and forehead are pressed against the monitor. A low moaning rises from her; saliva beads from her mouth.

Katherine yanks again at her arm.

"Please! Come on! Come—"

After a brilliant, blinding flash of light, the room is plunged into blackness. Edna's body thuds back against the wall, slides to the floor with a whoosh and thump. Then nothing. It takes Katherine a moment to realize that it's not just her room. The blackness is too deep, too encompassing. She hears the flatlining machines, the sharp, controlled orders of the nurses and technicians and doctors.

She pulls down her sweater over her cold and sticky stomach, and heaves herself off the bed. Feeling through the darkness with her fingertips, she reaches out and manages to grab her bag, which she left on a chair. She slides her hand against the smooth expanse of door and utters a tiny prayer of thanks when she encounters the jutting metal handle that yields down to her pressure. The hallway is not completely dark; there are tiny emergency lights at intervals along the wall, like phosphorescence in the ocean. She imagines it's how a plane's aisle must look when it needs to make an emergency landing. Out here, it's much louder. People call to one another, and they're not running, exactly, but walking quickly. A woman in scrubs moves fast past Katherine. She looks competent even in the dimness, so Katherine reaches out for her arm.

"Yes?" The woman sounds impatient.

"A technician fainted in my room." Katherine jerks her head at the door behind her. "There."

"What?"

"Her name is Edna. She was giving me an ultrasound and she fainted when the lights went out."

"Fainted?" The woman doesn't ask any more questions, or pause. She turns around abruptly and opens the door. "Wait there!" she barks over her shoulder at Katherine.

But Katherine doesn't wait. She makes use of the darkness to walk past the doors and down the stairwell. She wants to run, but she takes her time. The last thing she needs is to fall.

Don't think about it, she tells herself. *Just take it one step at a time, take it one step at a time, one step at a time.* It becomes her mantra, and she focuses on nothing else. Then finally, finally, she's out of the emergency exit in the stairwell and into the wonderful gray tail end of winter. It's wonderful because she is no longer inside that building. She is outside and moving far, far away. Into a black cab, all the way back to her house, all the way up the stairs to her bedroom. Where a woman is frozen by the bed, looking down at something in her hands.

"Mrs. B?" Katherine asks quietly.

The woman turns around. Her hands are small and pale, but it's easy to see what she grips. Palm crosses.

It's Mrs. B's expression that Katherine will think of later that night. She said very little, made no protest as Katherine gently but firmly guided her downstairs. Shock, yet also something else. Now Katherine lies in bed and tosses from side to side, not wanting to admit what that was. Yes, there was fear—she's losing her job. But it's more than that. *Relief*, Katherine admits. *She seemed relieved. Why? Why relief? She was about to be fired!*

Finally, the answer comes: *She was frightened of you. You scared her.*

And then, *Screw her, she was crazy*, Katherine fumes, and closes her eyes again. Whatever she was, she's gone now, and there's no real harm done.

She hopes.

27

Katherine

Two knights on horseback face each other in the field, one is clad in black and the other in red and yellow. Brightly colored flags snap in the wind as a weak sun shines down upon them. After a blare of trumpets, they ride full tilt, thundering down the turf, their lances aimed straight at each other. The black knight strikes true, hitting the other's shield dead center. The knight in red and yellow plummets with a great cry as his horse gallops away, empty stirrups flailing.

The crowd applauds and angles their cell phones for a better shot. Katherine, Niamh, and Lucas clap until their palms ache.

"Wasn't that amazing?" Katherine is deeply impressed.

Lucas nods so hard it looks like he's headbanging.

Niamh smiles at him. "Can you ride?"

He shakes his head solemnly.

She turns to Katherine. "You?"

"Not unless you count summer camp, which was a disaster."

"How so?"

"Well, as soon as the pony started to trot I let out this high-pitched scream, and it panicked and started galloping. By the time they got hold of me, we were both thoroughly traumatized. You?"

"I've ridden plenty . . ." Niamh grins, and murmurs in Katherine's ear, "Just not horses."

"Da-dum-dum." Katherine grins back and then glances guiltily at Lucas, but he's missed that particular exchange and still stares raptly at the field. "What did you think of that, hon?"

"It's so cool!"

"Agreed." Katherine thinks with a pang of her neglected sword-and-armor Christmas present. *Still, maybe their time has yet to come,* she tells herself.

"Now what?" Niamh asks.

Katherine, Niamh, Lucas, and Cordelia are on a day trip to a Game and Country fair. There are pens of cows and pigs and sheep, clay pigeon shooting and angling and vintage steam engines and tractors. There's even an event called horseboarding, where skate-boarders are pulled by horses, and also, gloriously enough, ferret racing. Not to mention archery and backswording, in case visitors want a less traditional method of killing people. In a small, enclosed area, you can pet bunnies if it all gets to be too much. It hasn't come to that yet, but who knows what the day has in store.

Lucas was beside himself when Katherine said he would be allowed to bring Cordelia with him. It seems that at least half the spectators have brought their dogs, terriers and hounds and mutts named Roger and George and Miss Marple. A country game show may be the doggiest place on earth. Lucas has found his people. They are amiable, mellow, jolly-hockey-sticks types, or what Katherine thinks of as the *very*-English English. Lots of tweed jackets and Barbour coats; old men in old checked flat caps holding walking sticks and striding purposefully on; gray-haired, stout, pink-cheeked women of that indeterminate age, some-where between sixty and one hundred and sixty, who are dressed for comfort in soft pants and shapeless sweaters and rainproof jackets. Not a fashionable bunch, though some of the younger girls, in their late teens and early twenties, sport a certain look in tight jodhpurs and riding boots. Plump mums and smiling dads in stained jeans and faded shirts hold the hands of small sticky-faced offspring.

After the joust, they wander through the craft tent, past an excess of wooden bowls and bags and cross-stitch samplers. They check out a demonstration done by the local blacksmith, which enthralls Lucas, and see a plethora of glassblowers, but the artisans that ultimately win their hearts are the chainsaw carvers. Large, grumpy-looking bearded men, they wield their instruments with grim concentration, but their sculptures are surprisingly delicate and detailed. Katherine admires a mermaid springing from a conch shell, a sleeping dormouse from *Alice in Wonderland*, and a woodland nymph with a coy expression playing a lute.

"Can we get that?" Lucas points to an orangutan holding a baby, both of them slung from a tree. "Or that one?"

She looks at the massive swordfish, springing red and grainy from an oak.

"It might be a little hard to bring back, honey, but let me know if you see something a little smaller, like an owl or a squirrel. There's no telling what might happen."

"An owl? Really?" Niamh looks skeptical, as does Lucas.

Katherine has to laugh. She puts an arm on Niamh's shoulders, takes Lucas by the hand. "Sure, I'm feeling expansive."

She feels expansive because it's the first time she's seen Lucas truly happy and relaxed after what happened with Mrs. B. It's great to be out with him and her friend Niamh, especially because it's hardly raining at all.

"I'm hungry," he announces.

They head off toward the main eating area, ringed with little food stalls and small tents, where wooden tables are set up on the damp, patchy grass. Lucas gets Thai noodles, Niamh opts for a falafel sandwich, and Katherine gets two sausages, one for Lucas just in case the noodles aren't up to scratch, and a hot, flaky chicken-and-mushroom pie. Her appetite for animal flesh is immense, her hunger endless. She wonders if she lacks iron, thinks she really will have to ask Dr. Edwards.

"I think I'm going to grab a beer, want one?"

Niamh shakes her head. Katherine thinks about justifying this craving but can't. She has looked it up on the Internet but got nothing from the tangle of mixed messages. Is it the potassium, the vitamin B, the phosphorous? Before her pregnancy she was all about the wine or whiskey, but now she craves the dank, fizzing bite from the marrow of her bones.

The guy serving the ale doesn't blink. "Dark or light or red?"

"A half-pint of red, thanks."

Katherine takes a tentative sip; it tastes cool and rich, right somehow. As she walks back to Lucas and Niamh, stepping carefully so as not spill her drink, she passes a table packed with guys who seem to be louder and drunker than everyone else. Katherine guesses that they can't be much older than teenagers. Pale underneath their hoodies, dark gray and black, they're getting some looks from people around them. They don't really fit in with the rest of the scene, which is decidedly family-oriented. Their eyes crawl over Katherine as she makes her way back to Lucas and Niamh, who are watching as she gingerly negotiates between the tables with her cup. She thinks she hears the words "lush mum" amid laughter.

Katherine sits back down, trying hard not to care, trying to remember when she was that age. It seems a world ago.

"Want a sip?"

Niamh shakes her head regretfully.

"Guess I'll be drinking for two."

Another phrase drifts out, she can't catch it, but the mirth is unmistakable. Katherine takes another sip and puts the cup down, her taste for beer gone. *Pregnancy makes you vulnerable*, she admits. *You're putting it all out there whether you want to or not.*

Lucas is engrossed with feeding Cordy a bite of roll, but she can sense Niamh growing angry. "It's not worth it on your blood pressure."

"Yobbo shites," Niamh hisses, then glances guiltily at Lucas, who is still mercifully looking down, all attention on his dog. She turns to Katherine. "Sorry, you can take the girl out of the council estate, but you can't take the estate out of the girl."

"Ignore them," Katherine tells her and laughs as she hears herself. "Didn't you used to hate to be told to 'ignore them?' It's crazy what comes out of my mouth these days."

Niamh sighs faintly in agreement. "If I see someone smoking near me, I have to be physically restrained from lecturing them about the damage they're doing, and that's me, Niamh Walsh, former champion chain-smoking, pint-chugging party girl."

"Those were the days." Katherine holds out her plastic cup for Niamh to clink it, and they share a little toast.

The louts at the nearby table burst into another round of hoots and guffaws. They've found a new target. Katherine glances around and sees two heavy teenage girls at another table, looking miserable.

Niamh stops smiling. "Then again," she says, "some people just need their heads kicked in."

"Yeah." Katherine stands up. "But you'll have to put your ass kicking on hold because we have a dog show to dominate."

A whole arena is set up for the dog show, and it's filling with Great Danes, spaniels, terriers, mastiffs, and more Labradors than one can shake (or throw) a stick at. The categories range from prettiest puppy, sweetest bitch, and handsomest boy to most sensitive ears, most musical bark. Clearly the intent is for everyone to be a winner. Rosettes are to be given for first to fourth place.

A call beckons judges over the loudspeaker, and Katherine helps Lucas to volunteer. He is judging "Happiest, Waggiest Tail." When not giggling, he seems to be taking his responsibilities extremely seriously. Niamh and Katherine watch him as he goes down the line, meeting the dogs one by one.

"He seems to be doing well?" Niamh offers.

"You mean after the whole firing—Mrs. B thing?"

"Yeah."

Katherine turns to see Lucas petting a small mastiff with a tail moving in a frenzied blur.

"How's he taking it?"

"Hard. He doesn't understand why I had to let her go and I can't tell him, 'Oh, she just happened to be a religious lunatic hiding crap under and in your bed.'"

"It's really creepy." Niamh shudders. "I don't know how you stood for it for so long."

"I wouldn't have, but Sael talked me down." Katherine still feels angry for not trusting her instincts earlier.

"So what did you tell Lucas?"

"I told him that it had nothing at all to do with him, that we had had a disagreement, and that she would be working somewhere else."

"Sounds a bit like explaining a divorce. What did he say?"

"He asked if he could go and visit her."

"Ouch."

"Yeah."

"He also asked me if I was mad."

"Oh, that's heartbreaking."

"I know. I told him, 'No, honey, I'm not mad with you.'"

"Poor guy."

"Anyway, we're going to find someone new. Well, *Georgiana* will find someone new, bless her flawless, efficient heart."

"Still perfect and gorgeous?"

"Yup."

"Pity."

Lucas has finally decided to give the rosette to a particularly fetching husky whose tail is extraordinarily waggy.

"Good call, honey! Nicely done!" Katherine tells him as he returns.

They stay to watch the dress-up competition, which is won by a spaniel wearing a pink tutu and an expression of shame. Then it's their turn. After much discussion, they've entered Cordelia into the "Pretty Puppy" category.

"Not that I'm competitive, but Cordy had better win something good or heads will roll. Just saying."

"Well, I've checked out the competition and I think she's the front-runner."

This proves to be true. Although there was a moment of tension with a wirehaired terrier named Norma, it is announced that Cordelia has earned the title of "Prettiest Bitch" among the puppies.

Lucas is horrified. "They're calling Cordy a bad word! They said the *B* word, Kat, they said the *B* word!"

Katherine and Niamh burst into laughter at this, and he looks up at them, bewildered. Katherine blushes, but speaks in a bright, practical tone, cursing her puritanical roots.

"That's the English word for female dog. It's okay when you use it like that. It means she's the prettiest girl dog." Niamh is still laughing. "Oh, shut up."

Despite this little misunderstanding, the three are in no hurry to leave Dog World, and they explore the stands, where in a flush of victory they buy some rawhide chew sticks and a bright orange-and-black squeaky snake for their champion, a purchase Katherine almost immediately regrets. After this they amble back to watch the "Dog Most Like Its Owner" competition. A bulldog and a beefy man who could be father and son, or at the very least cousins, win. Finally, even Lucas seems a little "dogged" out, and they make their way to the falconry show.

The field where the knights earlier fought each other has now been cleared, and a series of different-sized posts have been knocked into the earth, Katherine presumes for the birds. A big and grizzled man, wearing a white shirt, a vest, and khaki pants, stands in the middle of the field.

"Welcome to the falcon show! My name is Kevin Brixton!" he booms into a microphone.

Niamh nudges Katherine. "Rugged, just my type!"

Katherine has to bite her lip to keep from laughing as Kevin launches into a long explanation about falcons and hawks, eagles and kites and owls. She allows herself to drift a little, content to watch the huge, powerful birds as they dive and soar above the heads of the crowd. *Beautiful*, she thinks, *free.*

Lucas tugs on her hand and brings her back to the present. "Look," he breathes in ecstasy.

Five fat owls waddle around, blinking their large eyes. They are completely adorable. One is called Percy, who teeters along, squawking for treats. Percy is not a big flyer.

"It's called a parliament of owls." Kevin grins. "They look mean-ingful, but there's not much action."

He's clearly trotted this joke out countless times, but the dutiful crowd laughs. People are being kind today.

"So, we need some kids and their parents up here, to help Percy fly. We'll need a long line of you to come into the field and lie down on the grass, side by side." He grins again. "Hard work, I know, but any volunteers?"

Children start tugging their reluctant, smiling parents to the field.

Katherine looks to Lucas. "Want to?"

Lucas shakes his head. She turns back just in time to see a large guy wearing a gray tracksuit, one of the "yobbo shites" gang, pushing his way to the front. He weaves back and forth, clearly drunk. The audience murmurs uneasily.

Kevin addresses him through his microphone. "Sir, are you a child?" The man looks up and blinks drunkenly. "Or a parent of one of the children?

"God, I hope not." Niamh's jaw is set in a grim line.

"Well then, this exercise is not for you." Kevin stares hard at him.

The guy stands there, watching as more little kids and some parents come to the field and lie down. He senses the crowd is against him. Finally, with a grunt, he pushes his way back to his friends, who rib him mercilessly. No one's sure why he wants to participate, but there's something unsettling about it. Kevin continues with an air of calm triumph. When the line of prone bodies is long enough, Percy is encouraged to swoop over them, which he does. Everyone cheers the little owl's efforts.

After the owls are done, the show continues with the main draw, the birds of prey demonstration. But the hoodies, as Katherine thinks of them, are not to be cowed. They whoop and raise their hands in the air every time a hawk or falcon flies over their heads.

Even Kevin is growing annoyed, though he's trying to play it cool. "I know it's exciting, but please let me remind you not to try and touch them."

"Whooh!" calls out one of them. "Very fancy, tastes just like chicken!"

Kevin no longer sounds jocular. "Please don't touch them, these are very special birds in a delicate situation, and only experts can handle them."

"Jesus, what I wouldn't give for those birds to have a go at them," growls Niamh.

Spectators around them shuffle and mutter, one person even ventures a "Stop it!" which is radical for the English, who, Katherine has learned, are agonizingly mild and polite.

"Aren't there any sort of country fair police?" Katherine has a momentarily delightful image of ham-fisted farmers riding on tractors with sirens, booting these yobbos' butts off the premises.

Niamh shakes her head. "Probably security will be along in a minute. But it will be a shame if he has to stop the show on their account."

Lucas is solemn. "Kat, why are those men acting like that?"

"Because they're jerks, honey." She speaks lightly, but she can feel the anger building within her. It's been such a wonderful day, Lucas reaching for her hand, which he hadn't done in ages, and now these assholes are ruining it for everyone.

"Sorry, folks, but we're going to have to stop the show."

The audience groans.

"Louts!" a pink-cheeked woman huffs. "They should be kicked out."

"Kat, why are they being jerks?"

"I wish those birds would have a go at them," Niamh says again.

"They should be taught a lesson!"

Katherine thinks of the birds. She thinks of them wheeling, dipping, and diving, feels the cold currents of air surging under their wings, sees the hard earth down below, the people so small and insignificant, the hooligans' ugly, pale, jeering faces gazing up, their bulging eyes squinting, their yellow-toothed grins, their fumbling fingers reaching out, they have no respect, no understanding, no grace—

Someone should teach them a lesson.
Someone should teach them a lesson.
Someone should.
Someone is—
Screaming.
Someone is screaming.
Someone is screaming and screaming.
And screaming, and running, hiding their faces, and—

Katherine blinks. She sits, staring at the television. They've been running the story all evening.

Falconer Kevin Brixton is mystified. "In my twenty-four years of working with these birds, this has never happened. I mean, I can't 'sic' my birds on people. That's ludicrous."

Eyewitness reports claim that these birds of prey, part of a country fair display, attacked a group of men who were drunk and trying to touch them, despite repeated warnings to stop, while they flew above the audience.

"He was about to cancel the rest of the demonstration."

"I've never seen anything like it! All the birds suddenly dived into the crowd for them."

"Total chaos."

"Everything went crazy. One moment it was fine, and the next—"

Officials say ten spectators were injured, with three in critical condition, all with significant facial wounds. Their condition is not yet disclosed. It is not yet known if any of the birds will be euthanized. While most eyewitnesses and officials describe the phenomenon as a freak occurrence, triggered by agitating behavior, some are already saying that there is more to the story, including the controversial religious group Heaven's True, an international organization with a growing membership in the UK, which has already released a statement on its website.

"It's a sign. The Bible says, 'Behold the fowls of the air, for they sow not, neither do they reap, nor gather into barns, yet your heavenly Father feedeth them.' Jesus is coming."

Sael comes down the stairs. "Want me to turn that off?"

She starts. "Sure."

He reaches for the remote, presses a button, and there's a blessed silence.

She turns to him. "How is he?"

"Asleep."

She sighs. "Good."

He walks around the couch and plumps down next to her.

She leans her head back. "Thanks for checking again, I think he'll be okay, but . . ."

"But it was a hell of a day," he finishes.

She shrugs. "Yeah, that's about the size of it."

"What really happened?"

"I honestly don't know. One minute these drunk guys were trying to touch the birds and the handler was telling us the show was over, and the next the birds went totally beserk. It was chaos."

"God."

"I know."

"How's your friend doing?"

Katherine frowns. "I've called and texted, but no answer. Her husband eventually wrote back, said she was sleeping."

"But?"

"I don't know, it just feels wrong somehow. I'm worried about her. Maybe I should go there myself?"

"Katherine, if he says she's sleeping, she's sleeping. It was a traumatizing day. I'm more concerned with how you're doing and handling everything."

"I'm fine." But she doesn't look at him.

He stares at her. She's tilted her head back and is massaging her temples, her eyes closed.

"Listen, you only have to say the word and I won't go." He sounds uneasy.

"Sael, I told you, I'm fine."

"I'm not comfortable with it."

She opens her eyes, sits up. "But you *should* go. You've been planning it for ages, and it's important for the company, right?"

"Yes, but that doesn't matter."

"What?" Sael's voice rises with barely checked frustration. "You're more important than the company. Jesus, Katherine, why would you think otherwise?"

She doesn't answer him for a long time. "It's just good to hear you say it," she replies eventually.

"That's it, I'm not going." Sael's jaw is set.

"Sael, please, you should go. You've been working too hard on your presentation not to. And anyway, I don't want to cancel Wales."

His face registers confusion, then settles. "Oh yeah, you and Lucas with Matthew and what's-his-name?"

"John."

"Right. What's the deal with that again?"

"We're all going off to Wales for a week to check out some castles."

"How is that going to work? I don't want you running up a lot of steep, damp steps."

She laughs.

"I'm serious!"

"I know. It's just nice to hear you being protective."

Sael stirs uneasily; he opens his mouth, but she places a hand upon his shoulder.

"I promise you, I'll be *extra* careful. No running up damp steps," she tells him gently. "Besides it would break Lucas's heart if we couldn't go. He loves John and Matthew, and I think it will help him."

"With this whole Mrs. B thing?"

"Yeah."

He nods, frowning.

Sael has admitted to Katherine that her instincts were right. He should have listened to her and dealt with it sooner. There's nothing to be done now but move ahead. Still, Lucas has taken it badly. They had clearly formed a close attachment.

"Anyway, I organized it so that it overlaps with your trip. By the time you come back we'll be home again. Safe and sound."

Sael sighs. "Okay, but Katherine . . ."

"Yes?"

"Promise me you'll be careful. I want you to keep me posted, let me know how everything's going."

She smiles, and her face lights up. "I will, I promise."

"I don't know what I would do if anything happened to you." He drops his voice as he glances down at her considerable swell. "Or him."

"Him, huh?"

"That's right."

"Not a girl?"

"Nope."

"How can you tell?"

"I just have a feeling."

Katherine laughs. She never said how it went with the ultrasound, only telling him all was well. She had mentioned early on that she wanted to keep the gender a surprise. Sael seemed happy to let her. There are few enough nice surprises in the world these days.

"Well, there's a fifty percent chance you're right." She eases herself up. "I think I'll hit the hay myself. When are you coming to bed?"

"I'll be there soon. I just have to finish this."

"Okay."

She heads up the staircase.

"Katherine?"

She looks back. "What?"

But Sael doesn't answer and she can't decipher the myriad of emotions running over his face. There's an endless pause before he seems to return to his normal inscrutable self.

"Sleep well," he finally says.

A few hours later they are standing by the front door. He's in a suit and an overcoat, and she is still in her slippers, her dressing gown barely covering her swollen stomach. *How 1950s we must look*, she notes with a small smile.

"Well, there's my car."

"I know."

He stares at her, as if trying to memorize her features. She too feels like this is the first time they've really *seen* each other in a long while.

"Are you sure it's okay if I go?"

"Sael, it's only ten days."

"I'll be back before you know it."

"That's right."

"Well, if you're absolutely sure."

"Go." She gives him a little push. "We'll be fine!"

"Okay, okay! I get the message!"

He gives her an awkward hug. They kiss, bump noses, laugh, start again to do it properly, but the car is waiting. He's pulling his bag, heading out of the door and down the first step. He turns back just once and sees her still there in the hall, smiling faintly at him. Then he shuts the front door behind him and is gone.

Katherine stands, listens to the purr of the engine, Sael's voice, the driver's, and then the rumble of the car pulling away. She hears the house settling down around her, the tick of the clock, the hum of the fridge, the swish of other cars down the rainy streets. Then she sighs, bends a little to collect the pile of mail on the entrance hall table. Stuff that Sael didn't get to yet.

She sits at the dining room table, absentmindedly leafing through bill after bill after bill in the stack until she comes to a thick cream envelope different from all the others. She slides her thumbnail underneath the flap, which tears neatly open with a satisfying little rip, before turning it over to see that it's addressed to Sael. *Oops.* She wonders who would be writing to him. When did she last handle a real letter? There's no return address. She finds herself taking out the pages, and idly she begins to read.

Dear Mr. de Villias,

Forgive me for writing, but I thought an old-fashioned letter might be my best chance to reach you. If I wrote you an email, you might just delete it or alert the agency without reading it, which you are fully entitled to do, and you may do the same now, but regardless of whatever action you decide to take I hope that you do finish this letter first.

Please understand that I mean you and your family no harm. I would sooner end my life than harm a hair on Lucas's head. I would not be writing now but for the fact that I am truly concerned, even frightened, for his safety.

Many weeks ago, when you first arrived and I began working here and spending time with Lucas, he told me that he was scared of a lady who came and visited him at night. He said she would come into his room and stare at him with a mean smile, that her eyes were full of bad thoughts about him. Naturally I thought that this was a make-believe person, the fantasy of a child.

I would have told you both immediately, but he made me solemnly promise that I wouldn't tell you or Katherine. He said that the lady would hurt you both if I said anything. I promised him, as he seemed very upset at the idea of discussing it with the two of you, but I now realize that was a mistake. I should have alerted you to this at once. I believed that because he had confided in me, an adult, who listened, he would feel better. Children sometimes take odd fancies and notions, and I believed that this was the case. However, I now have reason to know that I was wrong. As the weeks went on I began to understand why Lucas had told me to keep it a secret.

I don't know how to tell you, other than just to write it.

I believe that Lucas's "lady" is KATHERINE.

I will explain. In the past months I have found Katherine's behavior increasingly erratic and strange. Sometimes I would turn around and she would be standing there, just watching me. I wouldn't even hear her come up behind me.

When I tried to say hello or make small talk, she would grin in a way that I can only describe as menacing.

On more than one occasion, I opened the door to Lucas's room to find her sitting alone there in the dark. Lights off, curtains drawn. Of course she has every right to sit and stand where she wants to in her home, but something seemed unnatural about it, as if she was trying to frighten me.

Sometimes I would refer to a conversation that we had had and she would have no recollection of it at all. She would ask me if I had seen an object she was carrying only a few minutes ago. I tried to raise this with her several times, but she would always change the subject.

I would go downstairs to find the stove on with an empty pot on top of it. The third time this happened, I spoke with Katherine about it, telling her that I had turned the stove off and had she turned it on by mistake? She told me that she hadn't left her room because she had been taking a nap, despite the fact that I had seen her downstairs only a short while before that.

Another thing I began to notice was that raw meat was

disappearing from the fridge. As you know, I did the food shopping after some discussion with Katherine, so I knew what was in the fridge. After this had happened a couple of times, some ground beef went missing and I asked her if it had been used to feed Cordelia. She told me that she didn't know what I was talking about. Later on that day I was cleaning her bathroom and I found a bowl next to the sink with the remainder of the raw beef.

One afternoon around the same time I came downstairs to make some tea and heard Cordelia growling. I was concerned, and when I went to see what she was growling at, I realized that she was growling at someone or something behind the couch. I was terrified until I saw in the mirror that hangs on the opposite wall that the person hiding was Katherine. She was crouched over with her hair hanging in her face, and I was upset but decided to ignore her. At that point I was already uncomfortable around her and I thought it might be a practical joke, albeit a bad one. I do not know if she saw me before I went upstairs again. When I came back down, she had left the house.

I tried to rationalize everything because I have had children too and I know pregnancy can be difficult, but I was concerned about Lucas. He seemed to be more and more afraid of her. Sometimes he would even flinch when she reached out to touch him, or look anxious when she called to him.

I had finally made up my mind to speak with you when Katherine discovered the Bible and the figurine and the crosses that I had placed in his room. I apologize for this again, but I didn't know what else I could do to protect Lucas. I understood then that I had left it too late, and anything I said after that would not be taken seriously. I wanted to leave, but I was afraid for Lucas and did not want to abandon him.

I did not say anything at the time of the incident with the palm crosses, knowing that I would not be believed, but I need you to *know that I did not make those palm crosses, nor did I place them under Katherine's pillow. The only explanation I can think of is that Katherine made and hid them herself. I am so sorry to have to tell you this, and even more sorry I did not come to you the moment I had my suspicions. I found myself overwhelmed and frightened and unsure of what to say.*

I only want Lucas to be happy and safe, and that is the reason I am writing to you today. I am not sure what you have been told about me, but my son James died of leukemia at the age of nine. I have come to love Lucas. He reminds me of James. But I assure you that my grief over his death is not influencing my perception of what I have seen or experienced. Although I loved my son with all my heart, he passed many years ago, and I have now learned how to live without him even though that is something I would have never thought possible before he died.

I do not believe that Katherine is aware of what she is doing, but in my opinion that only makes her more dangerous, not just to Lucas but also possibly to you and even herself. I have come to care deeply for you and your family. I promise that I will not reach out to you again. If you wish to contact me, you have my number. But I had to let you know. I could not live with myself if I did not.

May God bless you and keep you safe.

Alice Bailey

Katherine sits at the table for a long while. Then slowly, and with great deliberation, she rips up the pages. First into halves, then quarters, and then smaller and smaller, her hands moving in a frenzy, her face still. Then she gets up and gathers the pile of shredded paper and throws it in the garbage.

She climbs up the stairs, a little smile playing on her lips as she thinks about what to pack for Wales.

Third Trimester

28

Katherine

"Now listen up, because this is important! What music does everyone want to hear? I'm taking requests. Apart from John, he's not allowed."

"As the driver I call that a cheek!"

"Darling, no one here wants to listen to Hildy."

"Hildy?" Katherine asks.

"That's what Matthew calls her, Hildegard von Bingen," John explains. "A medieval abbess, very powerful—"

"Yes, yes, very meaningful." Matthew sighs. "The gist is that she had migraines, and wrote a bunch of trippy poetry that she set to music. It's fine for two seconds and then you want to kill yourself."

"I wasn't going to suggest her anyway," John says coldly.

"Liar! Who *were* you planning to suggest?"

John opens his mouth, pauses, closes it again.

"I thought so. All right, I have the Beatles, Amy Winehouse, Ella Fitzgerald, Elton John—my God, what's that old queen doing here? Stone Roses, Rolling Stones, Bach's *Goldberg Variations* ... Katherine?"

"I don't know, they all sound great." She's not about to insert herself into a contentious conversation that has been clearly going on for years.

"Useless." Matthew twists farther around in his seat. "Lucas, you're our last hope. Who would you like to hear?

"Elton John." Lucas is firm.

Matthew looks surprised, but manages to recover. "Then Elton John it is. May I ask why?"

"Because he's a queen."

John and Katherine giggle. Now Matthew is the one who is speechless.

"What?" Lucas turns to her, almost angry. "He did say that."

"You're right, honey, he did." She reaches over and kisses the top of his head. He doesn't wriggle away like he has been doing in the past few weeks. Like his holding her hand at the fair, this is a victory.

In the rearview mirror, Matthew meets her eyes and winks. *No need to look so smug*, she thinks, but she winks back. Maybe a change of scenery is what they needed, after all.

Wales is green.

Wales is rolling hills rising into mountains and then undulating down again.

Wales is winding footpaths and cobbled streets and flowering hedgerows. Wales has smaller roads, which Matthew and John negotiate flawlessly. They talk and laugh softly in the front while Katherine and Lucas nap in the back. It feels like the kind of family trip Katherine longed for growing up.

I am happy again, she realizes. The farther they travel from London, the lighter she becomes, as if she is shedding all the troubles and worries that have been weighing her down.

In the last of the sunlight, they drive up a small road that seems barely fit for one car, ending up on a quiet street lined by a row of pretty houses that face the sea.

"It's the Irish Sea," John tells them.

"I thought we were in Wales?" Lucas turns to Katherine.

She shrugs. "I don't get it either, babe."

The bed-and-breakfast is run by a pleasant woman called Sue, a former teacher who still has that firm, smiling air of authority as she shows them around the house. Their rooms have a strong pine theme, with old pine chests and old pine beds, flawlessly made, and framed illustrations of birds upon the pine-paneled walls. The bathrooms are impeccable, and there are heated railings where you can hang up your towels. Out of the windows, in the distance, Katherine can see small white sailboats cresting upon the water, and even farther out in the other direction, gentle mountains dip and rise. After they unpack, they wander down the road to the main stretch of the village. It's early evening and already very quiet.

There's a small restaurant nestled among the white houses with the dark beams. They order fresh fish-and-chips, whiting with tartar sauce. Everyone has huge appetites. Meandering slowly back along the pier, they take in the evening's hues of blue and purple and laven-der. Gulls cry far above them as they breathe in the salty air.

"I like it here." Lucas takes Katherine's hand.

"Me too!"

Full and sleepy, they are soon safe under the crisp white sheets. Katherine falls into a deep and dreamless sleep. The light slanting in through the windows wakes her, and she lies for just a moment longer, content to think about the day ahead and listening to the footsteps of the other guests. Sue has prepared a fully cooked English breakfast, sausage and bacon and eggs and toast. Katherine and Matthew have tea, and John has coffee, and Lucas has orange juice. The orange juice is freshly squeezed, and white porcelain bowls filled with fresh fruit and cereal sit atop a red-and-white tablecloth.

"Food always tastes nicer when somebody else makes it," announces Matthew.

The first castle is only a short amble from the B&B. The roads are quiet—it's early in the season. They walk past pale pastel houses, neatly parked cars, and old people sitting out in the sun, already eating ice cream.

After they collect their castle passes, they stroll past the clothing shops and teashops and finally, finally . . .

"The castle!" Lucas is very excited. "Look, Kat, there's a moat! A moat!" He squeezes her arm and stares at the green body of water. "Do you think there are alligators and sharks in there?"

"Absolutely." She ruffles his hair. "So don't fall in!"

Over the drawbridge and through the main arch, the keep of the castle squats on velvety green manicured grass. Together they gaze at the moss-streaked, weatherworn stone walls soaring above them.

"Do you ever wonder what it would have been like to live here?" John asks her.

She nods. "All the time."

Matthew and Lucas have gone ahead.

"Be careful!" she calls.

"We will!"

"Shall we climb the battlements?" Katherine suggests to John.

Cut deep into the walls, the stone staircase spirals a little steeply, but it's not hard.

"Is this all right?" He glances at her stomach, concerned.

"It's fine." She holds on to the rope and half pulls herself, half climbs up. At the top they look out on the meadows flocked with sheep and cows.

"Not so different from times past." John walks along the parapet a little, while Katherine stands still for a moment. She breathes in, filling her lungs with air. She closes her eyes. She feels good, better than good. She feels like she's come home.

"Kat! Kat!"

She opens her eyes.

Lucas is waving to her from the battlements on the other side of the castle. Next to him, Matthew aims his invisible bow at her, releases an arrow, and she clutches her heart and pretends to collapse.

Later that afternoon, they pull into the parking lot of the Hidden Gardens, an estate containing three gardens cultivated in the early nineteenth century. Matthew has heard from friends, as only Matthew would, that it's out of this world.

"Look, Kat, look at the sheep!"

"I see, I see."

There are sheep everywhere though, to be fair, the parking lot is a field.

"I want to pat one."

"I don't know if you can get close enough, and they might be smelly."

"Oh." He looks disappointed.

"But you're welcome to try." Katherine grins. "Mutton ventured, mutton gained!"

"It would only be a sheep thrill anyway," Matthew drawls. "They're probably on the lamb."

"For crimes I shear-der to think about!"

Now Matthew and Katherine are truly cracking up.

Lucas, bewildered, turns to John. "What's going on?"

Without a pause, or even a change of expression, John replies, "Bleats me." He eyes Katherine and Matthew, who are still giggling. "Wool you both stop making baaaa-aaad sheep puns, please?"

He takes Lucas's hand, and they both start off toward the reception.

"That was pretty lamb-tastic." Katherine stares at their retreating figures, dazzled by the brilliance of the delivery.

"That's why I love that maaaaa-aaan!"

Katherine groans as she and Matthew follow them down the hill.

The gardens are incredible, with an endless display of colors both delicate and bold. Gravel paths lead through the carpets of ferns, elephant ears and moss to quiet pools and even a waterfall. Small nooks with peaceful benches are shaded by sculpted hedges and surrounded by every type and hue of rose.

Unfortunately, they aren't the only ones who've heard about this paradise. Wrinkled and determined in practical, primary-colored clothing, with caps and hats to shield them from the weak sun, a slow-moving mass of old people wielding walking sticks and crutches blocks the paths. They seem determined to peer through binoculars and examine each and every petal on the giant red poppies, altogether traveling at the rate of ancient tortoises in a traffic jam.

Matthew and Lucas make a game of passing them, sometimes running ahead when they hear the scrape of a stick or walker on the gravel, sometimes ducking down another path. John and Katherine, however, take it slowly.

He smiles ruefully. "Both of them children, with Lucas slightly more mature."

"Yes." She laughs. "This is gorgeous, isn't it."

"It is."

"Pity I barely know a rose from a sunflower."

"How are you feeling?"

"I'm good."

"Any kicking yet?"

"No. Not that I've noticed anyway. I've made an appointment with the OB next week, I guess we'll see."

"It must be very strange, to have something growing inside you, something of you and yet not."

"It is. I guess part of me, maybe most of me, can't really comprehend it. It's like there's an alien inside me, taking in my nutrients and siphoning off proteins and fats and calcium. It's changing and developing, and it needs me to survive, but it remains a total mystery."

"In some ways it's not fathomable." He pauses and then continues, "Matthew wanted children. But I didn't. I always felt that it was too much of a responsibility. And in some ways, many ways really, I'm far more selfish than Matthew is."

"I hear you."

"However, seeing him with Lucas, well, it gives one pause."

"There are rough days too."

"I'm sure."

"Still, there's a lot of joy."

"Speaking of . . ."

She follows his gaze down toward Matthew and Lucas, who have taken a break from their game to admire the flowers growing a little way off the path. Lucas points to a beautiful purple-blue flower growing straight and tall, and Matthew reaches out his hand.

"He shouldn't be touching the flow—" John turns. "Katherine, what's wrong?"

"Hey!" Katherine calls out, but she's too far away, and they don't hear her. "Hey!" And then she's running, or trying to.

"Katherine, wait! What's going on?!"

But she doesn't respond to John, only trying to get to them as quickly as possible, skidding on the gravel that's turned slippery under her feet. As fast as she runs, they seem to be slipping farther into the distance. She has to warn them, but she struggles to find air—there's a stitch in her side.

With her last puff of breath, she cries, "DON'T TOUCH IT!"

Finally, they look up, gaping.

She is gasping. "It's poisonous!" she wheezes.

Matthew pulls Lucas away from the flower with a speed that is almost comical, their eyes cartoonishly round.

"Poisonous?"

"Yes." Her heart is slamming against her ribs "It's monkshood. It's highly poisonous."

"But"—Matthew is stammering—"we weren't planning on *eating* it."

"I know, but sometimes touching it is enough."

Now John is by her side. "Jesus, Katherine, are you crazy? You could have fallen!" He rounds on Matthew. "As for you!"

"I'm sorry, I didn't think."

"My God, of all the stupidity! There's a reason why there are signs saying 'Don't Touch the Plants'!"

"I'm sorry," Matthew repeats in a small voice. "Katherine?" He turns to her. "Truly, I apologize."

She looks at Lucas, whose lip trembles. He is about to cry. She breathes in, breathes out, allowing her heartbeat to steady itself. "It's okay, honey, he didn't know."

"Lucas, I'm sorry." Matthew is distraught. Katherine has never seen him so emotional. "I really am."

Lucas doesn't take his eyes off Katherine. "You're not mad?"

"No, sweetheart, I just got a bit frightened."

"And ran like a maniac." John glares at Matthew, and then shakes his head. "Come and sit down, Katherine."

"I'm fine now."

"For my sake."

She allows them to lead her to a bench. Matthew is rife with abject apologies. "That is the last time I touch any plant again. Even apples will be off-limits."

John rolls his eyes, but the corners of his mouth twitch. "Honestly, the pair of you."

Lucas still seems spooked.

John sighs and stands up. "Come on, Lucas, if you're hungry for something unhealthy, let's see if we can get you an ice cream."

Lucas brightens considerably and waits for Katherine to nod her assent. As the tall man and the little boy head off in search of a treat, Katherine and Matthew sit on the bench for a moment or two longer.

"I'm really sorry," Matthew repeats. "We both thought it was gorgeous. Why are the beautiful ones always the killers?"

"I'm just glad I got to you in time."

"Who is Thomas?" Matthew still sounds shaky, but his voice has a tinge of curiosity.

"What?"

"You kept calling, 'Thomas! Thomas!' I think that's why we were both so confused at first."

"What do you mean?" She wonders with some new annoyance if this is a diversionary tactic.

"You were shouting, 'Thomas, Thomas, Thomas.' Who's Thomas?"

"I was calling *Lucas*."

"It really sounded like Thomas. It doesn't matter, though." He pauses for a second. "But how did you know?"

"How did I know?"

"About that plant—monk's breath?"

"Monkshood," she corrects, absentmindedly. She's still thinking about calling out a stranger's name. Why Thomas? She doesn't know any Thomases.

"Yes, monkshood. I wouldn't have thought you were into botany."

"School project," she lies. In truth, she doesn't know how or why she knows that monkshood is poisonous. Or even what monkshood *is*. At that moment she just knew something terribly, terribly bad was about to happen, and she doesn't want to dwell on it. But her mind needles her. *Who is Thomas?*

"Well, I have failed to kill your charge." Matthew offers her an arm to help her up. "Shall we?"

Despite his crooked smile, Katherine can tell how bad he feels. "Don't worry," she tells him, "there's always tomorrow."

He laughs at this, and together they go to join the other two for ice cream.

They settle into a routine, and the routine is castles. Conwy and Criccieth and Caernarfon and Dolwyddelan.

"Those names sound like crickets having an orgasm," says Matthew.

Castles on the craggy coast, defiant against the sea. Castles inland, rearing majestically amid fields filled with fat, complacent sheep. Castles that seem untouched by time; castles that are merely bleached skeletons, ghosts of their former glory. The bigger, better-preserved castles crawl with couples pushing strollers and old people pushing walkers, talking to one another, taking endless pictures. At Conwy Castle, a man dressed in a tunic and leggings teases the little kids, dolling out "fun facts" as patient parents stand in a circle around him, beaming when he interacts with their offspring. Lucas is shy but happy to listen. John tries not to roll his eyes at the generalized information.

These larger castles have exhibitions, displays with recorded sound, medieval songs or looping cries of battle that play to largely empty rooms. Katherine thinks that there's something cheesy about this. It feels odd to watch outdated documentaries in these huge, historic cradles of death and life and defense. She collects all the pamphlets, but she doesn't really read them. She much prefers to stride across the flagstone courtyards and climb the narrow spiral staircases, cold and gray and curving—she feels like she's inside an ancient conch.

"Do be careful, Katherine," John frets repeatedly.

"You're like a mountain goat," teases Matthew. "Up, up, up to the very top!"

She loves to look out over the countryside, feel the wind upon her cheeks and in her hair. She loves to think about how everything has changed, wonders if anything remains the same. She presses her palms against the stone, shuts her eyes and listens to the gulls. She breathes in. Here she is free. Here she is herself. Then she descends again and feels the better for it.

"Castles are clearly good for you," John remarks, noting the glow in her face, in her eyes.

In between castles, they have tea in the local teashops. Crumbly scones, and real jam with fruit and pips, and clotted cream. No tea bags for them, only proper loose tea leaves.

"I'll read you your fortune," Matthew tells Lucas, before squinting at the dregs of his cups and predicting lots of adventures and good fortune ahead.

"The teapots have their own sweaters!" Lucas cries when encountering his first tea cozy.

On one afternoon they travel to a Tudor house, just to have a break from castles. It's beautifully restored, with a steeply pitched gable roof, and dark curling decorative timber on the bright white walls to the low ceilings, and a steep dusty priest hole built into the fireplace. They chat with a small bird of a woman who is eager to share all she knows about the kitchens. She shows them the spits, explaining how the spit boys would have used them, and a totally preserved rack for meat.

In the hallway, another woman discusses the misconception of the words "rushes," and "threshes," and "threshold." "People say that's where the word 'threshold' came from, though this is actually not the case."

John nods in approval, Matthew rolls his eyes, and Lucas and Katherine try not to giggle.

They also a visit a supposedly medieval-era house, but it has been ransacked to death over the years, and now it is only a shell, all the items in it dating only from the seventeenth century onward. Their guide, upon learning of John's academic credentials, is so embarrassed that he can barely make eye contact and speaks through the side of his mouth. Afterward Matthew chides John for being snooty.

As the days wind down, they walk through the main streets of the villages and towns, eating huge newspaper messes of fish-and-chips and ice cream. Katherine discovers elderflower cordial, which she loves. They try one or two fine dining experiences, and while neither is bad, the simple fare is better, and so if they want a break from fish-and-chips they stick to pubs, where Katherine orders steak-and-kidney pies, loins of lamb and beef.

"Bloodthirsty, aren't you!" Matthew jokes. "Your child is going to be Attila the Hun!"

"Or maybe they'll rebel and be a vegan?" John suggests with a faint smile.

"God forbid!" Matthew and Katherine say at the same time, and Lucas wants to know what a vegan is.

"It's like a walking vegetable," Matthew explains, and John laughs, and then they wander home, and Katherine is happy, and when she sleeps it is long and sweet and dreamless.

She tries to keep in contact with Sael, but it's hard. The B&B doesn't have the best Internet.

"Probably part of its rural charm," sighs Matthew as he waves his iPhone through the air, determined to catch a signal, like a lepidopterist after a rare species of butterfly.

But Katherine has to admit that there's a lot to be said for being out of the loop, no politics or reports of world disasters or corruption or more insane media coverage concerning Heaven's True.

Still, she sends Sael little emails and pictures whenever she can. They call each other, but the connection is notoriously bad, calls dropped, lots of delayed feedback. The beauty of Wales, the joy of their everyday adventures, is somehow flattened through the distance. Katherine also tries to get ahold of Niamh, with even less success. She's sent a lot of texts and messages but gets no response. She's not sure what's going on, and decides to go and visit her in person when she's back. Maybe she should worry more, but it's been so long since she's felt so lighthearted and carefree.

It's a real shock to realize that they've come to the end of the week. It's their last day, and for the first time, it's raining.

"I don't want to leave," Lucas says.

"Me neither."

"Well, in a sense, it's good because any more of these breakfasts would kill me. I must have gained a stone at least," Matthew claims.

"No one's forcing you!" snaps John.

Matthew and Katherine exchange glances. Unusual for him.

"You have a stone? Can I see it?" Lucas asks Matthew.

They all laugh and the tension is blown away.

Maybe going back home is not so bad. Katherine thinks about the conversation she'd had with Sael before they left. There's still hope. Maybe they can work it out, make a *real* home again.

"One more castle to go, or are we castled out?" John looks down at his map.

"Katherine?" Matthew side-eyes her with a knowing grin.

"Maybe just one more?" Katherine knows she will *never* be castled out.

By the time they arrive at their final castle, the rain is coming down in earnest. They huddle together in the reception–slash–gift shop–slash–office, undecided whether or not to venture out and explore. Apart from a glum-faced couple arguing in low hushed voices, they are the only ones here.

"I don't know, should we do it?"

"It's kind of miserable."

"But on the other hand, we paid."

"It's not raining that hard, I guess."

"Kat?" Lucas raises his voice above the rising debate.

"Yes, honey?" Katherine peers down, dreading the inevitable words.

"I need the bathroom."

"I guess that settles it." Katherine turns to John and Matthew.

"I'll take him," offers John. "You get your fix."

"May as well, since we're here. But we won't stay long." She is eager to reassure him. She turns to Matthew.

"Coming?"

Matthew has other plans. "I'll check out the gift shop."

Katherine and Matthew both know he's really checking out the pretty boy behind the counter, the one who's pretending not to notice his appreciative gaze but blushing nevertheless.

"Bad boy, behave," she murmurs.

"Life is too short to behave."

"Well, buy me some postcards at least. I'll just stretch my legs."

The courtyard is cool, the grass a brilliant green. It's a mild rain, sprinkling and damp. Intimate, even, as if it has shut out the others and made this castle only hers. She feels like running and running, or turning a cartwheel.

She walks to the nearest tower, and climbs up and up and up the stone steps, right up to the parapets, where it's wonderful, quiet, as if she has climbed away not only from the earth but from time. As if she is no longer in the twenty-first century but above it. She has an urge to go higher, as though it were possible for her to touch the sky. Standing against the battlement, the emerald wash of land beneath her, she closes her eyes, releases her thoughts into the wind as it blows raindrops across her face. Arms outstretched, she lets memories float over her brain. Horses' hooves pummeling the turf, the clash of blade on armor, sparrow hawks circling and wheeling and crying and crying and screaming—

Screaming. Somebody is screaming!

Katherine opens her eyes. She is no longer safely behind the crenellated wall, but perilously perched out on a small ridge of stone. She gasps, shrinks back, trembling fingers scrabbling for a sure hold in the slippery rain. Only after easing herself backward until she is once again behind the wall does she allow herself to look down. She blinks once, twice, not taking it in.

On the ground below, John kneels, rocks Matthew's broken body back and forth in his arms, weeping, his tears dissolving in the rain upon his face as he screams.

A little boy looks up at her. It's hard to make out his expression through the blur of the rain, but she already knows. It is fear.

29

Katherine

The hospital is mercifully small. It doesn't take her long to find where Matthew is. He cannot be moved yet.

It's a wonder he's still alive.

She came as soon as she could. She had to get Lucas down, had to make sure he was sleeping. Sue will keep an eye out for him. Her normally composed mouth had trembled, her eyes were bloodshot, as she told Katherine to call her if there was anything, *anything* she could do . . . Katherine had wanted nothing more than to lay her head on Sue's shoulder and cry, but she knew that she might never let go. She's tried to call Sael, but she can't get ahold of him—he's probably already flying home. John asked her to come to the hospital, and she cannot refuse him anything now. He meets her at the nurse's desk by the entrance to the ICU.

Katherine is shocked. In only a few hours, John has grown old. There are lines around his mouth. His eyes are shadowed; his skin is waxy and gray.

"Katherine." He swallows.

"I came as soon as I could."

"Yes," he says. "Where's Lucas?"

"In bed, asleep. Sue is looking after him."

"Good, good." But his speech is mechanical.

They walk together down the corridor. She pauses nervously at the door to Matthew's room.

"Come in."

"Are you sure?"

"Yes."

The man in the bed cannot be Matthew. He's too small, too pale; his arms are snaked in tubes hooked up to an endless array of machines that bleep and beep.

"Oh my God." Her eyes prick with tears and she moves toward the bed. "Oh, Matthew."

John mutters something under his breath.

Katherine doesn't even hear him at first. "What?"

"I said, I hope you're happy."

Her head whips up. She stares at him. "What do you mean?!"

His eyes never leave her face. His voice is low, but the words are sharp as nails. "It was raining, for fuck's sake. Hadn't you seen enough castles?"

She has never heard him swear before, and it scrapes her raw.

"He came to get you." There is something in his eyes that she doesn't understand, doesn't like.

"I never saw him," she stammers. "John, I swear I didn't or I would have come back with him. John, you *have* to believe me."

"It doesn't matter now," he hisses slowly.

For a few moments she only watches him until the silence becomes unbearable. "John," she whispers, "I promise I never saw him."

"Stop crying." He speaks quietly, without emotion. "He doesn't need your tears."

It is as though he has struck her.

"There's only one thing he needs from you." He pauses. "Heal him."

"John, what are you talking about?" Her heart contracts, and her arms crawl with gooseflesh.

"You heard me." His eyes blaze in his white face.

"I don't understand!" Instinctively she raises her palms up.

"Heal him, heal him like you healed *me*." It's not John who stands before her but the construction worker, only far more dangerous.

"Like I healed you?" There's a dangerous wobble in her throat. She takes a step back, trying to get to the door, but—

He's next to her now, grabbing her wrist. He's pulling her toward Matthew's bed, his grip is horribly strong.

"John, let go! You're hurting me!" She is squeaky with panic.

He isn't listening. "Look at him."

Katherine ceases to struggle and stares down at the lifeless figure.

"He's a vegetable."

The harshness of his tone makes her wince. "John, stop."

"No. I won't stop. The love of my life is a vegetable. He'll never walk or talk or laugh or love again. He'll never breathe without machines." He closes his eyes. "Unless . . ."

"Unless?"

"Unless you heal him."

Oh Jesus, he's gone crazy with grief. He's out of his mind.

"In my study, that day when I first met you . . ."

"What about it?" *Keep him talking.*

"Katherine, I had just been diagnosed with Stage III pancreatic cancer."

"Oh my God! Matthew never said anything!"

"Matthew didn't know. I couldn't bring myself to tell him yet. He just sensed something was wrong."

"John, I—"

"We were in my study, and you became light-headed, and I grabbed you, and you . . . you *did* something to me."

"No, I didn't—"

"You did, because afterward I felt . . . different. I went to the doctor and asked them to retest me. They thought I was in denial, but I insisted, and you know what?" He's breathing hard, and his breath is sour.

The thought randomly comes to her that he needs to drink more water, that Matthew would have made him drink more water. "What?"

"It was gone, as though the tumor had never been there in the first place. The doctors couldn't believe it. No one could."

"John, please, I don't know what you're talking about!"

"Yes, you do."

"John, you have to stop this." Any second now she's going to lose it—She tries to pull away, but John's grasp is iron.

"Look. At. Him." With each word he jerks her arm. "The love of my life is a vegetable. They say that he'll never walk, never breathe again without machines. You understand? Katherine? You get it?" He tugs her closer, his other hand clamped to the back of her neck.

"I don't know what you are, and I don't care. I know what you're capable of. You fix him. Heal him."

"John, stop it. Stop it! Let go!"

But now he's pressing her face down toward Matthew, close toward his yellow-blue lips, bruises blooming stark against his white skin.

"I can't! Let go! Let go!" Her voice rises to a shriek.

Suddenly, a nurse appears at the door. "What's going on?"

"Please." Tears stream down his face "Please, you can give me back the cancer, I don't care, please, only save him!"

"Sir!" The nurse is by his side, trying to pry his hands off Katherine. "Sir, I understand you're upset, but you need to let go! Sir! Excuse me!" she calls out. "Bryn! Bryn! Over here now! I need some help!"

"For God's sake, heal him! Heal him!" But his grip is loosening. "Take me, take me instead. Don't take my heart, don't take my love."

Katherine manages to pull away as a large orderly arrives. The nurse puts her arms protectively around John as he sags over Matthew's bed.

"You'd better go," she tells Katherine over her shoulder.

John's agonized cries echo in Katherine's ears as she runs from the hospital room, follows her down the passageway and out, out into the wet night.

The guesthouse is very still and dark. Everyone has gone to bed, even Sue. It's just as well. Katherine doesn't think she could bear to face anyone now, as kind as they might be. She tries Sael's phone again, and again it goes straight to voicemail. *What would you say if he answered?* she wonders. She has never longed for him as much as she longs for him right now, longs to feel his arms around her, longs for him to tell her that everything will be okay. But there's a little boy upstairs who needs her.

Katherine tries to be as quiet as possible in the bedroom, but the floorboards creak underneath her. She undresses as quickly as she can, hurries into the bathroom. A face she hardly knows peers back at her from the mirror. Milky skin and long, dark hair. The rims of her eyes are red, but there's something else. She draws closer to her reflection.

She is standing in a bedroom. It's not her bedroom. It's one of Sue's bedrooms. She's in the bed-and-breakfast and it is still nighttime and she is standing over Lucas's bed. He is asleep.

She clutches something white and soft. A pillow.

She's holding a pillow, holding it above Lucas's head. Lucas sighs, although his thumb is in his mouth, rolls over, eyelids fluttering a little as he dreams.

What are you doing?

Katherine manages to make it out of the bedroom and into the bathroom. She sinks to her knees, balls up on the tiled floor.

Oh God. Oh God. What was that? What's happening to you?

All she wants to do is sleep. Sleep calls to her, pulls at her with strong fingers. *It was nothing*, sleep murmurs. *Nothing, you were dreaming.*

She pushes herself up. Goes to the sink. Turns on the tap. Splashes cold water on her face. It shocks her.

In that moment, she knows. *No, it wasn't a dream.*

The last thing she remembers is staring at the mirror. She wants to look in the mirror again. The urge to see her reflection is strong, almost overwhelming. She splashes more cold water, but it's less of a shock now. If she can't look at herself, she may as well go to bed. She needs to sleep, she must sleep.

You can't. You can't be alone with Lucas, she realizes.

What is she to do? She can't reach Sael. *Think, think, Katherine, think.*

And then, as late as it is, she fetches her phone from the bedroom and dials. She has no choice.

The woman on the other end picks up immediately, almost as if she has been waiting for Katherine's call.

"I need you. I know it's late, but I need you. I need you to come and get us. Please, help me."

"I'll come tomorrow first thing," Niamh reassures her. "Do you think can you hang in there until then?"

Katherine tries not to burst into tears. She doesn't think she has ever been so relieved. "Yes," she exhales. "Thank you."

"You had to be in Wales, didn't you?"

Katherine manages a shaky laugh. "I guess I did."

"Typical. Well, text me your address and I'll make a plan."

"Niamh, thank you so, so much."

"Oh, shut up, you daft cow. Go to sleep, I'll see yez soon."

Katherine, still smiling, hangs up.

Then her smile fades. She can't sleep, at least not in the same room with him. The bed is singing its siren song, but she takes the coverlet and a pillow into the bathroom and shuts the door behind her. She locks the door and removes the key. Then she plugs the sink and runs the cold tap until the sink is full. After she drops the key in, she thrusts her hand down, wincing as she reaches through the cold water. That should wake her up if she tries to, tries to . . . But here Katherine falters. She does not look in the mirror. Although she wants to, although the pull of it is a physical ache.

No matter what happens, she must not look in the mirror.

Instead, she puts the bedding in the bath. She angles her cumbersome body as best she can and closes her eyes.

Why were you standing over Lucas's bed with a pillow? Where were you when Matthew fell?

But she can't think about that now. She just has to make it through till morning.

It will all be okay tomorrow, she reminds herself, *if you can just make it through the night.*

30

Sael

They offer him a choice of beverages. Champagne, wine, a beer?

He asks for water. He has a lot of work to do, but more than that, he needs a clear head. He needs to think. The clouds skim under him; then he leans back, closes his eyes. Just for a moment he'll enjoy the silence, the stillness. The captain says it should be a smooth flight now that the storm has cleared. The storm that caused hours of delays, that couldn't have come at a worse time.

In just under thirteen hours, he'll be home. He's not sure he thinks of it as *home*. He thinks of it as back to Katherine. And is Katherine *home*? Surely *home* should be a place of safety, of comfort, of peace—and Katherine? Katherine is none of those things.

He was just beginning to come to terms with what had happened. The damage wrought, the trauma. David dead, killed by Katherine. Self-defense, he knows that, at least on the surface, but there was still anger, and still more anger at David himself. David, a serial killer, the Sickle Man. And he never knew. Never picked up any strange vibe or feeling or clue. If he could just sit down with

David one more time and ask, *Why? Why? Why? Why did you do it?* How could he not have known?

Because he had met Katherine and she had thrown him into chaos. Refusing to play his games, introducing her own. He was obsessed, possessed. And jealous, jealous of David, his best friend, whom he betrayed and then who betrayed him in turn. It could not be repaired. The only way forward was, well, forward. He got the name of a great shrink. He hadn't believed in them, thought therapy was for the weak, but she was good. She called him on his shit, but didn't judge him.

True, sometimes she did say, "And what do you think about that?"

But really, it was a fair question. What *did* he think? What *did* he feel?

"You need closure," she had said. "You can't hide from this. I guess you could, but ultimately you'll have to make peace of a sort with it, whatever that peace looks like for you."

And the job offer had come up: challenging, hard work. An opportunity in all senses of the word.

"Hard work is excellent." His shrink was a fan. "But before you go, I think you should tie up loose ends. This will give you the motivation, an opportunity to set things right."

He had been a nervous wreck trying to work out what would be best. A public place, a neutral time of day. Nothing says closure like coffee in a diner at four p.m. No possibility for one drink to lead to another and into his bed. No, he would act like an adult. And maybe she wouldn't even reply. God knows he had shut her out, pushed her away. The woman he loved, had wanted to marry.

But when Katherine walked in, all his carefully drawn-out scenarios dissolved. She looked different, although he couldn't put his finger on how. It wasn't just him either. He saw the way other people watched her. There was something about her. A glow? Could it have just been that? A man in a diner booth had seemed to upset her. He had wanted to know what was going on, wanted to defend her. At the same time, he wanted to attack her himself. She was bringing out everything that was uncertain and uneven and roiling within him. Part of him, a large part, wanted to leap across the table and lift her up, kiss her and fuck her. Bury his face in her neck and weep. Hold her. And he wanted *her* to hold him and tell him that it would all be all right. But none of that had happened. They sat across from each other and made polite conversation. She seemed to be coping. He hadn't even thought of Lucas. What must that be like for both of them? She became more animated, warmer, when she spoke about him. He was jealous, a shameful thing he kept from even his therapist. Lucas, what a strange little kid. He had known about David somehow, and he would now have Katherine for life.

And he, Sael, would have closure. She seemed to take his announcement about leaving calmly enough. But what had he expected? Tears and begging? *Oh, Sael, please don't go?*

"That's on you," his shrink said. "Those are your projections, your fantasies, your fears and hopes."

It was sad saying good-bye.

"You're allowed to be sad," his shrink told him. "But also you're allowed to move on, and let go."

Then he had seen them both weeping on the sidewalk, and over hot chocolate everything imploded.

Now he understands his mistake.

He had been so focused on them coming that he forgot to think about what it would be like when they came. He didn't know how Katherine had changed.

She was prickly and unpredictable. He never knew what would set her off. He supposed it was the hormones, but that didn't make it easier to live with. And she seemed so lost, so purposeless. He wanted to comfort her and he wanted to shake her. After all, it was due to him that they were there, but she was a grown woman; she had also had a choice. What else was he supposed to do? And Georgie had been easy to talk to.

George, Georgie, Georgiana.

He had thought it was funny he had assumed Georgie was a man. Her initial emails *had* been pretty gender neutral in tone. She had been a godsend. Organized, funny, easygoing, with a self-deprecating sense of humor, her dry, delicious accent like a spritzer, her sudden infectious laugh. With Georgie, he never worried about what would piss her off or hurt her. She didn't look at him blankly at times, as if she didn't know him. She remembered past conversations. Maybe it was all smoke up his ass, but she seemed to take a genuine interest in his thoughts, opinions, what he felt. She knew the world he was in, appreciated the pressure he was under, what it took to do what he did. It would have been so great if she and Katherine could have become friends, but of course Katherine wasn't having any of that. That moment in the kitchen seemed frozen in her mind. She took everything the wrong way, even with the dog, which ultimately had been for her. He didn't know what he had done wrong, only that he had miscalculated *badly*.

Yes, Georgie was beautiful, and yes, she was young, but it wasn't just that, not by a long shot. She knew how to make him laugh, how to make him relax. He found himself eager to go to work, to connect. He honestly couldn't pinpoint when the texts, in the beginning so businesslike, began to turn more playful. Nor could he say exactly when they started to get lunch, and when it had become less about work and more about their day, what they had done on the weekends. The more he looked forward to coming to work, the more he dreaded coming home.

He thinks of them as the night visits.

He had woken with a start to find Katherine straddling him. She had covered his mouth with one hand, and with the other she had reached down and taken him, stroking and pulling with a confident, almost painful firmness, and then she had slid down and taken him inside her so fast it almost took his breath away. He had almost cried out with the surprise and the shock of it, but she pushed her palm hard against his teeth and thrust and thrust against him. And almost before he could regain himself, she had dismounted, rolled off, disappeared. At first he thought she had gone to the bathroom and would be back, but as the minutes stretched on into a growing silence he realized that she would not be returning. In the morning, he almost wondered if it had been a dream. She made no mention of it, so neither did he.

But two nights later, it happened again. This time he woke to her sucking his dick. He would always wake out of sleep, with her sometimes upon him, sometimes taking him into her mouth, or in her hands. Always in silence. If he tried to say anything, she would cover his mouth. It was rough; there was an undercurrent of violence. She was almost feral in her hunger for him. Her hunger was frightening. It was immense. Yes, there was a part of him that wanted it, craved it, desired her, but more and more he began to fear these encounters. He would look up at her as she rode him, and she seemed so cold and so fierce. She kissed him as if she could and would consume him.

He now sleeps in the room he's taken as his office. He is going to bed later these days and he doesn't want to disturb her. If he's honest, though, he knows that it's more than the work. There's something dehumanizing about these interactions and he wants to avoid her.

Meanwhile, Georgie asks him how he's doing, asks him how his day was, how the meeting went, how Lucas is getting on at school, how Cordy is doing. Meanwhile, he's staying later at work. Meanwhile, he and Georgie eat takeout, Indian, sushi, food that Katherine can't eat in her pregnant state. Meanwhile, he needs to go to Hong Kong for ten days. So does Georgie.

It had been coming for a while. And then they were there, together, miles away from everyone and everything. It made sense, after the second day, to have a drink, or two or three, and then to ride up in the elevator, only she wasn't stopping on her floor; she was coming to his. They continued to make small talk there, as if this was normal and they did this all the time. Then he opened his door with the sliding card, and they were in each other's arms.

"At last," she had breathed into his ear, "at last."

And after they had made love, she had stayed. Holding her, he couldn't believe he had missed it so much. Another body pressed against his own. Someone to watch over and to protect.

He didn't think he felt guilty. Georgie was Georgie, and Katherine was Katherine. She had known he wasn't happy, had known it for a long time, and that was all there was to say. It was only when, toward the end of the week, Katherine sent him a picture of just her smiling up at him in front of yet another castle that he began to feel that gnawing sensation. Because being with Georgie reminded him of how much he loved Katherine. After that, every time he holds Georgie close, or kisses her, or enters her, it's Katherine he holds, Katherine he kisses, Katherine he enters.

He has to tell Georgie.

He feels sorry for Georgie, but she's beautiful and she's young and she's smart and she's rich, and she'll find somebody else. Someone who appreciates her, someone who doesn't have a pregnant partner, someone who isn't already in love. He will get home and he will tell Katherine everything. He will make them sit down and talk, no matter how hard it is. He only prays it isn't too late.

He can't sleep with the longing to tell her. This is the longest flight of his life. And as soon as they land he tries to call, but his phone is dead. Something has gone wrong with the charger on the plane.

He's caught in traffic, tapping and tapping his fingers.

And then he's home, finally home.

"Katherine?" he calls. "Lucas?"

No answer, but he's moving through the house, dark and silent, still calling. He plugs in his phone, stares at it with hatred until it charges up. There's a message from Katherine. An accident. A bad one. Matthew has fallen from the parapet. He's in the hospital. Can't be moved. She's trying to work out how to get back. She and Lucas are okay. She doesn't know why she can't get hold of him. Hopes he's okay.

Sael has to sit down. His legs won't hold him. An accident, but thank God they're okay. He calls her, but it goes straight to voice-mail.

"Katherine? Hi, I'm so sorry, there was a massive storm and we were delayed, and then my phone died. Listen, call me back as soon as you get this and we'll make a plan. I'll come and get you guys. I'm so sorry about Matthew. Just hang tight, I'm coming. I—"

Say it, you shithead, just say it!

"I love you."

He hangs up the phone. He's exhausted. He'll have a shower; then he'll try her again, work out where she is, how to get to her. His head is pounding, his ears are ringing, and no, it's coming from the front door, someone is there.

Sael opens the door and sees a large man, possibly in his sixties and on the heavy side, standing there. Shadowed eyes gaze from the lined wreckage of his face into Sael's own.

"Yes?"

"Are you Katherine's husband?" the man asks, and Sael nods.

For all purposes he *is* her husband and she, his wife. They're only missing the paper and rings that makes it official.

"I'm Cathal."

Sael stands there blankly.

"Niamh's husband?" the man says.

"Niamh?" Yes, that rings a bell; then something registers. Niamh is Katherine's friend, also pregnant. But why is her husband here? Did Niamh go with Katherine to Wales? He doesn't understand what's going on, only knows that something is not right. Is very far from right. "Is something wrong?"

The man's haggard face tightens with strain. "I don't know. I'm looking for Niamh, but I think, I think, they might be together."

"Come in," Sael says, holding the door.

31

Lucas

Lucas is having a bad dream.

He's walking through the woods, tangled and green, with Cordelia by his side. Sunlight shines through the leaves. They hear a whistle, and Cordy runs ahead.

"Wait, Cordy, wait!" he calls, but Cordy is bounding ahead, and there is a clearing.

In the clearing stands a lady. She has long dark hair and wears a long green dress. Lucas thinks he's seen her before. She stands there, stirring a big pot, like the witch's pot he saw in the Halloween parade back in New York. The lady dips in a large spoon and pours out some food into a bowl. It's a dog-food bowl, Cordy's bowl. She holds out the bowl for Cordy, but Lucas knows that the food is bad. It's like chocolate for dogs, but it's much worse.

Don't eat that, Cordy! Lucas tries to shout, but he has no voice. *Get away from her!*

He's sprinting, but he knows that he will never be in time. The lady grins at him through the trees, and Lucas sees her teeth are red. He screams, and then he's awake.

He's not in the woods. He's in Wales. He's in the room he shares with Kat.

"Kat?"

She's not in her bed. Lucas can tell by the light that it's not early in the morning. Where is she? She must be in the bathroom. He turns and sees the closed door. That's it. In a moment she'll come out of the bathroom and come over and sit on the bed and say, *Want to talk?* Because it's important to use his words, it's important to share his feelings when something bad happens. And something really bad has happened.

He lies there and waits for the bathroom door to open. He waits and waits. Nothing. The brown door is closed. Lucas begins to wonder if it's ever been open. He gets up and goes over to the door. Maybe Kat is in the shower. When Kat is in the shower she likes to sing. She gets embarrassed about this, but Lucas likes to hear her sing. She'll sing him lullabies; she sings funny songs in the shower.

He doesn't think she'll be singing today.

He gets up and presses his ear against the door, but he can't hear the shower. Maybe she's on the toilet. That would be bad to hear because that's private, but still, it would mean that she was there. Again he puts his ear against the door and listens; again there is nothing.

"Kat?" he whispers.

Still nothing. So Lucas raises his hand and he knocks, lightly at first and then louder. He's scared now. "Kat! Kat!" he cries.

He wonders if he will have to go and get Sue, the tears are starting to come, when there's the clink of a key in the lock. The handle slowly turns and the door opens, revealing Kat. Her skin is pale and her eyes are pink and swollen.

"Kat? Are you okay?"

She stares at him for a moment like she doesn't know who he is, and then she tries to smile. Somehow, this is worse.

"Yes, honey."

"Did you see Matthew?"

Kat winces. "He's still very hurt."

"Can I see him?"

He is not surprised when she shakes her head. "Not yet, my love."

"When will he better?"

"I don't know, baby."

"Is John here?"

"John is with Matthew."

Lucas swallows. He wants to tell Kat something. "John was screaming," he whispers, "screaming and screaming."

"That must have been very scary."

He blinks.

"It's okay to admit you were scared. I was scared too. He was just very upset about Matthew."

"Is Matthew going to be okay?"

Kat bites her lip. "I hope so." She sniffs and wipes her eyes with the back of her hand. "Now," she says in a clearer voice, "why don't you go downstairs and ask Sue for some breakfast? You must be hungry."

"Don't you want to eat breakfast?"

"I'll grab something later. I'm not that hungry and I need to pack up."

"Pack?"

Kat's smile is watery. "We're leaving today. I made a plan."

He wants to ask more questions, but Kat frowns and closes her eyes and rubs at her forehead like her head is very sore, so he doesn't. He goes downstairs, where Sue is cleaning up some breakfast dishes.

"Hi, Lucas," Sue greets him, "Where's Katherine?"

"She says she's not that hungry."

Sue frowns. "Poor thing, you've all had such a terrible time. Maybe I'd better check on her."

"She's fine." Lucas thinks Kat wants to be alone right now. "She's just packing."

"Packing?" Sue frowns.

"She says she made a plan."

"I'll speak to her after I give you breakfast. You're both welcome to stay."

Lucas smiles. That would be good. He likes Sue. He feels safe with her.

Sue gives Lucas cereal, yogurt, and fruit. Then she leaves him to eat it and goes upstairs to talk with Kat. Then he hears the stairs creak. Sue and Kat are coming downstairs together, carrying their suitcases.

"Now that's taken care of, why not have something to eat?"

"Thank you, but I'm not sure I could manage it," Katherine replies apologetically.

Sue is understanding. "At least let me make you some tea."

"Well, maybe a cup, thanks. Then I'll settle up with you, and I'll settle John and Matthew's room too."

Sue nods. She looks sad.

Katherine turns to Lucas. "If you've finished your breakfast, why not go upstairs and check our room to make sure I didn't forget anything?"

He's proud of the responsibility.

The room looks fine, apart from one of the beds, which has no bedding on it. Lucas hesitates at the open bathroom door. Still, he wants to see, wants to know. He peers around the door. There's nothing, nothing wrong, and Lucas wants to laugh at himself for being so silly except—

There is a duvet and a pillow in the bathtub. Was Kat sleeping in the bathtub?

Also, he sees something on the mirror, a circle with a line through it. The circle and the line look like scratches but deeper. Lucas wonders how it got there, how you could be so strong as to scratch a mirror like that. He remembers seeing the glassblowers at the fair, watching them use long sticks of metal in the ovens, how long it took to shape something.

He stands on tiptoe, puts up his hand to touch the smooth, cool glass. Something faint red is in the center of the circle, underneath the line. A thumbprint. He learned about thumbprints in school. Everyone has their own thumbprint; no two are alike. They had used paint and made thumbprints and given the thumbprints little faces and stick legs and arms so they looked like silly little people, but this thumbprint doesn't have a face or legs or arms. He stares harder. It doesn't look like paint either. It looks like—

"Lucas!" Kat's voice drifts up the stairs. "Time to go!"

He starts guiltily, as if he were doing something bad. He would have liked to look more at the circle, and the thumbprint. He doesn't think Sue will like it. *He* doesn't like it. It looks . . . wrong.

"Lucas!"

All of a sudden, he doesn't want to go. He wants to stay here with Sue, where it's safe.

"Come on, honey, let's go!"

Slowly he heads down the stairs.

Kat is there, her hands on her hips. "What took you so long?"

"Sorry," he mumbles.

"Time to go. Say good-bye to Sue."

Lucas peers up at Sue. "Good-bye. Thank you."

Sue smiles, bends down. "It was my pleasure. Come back soon." She straightens up and turns to Kat. "Please let me know how he is and how everything goes."

Lucas knows Sue is talking about Matthew.

Kat takes a breath; she seems like she may cry. "Thank you for all your kindness."

Both women hesitate. Then Sue swallows, and Kat takes his hand, and they walk out into the sunshine toward the car. Kat opens the car door for him, but he pauses. The driver briefly glances at him.

"Don't you remember Niamh?"

He stares at the woman. This can't be Niamh. The Niamh he knows is laughing and pretty with a big belly because there is a baby inside, like Kat's belly. This Niamh is pale and thin and her hair hangs straight, doesn't bounce. It's dirty. Why would Kat let them get in the car with someone like this?

The question comes before he can stop it. "Where's your belly?"

Niamh's face darkens. "Get in."

Lucas gets in and sits in the backseat, trying not to cry. Kat makes sure he is buckled up and then goes to the front of the car. She is moving very slowly.

She gets in and addresses Niamh. "Thank you for doing this."

Niamh nods.

Kat closes her eyes, leans back. "I didn't know who else to call."

Niamh presses a button to start the ignition, and Kat closes her eyes; her head rolls.

"Kat?" he asks. "Kat?"

"Let her sleep," Niamh tells him.

And they drive.

32

Lucas

Niamh sings to herself.

"Rock-a-bye baby, on the treetop . . ."

It sounds strange in the daytime when there are no babies around. She has a pretty voice and she doesn't sing loudly, but it makes Lucas feel uncomfortable. He sits in the backseat and stares out of the window.

He tries to remember when it all first began. It started soon after they had come to London on the big airplane. He would wake up in the night and realize she was standing in the doorway, watching him. She looked like Kat, she wore Kat's clothes, but when she came to him in the dark, she wasn't Kat. His bedroom would turn cold. He would shut his eyes tight and pretend to be asleep, and eventually he would hear her leave.

Kat knew there was something bothering him, but she didn't know what. And he couldn't tell her. He couldn't tell anyone, but the knowledge grew like a balloon inside him. Tighter and tighter and tighter, until he thought his chest would burst.

Once Mrs. B had asked him, "Is it Katherine?"

And he had to say no, because Kat would never hurt him. Kat loved him. But Kat was no longer Kat. At first, it had only been at night, but more and more, Kat was like somebody else. But who?

It was like new shoes. He and Kat had bought him nice shoes before he started at his new school, but they were a little stiff and they hurt his feet. The salesman had said that sometimes shoes have to get broken in.

"Why broken," he had asked, "when they're supposed to be new?"

"He means you have to wear them for a little at a time every day," Kat, the real Kat, had told him. "The longer you wear them, the more comfortable they get. But you'll let me know if they stay sore? Maybe you do need a larger pair."

But the salesman was right. He had worn the new shoes around for a little bit at a time, and then for longer and longer, and then he began to forget he was wearing them at all. That is what is happening now with Kat. Whoever is inside Kat is breaking in her body. Wearing her skin. First just at night, and now in the daytime too.

"When are we getting to London?"

New, thin Niamh doesn't answer. The car makes a tick, tick, tick noise as they turn onto another street.

"We're not going back to London, are we?" he says to her.

She doesn't say anything, but he knows he's right.

He looks at Niamh. She doesn't have a belly anymore. If her belly is gone, then maybe her baby is gone too.

"What happened to your baby?

She flinches. Lucas has a very bad feeling.

For a long time he looks out of the window at the other cars. He wishes he were in any of them. And a growing need, a pain, starts in his bladder.

"Kat?"

She doesn't move.

"Niamh?"

No response. As if he isn't here.

"Niamh?"

Again, nothing, but now he must say it.

"I have to go to the bathroom."

Finally she glances at him in her rearview mirror.

He makes sure he looks straight back at her, even though he really doesn't want to. Her eyes are dark.

"Please?"

"You can't hold it?"

He shakes his head. "How long until we get to our house?"

It's now that he knows for certain that they're not going to their house or her house or anywhere Kat wanted to go.

"Please," he begs. The pain is getting worse. "Please don't make me go in my pants like a baby."

She bites her lip.

He can see she's unsure. "I'll be fast," he pleads. "I promise."

"You had better be," she responds.

The green rest stop sign says WELCOME.

They turn in and find a parking space.

"Okay." Niamh turns off the car. She turns to Lucas. "We're going to be quick. Like five minutes. Got it?"

"Okay."

"Don't talk to anyone. You don't say a word. Understand me?"

"Yes." He is suddenly sure she would hurt him if he did.

It's very quiet. They walk quickly toward the bathrooms.

"You have five minutes," she tells him.

By now his need is so great that he almost doesn't make it to the toilet. Afterward, he just stands there. What can he do? What can he do? The tears come.

Don't be a baby, he tells himself, but it's no use. He rubs his eyes furiously.

Then there is a tap on the wall of his stall.

He peers up. Directly in front of him.

Another tap, lower down the wall.

He bends down and then farther down until he sees into the next stall, through the gap between the floor and the wall.

Those feet. Bare and brown. He remembers them. He would know them anywhere. "Momma?"

"Lucas! Come on!" Niamh must be in the doorway of the bathroom. She sounds angry.

"I'm still using the bathroom," he calls back.

"Hurry up!"

A hand, Momma's hand, appears next to her feet. She drops a crumpled wad of toilet paper on the floor. Spots of ink have seeped through. He grabs it, unfolds it.

LOOK
IN
BAG

"What bag?" he whispers.

No answer.

"What bag? Momma, what bag?" There is no bag here.

A knock on his stall door.

"Lucas! Stop playing around! Let's go!"

He hastily throws the toilet paper into the toilet and flushes, unlocks the stall door.

Niamh is furious. "I said let's go! What were you doing in there?" She peers suspiciously into the stall.

"Nothing," he says. "I just really had to go." As he walks out, he casually tries to see into the stall next to him.

The door is open, and the stall is empty.

Niamh allows him to rinse his hands, and then he is marched out. She squeezes his arm so tightly that he almost cries out.

They have taken about ten steps outside toward the parking lot when she slaps his face, hard. "I told you to hurry up!"

Then she half drags, half pulls him along to the car. Kat is still inside, asleep.

Niamh turns to Lucas. "Get in."

His face is stinging and his arm aches. He sits quietly, not moving. Niamh buckles up and turns to him.

"I hope you enjoyed your little bathroom break because that's the end of it. We're not stopping again."

He doesn't reply. He needs to put on his seat belt. It takes him several tries, but he keeps at it, and on the fourth try the buckle clicks. As he pushes it, his eyes fall on his knapsack there on the floor. His knapsack, his bag.

Look in bag.

He waits until they've been driving for a while.

Niamh has stopped singing, but now it's worse. She's talking and listening to someone. Someone he can't hear. Someone he can't see. Niamh nods. She murmurs, "Yes, I understand. Yes, I will." She cocks her head on one side. She laughs. This is worse than the singing. It's like she has an imaginary friend, but Lucas knows that just because you can't see or hear them doesn't mean they're not there.

He reaches down and unzips the zipper as slowly as possible. She doesn't hear him. Maybe she has forgotten that he is here.

With one hand, he digs around inside his bag. Only feels clothes, the clothes that Kat packed for him.

Look in bag.

But nothing in here can help him. His hand digs farther, and then his fingers feel something different. Something sharp. As slowly and carefully as he can, he maneuvers it up through the clothes and then peers down. It's red, rusted, but he knows what it is.

It's John's knife. Matthew had shown it to him when he and Kat came to their house before they all went to Wales.

"What do you think of it?" he had asked. "I got it for John as a present."

Lucas hadn't known what to say. It didn't look like any normal knife to him. It had a strange red color and deep curls carved upon its handle. Momma and Kat had always told him not to touch knives. He wouldn't want to eat with it or even hold it, but Matthew was very proud and he didn't want to hurt his feelings.

"It's pretty cool?" guessing that's what Matthew would like to hear, and Matthew rumpled his hair and said, "Exactly what I thought."

How did John's knife get into his bag? Did Momma put it there?

He doesn't know. But if his momma did that, there must be a reason.

Niamh has started to sing again.

"When the wind blows . . ." She giggles like the song is a funny one.

Lucas closes his eyes. He wishes he could close his ears against Niamh's singing.

He tries to sleep.

33

Sael

The radio weather reports grow worse. Drivers are warned to proceed with caution. It's the word "caution" that gets him. "Caution" because the forecasters don't really seem to know what's approaching, only that it is an unusual weather pattern. Not at all typical for this time of year.

"If we were in the States," he says to Cathal, "the news would be going crazy. Full-blown panic mode."

Cathal nods but says nothing, keeps his eyes on the road. He looks as tense and unhappy as Sael feels.

It was one of the strangest exchanges Sael has ever had. The man introduced himself as Cathal.

"Niamh's husband?"

Somewhere, a bell in Sael's head rang. "Oh yes! Your wife is also pregnant."

Cathal's expression was unreadable. "Didn't she tell you?"

"Tell me what?"

"We lost the baby."

"Oh my God." He feels as though he's been punched. "Katherine never told me."

"I wonder if she knew. I don't think Niamh told her. I don't think she told anyone." Cathal grimaces.

Sael senses he should get back to the matter at hand. "So how do you know they're together, and how are we going to find them?"

"Because I've tracked her phone."

"Tracked her phone?"

"I work for a company that specializes in mobile securities. I installed our new app on her phone." He reddens under the other man's gaze. "Look, think of me what you will, she's been in a bad way and I was worried. I woke up and she was gone. I called her, but it went straight to voicemail. Her location showed that she was on her way to Wales. I remember her saying something about Katherine taking a trip there."

Sael doesn't question Cathal further, only asks, "How bad?"

"Bad." He looks away.

So now they're in Cathal's car and driving to Wales. And they are not proceeding with caution. They have thrown caution to the winds and are speeding full tilt, trying to catch up to the blue dot on the screen. During the ride, Cathal filled him in on just how "bad" it had gotten.

They had been trying for ages to have a child. Margot, his first wife, had no difficulty conceiving Bella. Bella now a teenager who goaded and jabbed at Niamh. Cathal thinks this might have added to the pressure. Niamh had always been a little insecure when it came to his first marriage, his wealth, his background, though he had told her time and time again that he loved everything about her. She had believed that a baby would secure their life together, give it solidity, even a respectability she publicly scorned but clearly longed for. Life became a never-ending stream of specialists and treatments, injections, medication, poking and prodding, soulless clinical rooms, invasive questions, and negative test results.

She had borne it so bravely, much better than him. And when she finally conceived, it had seemed like a miracle. They were so happy. Until the night a few weeks ago when she shook him awake, their bedsheets soaked bright red.

Afterward, she has turned her face to the wall. Refused to see the visiting midwives, to talk with her family, to contact her friends. Yet when he passed their room he would hear her voice, low but animated, talking with someone.

"Grief takes everyone differently," his mother had told him.

"Just be there for her," said her sisters. "She'll come around."

At three a.m., her side of the bed would be cold, empty. Muffled murmurs coming through the locked bathroom door. Her hip bones began to protrude through her stained pajama pants; lank strands of greasy hair fell over her eyes. He begged her to seek help, pleaded with her.

"She'll help me. She'll see me through. She knows what to do."

"Who is she? What are you talking about?" He kept asking.

Niamh's gaze sliding up and away and over his shoulder. Looking at someone or something he couldn't see. She smiled as if to reassure an invisible presence. He had felt like a shit downloading the software onto her phone, but he can't pretend he trusts her anymore. He is afraid of what she may do to herself.

Sael wants to go faster, as fast as possible, but he knows that if they are stopped now by a traffic officer, that's the end of it. The English are serious about their driving laws. It will slow them down, use up time they don't have.

He looks out of the window. The sky is yellowing. *Something is coming*, he thinks. *Something is coming. I hope we make it.* But he doesn't have a good feeling.

They speed along without saying anything for a long time, and then Cathal glances at the blue dot and swears and brakes and puts on his indicators.

"They've gone off the motorway."

Sael grabs the phone, starts navigating. "Left. Okay, stay here, they've taken a right."

They are heading down smaller roads, and the sky grows darker and darker.

"What's around here, do you think?" Sael's own words sound wrong, cracked and strained.

"Fuck if I know," says Cathal.

And then they see a sign. It's in Welsh, a string of letters full of L's and W's, but the symbol of the little walking man tells them all they need to know. There are footpaths for hikers all around here.

"Why in God's name would they be here?" There is a bewildered note in Cathal's voice that frightens Sael.

Then they see a lone car parked along the shoulder of the road, the passenger front door open. Cathal pulls up sharply behind it.

"It's hers," Cathal says. He almost doesn't turn off the ignition because he's trying to get out so fast.

There is something horrible about that open door. Sael hurries toward the car, glances inside, sees that their phones are there, also a bag that has some sandwiches and a bottle of water in it. But why wouldn't they take that with them?

Cathal is already half running down the road, looking desperately to either side. Sael also begins to trot, but there's no sign of any of them. A wind is blowing, lifting Sael's hair; it's warm, weirdly intimate. It only adds to his unease. He has an urge to call out, but knows in his gut that to do so would be a mistake.

Cathal has stopped. "Fuck," he breathes.

Sael is about to ask when he sees for himself: two footpaths steeply diverging.

"We'll have to split up."

"Wait, what's this?" Cathal is bending over something in the grass, something red and soft.

Sael's stomach twists over in a greasy lump. "It's Lucas's," he says. "It's his shirt." He remembers buying it for Lucas, a Polo shirt, a ridiculous amount of money to spend on a five-year-old, but he hadn't been able to resist himself. He looks around wildly, then gives a cry as he steps on a small pair of jeans. He holds them up so Cathal can see.

"Thank Jesus," Cathal says. "Let's go, the light won't last for long."

34

Lucas

Lucas opens his eyes. Noises are coming from Kat. He remembers taking Cordy to the vet, and this huge dog—it was called a Doberman pinscher—kept growling. It's a sound full of teeth, like thunder but lower. Lucas didn't think a person could make that kind of noise.

"What's happening?" His question comes out before he can stop it. He didn't mean to ask one because he is terrified of Niamh.

"We're close." She sounds very excited, like a kid on his way to Disney World. "We're almost there!"

He is afraid to ask any more questions. He stares out of the window for clues about where "there" is. They've turned off the motorway now, onto a narrow road bordered by pine trees, and there aren't any other cars around. The sky is deepening into a yellowy purple like a bruise. It must be windy because the pine trees sway.

The humming and growling noise grows louder. Kat is panting, like Cordy. In between she groans hoarsely and clutches her belly.

"We're here," Niamh announces abruptly.

She pulls the car over to the edge of the road, then grabs her bag, gets out, and runs around to the passenger side of the car. She pulls the door open, and Lucas smells the faint tang of salt on the blustering wind.

They must be near the sea.

Kat half falls, half scrambles out of her seat. Niamh offers an arm, and Kat takes it, leans on her. Together, Niamh leading, the two women begin to move down the shoulder of the road. And then they stop at a gap in the pines, where a footpath cuts away into the trees.

Lucas realizes that they are abandoning him. He doesn't want to get out of the car, but he doesn't want to be left here either. He's hungry, and he's tired. He has to go. He unbuckles his seat belt, picks up his backpack, hoists it on his shoulders, and runs to catch up. But he doesn't want to get too close.

How will anyone find them? How will he find his way back, if he and Kat escape?

The wind is warm, too warm. It may blow him over if he doesn't lean into it. Lucas doesn't know how long they have been walking, only that it is darker now, and he is running out of clothing. He hopes the wind doesn't blow his clues away.

Ahead the footpath curves to the right, to the sea, but Niamh and Katherine aren't following it anymore. They keep going straight, up the slope of a hill that rises out of the thinning trees. He hesitates, drops his sweater at the base of the hill, near the path, and then abandons it to follow them. He doesn't know how much longer he can keep going. He's so tired, so tired.

In the last of the sickly light, Lucas can see the trunk of a great tree on the brow of the hill, and rising behind it, in the not-too-far distance, the dark gray bulk of a castle. But it is different from the castles he visited with Kat and Matthew and John. It scares him, and then he understands why.

Flags are fluttering at the top of the turrets. This castle isn't old, dead, like the others. This castle is alive.

As he climbs the hill, he hears the first wet cough of thunder. He gasps for air, a sharp stabbing pain in his side.

The slope is leveling out, and he can see Kat now. She is on her hands and knees near the base of the tree, and it looks like she's struggling to breathe. Niamh kneels beside her, rubbing her back with one hand. The other she holds, palm up, in front of Kat's face. She appears to be feeding Kat something, like he sometimes feeds Cordy. He creeps closer, but when he sees the smile twisting Niamh's face, he begins to run.

"Stop! Stop, Kat! Don't eat that!"

But Kat doesn't stop. She doesn't even hear him. She is licking Niamh's palm clean.

"Stop!" he screams, tries to push Niamh's hand away. "It's poison!"

Niamh looks up at him in surprise. "Poison?" She laughs. "I would never give her poison. That could hurt the baby. These are herbs that are supposed to induce labor."

"Labor?" The word makes no sense to him.

"How a baby arrives. The baby will be coming soon." Her dark eyes are shining.

Lucas knows babies are born in a hospital. Kat had explained it to him, how she would go to the hospital when the baby was ready to come out, how a doctor would help her. She should be in a *hospital*. There should be adults, a doctor, not just him and Niamh alone, outside on a hill in a storm.

"How can we stop it?"

"*Stop* it?" Niamh glares at him. "Why would we stop it? We can only wait and let her have my baby."

He stumbles back, almost falls over himself. *My baby*? This isn't her baby. He doesn't know what happened to her baby, but this is Kat's baby.

Is she going to take Kat's baby?

35

Lucas

Kat moans, writhes, sweats. Her cheeks are flushed; her eyes are filmy, unfocused. Niamh is sweating too as she gazes intently into Kat's eyes, brushes Kat's hair away from her face.

But Lucas is not watching Kat's face anymore. Instead, he is looking at Kat's necklace. It is shimmering, pulsing with light that radiates outward. He's glimpsed it before. She never takes it off. It's strange, a rough silver circle pushing into itself. It makes him think of a snake. And now it makes him think of a halo.

Lucas wants to know if Niamh notices this, but she's still on her knees by Kat's head, rocking back and forth as she squeezes Kat's hand. Very slowly, very carefully, he leans forward into the light. He has never seen her necklace up close like this before, and only now does he realize the circle *is* actually a snake, a thin silver snake that is feeding on its own tail. Its scales ripple; its tiny red eyes gleam.

Niamh moves quickly, like a tiny monkey he once saw at the zoo. One moment she is clutching Kat's hand, the next she is standing up, peering out into the gathering darkness.

She cocks her head to one side. "All right," she says, only she's not speaking to anyone that Lucas can see. "I'll deal with him. See if I don't." She turns to him. "Hold her hand, stay with her. I'll be right back."

He nods.

She looks at him, and her eyes are dark and shining, like the snake's. "If you make a noise, I'll kill you."

Then she walks into the darkness.

Lucas counts to five. He's almost too scared to move, but this is his only chance. The necklace is bad. He reaches into his backpack, closes his fingers around the handle of the knife.

It feels strange in his hand, not cold but warm, alive. He gingerly touches the chain. It burns his fingertips, and he drops it back against her neck. Then he bites his lip and takes hold of the chain again. Kat cries out, and Lucas can see that there are little drops of blood on her skin, as if the chain had been stuck on her flesh. His hand shaking, he takes the knife and slowly, oh so slowly, slides the blade underneath the chain.

"She will never take our baby."

He freezes. Slowly turns.

The most beautiful woman he has ever seen sits in the gnarled roots of the tree. Her hair is long and dark, like Kat's is now, and her dress is green. She is looking into the darkness where Niamh has run, and slowly shakes her head.

"What?"

"I said she could have the baby if she did what I told her. I lied."

She sounds amused, like she's telling a joke. Then she turns to stare at him.

Lucas is cold all over. He wants to throw up. His bladder lets go and a warm trickle runs down his leg. He doesn't even notice. He can't move.

She is worse than any of the other ladies who used to come to him. She is the one who wears Kat's skin.

"And what do you think you're doing?"

She doesn't sound mad or surprised. She sounds interested.

"What?" It comes out as a squeak.

"What are you doing with that knife?"

Lucas looks down. He had forgotten he was holding it. "I don't know."

"Are you going to kill her?" She smiles.

"No!" Lucas is shocked.

"My mother was killed in the woods," she says lightly. "By the same person who killed *your* mother."

Lucas does not know what to say. He glances miserably away and then back. *Momma.*

"I was not much older than you," the woman continues. "My mother and I had gone to the woods to look for mushrooms."

Before he can stop himself, the question comes out. "Who are you?"

"My name is Margaret."

"Are you a ghost?" he whispers.

"In a way. I lived a long time ago, but a part of me never died." She rises to her feet, steps forward. "Now drop that knife." She does not sound interested anymore. "Drop the knife, or I'll make you wish you were dead and buried with your mother."

36

Sael

Halfway up the hill, they see a castle silhouetted against the seething marbled sky, and beneath it a huge tree. The tree is bathed in pure white light.

Sael was the one who realized that Lucas had been leaving clues for them, shedding his shirt, his jeans, with a purpose, to mark a route. Sael remembers reading *Hansel and Gretel* to him and his heart twists. He had spotted the small blue sweater a little way off the footpath, guiding them away from the sea and up the hill.

"I've never seen anything like it." Cathal's words are barely audible against the rising howl of the wind.

Cathal grabs Sael's arm and pulls them both down to the ground.

"Stay low," he whispers.

Now both of them are crawling on their hands and knees through the gloaming. As they near the tree, Sael can make out two figures underneath its branches. Katherine's face is a mask of pain, and her screams cut through the keening wind. Lucas is bending over her.

Sael forgetting everything scrambles to his feet. "Katherine!" he shouts. "Lucas! Katherine!"

When Lucas turns around, Sael can see that he's holding a knife.

Before he can ask why, Lucas cries, "Sael, look—"

The world goes dark.

37

Lucas

Niamh is running, running, out of the darkness behind Sael, raising a thick, jagged branch higher and higher.

"Sael, look—"

But Lucas is too late. Niamh smashes the branch into the back of Sael's head, and he crumples, his eyes rolling backward. She shrieks triumphantly, lifts the branch high again.

She means to kill him. Lucas screams.

Niamh looks up, sees him with the knife near Katherine's throat.

"No! You will never take my baby! Never! Never!" she cries, dropping the branch.

Then a huge man rushes up, tackles her, pulls her down. Together they fall to the ground.

Niamh is still howling.

38

Lucas

Lucas knows there is no time to wonder about Niamh, or who the man is. He focuses again on Kat, the chain resting on the edge of the blade. And he pulls up, up.

Kat is suddenly staring at him, reaching her hands out and fastening her fingers around his throat. She is laughing and laughing. She is not Kat now but the woman who comes to watch him at night. She squeezes his neck tighter and tighter, squeezes and squeezes, and he cannot breathe, he cannot move, he cannot breathe, spots of color dance in front of his eyes as his vision fades, but he must, he must do this.

Exhaling everything he has left, he yanks the blade of the knife up against the chain, away from Kat's neck, and it breaks in two with a great crack. There is a brilliant flash of light, and as a blast of wind blows him back, he sees the silver circle slide off the broken chain and roll away into the roots of the tree.

He lies there in the night, gulping air. It burns to breathe. His throat is on fire. His whole body hurts. He keeps his eyes shut.

After a long time he realizes that he can't hear the wind anymore. In the silence, something soft touches his face, once, twice, a third time. Cool, but not wet. He opens his eyes. All at once the tree has bloomed, and tiny white blossoms are falling from its branches. They land on his hair, slide down his face, like kisses. He sits up.

When the petals reach the ground, a thin beam of white light shoots up, like a seed has sprouted and is poking through the earth to reach the sun. As the blossoms snow down, more and more and more lines of light flower, until he and Kat are cradled in an orb of light, blocking out the darkness.

The Light is beautiful. The Light is safe. And there in the Light he can make out a familiar shape. She's standing there, smiling at him.

"Momma?" he gulps, and she holds out her hand and he goes to her. "Momma."

"My brave boy," she whispers. Her voice is full of warmth, her eyes full of love.

He is crying now. "Momma, take me with you."

She holds him close, but shakes her head.

"Please, Momma, why won't you take me with you? I want to go with you!"

"I cannot take you with me. You still have work to do."

He bawls, desperate.

"Lucas, do you know what your name means?"

He shakes his head, still crying.

She puts her hand gently under his chin and lifts so she can look into his eyes.

"It means 'to illuminate, to light up.' You are a Bringer of Light. You will light the way. You are a Prophet."

"But Momma, please, *let me come with you*."

She shakes her head again. "You must look after the baby. You must keep her safe. You are the Watchman and the Lantern. That is your destiny."

He cannot speak only gaze at her, take her in and in and in.

"I am very proud of you. You are my joy. You are my son. Know that I will always be with you. I love you always and forever." She leans down and kisses him on the forehead. "Now rest," she says, "and I will hold you."

He doesn't want to sleep, but he is so tired, so very tired.

He closes his eyes.

39

Katherine

As she bears down and bears down and bears down, there is no pain, only joy. Only joy, only waves and waves and waves of love.

Her baby. Her life. Her love. Streaked with blood and covered in white, she lies on Katherine's chest, nestled between her breasts. Katherine's skin and her skin.

At her faint, mewling cry, Katherine laughs because it is the most wonderful sound in the world. Time has stopped. There is nothing but Katherine and her baby together, here and now and forever. She gazes rapturously at her daughter's tiny nose, her perfect mouth, her little eyelids, her soft, sweet curled fists. She inhales her daughter's scent. Kisses her flushed cheek.

She puts her child to her breast. The baby suckles a while and then sleeps.

Katherine has never been so happy. She has never loved so much.

It may be minutes or hours or years later when she looks up and sees a woman standing in front of her. Looking at her is like looking into a mirror, yet different. Her dark eyes are fixed upon Katherine and her baby.

They stare at each other for a long time, and then Katherine speaks.

"Why me?"

"I waited for you, I waited in the ring brooch. And you released me. You are a Vessel, as I was a Vessel. No other body could hold me. It was the only way. We come from the same lineage. Our destiny written golden in the sky. We were born to carry the Child, and now we have."

"What do you *want*?" Katherine's entire body trembles.

"I want to live," Margaret tells her.

"You have already lived! Why did you come back and make me do such terrible things?" Katherine's throat is raw. "You made me push Matthew. You destroyed Niamh's life!"

"You still mourn for the sodomite, for Cecily? They were weak, pathetic. You are better without them."

"Cecily? Who is Cecily? I am speaking of my friends." Katherine bites at her lip in confusion; then a new surge of horror and rage breaks through and her voice swells to a ragged shout. "You tried to kill Lucas!"

"Let me remind you that I saved your life."

"You saved yourself."

"Yes, and in doing so, I saved you and your child. Do you know what I lost? Do you know what I gave up? I had to kill my own child."

Katherine swallows. "How could you do it?" she whispers.

"There must always be a sacrifice.

Katherine stares at Margaret lost for words. Margaret continues in her numbed silence.

"I know you think you would not be capable of such an act, but I will share my strength with you. Soon you will have my knowledge, my power. You will learn the ways of the Travelers, and then you will never know fear again." Margaret smiles. "You see, I know you, I know you intimately, and I know the burdens that weigh upon your heart. But now there is no need to wake in the night nor give way to despair. And your child will be safe."

Katherine stares down at her tiny, sleeping daughter.

"She will never feel pain. She will never know loss. She will want for nothing," Margaret continues.

Instinctively, Katherine tightens her arms around her baby. She is afraid, but she knows this woman speaks the truth.

"Together, we will give her everything. Together we will watch her grow and prosper, and when the time comes she will rule. She will rule over this world and all the worlds to come. And she will be revered, and we, as her mothers, will be revered. Only think of the power. We will be worshiped as the New and Rightful Trinity: the Mother, the Child, and the Spirit."

Katherine bends forward and very gently presses her lips against her child's forehead. She looks up at Margaret. "No."

"No?"

"No. She must live in the world. I want to her to have a normal life, to go to school, to make friends, to ride bikes. I want her to watch puppet shows and eat peanut butter from the jar and play in the ocean. I want her to live as a person, not be worshipped as a goddess."

"What kind of mother are you?" Margaret is filled with scorn. "What mother would deny her child the world?"

"A good one, I hope."

Katherine's eyes swim with tears, but she cannot waver now. She hopes this woman doesn't see what she has just seen. Slowly she lowers one arm, the arm closest to the tree. "A mother who believes that her child has the right to choose her own life, to make her own destiny."

Margaret laughs. "It makes no difference if you deny me. I am here entwined within you forever and ever and ever."

"No." She slides her palm across the earth until her fingers find the knife.

"What are you doing?" Margaret has noticed the blade.

"The only thing I can."

"Stop! You cannot do this!" she screeches.

Katherine makes no move to wipe away her tears. She cannot let go of her daughter, and she cannot abandon her plan now.

"You saved my child, and now I must save her too." She raises the knife.

"You will never rock her, never hold her close. You will never watch her grow. Do this, and she will never know how you loved her."

"There must always be a sacrifice," Katherine repeats.

She turns and with great deliberation thrusts the blade down hard and fast directly into the ring brooch, which still lies among the roots and dark earth.

Margaret screams.

There is a thunderous crack.

Then all is still.

40

Sael

Sael opens his eyes to light, soft white light. His squints; his hand drifts up slowly to caress his head; he turns toward the tree and sees Katherine half sitting, propped against the roots, holding—

He tries to leap up, almost falls, clutches his head for a moment, bends over, takes a breath then.

He runs toward them.

Katherine smiles at him. "Meet your daughter."

His daughter. His own daughter. His child. "She's all right?"

"She's fine."

"She's perfect." Sael is hushed, awed.

"Yes, she is."

"You're okay?" He stares at her. Her face is very pale, but she looks so beautiful.

"I'm fine," she tells him.

But she is not fine, he can tell. "Katherine! Jesus Christ, why is there so much blood?!"

"There's always blood." He could swear she sounds almost amused.

"Yes, but . . . but Katherine, what happened?"

"Does it matter, for now?"

He opens his mouth, shuts it, opens it again. "Yes. No. I guess, I guess . . . right now it doesn't matter." He cannot take his eyes off his daughter, cannot stop drinking in every detail.

Then, suddenly, he realizes. "Lucas! Where is Lucas?"

Still smiling, Katherine nods her head toward Lucas, who is curled up in the roots of the tree. "He's sleeping."

"And he's okay?"

"Yes, he's okay."

"Thank God. Poor kid." But he is already drawn back to his daughter.

"Do you want to hold her?" Katherine asks.

"Really?"

She laughs. "Of course, she's your daughter."

He reaches out, and very gently he lifts her, takes her in his arms. Cradles her close. He feels as though he's in a dream. "I have to get help," he says.

"There is no hurry," Katherine reassures him. "I think I'll go to sleep for a little bit. But do me a favor?"

"Anything."

"If Lucas wakes and I'm still sleeping, tell him I love him and I'm proud of him."

"I will." His heart is so full of love he thinks it will burst. "Katherine?"

"Yes?"

"I love you."

She looks at him, and in her eyes he can see she is Katherine again, the Katherine he fell in love with and loves with all his heart, the mother of his child.

"I love you too," she replies.

"What do you want to call her?"

She's already drifting off. "I was thinking . . . Mia."

"Mia?" He likes it. "What does it mean?"

"It means 'mine.' It means 'wanted child.'"

Then she smiles and closes her eyes.

Thomas

Thomas sits on the small bench, staring at nothing. Father Martin is talking to the abbot, so he, Thomas, must wait. A month or two ago he would have gone mad with impatience, itching to explore the monastery and bursting with questions.

Things are different now.

Some priests pass by. He feels their eyes upon him, hears their whispers. He cannot make out their exact words, but he knows of what they speak. The story has swept through the abbey like fire.

Fire. Thomas shudders. If it had been anyone but Father Martin who told the tale, Thomas would not have believed it. But it had been Father Martin who awoke to find a huge white bird in his cell. He was startled but not frightened, not at first. He had risen from his bed and followed the bird away from his cell and away from the monastery to the castle, where black smoke coiled against the orange sky. Father Martin did not say much more about what he saw that night. He does not have to. Thomas remembers more than he wants to. Some nights it is so vivid, more than he can bear.

He had emerged from the Great Hall into the castle courtyard, his head reeling from the splendid sights, his ears ringing with music, and had almost tripped over Warin the Baker, who was splayed senseless on the ground. Thomas was readying to sprint for help, but he spied a wooden cup still clutched in the man's hand. Thomas crouched low to peer into Warin's face. The baker was alive, his mouth stained purple, exhaling breath sweet and sour and pickled. This surprised Thomas, for he had not thought his friend the kind of man who drinks himself into oblivion.

But it was not just Warin. For the first time, Thomas looked around the courtyard with dawning unease noting body after body lying upon the cobbles. Rank had been forgotten, for in their unguarded state they were all equal: guard, scullion, cobbler, wife, child. Their limbs splayed at awkward angles, some in states of undress, others with vomit crusting their chins. He had broken into a run and almost careened into a woman bent over yet another body. It was Dyl's wife, bent over her husband, pleading and scolding by turns but to no avail.

"What happened here?"

Sobbing, she told him. Lord de Villias had been in a generous mood. He had gifted a cask of the banquet ale to his people, and the guards had somehow got their hands on a second, determined that everyone should share in the good fortune.

Margaret had not let Thomas drink the ale. And he knew. He knew what she was capable of.

He stared down at Dyl's wife's tear-streaked face, asking only one question: "My brother? Have you seen my brother?"

But even before she shook her head, he knew the answer.

And so he ran on and on, past the fallen. *It looked like the bandit camp that night.*

"Rudd! Rudd!" he called.

No one replied. The silence was deafening. The ale must have worked upon the guests too, but Thomas did not care. He cared for no one but "Rudd! Rudd!"

He found Rudd curled up like a child near the steps leading down to the kitchen. Thomas could tell by the rise and fall of his massive chest that he was alive, but as much as he shook Rudd's arm or slapped his face, Rudd would not wake.

On the night Margaret had helped him rescue Rudd from the bandits' camp, Rudd had only tasted a little of the tainted stew, but even so it had been a struggle getting him to safety. Thomas groaned. There was nothing to do but hold his brother's hand, to wait for the effects to wear off. For all Rudd's strength, he was utterly defenseless, as gentle and as helpless as a kitten, and Thomas loved him for it. He drifted into sleep, his head upon his brother's enormous chest.

Thomas was caught in a nest of snakes hissing, their scales crackling and sparking as they writhed. He woke from his dream to a living nightmare.

The castle was on fire. Flames licked around the timber beams of the courtyard stables, devouring the hay while the trapped horses whinnied and kicked in desperation. Fire flowered into red and white blooms that consumed the castle from the inside, bursting through its windows to light up the night.

"Rudd, please!" he had pleaded. "Please wake." He sobbed and yanked and sobbed, but they were too late.

"Margaret!"

Her name echoed through the courtyard, rose above the roar of flame. Thomas peered up through the smoke and sparks at a figure standing high above them.

Lord August, disheveled, his handsome face smeared with soot but otherwise unharmed. The ring brooch pinning his cloak glinted and gleamed. "Margaret! Margaret! Bring her back to me!"

Lord August had gone mad. Thomas turned away, prepared himself to die. "Rudd, I love you," he whispered. *"Margaret,* I loved you too."

As his lids lowered, swollen from the thick black smoke, he thought he saw a huge white bird gliding toward him. Then he was coughing and coughing and coughing.

"Good, my son, good," urged a familiar voice. "Bring the foulness forth."

Thomas hurt; he was in pain. He reached for Rudd, but there was no one, nothing. Only darkness.

And when he finally came to in the sanatorium, many nights and days had passed. Father Martin comes now to sit by his side, tend to his wounds. At least those wounds that can be seen. There is an ache cleaving his heart that will never ease, a sorrow that will never cease. Still, the days here are pleasant, quiet enough.

It is night when she comes to him. The dream is always the same.

He stands upon a sheer cliff, watching the sea as it breaks against the rocks below. Only it cannot be the sea, for the water is a deep and dark red.

"It is blood." Margaret appears beside him. She speaks calmly, without passion. "It is the blood of all mankind."

"How did this happen?"

"War, Plague, Famine, Death." She is dreamy, as if what she says is of little consequence. "Man brought this upon himself."

Thomas turns away from her terrible beauty, past the spiky cliff line down to the uneven shore below. There, where the red waves crash upon the stones, he sees a small figure facing out to sea. "Who is that?"

"The one who could save them, or damn them. She could lead the armies of hell or unite the hosts of heaven."

Then Margaret turns to Thomas. The sky behind her is ablaze with stars against whirling clouds of impossible colors. Her eyes are black pools; her voice is a buzz, a hum, both less and more than human. "You must tell the story."

"What story?"

"My story. You must warn them of what is coming."

"But," he quavers, "how can I do this?"

"War is coming. The War to end all Wars. Do you know where you stand?"

And in the starlight, he sees that her face crawls with bees.

He blinks, sees Father Martin's anxious face peering into his own. "I am sorry, Father. I must have fallen asleep."

"The fault is mine. I have left you too long. However"—Father Martin grins with delight—"I hope it will have been worth the wait. I have wonderful news! Father Abbot has given his permission that you may stay!"

"Stay?"

"And more than this," he says. "You will be taught Latin with the sons who are sent to learn here. You will be taught to read and write."

Thomas cannot speak.

"Yes, it is even more than I dared hope for!" the priest continues, beaming. "You are to be a scribe, to help transcribe our most holy works. Is that not good news?"

You must tell the story. War is coming. Do you know where you stand?

He does his best to smile. "Yes," Thomas answers, "that is good news."

And he tries, with all his heart, to believe it.

ACKNOWLEDGMENTS

No writer is an island and, as usual, there are a multitude of people I need to thank for their endless help and support. To my stellar agent Alexandra Machinist; our lunches are a thing of beauty, and I truly value your razor-sharp instincts, advice, and encouragement. Massive thanks are due to my newly-wedded editor Hannah Wood, whose tireless passion, drive, and dedication know no limits; and to the amazing team at HarperCollins who always has my back, especially hard-working copy editor Mary Beth Constant. I also want to give a shout-out to Avi Burstein, for his creation and maintenance of my beautiful website. Thanks to Venetia Strangwayes-Booth for your invaluable advice regarding midwives in the UK and traveling in Wales; and to Joanna and Dermot Strangwayes-Booth for setting me straight regarding medieval England and the proper use of titles. I also want to say that Ian Mortimer's book *The Time Traveler's Guild to Medieval England* was a real godsend.

I want to acknowledge my fellow writers who supported me when times were tough, especially Sarah-Jane Stratford, Anne-Sophie Jouhanneau, Heather Haddon, Mariana Elder, and my fabulous collaborator and 'other sister,' Dr. Reverend Kathleen Tagg. I have always been grateful to belong to two thriving artistic communities: The Dramatists Guild of America, and Paragraph: Workspace for Writers and for all the incredible help they provide. Thanks to the people of Wales for the hospitality they showed to me and my mother as we traversed their rolling hills, explored their castles, and ate their delicious steak and kidney pies.

In between writing *Love Is Red* and *Crown of Stars*, I got married and had a baby. This opened the door to a whole new world of supportive and amazing people I have to thank. To the incredible South African doctors in making sure I was as good as new, Dr. Marshall Murdoch and Dr. Trudy Smith—I wish you lived here! To the wise and wonderful community of the Hudson River Park Mamas who offered support, advice, and gave me some truly great friends, Hollie Greigo, Amapola Manrique, Louisa Wyatt, Kirsten Arnfast, and my dear Marissa Long, who's been with me through all the incredible joys and sleepless nights. To Mike Javett for his generous support, and the entire Suzman family for always being there. To the Arismans, who cheered our family up with many marvelous brunches, and to Areta Pawlynsky for her words of wisdom regarding work and motherhood.

To my family in Mexico—Amira, Armando Sr, Moni, Joni, and Santi—gracias por su inagotable amor y amabilidad. And thanks to my brilliant, blazing sister; my intrepid, entrepreneurial father; and my amazing mother. I have the best family in the world. You get me through the hard times. There are none better.

Most importantly, thank you to my husband Armando. It can't be easy being married to a writer, but I could not do this without you. Your love and strength keep me sane. Each day I wake up knowing how lucky I am that I found you. You make my life a happy and joyous one. I louve you. And, finally, to my shining girl, Emiliana. Emi, you're the light of my life, the apple of my eye, the foam of my flat white. I couldn't be prouder of you or love you more. And if your daycare teacher is correct, at the rate you're going, you'll be reading this next year. Mommy loves Emi. Now, forever, and always.

ABOUT THE AUTHOR

A native of South Africa and the author of *Love Is Red*, Sophie Jaff is an alumna of the Graduate Musical Theater Writing Program at NYU's Tisch School of the Arts, and a fellow of the Dramatists Guild of America. Her work has been performed at Symphony Space, Lincoln Center, and Goodspeed Musicals. She lives in New York City.

ALSO BY SOPHIE JAFF

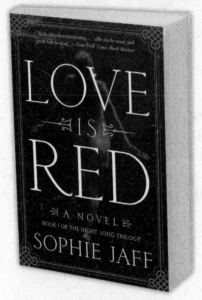

The Nightsong Trilogy, Volume Number 1
LOVE IS RED
A Novel

Available in Paperback and E-Book

"Ridiculously entertaining.... Jaff's woozy supernatural saga is
effectively scary and great fun to read." —*New York Times Book Review*

Katherine Emerson was born to fulfill a dark prophecy centuries in the making, but
she doesn't know it yet. However, one man does: a killer stalking the women of New
York City, driven by darker, much more dangerous desires than we can bear to imagine.
He takes more than just his victims' lives, and each death brings him closer to the one
woman he must possess at any cost.

As the body count rises, Katherine is haunted by harrowing visions that force her to
question her sanity. With this unforgettable novel—one that combines the literary and
the supernatural, fantasy and horror, the past and the present—Katherine's moment of
awakening is here. And her story is only just beginning.